Patricia Grace is the author of four novels, including *Potiki* (The Women's Press, 1987), winner of the New Zealand Fiction Award and the LiBeraturpreis from Frankfurt, Germany; *Mutuwhenua: The Moon Sleeps* (Livewire, 1988); and *Cousins* (The Women's Press, 1993). She has also written four short story collections, including *The Sky People* (The Women's Press, 1995), and several books for children.

Patricia Grace was born in Wellington, New Zealand, in 1937. She has taught in primary and secondary schools and was the Writing Fellow at Victoria University in Wellington in 1985. She is now a full-time writer and lives on the ancestral land of her people of Ngati Toa, Ngati Raukawa and Te Ati Awa, and in close proximity to their family marae complex in Plimmerton.

Also by Patricia Grace from The Women's Press:

Potiki (1987)
Mutuwhenua: The Moon Sleeps (Livewire, 1988)
Cousins (1993)
The Sky People (1995)

PATRICIA GRACE

baby no-eyes

Published in Great Britain by The Women's Press Ltd, 1999
A member of the Namara Group
34 Great Sutton Street, London EC1V 0LQ

First published in New Zealand by Penguin Books (NZ) Ltd, 1998

British Library Cataloguing-in-Publication Data
A catalogue record for this book is available from the British Library.

ISBN 0 7043 4616 8

Printed and bound in Finland by WSOY, Finland

*To the memory of Frances Warren
and Muriwai Crozier*

Acknowledgements

My love and thanks go to Emma Mikaere, Moana Jackson,
Aroha Mead, Ken Mair, Taki Anaru, Tania Te Rei,
Miki Rikihana, Matiu Baker, Kerehi Waiariki Grace,
Ola Hiroti, Irihapeti Ramsden, Jo-Anne Grace,
Kohai Grace, Rakairoa Grace, Raniera Grace, Brian Gunson,
Mahinarangi Tocker.

Thanks also to the staff of Te Puna Matauranga o Aotearoa,
National Library of New Zealand and the Turnbull Library.

Author note

The events, as described in the book, that take place in the pathology
department of a hospital, are a description of actual events,
occurring in 1991 in one of this country's hospitals.

In the process of writing the book I went to do research in the
pathology department of the Wellington Public Hospital. I wish to
make a disassociation of Wellington Pathology from what has been
described. The Wellington establishment had people, policies and
practices in place which would not enable what has been described,
to occur.

I wish to express gratitude to the people there who have an
obvious and justified pride in their department, and a love and
respect for the work they do. I especially wish to thank Professor
Linda Holloway and Doctor Brett Delahunt who spent much time
with me, showing me through their department and helping me
understand the hospital processes and protocols that are carried
through prior to the dead being given over to their relatives.

PROLOGUE

The first thing I knew was bumping along, the sound of my mother's feet going lap lap, and breath coming and going fast in and out her nose. Lap lap over a hard, smooth surface, such as a road.

My mother the frog. (And someone else.)

It was a black-with-rain boulevard where we bumped along at drizzly dawnbreak. High wet trees. Houses of white stucco, stained wood, blond and brown brick, wrought iron and Decramastic tile.

Boulevard?

All right, road. Straight, wide and tree-lined, with fine gates and front fences. Magnificent gardens.

Haw.

Let me think. Azaleas, rhododendrons, kaka beak, hibiscus, jasmine, japonica, kowhai. Not too clipped, all a bit wayward, but full on you know, making a statement. It wasn't dark enough to not understand all that. Nothing skimped in road, footpaths, houses, gardens – which is why I wanted to say boulevard. It swooped. It was grand.

But anyway, road. Street. Long, wide and swooping. Lap lap, bounce bounce, and towards us came a glossy dog with a rainproofed owner lap lapping too, their lifted faces glistening in the bowl of streetlight as they passed under it, passing us by.

Beyond all that, and beyond dawn, we came to a crescent, more skinny and pinched than where we'd come from. We could see in the brightening light that here the gardens were all colour coded. Like – white pink and violet through to weakish purple, then back again to white. They were shaped up and down via rockeries – white purple pink, pink white blue, white cream lilac, colour code, colour code, colour code. Lap, lap, lap.

Not the lawns though. No coding there. Over the clipped green lawns were mats of kowhai flowers and scatterings of old grapefruit and mandarins. Piled on top of it all were browning camellia heads – down every frontage, coagulated. So much it made you want to heave, throw up, chundalucka, technicolour yawn.

Those lawns.

Could've brought on a nosebleed.

My mother the frog could've haemorrhaged, and I could've . . . 'Go Mum. Led's ged ouda hia,' I said. Lap lap lap, lappity lap.

Apart from the glossy dog and rainproofed owner we'd not seen anyone. It was as though there were no people living in any of the houses, or as though they'd all been whisked off to outer space.

I've heard of that. People get taken, whole streets, whole towns of people. After a time they're sent back to earth but are now inhabited by other beings who are going to take over the world. These people, the returned ones, don't like to be inhabited. They want to be how they were before instead of how they are now, because they still have some memory of that, but there's nothing they can do. There's no one to help them or believe them. Yes, all these ones from this crescent and that boulevard had been whisked off, which accounted for the stillness and the silence.

Woman with the dog?

She could've been one of *them,* one of those aliens already returned with a dog as an alibi. She could've been already a hundred years old, could've been marked in some unusual way – by an unjointed thumb or equal-lengthed toes. Horror beings could've grown from her armpits, or her face could've turned to slime. Who knows? 'Come on Mum, geddus ouda hia.'

Just kidding, just kidding, about ouda spaze. Because all the cutting, clipping, pruning, planting, colour coding was evidence wasn't it, that there must be cutters, clippers, pruners, planters, coders somewhere? Like, you don't see mice in your cupboards but you know.

My mother, unlike the dog woman, wasn't showerproofed even though she's a frog. She was wearing an Indian dress. What I mean by that is that she had on a maroon cotton dress with an embroidered, mirrored bodice tied at the throat with a string of bells, and a skirt coming from bustline to shins with tassels round the hem. The hem dipped at the back and flopped about her ankle hollows, but was dragged up at the front by the shape of us. Jandals on her feet. Cheapo.

She lapped along with her orange backpack of things, her black hair crinkling in the drizzle; wide, freckled face; frog mouth; eyes magnetised under double-glazed glasses; body short and wide.

Me? I was waterproofed completely.

After a while the drizzle stopped and in the dribbly sun my mother steamed, lap lap lapping, until we left all that behind – that boulevard, that crescent, that colour coding, those clotted lawns.

Those aliens.

We hiked through a park and came out the other side to Main Street where the traffic was nose to bum like sniffing dogs – it was that time of morning. My mother looked for lights to let us over. (Someone holding her hand, waiting with us.) Wait, Wait, Wait, Wait, Cross. We were heading down.

Plunging really. All the cars and us, walled on either side. Down in diesel, petrol, rubber and my mother's steam, her feet lapping, getting faster and faster until I began to punch and kick, pull her tight so that she slowed down, and she laughed.

At the bottom we were the last ones into a bus that sidestepped out from the kerb, pulled us through streets and lights to the motorway where it loosed itself, taking us along. Smoothly we went – karm, karm, karm, karm.

My mother sat back and made us comfortable in the staticky upholstery and leaned her head against the tinted window which reflected her into a double-headed frog. She closed her frog eyes, pleased with herself, and went to sleep while I went slow, slow swimming, hi-aa

9

hei-aa, hi-aa hei-aa, then curled myself and went to sleep too, karm, karm, all the way, all the day in the bus.

After that long sleep we were in a new city lappity lapping along a grey platform and into the echoing railway station where my mother stopped, swung the backpack down and took a leather jacket from it to put on. She took money out of the backpack pocket, bought a double-decker burger, a paper cup of coffee and sat on a slatted seat. (Someone else too.) But ha, hot coffee, warm food. It steamed her glasses making her see misty people walking to and fro. We were waiting for it to be time for *them* to be home so we could surprise them. But who were *they*?

Out and down the steps under the big clock, between the salty pillars and into the getting-dark wind, she found us a taxi.

Along the waterfront we went, the big moons of lights pale in the new dark, traffic lights like jewels, one set after another. We turned, swapping from lane to lane in this smart taxi, following on the heels of cars, until leaving all that we turned up a quiet hill on a road that was narrow and ragged. At the top we stopped.

Mum paid the taxi driver, opened a gate and lapped along a path to the back of a house that was tall and thin. It was painted blue with dark blue facings. There were three concrete steps leading to a dark blue door. My mother didn't take us up these steps. Instead she sat herself on the lid of a rubbish bin by a flax bush in the little yard, 'I'm back,' she yelled.

This was my mother the frog, with me, the tadpole, wiggling, swimming, jiggling, turning round inside.

'Paani, Paani. Mahaki, it's Te Paania. Come and see what she's brought us.' It was Dave, hugging our m″other and smiling all through himself, 'What's this, what's this? We never thought God would give us a baby,' which is what I heard with my own little baby frog ears, coming from holy Dave.

'Come on, come on in Paani Girl,' said Dave and Mahaki, taking her pack, patting and poking me, putting their ears down on her stomach to listen to me. Kissed me too, they did, through the Indian dress and all my weatherproofing – but who were *they*? I flipped and squirmed,

screwed myself up tight, kicked and boxed, went into spasms and my
mother laughed like anything – laughed and laughed and flopped herself
down. They gave her cushions, put her feet up and questioned her.

'What did you do? Did you ...?'

'Run away in the dark?'

'What did he do?'

'Did he ...?'

'Put you out in the street?'

'Why?'

'Why did you ...?'

'Why now?'

Good questions. You might think she was running away from
beatings or other forms of cruelty. You could think she'd been treated in
some deliberately unloving way. 'I was bored,' she said, 'and lonely, and
children need a great chance in life – need a family, stories and languages.
Someone to give them a name. I woke up this morning and knew it was
the right day to come.'

'We've done up upstairs, got it ready for when you were supposed to
come the last time.'

'O sorry about that,' Mum said, though she didn't seem to mean it.
Then she said, 'I wrote Glen a letter. He won't mind. He'll find someone
else, someone unencumbered. He falls in love at the drop of a hat ... I
wrote to Gran Kura too.'

Who? Who?

'We'll grow silverbeet and carrots,' said this Dave.

'And trees,' this Mahaki said.

Who are they Mum, these gooey galoots?

A week after our return we had a party for me, a baby shower.

Well, what came up the hill, up the path, up the steps and in the
door that party day were marvellous friends in denim and leather, silk
and cotton, tracksuits and tuxedos, all kissing and laughing – bringing
bread and cheese and dips and drinks, boil-ups and watermelon.

What else? Clothes for me. Stretch-'n'-grows galore. Bibs, feeders,
naps and Treasures. And toys, teething rings, soaps and powders, baby

bottles, rugs and a big tiger blanket. Everything. All this was piled in a yellow room that Dave and Mahaki had painted when they thought Mum was coming back that first time.

And while the music played, while my mother sang and laughed and danced, I swam round and round, flipping and turning in slow, slow motion. Hi-aa, hei-aa.

The next day Gran Kura arrived with her bag, her oil, a fish and a little tree.

'Mum, Mum, we're all ready, everyone's here,' I said. 'Let's get this over and done with.'

1

KURA

There was a suitcase on the verandah. The leather was cracked and flaking and both straps were broken.

Josie, who was the great-granddaughter of the man-who-was-a-ghost, had called to see me. As well as being the man's great-granddaughter she was his great-grandniece also.

It was a cold day with the wind coming in off the sea, so we stayed inside all afternoon with the chip heater going. This heater was installed at the time when Joe and Gordon renovated the kitchen for me. I didn't see the suitcase until Josie was leaving.

'Don't forget your bag,' I said.

'It's yours,' she said. 'I was just returning it.'

'It's not mine,' I said.

'You gave it to Luddie and Tom when Laina was going to boarding school. Laina gave it to me for Timmy. Now I've brought it back.'

'Keep it,' I said. 'I've got no use for it. I don't know what it means being there, don't understand why it should come back to me again.' But even as I was saying this I knew that because of what had happened recently, my life was changing.

She hugged me and gave me sticky red kisses, her big head above my head, her wide self around me, her soft, unsuitable skirt lifting and flapping. She clopped across the verandah in high heels which were wrong for her size and which unbalanced her on my new verandah boards. All that her bright lipstick, her frothy clothing and her unfitting shoes did for her was indicate the kindness of her heart. 'We'll come and get it if we ever need it,' she said as she left.

Having the suitcase there was unsettling. Where was I going with a suitcase and what turn was my changing life to take? I left it where it was, reluctant to take it inside. That night the wind toppled it and the catches came undone. In the morning it was there gaping, ready to have belongings put inside.

When Joe and Gordon came to fix up my house they wanted to pull my verandah down because it was rotten and dangerous. They wanted to pave out front and make a patio – which they described in such a beautiful way that I was almost persuaded.

'No, leave my verandah,' I said. 'My grandmother sent Jack off from there and Marty was propped by its posts.'

They put down a new floor so that my foot wouldn't go through the old boards, and in the front wall of the house they put in new aluminium window frames and a glass sliding door.

A year later they came and did some alterations to my kitchen – put in a bench and some new cupboards, replaced the wood range with the chip heater and installed an electric stove. They asked again about the verandah. 'The day after my burial,' I said, 'you can pull the whole lot down and make something new and flash for you, or for whoever will live here then.' They laughed and said they'd replace the posts so the roof wouldn't fall down on me.

I must have had an idea even then that my verandah wasn't finished with, that it had to be there for the day when Shane would step up on to it, that the steps had to be there to thump under his heels, that its boards had to be there to allow the sun to slope across them the way it did. It had to be partly enclosed the way it is, and shaded at one end by the clematis. In a more open place Shane's demands could have leaked away into the garden to be eaten by flowers, or could've scattered across the yard and gone out with the tide.

Also, Shane needed the protection of my verandah to allow his words to come. Joe and Gordon, who were ready to knock him down, were unwilling to do this on my verandah. But if the verandah had become a patio, built by them, cement and gravel rolled around by them in their concrete mixer, concrete watered and trowelled by them, walled by them on the wind side, then they could've laid Shane out on it and not been troubled.

If Shane had been flattened, if there'd been blood, then that would have ended the afternoon. If I had not been jolted by what Shane stepped up on to my verandah and said, the little ball inside me would not have cracked. Words from it would not have escaped into my throat, remaining there until the tide had been slept out and in. The words would not have propped themselves between my lips ready to pour themselves out over the floor and under the roof of my verandah.

And what would my words have made of themselves in an open space anyway? If my verandah had been pulled down, how could we who were there have been grouped so conveniently together on a day of such strong sunlight?

Not long after Josie's visit, Pita and Bon's house burnt down and they came to live with me. They'd been there for a month when I came to understand why they were there, why the suitcase had returned to me and why it had opened itself ready for packing.

Death and birth ring on my phone.

This time it was birth. Te Paania rang to say that she was back in the house where she and Shane had lived, and that her baby was due in ten days' time. Why would she ring to tell me these things if she didn't need me, or if she didn't want me to come and live with her? Why would a suitcase have come to me and opened itself on my verandah if I was to remain at home? 'The house and the grandmother's things are for you and Bon now,' I said to Pita, who is my brother's son. 'There's more I have to do. Before I leave do you think you could get me a fish?'

I went out into the garden and found a seedling pohutukawa that I watered and spaded round. I packed the suitcase, lifted the tree onto

15

damp newspaper, patted soil round it, wrapped it in plastic and tied it. I put the fish on ice in a cool-bag and went to the cupboard for a bottle of my oil.

Then, with the bag and everything I needed, I went to live with Te Paania, arriving just a day before her second child was born.

2

TAWERA

There was a head at both ends like on those reversible dolls. One doll is a dark dancer in a red flouncy dress, big gold rings in her ears, bright red lips and large black eyes which roll sideways. On her head is a wonderful turban decorated with red fruit and bright flowers. Flip this doll, and the underside of the dancing dress becomes a sparkling ball gown for the blonde-haired, blue-eyed doll who has a demure look and diamonds in her hair. Between the two of them there are four arms but there are no legs. They are each other's legs.

However we weren't reversible dolls. We were my mother and me. My mother was squatting over a towel which Keri had placed in the centre of a large groundsheet of blue plastic that was spread over the floor. On the towel was a mirror that my mother caught sight of me in, excitedly, when she wasn't too busy. Behind my mother, rubbing her back, holding her to stop her from toppling over backwards, one left and one right, were Mahaki and Dave.

Neither my mother's face nor mine was ogling or demure. No. Both of our faces had eyes closed tight. Both of our mouths were open and yelling. One face was large, froggy and freckled, with these freckles now popping out to a third dimension – as if they could be rain splotches on a window some centimetres from an onlooker's face, or spots before someone's eyes, or kiwi dollars, or tiny flowers on invisible stalks, or little helicopters, or floating grit that could be whipped up by a vacuum cleaner. That face was Mum's.

The other face was small and purplish, screwed, wild, not spotted then at all – except with removable blood and water spots. That face was mine.

There were two arms her end. And her two legs, that could've been my arms for the time being, were spreading, spreading. She was heaving down. 'Here we go again,' Keri Pomana said to that other end's head, Mum's head. Keri was the midwife in green overalls and a white blouse with the sleeves rolled up. Karm karm. By her shoulder was Gran Kura. 'Slowly, slowly while we ease the shoulders. Deep, deep,' Keri Pomana kept on saying to the other end's head, while both ends' heads kept up their yelling.

'A boy,' they all said at last, as if I didn't know.

There we were, my mother and me.

Undolled.

Hi-aa.

And there I was, up by my mother's neck. She was holding me, laughing and talking. (Someone else too, pushing in. Who was that?) Keri and Gran were clipping and snipping, then Gran took me and wrapped me in a towel, while Mum moved on to the settee where Keri cleaned her and made her comfortable. Mahaki was grinning and talking to me over Gran's shoulder. Dave was looking at me too, but he was feeling ill and his face had paled to the yellow colour of eggy pancake mix. He had to go and sit down.

It was night and we were in our lounge that had been recently papered in mottled pink and grey, though the colours weren't noticeable in the light diffusing from the centre of the ceiling. There were wine-coloured curtains drawn across the windows, and on the floor, once the blue sheet had been taken away, were two colourful mats covering an old brown carpet. Two heaters going.

We were upstairs.

All afternoon my mother had been going down the stairs, out along the weedy path, around the clothesline and the scrawny, creeper-covered bushes, in again and back up the stairs. All evening she'd been in and out of bathroom and bedrooms, or she'd gone into the little kitchen where she'd leaned, gasping, on the window-sill by the coloured squares of glass that Dave had fitted into the frames at the time of glass-breaking Shane.

Gran gave me back to Mum and wrapped my placenta ready to put out in the garden under a little tree that she'd brought all the way from home with her. Dave came out of his chair, put a big blanket over the two of us (someone else in the blanket too. Who was that?) and went to help Mahaki make a cup of tea. My mother drank her tea, going ooh and aah, then we curled ourselves together and had a massive sleep.

When we woke my mother sat up and looked into my face. Her first words to me following my special appearance were, 'I want you to know you're not an only child.'

'I knew there was someone,' I said.

'You have a sister four years and five days older than you.'

'Now I see her,' I said, 'Shot. Two holes in her head.'

'You mean she has no eyes,' my mother said. 'You mean her eyes were stolen.'

So, I made a mistake about the bullet holes.

My sister was like this: four years old and dressed in K Mart clothes, that is, jade track pants tied at the front with pink cord, jade T-shirt with a surfer on it riding a great pink wave, coloured slippers fastened by velcro straps. She was thin and dark like Shane in the photograph, and not near as froggish as my mother and me, not speckled at all. She had straight black hair that flickered and glistened as her head moved this way and that. She had no eyes.

'All right Mum,' I said, 'tell us about yourself and about this sister of mine who has no eyes. Stolen? How come?'

'She died in an accident,' Mum said. 'If we're going to tell about the accident we'll have to tell everything.'

'We?'

'Gran Kura and me, and all of us in our different ways. You too, you'll have to do your part. It could take years.'

'All right Mum and Gran Kura and all of us, let's tell everything. Tell about ourselves, and about this sister without eyes who's already four years old. I know there's plenty of time but let's get cracking.'

3

TE PAANIA

After I told my family I was pregnant that first time, the time of big sister now four years old, I had a proper wedding. Me, not being beautiful, having a big mouth and a reputation for trouble, my family thought I was lucky to be marrying Shane – who was good-looking, had a computer technician's ticket and a good job, and who could fix any motor, appliance or machine.

Shane's family wasn't so sure that I was lucky, not that any of them said this in so many words. He'd settle down was what they said, anyone with work was bound to settle down. And with someone like you . . .? I think they thought I was all right.

My family?

His family?

It wasn't until our wedding day that we found out we both came from the same family, that Shane and I had the same great-grandparents. Gran Kura and my laughing grandfather were first cousins, and I guess if the old people had found out sooner about our close connections they may not have approved of the marriage.

Grandfather had left the place where he was born when he was fourteen. At eighteen he'd married our grandmother. He, and we, had lived in and near grandmother's community ever since. Although he had often spoken of his relatives and the place where he'd been brought up, grandfather had never returned there until I came out of hospital some months after our wedding. 'We had to marry him back,' was what Gran Kura said.

Anyway, I'm not so bad-looking in my own opinion. I had a good job too, which was something that no one mentioned. Also I was settled and managing to keep my big frog mouth from getting me into trouble. There was nothing unlucky on Shane's part in marrying me, was what I thought.

But also I agreed that I was lucky because I loved skinny, bad, unsettled, fixit Shane.

By 'proper' wedding I don't mean up the church aisle in a gown and veil, vowing in front of an altar with my back to the people all seated in rows behind. Nah. I bought myself a pink outfit, a frilly blouse and high heels, toned the freckles down with a dollop or two of makeup and had my hair thinned and piled. Shane hired a suit and bought a pink bow-tie.

Off we went to the registry office with our grandmothers, grand-fathers, parents and sisters and brothers. After that we went back to our place to a beautiful dinner prepared for us by Mahaki, Dave and some of their friends. We had an all-night party up and down the stairs, all becoming highly pissed among the boxes of glasses, the heap of pots and pans, the sheets, towels, cutlery and electrical appliances that were our wedding presents.

That was our wedding.

Most of the glasses had been smashed by Shane by the time our baby began to be obvious. Pots and pans were dented and bent and windows were broken, though nothing awful happened to me. 'You should get out now,' Mahaki and Dave said to me. 'When he's used up glasses and pots he'll start on you, flinging and banging. Kick him out. What is it in you that makes you love someone like him?'

When I'd first left home to live in Wellington I'd lived with my father's cousin and his family – sharing a household and a family, cooking, cleaning up, having friends and relatives coming and going, being involved with the daily lives of several people. I'd go off to night classes on some nights and look after children on other nights. It was like home in a different place. It was how I grew up, what I was used to.

Then I fell in love with this Shane, and we went and found a place where we would live together, in an upper storey of a house owned by Mahaki and Dave who lived downstairs. We were pleased about this, Shane and I. We would be together and become a new unit, which is what people in love are supposed to do.

After we'd put our clothes in the wardrobe and drawers, stocked the refrigerator and bought an iron, there we were, enclosed, two strangers, wondering what to say to each other – apart from, I love you Te Paania, I love you Shane, which is what two people in love are supposed to say. But what else? And what was two? What was this thing of being two? I didn't know anything about being two. Neither did Shane.

I'd wander in and out of rooms thinking there must be more. I could see that Shane was doing and thinking the same. We'd go out partying at night, or sometimes wander about town making purchases to give evidence of our life together, but every day there were walls to return to, and little rooms, and silence that neither of us understood. There were certain spaces in Shane that I hadn't fathomed. There were places in me that he couldn't know.

I returned from work earlier than Shane, and it was always too much for me to go upstairs to an empty flat, so I began calling in to have coffee with Dave who returned home at about the same time. We'd talk and listen to music and try out recipes. Sometimes we'd cook a meal that we'd all eat together when Mahaki and Shane came home, but we didn't do this too often. Shane was wary of Mahaki and Dave. Didn't like this different food, what he called typical queer-boy kai.

When I became pregnant it was Dave more than Shane that I discussed my doctor visits with, and who was more interested in the minute details of the scan pictures that I took home. I was unwell during the first weeks of my pregnancy and didn't want to go out at night any more, so Shane would go out alone. It was when he came home late at night that the shouting and crashing would begin.

Mahaki and Dave would hear the noise and come upstairs to see what was going on. Mahaki would get Shane in a headlock and threaten him with killing. 'I'm sorry, I'm sorry, I won't do it again,' Shane would bleat to them and me. 'I love you Te Paania,' he would say.

And after the biffing, crashing, shouting, the headlocking and threats, the promises, the 'I love you Te Paania,' Shane would go off to work the next day as though nothing had happened. After he'd gone I'd go out in the grass and shrubbery picking up pieces of glass and finding pots and lids. I'd put a piece of cardboard over the broken window to keep out cold and rain before hurrying off to my own job which started at nine.

Dave would come up within a day or two and put in new old glass. Well, glass from old windows, coloured pieces that had been taken out of buildings and cut down for me. 'Go home to Mum and Dad,' Dave would say. 'When there are no more glasses for him to see himself crookedly in, no more windows giving an ugly reflection, he'll look into your eyes and see himself in there to hit. One day it'll be you.' I liked the pretty gold, pink and blue windows that Dave fixed for me.

Down Shane would go after work, knock on Dave's door and thank him for the new window.

Mad Shane.

'I did it for her, not you,' Dave would say.

'Mm.'

'And you can bloody fix it yourself next time. Do you think I've got the whole world's glass at my fingertips.'

'Well, mm.'

'You're a nutter Shane. We should kill you.'

'Mm, right.' And he'd come up and eat, and not go out drinking that night. We'd sit together and set our four eyes on the television screen.

Which was another window you bet, to look into — where there was chasing across rooftops, down fire escapes and through warehouses, with goods tumbling from shelves; where there were guns banging and flashing; where there was roaring and screaming, tyres squealing, windscreens shattering; where there was blood, rape, rage, murder; where cars hurled over cliffs and burst into flame above high black rocks and churning seas.

Nights exploding. Pinning me to the settee some nights.

Shane.

Shane.

'What sort of a name will it have?' he said one night, the first time he'd ever been the one to bring up the topic of our baby. Then, before I could answer, 'Am I a cowboy?' he asked with a fist like a tight bag of stones.

'No,' I said.

'So why was I named after a movie?' The window was likely to go, a pot through it, a fist through it perhaps. But no. He flopped down on the settee. 'We're getting a car.' Whew. 'Then we'll go there and they're going to tell. Me. Tell us. My name. My things. Our stuff. Those secrets. That's that,' he said, the door handle coming off in his hand as he went out. Bangitty bang.

That week he pulled down a piece of the front fence and brought two old cars into the yard. For three weeks he spent evenings and weekends swapping pieces and parts from one to the other, then masked it up for a purple paint job. 'Get in,' he said when the paint was dry, and off we went to the movies. Afterwards we came home madly, past the limits in our car. Hey.

Hey Shane.

And on the following Saturday we were going to visit the family because there was something to settle that was to do with Him, His things, His name, Our stuff. I was pleased to be going, wanting to show off my big stomach and the new car, but Mahaki and Dave weren't pleased at all.

'Don't go with him,' Dave said. 'He'll smash. He'll kill you.'

'We knew,' his mother and aunty said, talking to me as though Shane wasn't there. 'We knew he'd settle.'

'That's why I come,' he said.

'A place to live, a car, money coming in . . .'

'Settle, what's mine, my name . . .'

'A baby . . .'

'Blow up the secrets . . .'

25

'Yes car. He's clever. It's nice . . .'

'Whatever there is.' He was getting wild.

'Purple?'

'Come on, drink up Shane,' his brother said. 'Don't gas so much, you're getting behind.'

In the afternoon, out from under the drinking tree and up onto Grandmother Kura's verandah, wearing a pair of shorts but shirtless, came long-legged, grasshopper Shane, stumbling drunk. 'You old grannies are a load of shit praise the Lord,' he shouted to Gran Kura.

'Watch it Shane,' his brother said.

'They got my stuff, I want it.'

'Want a sock in the face more like.'

'Where's our stuff?'

'You're all too soft for it,' said Gran Kura.

'What stuff?' Niecy asked.

'Our names, the secrets, our stories . . .'

'Our stories could kill you,' Gran Kura said.

'Am I a cowboy?'

'. . . or you could kill someone if we tell.'

'My name?'

'Shane. It's a name of your own.'

'It's a movie name, a cowboy name.'

'A name for today's world.'

'A name for Pakeha, a name for Pakeha teachers to like. To make me be like them. Where's my tipuna name?'

'To protect you. Like Riripeti, called Betty.'

'You think I need that? Protection? Not to be real, not to know, have it all hidden? You all think you got to whisper in case we hear, in case we know?'

'Every generation has its secrets to bear. What good is knowing?'

'What secrets?' Niecy asked.

'What good nothing?' Shane said, 'Nothing, nothing, nothing, alleluia. Look at this black face. Look, look.' Shane step-danced his silly arms and legs, showing us himself, his black face pushed forward in a fury. His brother was getting a punch ready to put on his sticking-out jaw.

'Let him say,' said Gran Kura.

'But what to go with it? Uh? Black, but what to go with it? Shane for a name. Shane, Shame, Blame, Tame, Lame, Pain. Nothing to go with this,' he prodded at his chest with stiff stick fingers, 'nothing to go with this. How can I be Pakeha with this colour, this body, this face, this head, this heart? How can I be Maori without . . . without . . . without what? Don't even know without what. Without what?'

'But do know how to be a whinge and a wimp,' his brother said.

'Like a cup.' Shane took a cup from the verandah ledge and waved it. 'Cup, cup. But what is it till it's got beer, coffee, something . . .?'

'Grow up man.'

'Yeh, come on bro, put a beer in there . . .'

'Or a coffee . . .'

'All yous. Look at yiz. Pissheads, dopeheads, roughnecks, no different from me only you got no mouths. Goody. Nice to grannies, load-a-shit grannies. They're thieves . . .'

'Leave the old people out of this, they got their ways . . .'

'Jesus-freak thieves.'

Gran Kura shifted in her chair and opened her mouth to speak. But Shane, part-paralysed grasshopper, trickling from heat, stumbling from drink, fell to the verandah boards in triangles of limbs, in a place where the sun was hot and went to sleep there.

'Shift him,' his mother said. 'Or he'll burn.'

'Let the silly bugger burn,' his father said, but he and Niecy picked Shane up by the triangles and set him down in the shade of the overhanging clematis, where he stayed asleep for some hours while the tide went out and came in.

We sat drinking iced water, cold beers and hot tea, and at low tide went down to collect pipi, shuffling our feet hard into the sand at the water's edge, bending to pick them when our feet felt the edges of the shells.

Back at the house we hosed the sand off the pipi, gave them a dunking in boiling water and sat out under the trees picking away at them, taking our time.

Gran Kura did not eat or drink or move during that time. Her lips, where words were gathered, were pushed forward and slightly parted.

When the sun began to drop we all made our way back on to the verandah. The tide washed in. We could hear the water up over the sand rattling at the fringe of stones. Shane woke and stood, sober and sore, rubbing his head and shifting his eyes. His back was ridged in the pattern of verandah boards.

There's a way the older people have of telling a story, a way where the beginning is not the beginning, the end is not the end. It starts from a centre and moves away from there in such widening circles that you don't know how you will finally arrive at the point of understanding, which becomes itself another core, a new centre. You can only trust these tellers as they start you on a blindfold journey with a handful of words which they have seemingly clutched from nowhere: there was a hei pounamu, a green moth, a suitcase, a birdnosed man, Rebecca who was mother, a man who was a ghost, a woman good at making dresses, a teapot with a dent by its nose.

Or sometimes there is a story that has no words at all, a story that has been lived by a whole generation but that has never been worded. You see it sitting in the old ones, you see it in how they walk and move and breathe, you see it chiselled into their faces, you see it in their eyes. You see it gathering in them sometimes, see the beginning of it on their lips, then you see it swallowed and it's gone.

But Gran Kura's lips had remained parted. Words, unswallowed, began to fall from them. 'There was a school,' she said.

4

KURA

There was a school. Our grandfather gave land for it so that we could have our education. It was what we wanted. The school was along by the creek where Staffords live now. It was there for our parents and us, and then for our children. But after our children grew up our school was left empty because many people had left the area by then. Their land was gone, and the children's children, who were only a few, had to travel by bus to the big school in town.

Our grandfather's mother was the eldest daughter of Te Wharekapakapa and Kapiri Morehua, both people of high birth and status – so it was through her parents that our great-grandmother came to have jurisdiction over land from beyond the foothills to the sea, and from Awakehua to Awapango. I mention this not to be boastful but only to tell you that we did not come from slaves.

Our school was painted light brown with dark brown window frames and door. There was one big room with a high roof, and a low porch on one end. Joined to it at the other end was a little low-roofed shelter. The big children were taught by the headmaster in the big room with its blackboards and big windows, its polished wood floors and varnished walls, while the primer children were taught by the headmaster's wife in the little joined-on room.

When I first started school this primer room had a board floor and one little window. Inside was a blackboard on an easel. Beside it was the teacher's desk. There were six desks in a row for the older children, and a table with forms on either side where the littlest ones sat. By the time Riripeti started school I was eight and had a desk of my own. When I took Riripeti to school on her first day I took her to the table where the little ones sat. That's where I put her. I believed it was the right thing to do.

I was up early that day. I hurried all morning because I had this important work to do – to take Riripeti to school. My mother and Riripeti's father were sister and brother, which in those days made Riripeti a sister to me. She was my teina.

That morning before I went to get Riripeti my mother said, 'Look after your little sister at school, help her, teach her what to do.' All right I was very happy. I was proud of this work I'd been given.

When I arrived at Riripeti's place she was ready, wearing a new dress that grandmother had made for her. Her hair had been plaited and tied with ribbons made from strips of the dress material. There was a hanky in her sleeve and a bandage on her knee.

Grandmother was there with Aunty Heni and Uncle Taare to see Riripeti off to school. 'Look after your teina, take her by the hand,' Grandmother said to me. 'Do as your tuakana says,' she said to Riripeti. 'Your tuakana will help you so that you'll know what to do. Listen to what she says.'

Then our grandmother said to me, 'We know you're a good girl. We know you'll do what you're told, we know you'll help your little sister and look after her. We don't want our children to be hurt at school. That's why you have to be very good. You have to listen, you have to obey. We know that you're clever and we know you'll learn. That's what our school is for, for you to learn, for our children to learn. You're very lucky to have a school and to be allowed to go to school. Look after your little sister.'

Perhaps I was told to take Riripeti to the headmaster or the teacher before taking her into the classroom, perhaps I forgot this, being too excited to hear.

Sixty years ago I was a tiny girl, small for my age. See that leaf – like that. Thin like that, without weight. You could see through me those days, just as you can see through that leaf now, but I was not too light and leafy to have this important job. I was this important girl, this happy leaf and I loved my teina with her new clothes, her hair in pigtails, a rag hanky in her sleeve. She was a black girl, six years old.

The teacher didn't notice Riripeti marching into school with me, and was busy writing on the blackboard when I stood Riripeti by Tihi at the little children's table. I was the one who told her to stand there. I straightened her, put her feet together, put her shoulders back and went to stand by my own desk. We said our good mornings to the teacher before we all sat down.

'Who is this?' the teacher said when she saw Riripeti sitting on the form. I put my hand up because that was the right thing to do, but the teacher didn't look at my hand. 'Who are you and where are your manners, coming in and sitting down as though you own the place?' she said to Riripeti, but Riripeti didn't know what the teacher was saying. 'Stand up when you're spoken to,' the teacher said. I wanted to whisper in our language so this teina of mine would know what to do, but I knew I wasn't allowed to speak our language so I made a little movement with my hands trying to tell her to stand. She didn't understand and sat there smiling, swinging her shoulders, swinging her eyes – to me, then back again to the teacher.

I knew Riripeti shouldn't smile so much. I knew she shouldn't fidget herself or roll her eyes. At that moment I didn't want her to be a girl so black that it would make the teacher angry.

'Get that smile off your face. Do you think this is a laughing matter?' the teacher said, taking Riripeti by the arm and standing her.

Riripeti could speak some English. Of course. We all could. But Riripeti had not heard words like the words she was now hearing. 'Go and stand in the corner until you learn better manners,' the teacher said, but Riripeti didn't know what she was being told to do. I wanted to call out to her but speaking wasn't allowed.

The teacher turned Riripeti and poked her in the back while she shuffled forward, but not fast enough, not fast enough, still swerving her head and eyes towards me – until she was standing in the corner at the front of the room where bad children always stood.

But how was she to know she was bad? She had said no words that would make her bad, spelled nothing wrong to be bad, given no answers to be wrong. 'Face the corner,' the teacher said, because Riripeti was still twisting her neck to look at me. She didn't know what she had been told to do. The teacher jolted her head round and gave her a smacking on the legs, then Riripeti stood stiff and still without moving, facing the corner.

At playtime, I ran with our cousins Kuini, Hama and Jimmy to hide in the bushes, where we put our arms round each other. No one from the little classroom played that morning. The ones not crying sat close together eating bread, turning the balls of their feet into the ground, watching their feet make dents in the dust.

After play the teacher turned Riripeti round and asked her for her name but Riripeti wouldn't say it. Instead she smiled and smiled and moved her eyes from side to side. So the teacher asked Dulcie, who was the eldest in our class, what Riripeti's name was. But then the teacher became angry with Dulcie too because she wouldn't speak the name slowly and loudly enough. The teacher gave Dulcie a piece of paper to take to Riripeti's family. Full name, date of birth, English name, it said. She turned Riripeti into the corner again, but allowed her to come out with us at lunchtime.

After school, Dulcie, who didn't live anywhere near Riripeti or me, gave the note to me to take home to my aunty and uncle. Her family was where the Beckets are now – that was their land then. I took the paper home and the next day gave it back to Dulcie to give to the teacher. It gave Riripeti's name, her date of birth and her English name, Betty.

On the way to school we taught Riripeti to say, 'Yes Mrs Wood, No Mrs Wood, Yes please Mrs Wood, No thank you Mrs Wood.' We thought it very funny that our teachers were called Mr and Mrs Wood, and once we were out of the school grounds Mr Mrs Rakau is what we called them. We had this silly song to make ourselves laugh: 'Mr Mrs Rakau, patu patu *wood*.' *Wood* was the loud word. It was the word to scare anyone with. We'd call it out to the kids we didn't like, call it out to the ones chasing us, or we'd jump out from a tree where we'd been hiding and call, 'Mr Mrs Rakau, patu patu *wood*,' and off we'd run.

It was no good. School turned out no good for Riripeti. How did she know her name was Betty? That second day she was in the bad corner for not answering when her name was called, and for not speaking when she was spoken to. On the way to and from school we'd tell her the right things to say, but even though she tried she still couldn't say the words the teacher wanted. She spent most of her time in the corner. Every day she was given smackings by the teacher.

Other children were smacked and caned and punished too, but not as much as Riripeti. We were much naughtier children than what she was, that's how we knew what to do. I knew my name was Kate at school. Minaroa knew her name was Dulcie. And we had ways of sending messages to each other with our faces, ways of guessing the teacher's mind, knew which lies were the right ones to tell. If the teacher gave us a lesson about the right food to have for breakfast, when questioned we would tell her that's what we had – bacon, egg, toast, class of milk. It was the right answer – bacon, egg, toast, class of milk. '*Glass*, *glass*, a *glass* of milk,' the teacher would say. After a while we could say it, making this choking *g* sound right down in our throats. But we didn't know it meant milk in a glass, didn't know what it meant. Didn't know a glass was right for milk and a cup was right for tea, because at home we had enamel plates and enamel mugs for everything. We didn't speak until we'd learned, didn't speak unless we had to because we were afraid our bad language might come out, but we became good at guessing the answers we had to give.

Riripeti was too good to guess what to say, too good to know what lies to tell, too good to know what to do. It was so difficult for me to be her tuakana. It was so difficult to take her to school every day with her footsteps getting slower and slower the nearer we came. By the gate she'd say, 'Kura, Kura, he puku mamae,' and she'd hold her stomach and bend over. Her face would be pale.

'Never mind, never mind,' I'd say. 'You got to go to school every day. We got to learn so we be clever.' I'd pull her along so that I wouldn't be in trouble with our mothers. I was trying so hard to do this important work that my grandmother had given me to do.

All the way to school I'd talk to her, tell her what to say and what to do. And she did know, she did learn. She was very brave and tried to do everything I told her. She remembered to speak in English, except that the teacher didn't know it was English she was speaking because Riripeti was too afraid to make the words come out loudly. 'Do I have to shake that language out of you, do I do I?' the teacher would say, shaking and shaking her. Then Riripeti would be smacked and sent to stand in the bad place. She did mimi there sometimes. Sometimes she sicked there, then cleaned it all up with a cloth and bucket. I would've helped her if I'd thought I'd be allowed. After a while it was only Riripeti who went to the bad corner. It became her corner. She smelled like an animal and spoke like an animal, had to go to the corner until she stopped being an animal. I could see that she was getting smaller and that it was only her eyes and her teeth that were growing. We didn't tell our mothers, or anyone, what was happening, but sometimes Riripeti was told off at home for her dirty wet clothes.

One morning Riripeti sat down by the track and said she couldn't go to school any more. Usually when she did that we would manage to persuade her, but that day I believed her. It was true that she couldn't go to school. Her spirit was out of her, gone roaming. Her hair was as dry as a horse's tail, rough and hard, her eyes were like flat shadows, not at all like eyes. I had seen a dying dog look like that, which made me think it might be true what the teacher said, that my teina was changing into an animal. 'Go home to aunty,' I said.

'No, I'll wait for you.'

'Go in the trees.'

So she agreed and I gave my bread to her. Down the bank she went, across the creek and into the trees where perhaps she would become an animal, a bird.

When Mrs Wood asked where Betty was I said she was sick, so Mrs Wood asked the other children too where Betty was, to see if I was telling the truth. 'Betty is sick Mrs Wood,' was what each of the children replied, but Mrs Wood was not happy with this answer. She became angry because how did we all know Betty was sick when we all lived in different directions? Sometimes it was difficult to know the right words to say.

After school I called to Riripeti by the track and I heard her coming. When she came up the bank I could see that her spirit had returned to her. It was looking at me out of her eyes, pleased to see me.

So that's what Riripeti did every day after that, hid in the trees. Mrs Wood was waiting for her to come back to school with a note and I felt afraid that we'd be found out. But the end of the year came. We had long holidays and Riripeti and I went to stay with our grandmother.

When our grandmother went to town she wore a grey suit and a cream blouse with a high collar and pintucks across the front. She had black Red Cross shoes which she polished the night before, on paper spread on the floor by the hearth. She had a black hat with a small turned-up brim.

In those days no one would take a Maori bag to town or to the shop, not even to a tangihanga, not even to land meetings. It wasn't like these days when you see these baskets everywhere – all colours, all sorts of patterns, not always pretty either. Sometimes they're ragged like the old ones we used for getting pipi, but even a Pakeha will carry a Maori bag now, paying a lot of money for one. In those days all the kete were on top of people's wardrobes with photos in them, or hanging on nails behind the bedroom doors.

Our grandmother had a good leather handbag for her money and combs and handkerchiefs. She had a deep cane basket with black and orange stripes around it for the shopping. Riripeti and I liked to carry the shopping. We were happy to go to town with our grandmother and to carry the basket between us.

We didn't go to town often because in those days we had our own store down the road with everything we needed. We all had our own killers, our own gardens and our own milking cow. So nobody went to town much, but our grandmother sometimes had business there and she'd take us with her for company. When she'd finished her business we'd go and buy whitebait, or whatever she wanted to take home, and then we'd make our way to the railway station where she'd let us buy something to eat. Not for herself. Our grandmother would never eat in town but she would let us buy a sandwich and a melting moment, which we would eat while we waited for the train.

That day grandmother took us to a shop that sold dress materials and bought remnants to make new dresses for Riripeti and me to wear to school. One of the pieces of material was brown with white spots on it, the other was plain dark blue. What a good day it was.

But on our way to the railway station Riripeti's feet began to slow down. 'Come on, catch up to Grandmother,' I said. Our grandmother was already going up the steps to the station. Riripeti stopped walking, 'I don't want a dress,' she said.

'Come on, come on,' I said pulling her by the hand and talking about the sandwich and the cake. I knew she was thinking about school.

There was a woman in our village who was good at making dresses. We only had to take material to her and she would make anything we asked, but it was our grandmother who wanted to make these dresses for Riripeti and me. Riripeti didn't want to watch Grandmother make the dresses or to have her dress tried on. Didn't want to talk about the dresses. She told me she wanted to go back to her mother and father and kept urging me to ask our grandmother if she could go home, but I wouldn't. I wasn't old enough to ask our grandmother a thing like that.

Riripeti's dress was the spotted one, mine was the plain blue. When they were finished we went home to our parents. The day after that was the day school began again.

Riripeti wanted to hide down by the creek on that first day but I wouldn't let her because I didn't want to be in trouble and didn't want to have to tell lies to the teacher. 'I'll tell aunty and uncle if you don't come,' I said. 'I'll tell grandmother.' She was too good not to listen to me. That was how I made her come to school.

But when we arrived at school we found out something that made us both cry. We found that I was to go into the other classroom, the one for the older children, and that Riripeti was to stay in the little room as before.

There were plenty of children crying that day – little children, big children. I don't know what for but some of it was to do with Waana who was Dulcie's little brother, brought up by their grandfather. The grandfather had brought Waana to the steps of the classroom and was talking to him, trying to make his grandson let go of his leg. The headmaster came out and said in a loud voice, 'I'd like to remind you Mr Williams that I don't allow any of that language in my school or in these school grounds.' We all got a fright because Waana's grandfather took no notice of the headmaster and kept talking to Waana. The headmaster became angry. 'I'm asking you to leave these grounds at once,' he said. 'Off you go and take your language with you. We're not having any of that in *my* school and in front of these children.'

'I go, yes, take my grandson too,' the grandfather said to him in English. He lifted Waana and off he went. Waana never came to school again. His grandfather hid him from the authorities, telling them that Waana had gone to live somewhere else.

Riripeti was silly, because when it was time for me to go to the other classroom she cried and put her arms around me. I promised her my bread, I promised her my dress, but she wouldn't let go. In the end I had to wriggle myself away, had to pull her hands off me and run because I could see the teacher coming.

It was when I ran off that Riripeti called out to me but forgot to speak in English. Well, all the holidays we had been speaking in that Maori language of ours, so perhaps that's why she forgot. Mrs Wood grabbed Riripeti by the shoulders and brought her to Mr Wood for the cane. We all had to stand in our lines and watch this caning so we would learn how bad our language was.

Riripeti wouldn't hold her hand out, which I knew was from fear and not from being stubborn. She had her eyes shut and stood without moving while Mr Wood gave her a caning round the legs, then Mrs Wood got her by the arm so she wouldn't run away. I thought what an evil thing our language was to do that to my teina.

It was a bad time for all of us. Some of us learned to be good and to keep ourselves out of trouble most of the time. Others were bad – swore at the teachers, got canings, or were sent home and not allowed to return.

Riripeti came to school every day. She didn't try to go and hide any more, and even though she began vomiting each day as we came near to school, still she came. She was always good. We were known as a good family. I'm not saying that to be boastful but just to let you understand about Riripeti.

One day during the holidays our grandmother said to Riripeti, 'Why are you small? Why are you thin?' And she took Riripeti to live with her, gave her wai kohua, gave her malt and Lane's emulsion and meat. Riripeti was all right too. For a while she was happy and we played together, then when it was near time to go to school again she became sick and couldn't eat. Her throat closed and wouldn't let any food go down. Her skin was moist all the time and she couldn't get out of bed.

Not long after that she died.

Killed by school.

Dead of fear.

My heart broke for my teina. Oh I cried. She was mine, she was me, she was all of us. She was the one who had died but we were the ones affected, our shame taking generations to become our anger and our madness. She was my charge, my little sister, my work that I'd been given to do, mine to look after. What an evil girl I was to let her die.

We never told our mothers and fathers what we knew. They thought Riripeti had a Maori sickness, thought some angry person had put a makutu on her – which was right perhaps, but they didn't know who. Or they thought it could've been part of the cursing of Pirinoa that was still being handed down and affecting us all.

After that I became sick too. I couldn't eat and I couldn't go to school. I went to bed and couldn't get up, just like Riripeti. I think I nearly died too. There were people coming and going, talking to me, talking amongst themselves, putting their hands on me, speaking that language over me – that evil language which killed my teina and which I never spoke again.

One day my grandmother took me out of bed, wrapped a blanket round me and sat in an armchair with me on her knee. She held me against her and rocked me. I think we stayed like that for days and nights. While she held me and rocked me she spoke to me of God's Kingdom. She told me about Riripeti's special place in God's Kingdom with the Lord, who alone was merciful, who alone was good. Riripeti

38

was heaven's bright gold. She talked about the journey that is life, how we must walk its pathways in goodness and righteousness, how we would all be together one day in glory. We all prayed together and the Lord answered our prayers.

Soon I was able to eat. Soon I could sit in the armchair on my own with pillows round me. After a time I was able to get up. Three months after Riripeti died I returned to school with God in my heart. There were new teachers there who were different in their ways, but I only stayed at school for two more years because I was needed at home.

So we children never spoke of what had happened to Riripeti. It became our secret and our shame. It's a story that has never had words, not until today. Today the words were jolted from my stomach by Shane, where they have been sitting for sixty years. They came to my throat, gathering there until the sun went down, when they spilled out on to the verandah in front of the children's children, who may not be strong enough for them.

We keep our stories secret because we love our children, we keep our language hidden because we love our children, we disguise ourselves and hide our hearts because we love our children. We choose names because we love our children.

Shane.

5

TE PAANIA

'Shane.'

It was quiet after that. No one moved or spoke, and the name grew inside a long stillness, a silence, and circled about in a darkness that was broken only by clematis flowers and the prickling stars.

Shane stood then, spread his stickish arms and turned as if to those flowers, as if to those stars. 'A-a-a-a-le-luia,' he said, not in a whisper or a shout, but in a voice that was moderate and cold.

Following this, others began to move but no one spoke. The sliding doors opened, the inside lights went on and light spread out over the verandah boards under the chair where Kura sat. Her lips were closed now, so were her eyes. She didn't move. There was water running in the bathroom and the kitchen, the kettle was being filled and put on to the element. Cupboards and doors were opening and shutting. Niecy, Gordon and Darcy went out to smoke in the dark and no one spoke.

In the kitchen Aunt Vera put hot water in Gran's teapot, swirling it, wrapping her hands round it to receive its warmth. Her face was in shadow. Beside her Uncle Joe took cups from the cupboard and put them out on the bench. He put out sugar, milk and teaspoons then went out to lean on the verandah rail, looking out into the dark.

'*Shackled by a heavy burden,*' sang Shane out there, cold and hard, to the frosted sky, *'Neath a load of guilt and shame . . .'* Then he came, thrusting his head through the neck of his shirt, casting his arms out of its sleeves as he leapt back up the verandah steps to the door. *'The hand of Jesus touched me,'* he sang, putting just his hands into the lit kitchen. *'And now I am no longer the same.'*

The kettle began to whistle. Aunt Vera emptied the hot water from the teapot, spooned tea-leaves into it, poured in the boiling water and put the lid on, letting her fingers rest for a moment on the bakelite knob.

'Let's go,' said Shane.

'It's late. Go in the morning,' Aunt Vera said, more to me than to Shane.

'We're off,' said Shane.

'Don't go,' Aunt Vera said, directly to me.

'It's all right,' I said. 'We'll get back, have a few hours sleep . . .'

'With him in that mood . . .'

'It's OK . . .'

'Well you're having a cup of tea and something to eat before you go,' she said and began pouring. Niecy came in. She was coming to stay with us for the two weeks of term holidays. Her bag and guitar were ready on the verandah. 'Bring Gran in,' her mother said.

The high tide washed up in half circles and the wave tops glimmered beside us as we made our way towards the river. Shane gripped the wheel, staring down on to the patch of light that the headlights made – light which illuminated the rutty tracks as well as the centre strip of dry grass, dock and thistle. He pushed along, swinging the wheel, bouncing through the holes, up and down the rough verges, in and out of the shallow, hand-dug drain.

Although I had heard grandfather speak of the place where he'd been born I had never been here before, hadn't known his side of our family. He'd spoken of the river, the sea, the hills – but mostly of the people.

So on our arrival the previous day I'd expected to see a number of houses and was surprised to see just the two – Gran Kura's house close to the shore, and Shane's parents' house, back from it, on a rise. Before the houses, on a track to the river, and set against the hills, were the meeting house and the old church with the graveyard behind it, both painted and tidy as though in use. 'They live in town,' Shane told me when I asked about the people. 'Come down when there's something on. The rest is leased out to eternity, or belongs to Pakeha farmers.'

Shane dipped the front wheels into the water then gunned through the river singing his alleluias, water jetting up at either side. He kept the motor pushing as we came up on to the metal road following the shoreline, then turned and began to take the hill, rally style. The high bank swooped to meet us on one side, the gully dropped away from our wheel edges on the other. At the top we came on to the sealed straight, and Shane took us, churning up dark, to meet the main road where we turned to follow the coastline again. We were alone on the road.

I closed my eyes and when I opened them there was traffic up ahead. Shane was putting his foot down – passing, passing, car car truck, then squeezing left again before the corner coming up. *'He touched me, O-o He touched me,'* he sang. *'And O the joy that filled my soul . . .'* We looped to the top of the hill, passing one car and then another as we came running down and into another straight. *'Something happened . . .'*

Car. Passing it.

'And now I know-oo . . .'

Truck. Passing, passing . . . Running out of road.

'He touched . . .' Running out of road Shane.

'And made . . .'

'Shane.'

'Shane.'

The night exploded into a silence so dark and pure that I knew nothing of it. It was lasting and without dreams, and when it came time to leave it, I did so reluctantly. The first sounds were of distant, undulating voices that carried with them a wavering grey light, and into this light came faces that were unrecognisable, that leaned into my face, that were distorted as though reflected from misshapen mirrors.

There was pain too, edged and jagged, intensifying as I lay there gauging it – and which once I discovered the depth of it I wanted to escape, reaching back towards that dark, quiet place where I'd been before, but which I couldn't find again in its purity. All I could find was a half-place of dreaming in which Pain spoke to me. 'Hold on to me,' it said.

'No, not you . . .'

'I'm all you have, hold on to me because there's nothing else to hold to.'

'Leave me . . .'

'Can't hold the faces which slip away from you like shadows, can't hold the voices which tremble, shudder and dissolve, can't hold light which is illusory. You need me.'

'Not you . . .'

'I'm all you have. Use me as a ladder and you'll find the way.'

'Why should I believe you . . .?'

'I'm all you have, hold tight and move up one slow step at a time.'

So I held, took a step and rested, clutching Pain against me like treasure. I took another step and rested, another and another, continuing until I thought I heard my name. It was distant, elongated and echoing against itself, so that I couldn't recognise the voice of the callers. 'Be encouraged but don't let that distract you,' Pain said. 'Keep hold of me. Keep going.'

I began to climb again, Pain broadening against me as I listened. I heard my name again, coming nearer, beginning to have its proper shape and size and to gain its true sound. There was dark light, which after a while became less grey. There were faces that shifted, shimmered, then became still. Someone laughing, hee hee, hee hee.

'Hee hee, you done it,' my laughing grandfather said.

'Get you out of this place,' my father said. 'Sooner the better.'

'Only the dressings . . . A few more days.'

'I don't know,' he said, his breath hissing out through missing teeth as he jerked his jersey down over his paunch, over the large portion of himself, over the slab from the meatworks.

'You're so fat,' I said, hoping to bring out a smile, but there was nothing from him. 'What don't you know?' I asked. His head was small, far away, rigged at the top of the meatworks.

'Who knows?' Eyes shifting from wall to wall to wall, as though there could be answers there. 'There was nothing like this back home when I lost my fingers,' he said.

'Dad, you don't have to be here,' I said. 'Don't need you all here taking turns to sit with me, bringing all this stuff . . . The kids need you at home.'

'Couldn't leave you by yourself in a place like this,' he said, eyes clapping out the walls.

'Why not? They've been good to me here, saved my life.' Ceiling, floor, ceiling, floor, wall, wall, doorway. 'Nothing bad can happen to me now.'

'Going for a smoke,' he said.

'Tell me first.'

'Tell you what?'

'What it is.'

'What what is?'

'What no one will say. Is it because you're mad at Shane?'

'He's dead. Useless being mad at him.'

'What is it then? Who?'

He pressed his palms down into the stool either side of him, eased himself up, shifting his eyes, shifting his weight, rolling himself to stand. Father, fat man, meatworks, shuffling out the door, diminished by his size.

'You used to be smaller,' I called. No response to that.

'I'll go, let you rest,' he said.

So I leaned back into the pillow where the dreams always waited, bringing me to a roadside where human-sized insects clicked and whirred and shirred their wings. They were glass-faced, brittle, marble-eyed. I was small among them. Above us the sun rolled, and in the light of it the earth blackened as the insects stirred the dusty verges for signs of plant or a drop of moisture.

When the stones and clay did not give them what they searched for they stood upright – pivoting, gyrating and rolling their marble eyes –

and began clawing, spitting, gonging their glass heads together until they splintered, until their shells cracked and their eyes spilled and scattered and became molten. I had to run from there. Now that he was part of the tide I knew I would never find him.

'Are you the arm and the leg?' asked the dressings nurse, snatching the curtains and beating them round their rails until we were enclosed. She had a wide face, grey eyes, a wide smile.

'That's me.'

'How's it going?'

'Like a train on fire.'

'Good for you.' She pulled the dressings trolley to the bedside and began snipping and tweezing the bandages.

'Did she say?' Dad asked as the nurse left.

'It's not up to her, it's up to the doctor, Monday . . . When's Mum coming?'

'Tonight.'

'I'll make her tell me.'

'Tell you what?'

'Whatever it is that you won't tell.'

The tea nurse whisked in with a compartmentalised tray containing dabs of coleslaw, potato salad, beetroot and cold sausage – bread roll and cheese, packages of butter, jam, mayonnaise and tomato sauce.

'She doesn't know enough to tell,' my father said. 'Neither do I.'

He went to the window where he stood, leaning on his knuckles, looking out so that I couldn't see his face, so that he wouldn't have to shift his eyes from wall to wall to avoid me. 'Only know what we saw,' he said.

There's an unborn baby in your life which is not truly known to you. It's a tumbler, it's a dancer, it's a fish. Even though it's part of you, it's apart from you – more separate than it is when it comes from your body at the time of birth.

Before that birth you might wonder what this baby will look like, whether you will recognise each other at once. You could wonder

45

whether you will deeply love this baby, because up to now you've had no great feelings of love. What you have weighing you down is a lump, a rock, a parcel, a load. You could wonder if you will be different once your baby is born – now that you have become a mother – someone different from who you were before. Sometimes you could worry about whether your baby will be 'normal' and how you would feel if there was a deformity, a sickness, an ugliness, a weakness. Would you be disappointed, horrified, angry, ashamed? And could disappointment, horror, anger, shame turn into a most special love? In the end would you lay down your life?

'So if it's not to do with Shane it must be to do with Baby, all this torment,' I said.

'There was no time. They had to go, take Baby back with Shane.'

'And it's all a big thing about nothing. Look, you don't have to be like this, didn't have to stay – once I was over the worst . . .'

'Couldn't . . .'

'Didn't need all this around me, all this . . . whatever . . . You look as though I died. I mean it's not that bad, can't be. Baby's dead, gone, but you know me, I can handle it.'

'It's different . . .'

'It wasn't as if I knew Baby – or not like it was a cot death or losing a baby two or three years old. If Baby was injured or messed up, or if there was something not right with her, I can handle it. Or if you think Gran Kura and Shane's family did something they shouldn't, well you can just say so. It's nothing I can't hear, or bear. Anyway, you don't have to have a snitcher on them just because Shane was a nutter.'

'We could've kept you home when you left school, put you in the freezing works pulling out livers.' It was an awful, bitter thing for him to say.

'Not all crazy, there's a few sane ones – Niecy, Aunty Vera, Gran Kura . . .'

'Said we got to hear it all, said you got to have a chance to cry for your family, got to know everything. But you were too sick, no time.'

'It's silly, nothing to cry about, except what's been cried for already.

OK, Baby was real and I wanted my baby, but I didn't know her. Having her inside me was just like getting ready to meet someone I didn't know, but someone I was looking forward to meeting. When I found out she was dead I was sorry but I wasn't surprised. Well, I was nearly dead myself. You couldn't expect a baby to live through that.

'No big feelings about it then, no big feelings about it now. Don't know if I'm supposed to feel more, don't know if I will feel more later – and don't know if I should feel guilty for not feeling more, but that's the way it is. It's silly Dad, you don't have to carry all this for me. It's not Baby I miss.'

'Hear it all from Kura.'

'It's nothing. You've all been around here too long, too many nights, too many corridors, too much takeaway food.'

'Let her know when we're coming . . .'

'What's the point?'

'And they'll wait for us there . . .'

'It's Shane I miss.'

6

MAHAKI

Mahaki called into Whitcoulls on the way home from work and bought a stack of coloured file boxes. He opened the boot of the car and put the boxes in there with the cartons that he'd brought from the office.

When he arrived home he lifted the first carton of papers from the boot, took it into the hallway and put it down by the stairs next to tins of paint and other packages that Dave had brought home. He wondered if Te Paania was in.

He went out for the second carton and returned with it, carrying the file boxes on top. 'Are they back?' he called to Dave as he went inside, putting the second carton down by the settee.

'No sign,' Dave said looking in from the kitchen. 'Want a hand?'

'It's OK.'

'Homework?'

'All this stuff filling up the office, and no time . . .'

'What stuff's that?'

'Biopiracy . . . Get it sorted. Then I might ask Te Paania to look after the files for me, keep them up to date, might like to once she gives up her job . . . So they're not back?'

'They could've left up there early this morning and gone straight to work. But still, they're usually home from work by now.'

'Could've.' Something spicy cooking.

'Coffee's hot,' said Dave. 'Or how about a G and T?'

'G and T,' he said.

He went into the bedroom and changed into his tracksuit, then to the bathroom where he scooped water from the cold tap, doused his face and ran damp hands through his hair. Get it all sorted, then he'd take a bit of time off to go and see his grandfather, or should go this weekend – which would mean he wouldn't be able to help with the painting. Would've enjoyed the painting. No, he'd better go and see the old man, see what was happening back home.

Nothing, that was the trouble. Nothing happening, and the old man had been ringing him every week, sounding more and more upset with each phone call. Get up there and find some way of persuading the Town Council to come and meet with the whanau. Surely with the climate as it was these days they could bring about the return of one measly piece of land that no one else had any use for, but which meant a lot to the old man and to themselves.

He returned to the bedroom then went out to the wash-house to put his shirt in the laundry basket. It was from there that he heard Dave call out – something urgent.

In the living room Dave had turned on television and was watching the news. 'Bloody idiot, bloody idiot,' he was saying. His face had paled.

There were pictures of a truck turned over in a ditch, police cars with their lights flashing. The camera moved over patches of blood on the road and on to a mangled guitar. Someone was being taken into an ambulance by stretcher. 'It's her,' Dave was saying. 'I told her . . .'

'No, it won't be,' Mahaki said.

'I told her not to . . . Look what he's done . . .' The on-the-spot reporter was having a word with an eyewitness.

'No,' Mahaki put his arm round him. 'It won't be . . .'

'He's killed her . . .'

'No it won't . . .'

'It showed the car.' The newsreader was remembering to keep a tight face as she gave an account of the road toll for the year so far. The phone was ringing.

'Shane's sister from hospital,' Mahaki said after he'd put the receiver down. 'Te Paania's in intensive care. Shane's dead . . .'

'Bloody good job . . .'

'And . . . they need my help, the family. I don't know what . . . Can you take me to the airport? Something about the baby.' He went to get his wallet and his shoes.

After the previous tenants had moved out he and Dave had put a notice about the upstairs flat on the supermarket noticeboard: Two Bedrooms, Fully Furnished, Inner City. There'd been no calls for a week, though when they'd gone into the supermarket two days later they'd seen that most of the tear-off phone number tags had gone. That Friday night Te Paania had rung asking if she and Shane could come and look at the flat in the weekend.

They made a time for Saturday morning, and Mahaki's first glimpse of Te Paania and Shane was from upstairs where he'd gone to open the windows. He'd watched them come up the hill together, arms about each other, turning now and again to look at numbers on the letter-boxes. Te Paania had been wearing jeans and a yellow shirt. He'd noticed the glasses and the dark, loose curls that she wore to shoulder length.

Near the top of the hill the two had stopped and separated. Te Paania had leaned forward then thrown her head back laughing, prodding her fingers into her chest as though the laughter was killing her. Shane, thin and leggy, dressed in shorts and a worded T-shirt, looked as though he wanted to join in the laughter but didn't know how. He'd stood apart from her, stuck in a half grin as though the laughter was too much for him.

The two of them had arrived a minute later, out of breath, at the top of the stairs with Dave, and after a quick look had arranged to move in that afternoon. Close up she was brown and freckled, big-eyed behind the heavy-framed glasses. Close up, he was bony and dark, and his shirt read DB Cool.

Come on, come on. One red light after another and now Dave had got them in the wrong lane – too upset to be driving. Te Paania critical, and what was it about the baby? 'Put your blinker on and squeeze over,' he said as they came up to another set of lights. Dave put the indicator on and signalled to the driver beside him who allowed him to edge over into the slow-moving traffic heading towards the tunnel. He wanted to say something to Dave. What?

Tunnel now, and traffic hardly moving, drivers amusing themselves by echoing their horns as they made their way through. Come on.

Out of the tunnel they were able to pick up speed down the long slope before turning and coming to more traffic lights. Green this time. Green again. If he didn't make it in time for the plane there wouldn't be another one until morning. Morning would be too late by the sound of it.

At last, the straight stretch to the airport. Looked as though he'd get there after all. What to say to Dave as they pulled in at the terminal? She'll be all right? She won't die?

'She's a survivor,' he said.

'Yes.'

'I'll ring.'

He ran, first to Ticketing then up through Departures, down the stairs and across the tarmac to the little plane with its propellers turning.

Two kids setting up house together. But fidgety, Mahaki thought. No sooner in the door than they'd be out again, shopping for nick-nacks as though they thought that's what it was all about – buying 'nice things'. Hmm, that jigged his memory.

First it had been mats and ornaments, then coffee cups and a coffee maker, place mats, fridge magnets, other items for the kitchen. They'd knock on the door before going upstairs, come in to chat for a while and to show what they'd bought. One weekend they'd gone on a pot plant buying spree, and the next week Dave had brought home shelving and hooks for them from work. They'd spent the following weekend putting up the shelves and hooks, and putting the pots and hanging baskets around. Seemed almost disappointed when the work was finished – as if they'd been trying to fill space and time and were now at a loss again.

Often they'd go out drinking, coming home in the early hours of the morning, clattering and calling up and down the stairs.

Then came the pregnancy. After that Shane went out mostly on his own. Te Paania hadn't felt well and though she still went to work every day, preferred to stay home and rest in the evenings.

But it wasn't that she liked to be alone. Often she'd come downstairs and spend the evening with them. Cheerful company, no matter how sick she felt. Mahaki had sometimes wondered if she preferred it when Shane went out and she was able to come and spend time with Dave and him. And because she worked close by – usually arriving home at about the same time as Dave – she'd come in and show him little things she'd gone out shopping for during her lunch hour. They were baby gowns, hats and bootees, matinee jackets, blankets and towels. Sometimes he'd come home early himself and there'd be hat, jacket with mittens at the end of each sleeve, and leggings, laid out all in the right order, like a flat baby. She'd stay downstairs drinking coffee, keeping Dave up to date on her visits to the doctor and the progress of her pregnancy. She'd wait with Dave until it was time for Shane to return from work. Te Paania and Dave – company for each other.

The little plane dipped a wing, turned, then straightened up, dropping towards the runway. The wheels touched, lifted, touched again, before pulling up and turning into the terminal. He waited in his seat until the pilot opened the door and let the steps down.

Baby?

Lost?

One night when he'd arrived home he'd found Te Paania and Dave with their heads together examining a copy of her eighteen-week scan. As he came in they'd looked up, their two faces excited, urging him to come and see. At that moment he'd felt older. It was as if Dave, who was his own age, and Te Paania, who was ten years younger, were suddenly his children. It had seemed as if they were looking to him for approval. He'd gone off into the bedroom thinking about this, feeling distanced, but also having doubts – about modern medicine, about scans. He wondered if Te Paania had had good information about the pros and cons of scans. What were the pros? Were there any cons? He didn't know, had never had reason to give it thought or study. All he did know was that there always seemed to be paybacks, somewhere along the line, for what was thought of as advances in medicine.

He'd gone to look at the little images, which at first seemed more like blurry pictures of the moon's surface than anything resembling a human being. If he had suddenly become father to Te Paania and Dave, did that make him grandfather to this? But then Te Paania had begun pointing out a head, an eye socket, a hand in front of a face, and somewhere along the way he'd found himself caught up, amazed by it all, no longer able to be a disapproving grandfather. Suddenly he'd become a father, or at least an interested uncle.

'Inside and out,' Te Paania had said. 'Arms, legs, face, sections of kidney, heart chambers . . . and here . . . first report.' It was a tick sheet showing that the baby had everything that it was supposed to have, and that it moved in all its moving parts.

It was while they were looking at the report that Shane had come in and they'd all reacted guiltily, doing what they could to draw him in. 'Yes, hmm, that's all right then,' Shane had said, almost as though humouring them.

On another night it had been colour charts he'd found the two of them poring over when he'd arrived home. Dave was keen on painting the spare bedroom for the baby and getting new curtains. Both were excited. Jonquil and off-white were the colours the two of them had decided on after a week of having their heads together. And Dave had had this idea about a coloured window which they were going overboard about.

But now? Well he'd have to find out what was going on, see what he could do.

The taxi dribbled its way up the hospital drive, over the slow-humps and past the arrows and signs and the hardiplank outbuildings, to the main doors. At the entrance there was a wooden seat chained to a rail, and a blue bin with a plastic bag opened up round its rim. There was a tin for cigarette butts beside the seat.

The hidden eye beamed him, the door slid open and he went in. Inside, he spoke to someone through a hole in a window, waiting while she brought up information on a screen.

He was in a foyer that had been refurbished with crooked, bubbling sheets of woodgrain, which reminded him of his office – done by an amateur carpenter. Perhaps a doctor did it. There was a glass showcase containing a kava bowl, a strainer and a root of kava. On one wall was a gold-framed portrait of Lucrezia. He took the stairs to the second floor and made his way along the corridor.

In the waiting room were Te Paania's parents, whom he had met at the wedding. 'Her grandfather's in there with her,' Te Paania's mother said. 'Stable, the doctor said, but still critical.'

'She's a survivor,' he said.

'Yes.'

'So what is it,' he asked, 'about the baby?'

'We don't know. Mum's there . . . You have to go out, down the drive, across to the brick building. Something . . .'

There were heart-to-hearts too. Dave had never liked Shane, well neither of them had, didn't know what Te Paania saw in him. Attraction of opposites? There was Te Paania, plumpish, laughing and laid back – then there was moody, unpredictable Shane, flinging his skinny weight around, knocking everything to pieces. Dave had tried to talk her out of the marriage. 'We'll look after you,' he'd said. 'Come to us if you change your mind.' Should've listened to Dave.

Lost?

He entered the brick building. Corridors. Patched-up walls and slits of windows, wheelchairs and trolleys parked along the way, faded pictures of rustic England.

A month ago Shane had brought home the cars. Without mentioning what he wanted to do he'd pulled half the front fence down and parked these two heaps in the yard, then got to work. To give him credit Shane was a worker. Single-minded. Mad actually. It was truly amazing what he'd done with the cars. Shifted the junk too, when he'd finished – put the fence and gate back in place. The gate had never been better.

Lost?

As in accidental birth? As in died? It didn't seem to be what Niecy had meant when he'd spoken to her – though there was no doubt the baby had been accidentally born, no doubt she was dead.

He went in. Kura and Niecy were talking to a doctor. Shane's young brother was there doing his nana.

7

KURA

The telephone and a green moth woke me.

It's because I have seen something of life that Niecy, sister of Shane, chose to ring me instead of ringing her parents, the parents of Shane. It's because of my age that she thought of me as the one to know what to do, the one able to tell the others, the one able to pass on sad news.

The moth touched the tip of my nose. I opened my eyes and watched it flutter across the room and spread its wings against the white wall opposite. The ringing in the other room sat me up and took me from my bed.

Though I went through the house without turning on any light, though I walked in the dark towards the ringing phone, the moth followed me, fluttering about my head as though I was a candle. 'What news do you bring?' I asked. 'Why have you come?'

I picked up the phone and the moth left me, flying about the room in zigzag pathways, shedding its green dust before landing on the window like a jagged green moon. 'Shane and the baby are dead and Te Paania could be dying,' Niecy said from the hospital.

I put down the phone, dressed and took a torch to walk to my daughter's place. My moth came with me, whirring its wings, tracking luminous powder through the dark. On every fencepost ahead of me it rested, and here and there I snatched sight of it in the deep grasses. 'Who are you?' I asked and kept talking to it along the way. But when I reached my daughter's house it dusted my face and flew away. I didn't see it any more after that.

It's because of our limited understanding that we are devastated when a young one dies. Like any sort of waste we see it as wrong. It makes us sad. Nevertheless, when we're old we get to expect death any day of our lives – our own deaths and the deaths of those around us – and people dying gets to be such an everyday occurrence that we can get through these times with reasonable ease. Your sorrow, your deep sorrow, is not so much to do with the one who has died but is more to do with others, the living. You have to help them through, you have to be there so that they see your old face, to be there because people know there is nothing you haven't already seen or experienced. Your job is to grieve and to help with the grieving at a time of life when you are past the time of feeling beaten on behalf of death – which you have come to learn is a part of life, one of its stages. They see you cry. They see you stop crying. They see a pattern and learn something from that pattern, coming to know that bad times pass.

For the time being, those close to death have to stay like moths in their birthing cases, protected. If there are arrangements to be made there must be other people to help with those arrangements; when the visitors come there needs to be people to prepare food; if there is money required there must be people to give it. The bereaved are wrapped, covered, until it is time to unwrap, uncover, get on with life, even though it may be a life different from before.

Fragility comes to the body eventually, of course, but not necessarily to the life of the body. The life can toughen from what it knows, from what it has met already, and it knows how to put its face this way, or that way, whichever way is necessary.

Except when there's something stray.

No, it's not someone's death that can traumatise – it's just that once in a while there's an aberration, something not seen or experienced before, that can break you. Once in a while there are circumstances to do with death which can make you cry in the depth of your heart.

*

'That's kids for you,' I said, to break the silence on our way to the hospital in the car. I said it to give some relief because grieving must have its rhythm, there mustn't be too much silence.

'You're saying it Mother,' Joe said. 'Nothing but a pain in the arse, these kids.' It was good of him to understand why I spoke as I did, good of him to recognise me, to know how I could help him to lift himself to face the death of Shane.

'That's him,' my daughter said, breaking her silence, lifting herself too. 'That's Shane.'

At the hospital Vera, Joe and Shane's brothers went to see about Shane and the baby, but I knew that I should stay with Te Paania. It would be several hours before her family arrived and it always needs a person strong in spirit to keep the ghosts away from someone as near death as Te Paania was at that time. So I placed myself there, as near to Te Paania as I was allowed to be. I put Shane from my mind, put the baby from my mind. I said my prayers and spoke to the dead who were there all round us, in and out like moths. I sent them away. This took all of my concentration.

When Te Paania's family arrived I sat them down and brought them out of their crying. I sent Darcy to get coffee and food and brought a nurse in to talk to them. While the nurse was speaking, Niecy came in. Niecy had been asleep in a ward when we arrived. She had a fractured arm, bruises and abrasions on her body and legs, but these had been attended to. When she left the ward she'd gone to see her family, and had now come to me with the message that Shane had been released to the undertakers but that the baby had not. There was some difficulty to do with the baby that I needed to attend to while the family was busy with Shane.

All right, but there was a discussion I needed to have before I could go and see about this.

I knew the right thing to do would be to take the baby home with us to be buried with Shane. Yet I thought that if Te Paania's family were angry with Shane for what he'd done, or for how he'd been in life, then they may not want the baby to go with him, even though it wouldn't seem practical to have two marae in different parts of the country preparing their ceremonies – one for a father, one for his daughter.

I gave Te Paania's family time to settle in, made sure the dead were well away, then said to her grandfather who is my cousin, 'There's the baby.' He understood what I was talking about.

'Our daughter's still alive,' he said. 'We have to leave Baby to you. If we took Baby it would only be to put her with our daughter because the worst had happened. But we still have our daughter. We have to stay by her. The dead go with the dead, the living keep the dead away from the living. So you have to take the baby with the father and have your tangihanga without us.'

There was no disagreement from the rest of Te Paania's family with what my cousin had said. His words were enough, it was truly settled. I had a job to do while they were busy with Te Paania and while my daughter and son-in-law were taking care of all matters to do with Shane.

A nurse showed me where to go. Niecy came with me. We found the right place, said what we wanted and were shown where to wait. While we waited I thought out what I would do so that Te Paania's family wouldn't be deprived of grieving for Baby, and so that I would not feel like a thief taking Te Paania's baby from them.

'I went to the hospital when Mona's baby was stillborn,' I said to Niecy. 'These hospitals have suites with special rooms where you can tend to your dead. We'll be able to wash Baby and get her ready ourselves. You can go out and buy clothes, and a blanket to wrap her in, and when we're ready we'll go and get Te Paania's family.' I told her how Mona's baby had been brought to us in a special little box, along with a spray of flowers which had been picked from the hospital garden and tied with white ribbon. 'The family'll be able to have turns sitting with Baby,' I said. 'And later, when a long enough time has been spent, we'll take Shane and Baby to the hospital chapel for prayers before taking them home.'

I was given this task while the others were occupied with Shane. I kept watch by Te Paania until you, her family, arrived. When the moment was right I talked to you about the baby. It was settled. You all agreed it was my job to see to Baby. I made sure I wasn't taking any rights away from anyone. I was to be the one to go and get Baby. We were the ones who were to be allowed to bring her home and give her her burial. This was serious to me.

It was a shabby room that we'd been shown to, painted dark brown and yellow, the dark colour going to a height above the reach of a person so that marks wouldn't show, or that's how I saw it. There were faded notices cellotaped to the walls. There were old cellotape marks where other notices had been. Also there were white spots, like eyes, dotted here and there about the walls, where holes had appeared in the plaster. You expected tears from them but there were none. There were two orange mats on the floor. You could tell by the hollows in them that they had been put there to cover missing tiles. I didn't like it as a place to wait for the dead.

There was plenty of time to notice all of this because it was more than an hour before a doctor in a white coat came out and said, 'Now we've had this request for a baby,' but he didn't say 'baby', he said 'body'. 'We've had this request for a body.' So there were these words that I didn't like, but never mind, I thought, these people have their words and we have ours. They are doctors, professionals, high-up people. Their words are different.

'Are you a relative?' he asked.

'The great-grandmother,' I said.

'There may be a problem,' he said.

'We've come to take Baby home,' I told him.

'There could be a problem with that, we'll have to see.'

'The father died in an accident,' I said as if to explain. 'The mother's in intensive care and we've come to get the baby.'

'You see it's not always the case,' the doctor said, 'where there's a pregnancy of this duration that people will claim the body.'

'The mother's parents know about it and have given me their permission.'

'There are other alternatives of course. But anyway I'll get the supervising doctor to come and see you. He'll be out in a little while. Very busy at the moment, it's been a bad weekend.'

As he left, Grandson Darcy came in, younger brother of Shane. 'What's all that about?' he asked. This grandson of ours isn't good in quiet places and I didn't really want him there. Instead of answering him I sent him to get a jacket for Niecy from the car.

There was another long wait before the supervising doctor came in. He greeted us, asked about Te Paania, took his time.

'Now there's a difficulty,' he said. 'It's been one of these horrendous weekends and we're actually having a little trouble locating the body. Do you think you could come back later this afternoon when we'll have a little more time?'

'We'll wait here,' I said.

'What do you mean?' Darcy asked.

'Or another alternative would be for us to arrange disposal. We could do that for you if you wish.'

'What do you mean, "trouble locating"?'

'We need time. The corpse has been mislaid, temporarily.' His words cut into me like knives. Never mind, I'd been cut before.

'You've lost Baby?' Darcy's voice was rising.

'Misplaced,' the doctor said. 'Something administrative . . . But as I said, you could come back a little later, when we've had a bit more time, or we could arrange disposal for you . . . if that would suit.'

'We'll wait for Baby,' I said.

'Get a lawyer,' the wild grandson said, his voice becoming higher and louder.

'Stop your noise,' I said even though I was feeling bad. 'They've got difficult work to do here and it's a busy time. Let them sort it out. We'll wait, do what we have to do, then we'll take Baby home.'

'Mahaki's a lawyer,' Niecy said. 'Mahaki and Dave should be contacted anyway. I'll go and ring.' She went off to look for a phone.

When Mahaki arrived nearly two hours later we were still waiting. Darcy was walking in and out giving his loud opinion to anyone who would listen.

'What's going on?' Mahaki asked.

'There's been a stuff-up,' Darcy said.

'It's taking a while to get sorted out,' I said to this Mahaki, who

61

wasn't my idea of a lawyer at all, with his tracksuit, his running shoes and his bushy head. He looked like a troublemaker to me.

It was another hour before an assistant came back and said that the body had been located and that the doctor would be out shortly. It was a relief to know that I was going to be able to get on with this task I'd been given.

But not long afterwards another white-coated man came in. He wasn't a doctor or a high-up person, just an orderly I think. He was sissy. 'They found Baby in a Wastecare bin,' he said in a loud whisper and a sissy voice. 'They've had someone going through the bin for the last hour, thought you ought to know.' Then he left. He was a liar, I thought. Darcy became quiet and we all sat without speaking, worrying about what the orderly had said.

When the doctor came out again he said that they needed to perform a post-mortem before they released the body.

'Well no,' said this busybody Mahaki. 'I don't think there's any legal requirement for that, not if you haven't done it already.'

'It's what we've decided needs to be done,' the doctor said.

'Well, can you tell me why it wasn't done before, before you lost the baby, before you put her in the Wastecare bin?' And the two of them had a discussion that I thought was none of this Mahaki's business. What was our baby to do with him? I was annoyed that Niecy had contacted him – but at the same time I noticed that the doctor hadn't denied that Baby had been found in a Wastecare bin.

'We don't want trouble,' I said, feeling upset with the way Mahaki was taking over without asking what we thought. He was shoving his hands into his pockets, jingling coins, staring the doctor in the eyes in such an ill-mannered way. 'If it has to be done it has to be done, doctor knows,' I said.

'We'll be as quick as we can,' the doctor said to me, turning his back on Mahaki. 'We've notified the pathologist and he'll be free to carry out the autopsy late this afternoon. I suggest you come back this evening.'

'We'll wait for Baby,' I said, and sat down.

I was ashamed that all these things were happening, that all these words were being said to doctors, that it was all taking so much time.

But even though I wasn't happy I still felt strong enough to do the job I'd been given. There was this and that going wrong, there was Mahaki meddling in our business, there was my grandson Darcy playing up, but I knew I could get through it all. I sent Niecy and Darcy out to buy baby clothes and told them to have a meal while they were out. Mahaki went away to use the phone.

They had all returned and were waiting there with me by the time our baby was put into my hands – but there was something else wrong.

'She's been born without eyes,' Niecy said.

'Hurt in the accident,' Darcy said, but I knew that neither of these things was true. I was so ashamed of what was happening. This was my job and this is what I was taking into my hands – a baby without eyes, a baby whose eyes had been taken out, a baby whose eyes had been stolen.

I held on to my feelings, not telling Niecy and Darcy what I knew. I prayed and prayed, reminding myself of other times when I'd had to wait a bad time through. At last I felt this deep wave of terrible patience spread through me. You hold yourself back, and by doing that you hold back others who won't react until you have reacted. You hold because of who may scream, shout, laugh, kill or cry.

How evil it is to be so good.

I should've screamed and cried, but I prayed myself into a deep, deep patience which stopped the cry in my throat. I thought that if I was patient, if I explained, then everything would be all right.

'Baby is not whole,' I said to the doctor. 'There's been a mistake. Baby has no eyes. I can't take Baby home to her family without eyes. What would people think of me? I have this duty, not only for my own family but the mother's family too. Before I came in here I spoke with my grandson's wife's parents who were sure I was the one to take care of this – but I can't take Baby like this for Te Paania's parents and grandfather to see. I can't take Baby home to the people like this, for burial.'

'I can get you the eyes,' the doctor said. 'It's not a problem.'

'Hold it,' Mahaki said as the doctor turned to go. 'First I'd like to know the reason for the removal of Baby's eyes.'

'There's no requirement for me to give a reason,' the doctor said.

'My clients . . .' I was angry with this Mahaki. We didn't need anyone speaking on our behalf. We were no clients of his.

'Could we please have the eyes,' I said. 'We have to take Baby home.'

What I had wanted was for Baby's eyes to be put back in, for Baby to be repaired, but as the doctor left with Mahaki after him, and with the words going on between them, all I wanted to do was to get the eyes so we could take Baby away from there.

The doctor came back with a plastic bag. And I hope that once you've learned all there is to cry for that you will cry for me also. Our baby had been discarded, our baby had been disfigured – but we can all understand that different people have their different ways, their different reasons for what they do. What we can't know is how different we are in our feelings and understandings – until something happens. The eyes were brought to us in a container inside a plastic supermarket bag. Our baby's eyes had become food. They were pies, lollies, pickles, plums, peas. It was the swallowing of chiefly eyes. I couldn't believe it at all. It was a terrible nightmare. You think that people know, think that they are high-up people, then you discover that all they are is different. To you they are empty, and you see it.

'And if you wouldn't mind waiting,' the doctor said, 'there are a few formalities. You need police permission before you can take the body away.'

'That'll be the day,' Mahaki said. 'E Kui,' he said to me, 'I think you should just take Baby and go. It's your baby. They can't treat you like this. You don't have to wait for any policeman . . .'

'Following an autopsy that's what we require,' the doctor said. 'Sergeant Hewton will be along shortly.'

'We'll wait,' I said, but these were just words coming out of me, coming from goodness. I wanted to cry out, could feel it welling up. There wasn't a prayer left in me but I wanted to call out to those who had died a long time ago. I couldn't be strong without them. I discarded the bag, took the little jar containing the eyes and tied them in a scarf I'd been wearing.

The doctor left with scissors flying after him, thrown by Darcy, which hit flat against the swinging doors, clanked onto the floor and spun across the room. I don't know where Darcy had found the scissors.

I kept my cry. There would be time. I knitted backwards to that place of patience until I found it. We sat down and waited. 'They don't know how we feel about being made into food,' I explained to Mahaki and Niecy. Darcy had gone. 'They have different words and different ways.' I felt embarrassed by what I was saying.

Then Niecy stood and held out her one good arm to me. So I gave Baby to her to hold while we waited. She wiggled her fingers for the jar with the eyes and I gave it to her. 'I'm going now,' she said. 'I'm taking Baby out of here, taking her home,' and she went. I'd been entrusted, yet here was my granddaughter, eighteen years old, deciding, taking and going.

It took Shane to open my mouth and it took his sister to move me. It took the two of them to stop me being this woman of evil patience and goodness, to stop me waiting there doing what I was told, to stop me sitting frightened of white coats, to stop me listening to people who gave themselves their own authority, to stop me letting them not tell me why they'd stolen our baby's eyes, to stop me demanding to know why they'd wrapped our baby's eyes like food, to stop me holding on to shame.

I stood and followed Niecy, at first tiptoeing along the corridors as though I was in a holy place, while Mahaki went in the other direction demanding. I could hear his voice sounding down the hallways as I went.

So there I was, this evil woman. I began wailing for my sins, walking along the corridors, following a green line which led to the main doors. Niecy was way ahead, not slowing down to wait for me, angry, leaving me behind.

It's not easy to learn that you are evil when you thought yourself good, to learn you're stupid when you thought yourself knowledgeable, to learn that those you thought crazy were not – and you killed them. I hope that as you cry you'll cry for me.

'Bernice, Granddaughter,' I called, but she kept on and on, not hurrying, not turning, not answering me, corridor after corridor. She stopped outside the front doors, holding on to Baby as though she thought I might take her and go back to wait for the policeman. 'You can't steal from us any more Gran Kura,' Niecy said to me. 'Otherwise why did Shane die?' She was calling me a thief.

There's a little ball inside me, a core. Round it are layers and layers, like bandages, that I've wrapped it in over the years so that it would remain hidden. Now, because of the children's children, and because my mouth has been opened, I must unwrap the little ball, find it, let the secrets free.

Shane wanted his name, and though this comes too late for him, I have names to give. He wanted his stories and I have these to give. I speak to you now in the language that I haven't used since the time of Riripeti. I will never speak English again. By the time I die I hope to be again who I was born to be.

8

TE PAANIA

Mum threaded a belt through the loops on my jeans and made a new hole with nail scissors. 'Those stick dolls we used to make,' I said, looking at my reflection. She pulled the strap through and buckled me up against my backbone.

'What's dem for, Kafaleen?' I said in a doll voice to the doll in the speckled mirror. Kafaleen manoeuvred the crutches and gave a two-step demo. 'For walk, Peaceful. Want a go?' she said. Mum followed up behind me – behind that Kafaleen in the mirror – stretching the neck of a T-shirt to put over my head.

'Leave it hanging,' she said smoothing it down. 'Cover the knobs.' I wriggled my feet into scuffs. It was hot. We were both trickling.

Out in the corridor, Grandfather, himself a stick doll, man-sized, waited with a wheelchair. He had a hanging face and big plates of teeth that clacked when he talked. On the handle of the wheelchair his hands were long and pale. His own belt was pulled in on half-empty trousers too, his tucked-down shirt filling the pants seat like a false behind.

'We're away Papa.'

'Hoo-oo,' he went, along the corridors to the big doors.

'Go man, geddus ouda hia.'

Out, out, into the air and sun to where Dad was waiting with the car. But two swings of the crutches, some settling and shutting of doors and I was enclosed again, huh, looking out.

'Out of here,' Dad said. He was trickling too. Off we went like runaways.

We left the hospital grounds and entered the town where the angle-parks that lined both sides of the street were already full. I was looking out on shoppers, workers on tea breaks, sun hot on them.

At the service station Dad manoeuvred himself from the car, worked the buttons and set the pump throbbing in the tank, while Mum went to buy food and Grandfather stepped out to have a conversation with a boy in a red shirt who had come across to wash our windscreen. Nothing I could do. People were juicing their vehicles, asking directions, looking for toilets, making purchases. In and out, through glass.

'Bread roll? L&P?' Mum asked, her face at my window.

'Later thanks.'

'For the road,' she said, showing me a bottle of water she'd bought.

'Discount,' Dad said, rattling a can of Coke as he levered himself back in. He took us out on to the street again amongst cars and vans and work trucks. Energy. All going places, all part of it.

Civic centre, through industrial to the bridges and railway lines. In the slow lane. Out on to the highway – sedately, in honour of my injuries, plates and bolts, my new bionic self – back the way I'd come that night in dead silence.

Here or here or here, fixed to a machine, in an ambulance with lights flashing and siren going, a baby with a heart like a geranium petal had slithered out of me. Had there been someone there to take her into their hands? This was something I didn't know. Shane in the ambulance too? Shane dead? Shane alive? I didn't know.

Wanted, Dead or Alive.

'There's a little light,' my grandfather sang. *'Always shining bright, By that window, At the end of the lane ...'* Hot air coming in the open window, smell of hot tarmac mingled with that of roadside plants and grasses, spruced and scented after days of rain. The sky was high and clear.

'Coming up soon,' my mother said.

68

'. . . *road is long and filled with many a turning,*' Grandfather sang, but I remembered nothing of this long road.

'Somewhere here?' my mother asked.

Long and clear.

But what had I expected?

An obstacle course of mangled iron, exploded rubber and shattered glass? Wheel marks burned black into the black tarseal? Hair and bone and blood? A chalk outline of a long-legged man, a big x painted in red?

X marks the spot.

Stake-out at the OK Corral.

Howdy pardner.

Dad slowed the car and halfway along the stretch he pulled over. My mother helped me from the car and we stood at the roadside, but what did I expect to do? Plant a white cross on the verge and decorate it with a necklet of flowers? No, not that.

Instead I watched, propped against the back of the car as my mother walked backwards and forwards across the asphalt, sprinkling water from the bottle. Grandfather followed her, chanting a karakia with Dad a few steps behind. I lifted my face to the sun which poured like syrup.

'That done it,' Grandfather said when he'd come to the end of his chanting and returned to the car. 'Hee hee, that done it. Gone.'

Alleluia.

Enclosed again and on, reversing a hill that I remembered. Up, unwinding it, then down the upside – to a straight that I remembered. Truck, car, car, purple alleluia. The ocean was steel chains beside us all the way to the turn-off heading to the top of the stony road.

'Where he nearly put us in the drink,' I said as we made our way downhill to where the narrow road narrowed even further, eyeing down on the river.

'Thought he was Stirling Moss,' Dad said.

'Madman,' Mum said.

'Horses, all horses,' Grandfather said. 'Horse track, that's all.'

We continued down the gully's ledge beside the bushes of rangiora, kawakawa and fern, all brightened by rain and sunlight. Across the gully the stands of manuka were covered in flowers – like looking down on stars as we descended, not flying.

Blackberry, foxgloves and broom. Time to notice all this as we turned towards the river crossing where the water was muddier and deeper than when we'd come roaring through it that night with water spreading up and out like wings. Debris had piled against the banks and in the shallows.

'So this is your country, Father,' Dad said. The wheels dipped, eased us across and out the other side.

'Capital City coming up,' Grandfather said. 'House of Parliament right there.' We turned towards the hills where the meeting house stood. 'Look like they flashed it up a bit since my day.'

The crutches made round dents in the ground as we made our way towards the house, called forward by the grandmothers, urged forward by the sea that swept up and back behind us. Rain earlier in the week had not affected this part of the land where the grass was dry and tufted, edged by hard, twisted flax and stunted bushes screwed into the gravelly soil. We paused at the place of lamenting where I leaned on my sticks and waited the time through. I didn't feel like crying, I'd done enough of that. I listened to the sounds rise and fall, felt the sun on me, breathed the salted air and began to feel part of the world again. We went with the others to sit down in front of the wharenui. The orators stood, welcoming us and having a crack at Grandfather for being away so long.

The wharenui was small and plain, sitting flat on the ground against stony hills on which there was a scattering of thin sheep. It was made of wide planks, painted white, with a green door and green window frames. One of the two front windows was curtained, giving the house a conspiritorial, winking look.

The only carvings on the outside of the house were the koruru at the apex of the widely pitched roof and the carved fingers at the ends of the maihi. From one of the carved fingers hung a bell.

Inside the house I was seated near the middle of the right wall, which is a see-all, hear-all place. From there I could see the faces about the circle, knew who had come in, who had left, who was waiting at the door, who was out smoking on the verandah, who was listening under the window. From there I could hear the whispers from every corner. It was a house without carvings, but the tahuhu, heke and pou had been painted in black and white patterns. Between the pou, and on the back and front walls, were the photographs.

Pillows were stacked behind me, a rug was placed across my knees and I found myself pleased to be there after all – if not to listen, then to rest in the presence of people.

Kura, seated on a stool by the door, was dressed in black. Her short black hair curled forward framing her face. Round her neck was a large greenstone ornament which hung from a black ribbon. Her body and hands were still but her eyes moved as they sought out the faces about the circle. The sea was running. There was a sharp smell of it coming through the open door.

I leaned back into the pillows and shut my eyes, my mind already made up about what I was going to hear – some story of misfortune caused by accident or abnormality to do with a baby. But my unknown baby was dead, gone, already cried for. This formality was all unnecessary, I thought.

It was a surprise though when Kura began to speak, because she spoke in Maori. I'd only ever heard her speak English before. My mother on one side, and grandfather on the other, began to interpret for me, knowing that my understanding was limited. But I wished they wouldn't bother, I knew enough to get the gist of what was being said.

So even when the word 'body', spoken deliberately in English, took hold of my breath and my ear, I gave it a shake, flicked it away from me, because it was as Gran Kura said, there were people who used a different set of words from what we would use.

However 'body' did not prepare me for 'arrange disposal'. 'Arrange disposal' did not prepare me for 'corpse' or 'mislaid'. What was happening here? I sat up, leaned forward, needing to know.

I was accustomed to pain, which at one stage had been my friend. Over the eight weeks that I'd been in hospital I'd not been completely free of it, but as I listened a new pain began to grow in me that was not like anything I'd felt before. It began in my head and was like a hot stone which moved down through the bones of my face, hollowing and searing them.

As Gran Kura continued speaking, the burning stone dropped, lodging at first in the upper part of my body until I thought my heart would burst. It dropped again, taking my heart with it to my stomach, where it broke and opened, reaching to every part of me.

I was breaking and opening and there was a cry that shouted through bone. After Gran's voice had stopped, after the pain had gone, I knew that my cast-out and plundered baby had been born to me.

I lifted her, felt the airy weight of her, smelled the smell that a new baby has – of warm soil – and when I put her against my shoulder and began to rock, she squirmed and nudged her head into my neck in a most tender way. I knew I would've laid down my life.

People drew in about me, put their hands on me, washed my face and hands as though I was a child. There were voices, the sea roaring on the sand, and I fell into a dream-filled sleep where a limbless doll, strapped to my shoulder, said in her squeaky doll voice, 'You have to find them for me.'

I walked, in the doll dream, along a roadway until I came to a place where there was rubbish all over the land. I began to walk over the debris with a stick in my hand, turning aside seaweed, broken bricks, branches, corrugated iron, tyres, containers, coats and baby clothes, fishing nets and rotting fish, concrete, posts, wire, sacks and boxes. I couldn't find what I was looking for, and the doll began to bite my neck and my shoulder and to wriggle and scratch. There was a cloud ahead of me that rolled itself into a large ball, came towards me and began to explode about me in muted colours. I was caught by it, unable to move. The doll freed herself from the strap that held her to me. She had grown wings on her limbless torso and flew away from me leaving a white trail. I stepped on to the trail, stumbling after her, calling her to come home, come home. But my voice was locked inside me. The words would not form.

There was light above the door with a pair of moths pitching about in it. People, except for Gran Kura, were on the mattresses sleeping.

'In a drawer in my bedroom,' Gran Kura said from under mothlight, 'I have a carved box that used to belong to my grandmother. In it I keep

72

jewellery and other treasured items that have been given to me to look after. I thought at first that I would put the eyes in this beautiful box for burial. In such a box they would be precious. But I found the box was too big and heavy for such little things.

'Inside the box was this hei pounamu that I wear today. It's a gift handed down from Pirinoa to our grandfather, who put it round the neck of his wife before he died so that it wouldn't be robbed from his grave. I had wrapped the hei pounamu in a square of embroidered silk. So I took the piece of silk, wrapped the eyes in it and bound them round our baby's midriff.

'Stomach eyes.

'It's a strange place for eyes to be, but they seemed safe there. And it's true, isn't it, that our stomachs give us sight. It's true that it's through our insides that we know what we know. When I'd done that we tucked her back in with Shane and had our funeral ceremonies. Tomorrow we'll go to the burial place.'

There were two hearts beating, one as pounding waves, the other as the tapping of insect wings. I shut my eyes again, rocking in and out of dreams.

9

TAWERA

'Take your clothes off and show me,' I said, curious about the stomach eyes. So she did a down-trou, pulled up her shirt and there they were, the two eyes either side of her belly button, her bb being a little bit of wrinkled forehead between these eyes. From the wide forehead the long face tapered down. It was an elephant face I was looking at, but with one very important piece missing. Her hands holding the shirt at her sides were the two elephant ears.

The eyes were a disappointment, though. I thought that they would be eyes that my sister could see the world with, except that she would see from a position lower down. I thought they would be eyes that pierced clothing, or jewel eyes. However, they were only two eye-shaped brown patches that didn't move, had no light, didn't see.

But the elephant was good. I thought she was very fortunate to have an elephant, though it wasn't as grand as the one Dave took us to see at Tudor Park when the circus came to town. How could it be? The one that Dave took us to see was enormous. It had a chain attached to its foot and was shackled to an iron ring that was concreted to the ground. It was like a live building.

The man who looked after the elephant was not a prince wearing a jewelled turban and red and gold robes like the princes in books, and he didn't have a long and interesting name. He was called Jason. Jason had a thin bright red face, yellow hair and rope eyebrows. He wore a tight white T-shirt and jeans with a studded belt. The bottoms of his jeans were tucked down into cowboy boots. So even though Jason wasn't a prince he wasn't a disappointment. He had a stick with a hook on it which he jabbed in behind the elephant's ear to tell him where he wanted him to go. I thought it might be cruel. Jason gave the elephant a scrub and a hose-down, then led him to a drum of water where he had a big drink. Sprayed water all over the place too, that elephant.

'You can't see with those eyes,' I said, trying not to make it sound like a criticism.

'See?' she said. 'What's see?'

'See is looking at something with your eyes and knowing what it is.'

'I can look at you talking,' she said. 'And know what it is.'

'That's not see, that's hear.'

'Explain hear.'

'Hear is listening to something with your ears and knowing what it is.'

'Well I do have ears you know, nobody took my ears.'

And then my sister said something. Something big, something bigger than an elephant, something enormous. 'I don't need to see,' she said. 'I don't need eyes. I have you to be my eyes.'

Ahh, ahh!

After we'd been to see the elephant Dave took me to the Family Fun Centre where there's a pinball game that I like to play. We put our money in and all the balls came rattling down. We pulled back the pin and fired the balls one by one. They went along and around all the pathways making the coloured lights flash, making the electronic sounds ring and ping and ding and sing. That's what I was like just then, when my sister said she didn't need to see because she had me to be her eyes. I was a pinball machine. There were coloured lights flashing all round me, bells singing all through me, a clamour in my head. I was so excited when she said it that I had to hold my raho, I did. I grabbed and held. This was the biggest thing for me. The biggest thing of my life so far was to be my sister's eyes. 'You can tell it all to me, everything you see,' she said.

Ahh.

What an important job this was for me. I thought I should begin right then by telling her about the elephants.

'First your elephant,' I said. 'You are very fortunate to be the owner of an elephant, even though you may not think it makes up for what I thought you had. That is, I thought that you had seeing eyes in the middle of your body, laser eyes, penetrating clothing, seeing everything at a level that no one else can. I imagined that they would be jewels, peridots, like in Dave and Mahaki's book about Earth and all its treasures. I had chosen peridots for your eyes to be like.

'The reason I thought of jewels was because Gran Kura said she had put the eyes in a silk scarf from a jewel box and tied them round your stomach for your burial. I imagined two jewel eyes, glinting and seeing, knowing everything.'

'Never mind about *see*,' she said. '*See* means nothing to me. I don't care about *see*. You said you were going to tell me about the elephants. I want to know about the elephants.'

I pulled her trousers down again and drew the shapes of the eyes with my fingers. 'These are the eyes,' I said, 'and in between them your button is a little wrinkled circle, a piece of jiggedy forehead.'

'What's *circle*, what's *wrinkled* and *jiggedy*?' she asked.

I drew the shape of a circle on her, then wrinkled some skin on her forearm and let her feel it. I guided her finger to her pito to touch the little elephant frown. 'But I have to tell you,' I said, trying again not to make it sound like a criticism, 'there's an important part missing. If you had a raho like mine, that would've been the elephant's trunk which flops down over its mouth like a long nose. It can squirt water too.'

'What's *raho*?' she said.

I pulled my own pants down and put her hand on my raho, let her give it a good pull. 'Well you could be the elephant with the nose and I could be the one with the eyes,' she said. I thought my sister was so clever to have thought of that.

I was excited about it. I showed her how to put her hands at her sides to make the elephant ears. 'That's good. That's all right,' she said, 'Now the big elephant, the one that Dave took us to see. You didn't tell

76

me about that. As a matter of fact you forgot all about me that day, left me behind, went running off. You got on Dave's shoulders, talked to Dave and not to me. You shouted and made stupid noises, didn't speak to me at all.'

'Well I didn't know then that I was your eyes,' I said. But I was ashamed. It was true I had forgotten her, didn't speak to her that day, didn't make room for her when I was up high on Dave's shoulders.

I took her by the hand and walked her along the bedroom wall. 'That's how long an elephant is,' I said. Then we climbed up on the dresser to show her the height of an elephant, walked across the end of the bed to show her the width.

After that we took our clothes off so that we could be elephants again. We went lumbering through the trees flapping our big ears, calling to each other, pulling down branches and turning everything upside down in the jungle. When we had done all that we went out to the kitchen to show ourselves to our mother who looked up from the papers she was studying. 'Put your clothes on Tawera,' she said.

'We're elephants,' I said.

'Put your clothes on.'

'She's got hers off too.'

'Both of you. Put your clothes on, it's bloody freezing.'

'She's got stomach eyes and no trunk. I've got a trunk and no eyes. All the trees in the jungle are down.'

'That could upset the monkeys,' she said. 'You'd better put it all back together.' She went back to staring at her pages.

We went to the bedroom and put our clothes on, but we didn't put the toys back in the box, didn't put the covers back on the bed, didn't put the clothes back in the drawers or hang the jackets in the wardrobe or put the shoes beside each other in pairs.

When we went back out to the kitchen Mum's eyes were still glassy on her reading. It was information that she had from the principal of the school that I would be attending.

In three weeks' time I would be five, and for some months Mum, Gran Kura, Mahaki and Dave had been discussing whether or not I should go to school. They'd been round schools like a band of detectives, looking for clues to find out whether I should go here or there, or whether I should be kept at home. They'd been terrorising the school principals and teachers with their questions and their demands but in the end seemed to realise that I would be all right at our local school. I could've told them that. During that past month the teachers had been letting me come to school two mornings a week to try it out and I'd had fun every time.

I took crayons from the kitchen shelf and sat up at the table making room for my sister beside me. She was a little dissatisfied with this because she really wanted to keep on with the elephant game. But I began to draw, outlining an elephant as high and as wide as the page, with a trunk from top to bottom. It had big ears, strong legs and a little tail. I explained it all to her and asked for her opinion. We thought of colouring the elephant grey, then decided it would be much happier to be red. So I coloured heavily with the red crayon, making sure there was no white paper showing. Beside this big elephant I outlined a smaller one. It had to be smaller so that the big elephant could still be seen on the other side of it. I coloured the small elephant blue, but it came out mostly purple because of the red behind it. We thought it would be happy to be purple, though my sister was getting niggly with me for not explaining colours properly.

There were still some white patches of paper showing round the edges of the elephants so I coloured these, making an orange and yellow jungle. When I'd finished I put it up on the door of the fridge with all my other drawings, attaching it with magnets.

'What do you think Mum?' I asked.

'I think it's excellent,' she said. 'But you've used the back of one of my pages.'

'If you want to read your page again Mum, you can get it down, read it, and put it back when you've finished.' She laughed.

Just then Gran Kura came in. Gran sat down on the settee, puffed out from coming up the hill and climbing the stairs. She'd been down to the school for Grandparents' Day because our friend Kawea, who is already five, didn't have his own grandparent to take to school. He borrowed Gran Kura. Gran Kura was going to be working down at the school on some afternoons in the new bilingual class, helping teachers with our language. She'd been amazed when the principal had asked her to do that.

I thought Mum wouldn't mind if I took another piece of paper. I started drawing a picture of Superman, remembering that I wanted to ask Mum something.

I was making the big S when Mum put her papers away and she and Gran began cooking. 'Did you tidy up your things?' she asked. I didn't answer. She had sausages cooking in a pan and was tipping some crinkly pasta into boiling water. Gran was at the bench breaking up a lettuce. I felt like complaining.

'Can I go downstairs for tea?' I asked.

'And me. What about me?' my sister said. She was niggly too.

'We, I mean we,' I said. 'Both of us, you know that.'

'You always forget.'

'I don't forget. I always mean *we* even if I say *I*.'

'Mahaki's not coming home for tea and Dave's going to be late,' my mother said.

I felt a bit grumpy about that too. 'They're always out, or late,' I said. 'I thought they were supposed to be my fathers. How can they be my fathers if they're out all the time? And there aren't enough sausages.'

'We're cutting up the sausages.'

'That doesn't make more.'

'Set the table please Tawera,' my mother said.

'And her.'

'The two of you. Set the table, please.'

Then I remembered that thing that I wanted to ask and thought I'd better stop acting up, being a pain. I set out four places at the table, put the salt, pepper, bread and butter in the middle and straightened our chairs, ready to ask.

'Set another place,' Mum said. 'When you hear Dave you can go and get him to come up.' That was all right, I did it straight away.

'Good,' Mum said, going from cupboard, to fridge, to warming drawer until the food was all on the table. I think her eyes were still dazed from her papers.

'Can we watch 'Lois and Clark' after this?' I asked.

'When you've tidied your jungle and had a shower,' she said.

'You're a pain, Mum.'

After tea we went into the bedroom and tossed toys back into the box, pulled the cover up over the bed, put the clothes away and tidied the shoes. We peeled off and got into the shower where we became elephants again, splashing and squirting water everywhere. Or we were princes, riding high, forgetting all about 'Lois and Clark' until Dave came in to get us out. He helped us dry the walls and the floor with a towel, helped us get our pjs on, then we went out and turned on television. It was quite boring waiting for Clark to change into Superman so we went to bed.

From my bedroom I can look through the doorway to a section of wall where we pin all our photos. There are so many photographs that there's not one bit of wall to be seen. Some of Shane, one of Mum on crutches, some of Mum and me, Mahaki, Dave, all their friends, Gran Kura, Gran Vera and Koro Joe, Niecy, Darcy and Gordon, my grandparents who are my mother's parents, the singing grandfather, my father, other grannies, other aunts, uncles, Brooke and January and all my other cousins. All of these photographs overlap in so many smiles and frowns and colours that sometimes I can't find the one I'm looking for, even when I stand on a chair. We say things to each other like, 'Where's that one of Mahaki? Not that one, the one of him laughing, the one with his arm round Mum, the one of him holding me.' Or, 'Where's the one of Aunty Mahu standing by the car when she was waiting for Janey to take her up North? Where's Jody's baby?' Etcetera, etcetera.

Even though there wasn't a photo of my sister, she looked like some of the people in the photos, especially Shane. She was eight now, and tall. She had a long forehead and black holes from where her eyes had been stolen. Her long hair was caught up into a high horsy tail at the top of her head. She had big front teeth. The holes where her eyes should have been were like holes burnt through wood with a red-hot poker – which was something Mahaki showed me how to do when it was winter time and we had a fire. He wrote my name on a piece of wood with the hot poker, then bored a hole right through it so I could hang it on my door. The holes were black round the edges from the burns. My sister had spaceship pjs, like mine.

When Mum came into the bedroom to see us I remembered something else I'd been wanting to ask about. 'Mum I'm nearly five,' I said. 'So far you've only told about her . . .'

My sister gave me such a jolt with her elbow. 'Talking about me as if I wasn't here,' she said. 'I have got ears you know, they didn't remove my ears.'

But I kept on with what I wanted to say.

'Who was buried but refused to be buried. All that . . . You and Gran Kura . . .'

'I have got feelings, you know.'

'And about you hobbling round on crutches, leaving and coming . . .'

'It takes time,' Mum said.

'That treasure box, those eyes . . . Mum, I'm nearly five and you haven't told me about my father. So far I've only heard about that Shane.'

That cowboy.

10

TE PAANIA

'I'm buried,' I said.

'No, not buried.' It was grandfather's echoey voice.

'I'm there, under, two of us in the deep dark.'

'You're here,' he said. 'You done it, remember? Hee hee, you come back.'

'Dirt in my throat, sand in my eyes. Baby . . .'

'Open them. Open your eyes.'

I climbed, pulled myself up out of dreaming, out of the hollow, beyond the quiet breathing in my ear, opened my eyes.

Grandfather was sitting on his mattress beside me with his back against the wall, my sticks making a cross over his chest, his arms folded over them. His short, streaky hair was damp and combed back. Light from a window was giving his face a shine, showing up the purple rings round his irises. He was like something from out of water.

'You been dreaming, fighting off ghosts?' he asked. He was wearing a green T-shirt and black track pants. His veiny feet, with their finger-like toes and yellowed toenails, looked artless, made him seem holy.

'I was being shovelled under, two of us . . .'

'You got a long way to go before that, or else you done all that struggle for nothing there in the hospital. Hee, hee, you got to put me down first.'

'Asleep and dreaming, or awake and not dreaming there's Baby – crying, sleeping, waking, breathing in my ear . . .'

'Course. She got to hang around for a while so we know she's a mokopuna, not a rubbish, not a kai. How do we know she not a fish if she don't hang around for a while – or a blind eel or old newspaper or rat shit. Huh. You don't expect her go away, join her ancestors, foof, just like that,' and he threw his hands up. 'Not after all that business.'

He used my sticks to stand, then leaned them up against the wall while he pulled the sheet away from his mattress and stacked it with the others in the middle of the room. 'You supposed to send it away, that baby. Kura and them didn't send that baby off. Got to send it off, otherwise trouble, get up to mischief, hee hee. Girl you got trouble.'

'Don't tell them Papa, don't remind them or they'll send her. They'll do it.'

'Ha ha, too late now.'

'Where are they? Where's everyone?'

'Breakfast.'

'You been waiting for me to wake up, get up out of that hole?'

He passed the sticks to me. 'We got to go over to the urupa after breakfast then get on the road, get home before dark,' he said.

Fresh flowers had been placed there for our coming. The dirt, piled high, was new and raw and I could feel it down inside me, taste it. Under all this rock and dirt and sand was Shane – in my mind elongated, flattened, pressed out like flowers, pinned like a butterfly: a specimen, dried and ironed, the juices gone.

The prayers had been said for all of us and now the gospel singers and their guitars had taken over.

Heavenly Lord I appreciate you.

The sun was warm on my back and people had begun to move around from grave to grave enjoying the warmth, or they sat by the headstones, in twos and threes, talking.

I appreciate you, Heavenly Lord I appreciate you . . .

Or?

Or in bits and pieces probably, dried and ironed. 'Was he messed up much?' I asked the cousins beside me.

'So bad they kept the lid on.'

'Except they took it off once.'

'To put Baby there.'

Baby, buried and not buried, buried but refusing to be buried.

. . . love and adore you, bow down before you . . .

'But Gran and Uncle Joe done that, put Baby in.'

'The staunch ones.'

I kept hold, listened to voices, refusing the dirt in my mouth.

'With the minister doing his thing, blahty blahty blah.'

Refusing to be buried. Climbing. People to hold me there.

'So, we never saw.'

'But Baby, before that . . .'

'We saw. All had a hold of Baby.'

'Baby was sweet.'

Sweet, keeping me there.

'Except what was done wasn't sweet . . .'

'Was cruel . . .'

'They think they can experiment on us brown people.'

'Look for cures for their own sicknesses.'

'See what we're made of.'

'Slugs and snails and puppy dogs' tails.'

'Get eyes for other people's babies.'

'Or sell them, get a lot of money.'

'From doctors in China.'

'Or they think they can find out if the mother's a druggy from her baby's eyes, is what I heard . . .'

I felt breath by my ear while the singers moved on to glory.

. . . set my people free, God said set my people free, God said set my people free . . .

'Hot that day.'

'Thirty-four degrees.'

. . . find the promised land, Glory glory glory glory . . .

84

'We brought them out on the marae for the service, then into the church for a bit more blahty blah, then here.'

'Hot as hell.'

Glory glory glory glory, Glory glory glory glory, Glory glory glory glory, Glory glory glory glory, To find the promised land.

Alleluia.

Shane.

Today the world looked different from what it had the day before when we'd set out from the hospital. The road unrolled ahead of us like a spilled bandage. On either side the paddocks were an intense, exaggerated green that I had forgotten belonged in the world except in plastic tags and flags and paint and labels. Now it jolted into memory, shocking, sticking against my eyes – this aggressive, bleeding green. I could hear crying.

Black and white jigsaw cows with their tails scything, stood to their knees in this greenness, curling tufts of it into their square mouths, chewing and swallowing it, vomiting it, swinging it back and forth in their furry udders, dripping it, plopping it – heavy, clotted green.

Further on there was a herd on the road. We came to a standstill as the animals divided around us, lifting their heads and opening their grey, foamy mouths to moo, rolling back their drunken eyes. Behind them a thin dog kept them turned. A man in a check shirt and a cap stood by the ditch with his arms extended. There was a sick, milky smell. It was time to talk, cry, sing. Mum?

In the less green places, the stubbled paddocks were daubed with sheep that were like dingy clouds, dirty sky reflections. Swabs. Dressings.

Mum, Dad, Grandfather?

'They were painting,' Mum said. 'Dad up the ladder, Papa stirring the tin, early in the morning before it got too hot, when the hospital . . .'

'Three boards and I got to come down,' Dad said. 'Couldn't hear what it was about the hospital. She was bawling. Had to come down to see what she's bawling about.'

'Ha ha, no teeth in her mouth,' Grandfather said. 'Fla, fla, fla.'

'It was Niecy who remembered our name so they could phone.'

'Then all of us bawling and getting ready. All the kids, everybody.'

'We said, "You all can't come, got to stay home."'

'All crying, no room in the car.'

'Had to ring up Dobby down the garage to open up and put two new tyres on. Fill up and away.'

'What colour?'

'Grape.'

'Mae and Tama picked it, grape they reckon.'

'But we haven't bought the grape yet. Just undercoat. White.'

White silence. Gauze and plaster, sheets and tubes.

Stacked pipes by the roadside and heavy gouges in the hillsides. Clay and rubble in fallen piles. The signs and marker cones were out and a man in an orange coat swivelled his STOP GO sign from red to green to let us through. Mud sprayed out from under our wheels as we passed the road machines scooping up slush, or which put out long arms to pick up boulders and branches, handing them on to trucks that waited with their engines running. We twisted our way uphill between wet banks. Yellow clay walls.

Surrounding me.

'What about window-sills?'

'Hyacinth, Mae reckons, and the doors, hyacinth.'

'That's if we got money left for hyacinth. If I still got a job.'

'And grape, if people still want meat.'

We wound down to the flats where we came up behind a truck carrying two layers of cattle, their black backs and ears visible above the top tray. Every now and then there was a lifted head and a rolled-back, frightened, cow eye. The eye of the driver found us in his side mirror. He put out an arm, waving us on.

Passing it, passing it.

Shane.

Wheels and wheels and wheels. Wheels and doors. Muck and milk smell. Crying. Passing it. 'Sing, Papa.'

'. . . *road is long and filled with many a turning* . . .' groaning through old teeth which tilted like rickety fences. '. . . *some day I wend my way back to where that someone . . .'* Dead trees stood and leaned. Uprooted stumps lay bleached or burned.

' . . . my dream come true, I will be there too . . .' I rearranged my bones, grasped hold of words, the cracked voice, held myself there.

And woke riding beside the full, brown river, which the week before had broken its banks and gone through the town. I knew the mud smell of it, and though the works had been closed for three years by then, mingling with the mud smell was the smell of rendered fat, the boiled offal of sheep and cattle, their stinking wool and hides.

Ghosts and the dirty river.

Beside it the fences were hung with debris, and the grass and weeds, though still clinging to the banks, had been combed sideways by the swift flow of water.

I'd been away from the town where I was born for ten years. Now I needed to return there to rest and recuperate, needed to get back to what was known and familiar and from there sort out what my life was going to be.

A dead sheep floated by, bloated – a sheep balloon – its stubs of legs pointing, like a macabre compass, in four directions.

We passed the Church of the Latter Day Saints and the High School where the headmaster had sliced us in half with his pink-sleeved, swinging arm. We entered the town where the roads were still yellow from water and mud that had flooded through. This was the place my mother had pushed me out of when I was fifteen. Out of the house, out of town was what she'd wanted. It wasn't for lack of love.

Shelving and goods had been brought out onto the footpaths outside the Trading Centre, the Discount Store and the saddle shop. Signs were out: Damage good's For sale, BUSINESS as USUAL, closed because of flood's.

Further along the river road, gardens had been flattened. People had brought their furniture and carpets out into the yards. We could see the watermarks under the window-sills of the houses as we turned in from the river and away from the low-lying land, bringing a baby home.

I'd thought at first it was because of the trouble I'd been in at school that my mother had turned me out, believed it was due to a lack of understanding on her part. But no. 'It's so you won't have to go and work in the freezing works,' she'd said.

'We got other mouths to feed,' my father, who isn't usually unkind, had said.

Of the two of them he was the one more upset over the trouble at school, trouble that my big mouth had got me into, trouble that ripping exam papers from corner to corner, straight across, any way at all, had caused.

Chop went the principal's arm at our first assembly when we'd entered High School in the third form. I don't know if it would've made any difference if I'd been on the left-hand side of the outstretched arm instead of the right.

'This half move to the right,' he'd said, looking along his long arm, 'and this half to the left.' Wave wave, went his arm this way. Wave wave, went his arm that way, until we had all moved further enough one way or the other to form a good aisle down the middle of the hall, ready for his next announcement.

'Those to the right will do cooking, sewing, metalwork and art, and will go to the Manual Block to be given classes, stationery lists and timetables,' he'd said. 'Those to the left will do shorthand, typing, woodwork and tech drawing and will remain here.' Teachers prowled up and down the aisle to make sure there were no defections.

'I want to do typing,' I'd said to my mates as we walked across the grounds to the Manual Block.

'Me too.'

'And me.'

'You tell them,' Jess and Maina said to me. 'Yes you.'

My mother worked from four in the afternoon until ten at night so that we wouldn't have to be employed in the freezing works, and though I hadn't figured out how her night-time job could prevent this, I now thought that if I wasn't going to be allowed to learn typing, how could I not work in the freezing works? I didn't think it would be so bad being a freezing worker like everyone else, but didn't want it to be a headmaster's chopping arm that decided it for me.

'Please, there are some of us who'd like to do typing,' I said to the teacher who was taking our names.

'You're out of luck,' she said.

'We don't want to do cooking, we can cook already.'

She didn't look up from the list that she was marking, didn't emphasise the word 'proper' when she spoke. She found my name on the list and ticked it. 'You'll learn proper cooking, Paania,' she said. 'You'll learn to cook proper food.'

I opened my mouth to call her a stuck-up bitch, but Jessie was too quick for me. She clamped both her hands over my gob, pulling my head back from behind. Tep and Maina each grabbed an arm and I was helpless. 'Stop horsing around,' the teacher said, 'I won't have any of that.' She kept her eyes on her book.

It was true that I could cook already. By the time I was ten I could prepare meals for the ten of us. Proper food. Flaps, hocks, neck chops and livers. Puha and spuds and doughboys. Proper meals. I could look after little children, wash them, feed them, put them to bed. I could wash clothes, have arguments, make school lunches, clean up the kitchen, boss younger children enough to help me.

Not bad for a frog.

Jess, Tep and Maina marched me, with my mouth still clamped, towards M4 for booklists and timetables.

We knew we'd been attacked but were not equipped to fight the out-stretched arm or the insinuations about not being proper. I didn't know then that a curse was a matter of potent ill-wishing, and that if we were not to die from it we needed to turn speakings back on those who spoke them in order to make them void. I didn't know, but I believe I had an idea of it, and that at least by opening my big mouth during those two years at school I showed some understanding of what I needed to do to defend myself. Even if I did it artlessly and without dignity, it was an attempt at dignity, a rejection of the idea of us not being proper people with ordinary hopes and a normal desire to learn and be part of the ordinary world.

I wasn't to be taken by surprise again. No one was able to shut me down from that day on. 'Mum, I did well,' I'd said, 'I did well at school.' She'd looked at me and pretended not to understand.

The school's ovens and utensils did not impress me, nor, after the first week or two, did the cloths and table settings and butter knives. Nor did the recipes. I felt like laughing when I looked at four pinwheel scones or a ten-centimetre pizza. It didn't seem like proper food at all.

However, there was something to appreciate. This cooking teacher who didn't think us proper, did however think that we could learn to be proper, or was determined that we would. Even though she seemed to think that she looked down on us from some great height – and I often told her what I thought about that – she had enough belief in what she did to think she could teach us. This was unlike others who thought that teaching us was impossible, who set us tasks of copying notes from the board and drawing maps and diagrams, which made us feel we were learning something but really only kept us quiet.

It wasn't her examination papers that I ripped up, swearing. It was the papers of some of the more pleasant, less sarcastic teachers, who spent hour after hour dictating notes to us without giving out any information, without assisting us to unlock any doors.

The smiling thieves.

At the end of each term I found myself staring at their test papers, staring at questions as though my staring would somehow turn questions into answers.

Finally, it was end to end, crossways, whichways, all ways. I heard myself mouthing. I had a ripping time.

Froggy out on the road.

Froggy on the way home.

Froggy fifteen years old.

The car turned in, my father walking the wheels up along the edges and ridges of the wheel tracks to the front of the house which had been scraped and primed. Three top boards white. Paint can and bucket of brushes behind a ladder which was lying on its side against the wall.

'Meatworks overalls and white boots, him up the ladder and me stirring. Ha ha, Girl, you got him down off there smart,' Grandfather

90

said, leaning his shoulder on me, leaning his head towards me, rattling my plated arm, squeezing his ringed eyes shut. 'Ha you fooled us.'

Mae, Tama and Georgie came down the steps and opened the doors, taking bags, getting me out and up the steps. 'What's so funny, Papa?' Tama asked.

'I didn't die,' I said. My brother laughed, helping me into the living room where a bed had been made up for me.

The room was smaller and darker than what I remembered. Mae's baby was there, standing bowlegged, holding the edge of the settee, fingers caught in the afghan-square blanket that covered the threadbare seat of it, lifting a foot, putting it down, lifting the other, practising.

Tama and Mae eased me into a chair, stood my sticks against the wall and went out while I let myself down into the noises of home – the unpacking, cooking, washing; voices from room to room; dogs in the yard rattling their chains; car doors banging. What else?

A baby noise close to my ear.

From the patched walls our younger selves smiled down from school photos – chopped, pudding-basin hairstyles, freckles and big teeth, wide mouths froggy and smiling. Strings of shells and plastic lei, puff-paint pennants, hessian wall-hangings, scenic calendars. I sank into it. 'Come on,' I said to Brooke, wiggling my fingers, but she couldn't, no matter how much she lifted one leg and then the other. Mae returned with nappies and cloths to change her, laying her on the settee on a towel.

Baby?

Yes, my own baby was dressed in a first size stretch-'n'-grow and hat, and was wrapped in a pink cuddle rug for the journey home. I unwrapped her now, took off the hat and flicked up her damp hair with my fingertips, cooling her. Her hair was long enough to stand up in half curls. There was a pattern, one row plain one row pearl, indented on one cheek where she had turned her head into the knitted bonnet while sleeping. Her hands were damp and there was wool fluff caught up in her fingers. Wash and change and feed. Scars, grafts, plates and sticks would not stop me doing those things for her.

'You want us to bring your kai in here?' Tama asked from the doorway.

'I want to come to the table like a real person.' I said, 'Don't need help, just my sticks.'

I made my way into the kitchen. 'Proper food,' I said.

'So hospital kai . . .?'

'Was OK.' Rattle, one-eared rabbit, bottles and pink medicine – Brookey things on the bench of worn Formica. Missing screws from hinges and missing screws from drawer handles made everything lopsy. Watercress, spuds. Flaps, neck chops, hocks. Where had the meatworks gone?

My father swallowed them.

Curtains on crazy wires, thin, torn. Mum. Worked, washed, used. Mum you're a curtain.

'So what's all this we heard?' Georgie asked. Eyes round the table fixed on Mum as she began to tell about Baby, who was, right then, talking in my ears.

In the night a baby cried but it was in another room. It was a sad bleating. Soon there was whispering, the creak of floorboards, and Mae, carrying Brooke, went through the living room – where I lay looking into the dark – and out into the kitchen. The light went on and I heard her walking back and forth talking while a bottle heated in the jug.

'Bring her here,' I called. So she came in and sat on my bed while she gave Brooke her bottle.

'She was sleeping right through before,' she said. 'But lately she's been up at midnight every night no matter what time I put her down. It's her teeth and her ears.'

'My baby's eight weeks,' I said. But I didn't say that this baby of mine smiled into my face and tightened and pointed her top lip to speak her sounds to me. I didn't explain how I felt every breath and every movement.

'I was keeping Brooke's clothes for her,' Mae said.

'I wanted you to come and stay, thought Mum would make you come, thought Dad would . . .'

'They tried but I wouldn't. I was going round with Matthew . . .'

'There's computer courses . . .'

'Wouldn't leave because of Matthew, then he left.' She laughed at her sentence.

I'd left home when my sister was ten. She was eighteen now, but still seemed not much bigger and looked not much older to me than that ten-year-old, except that she was tired and heavy-eyed. Her bony cheeks each had a little cross tatted on them. I knew she would have had a load of work since Mum and Dad had been away, as there were still two young brothers and a sister at school, and two older ones, without jobs, attending courses.

'I'll help you,' I said.

'Get yourself better first.'

She sat Brooke up beside me while she went away to clean the bottle, then returned, lifted Brooke, winded her and went back to the bedroom, leaving the empty space on the bed, the baby smell in the dark, the midnight chill.

I woke again in the grey early-morning light, to the sound of my father out on the steps farting and sharpening knives. I felt stiff and sore and needed to get myself going. I moved to the edge of the bed, pulled myself up with the help of my sticks and made my way out to the backyard, to the dark morning smell, the night river, damp grass and soil, damped-down dust, wet gutters and compost, duck mess and dogs.

A truck came up the drive, my father let the backboard down and the dog jumped up onto the tray. He was going with a neighbour to his cousin's farm where they would round up a few killers and a cattle beast to slaughter and butcher in an old milking shed. The meat would be delivered to customers the next day.

The door banged and the truck backed down the drive, clanking saws and knives.

11

KURA

There's the hei pounamu made of speckled greenstone. It's like deep, milk-green river water, where the surface is so still that it has a shiny, oiled look. But when you look below the surface of the water, whether they are there or not, you see lips, eyes, fins and tails of fish, tumbling and turning. The hei pounamu is for important occasions such as when a relative dies. It is something to be worn, not one of those treasures that is placed on the casket of the dead.

There's a portrait that hangs on my living room wall, of grandfather when he was about forty years old. The picture shows a solid-looking man, with a broad, dark face and a large, hooked nose like the beak of a kaka. His eyes are shadowed under heavy eyebrows, but one eye is more widely open than the other because his birth and circumstances surprised him – or that's what I used to think. He has a short, curly beard and thick black hair which is parted in the middle and draws back from his face in bunched waves.

In the portrait Grandfather is wearing a dark suit and cravat. From a watch-chain attached to a button on his waistcoat hangs this hei pounamu. Before he died he put it round the neck of his wife for safe-keeping, so that it wouldn't be robbed from his grave.

The hei pounamu was made specially for Pirinoa, Grandfather's mother, and was gifted to her when she was born, along with other ornaments that were gifts handed down. As well as ornaments, there were bird feather and dog hair cloaks and finely woven garments. All these were given to honour her birth because she was the eldest child of two most chiefly parents, both of different areas, who had been brought together to cement peace and consolidate land boundaries between the two peoples who had been traditional enemies for several generations.

Because of her high birth Pirinoa was brought up in a certain way. Aunts and grandmothers competed to have charge of her, those hunting or gathering or preparing food chose special portions for her, and as she grew she was tended and watched, and dressed in a way that was intended to show her beauty and her status. She was taken up and down the country to important gatherings where she became familiar with the histories and genealogies and everything to do with the life and the land.

When Pirinoa was fifteen it was decided that she should receive a moko. She was taken to an expert for this work to be done. At that time only her chin was carved, but because the lips are the most painful to have done, this was not undertaken until some years later, after she had married and given birth to children.

A woman of her status could not usually marry for love. Promises of marriage were often exchanged between families while the woman and man were still babies, or even before they were born. The two children would be brought up in a certain way with the future in mind. They had no choice in the matter.

However, no such arrangement had been made for Pirinoa. She was already past the age when most are married and have families, but no marriage partner had been found for her.

One day she made it known that she wanted to marry Billy Silk, a Pakeha whaler who she'd seen during a visit to a nearby township. It is said that their eyes met on this occasion.

What I've been told about Billy Silk is that he was a man of good humour who, though not tall, was wide in build and had exceptional physical strength. He had black hair and yellow eyes, and the first time some of Pirinoa's people saw him was when he walked out of the tide in their bay after a scow he was working on had cracked apart on the rocks north of there.

When Pirinoa made her announcement, there were some who wanted to go, then and there, to kill this Billy Silk, believing that he had taken her attention, had perhaps been meeting her secretly, had perhaps already made a common marriage with her.

However, the old women of the hapu became Pirinoa's advocates. They spoke of Pirinoa as a woman pining for her children who had been failed by her elders in that they had been unable to find a match for her. To those who disagreed the old women said, 'All right, marry her to old Rohipa, but be quick before his relatives choose their greenery. All right, obtain a promise from Te Rakaiapo whose grandsons are little children but who will be grown when we are gone, and by which time our daughter's children would have bled out of her. All right, ask for a man from Te Tonga who made a feast of our relatives and made music through their bones.'

After all this had been said the people sent for Billy Silk and his family.

Billy Silk came. He had no family.

'Every man has a family,' the people said. 'Everyone has someone to speak for him, only a cormorant speaks for itself.'

But there was a man of the hapu called Mehana, who was the son of Pirinoa's father's sister, which made him Pirinoa's brother. Mehana had been Pirinoa's companion during their childhood. He was an adventuring young man who had worked on whale boats and trading vessels, and who had made his way up and down the coast on one excursion or another. 'I'm this man's family since I've pulled oars with him at times when hands have been needed,' he said. 'We've been on the ale together and slept in the sand dunes together when the drink made old rope of our legs.' And he spoke at length about what gave him the right to be Billy's brother. People agreed that he would be family for Billy Silk, as well as translator, and the talk began.

A morning and an afternoon went by, during which time Billy Silk was given an account of family genealogies and histories. Portions of this were translated to him and he sat through it all, out of curiosity or politeness, still not knowing why he was there.

We have not been told about Pirinoa during all of this. I know that when Billy Silk was sent for she would have been taken and dressed. I imagine her in a high-collared dress such as European women wore, that Maori women liked to wear then also. Her hair would have been dressed with two huia feathers standing straight, one either side of her head. She would have had over her shoulders the kiwi cloak that had come from her father's people, and round her neck would have been the hei pounamu.

She would've been seated in full view under the overhang of the house, with her grandmothers about her and with others around, all curious as to what the outcome of the talk would be. Set apart would have been Billy Silk and this new brother of his.

When the people had finished what they had to say, Mehana stood and spoke about Billy. 'He's an Englishman,' he said. 'A free man, a man without a wife or children. He's nobody's slave. He's a son of Tangaroa, guardian of the sea, who saw fit to deliver him to our shores. He's a strong man, a midship oarsman, always the strongest of the crewmen, pulling the longest oars. When an animal is sighted and the shout goes up, it's his strength that brings us up quickly beside it. It's his strength that is needed to haul up alongside and get a line in. He's the one who must bring us up again and again to plant the irons. He's the one whose strength is needed to tow our animal to the big ship after it has only its own blood left to shoot out into the air. The reason his coat pulls so tightly across his back and chest, and the reason his arms bulge in his sleeves, is that there is no coat large enough to contain his strength. His legs are bowed outward because he has many strong children locked up in his groin. His man's piece is like a fist and an arm.'

Now there was a great deal missing from this talk. It wouldn't have gone unnoticed that apart from a clever reference to Tangaroa, Billy Silk's genealogy had not been attempted, nothing about his parentage had been disclosed, and no reason was given as to why he had left home and family and country of birth. Billy Silk could have been a street urchin, a runaway, a deserter or a criminal. Actually, what he was, it was found out later, was the son of a basketmaker whose family had come on hard times in England. Billy had spent much of his childhood at the docksides, watching ships load and unload, and at twelve had left home to go to sea.

'We've been up and down the coast together,' Mehana said. 'He knows the sea, he knows the people, he knows the business of trading. He has spoken of building a vessel and bringing trade right into our bay.'

There was a murmur at this announcement.

In those days marriage partnerships for men and women were made to honour both families. What you brought to a family must be not less than what the other family brought to you. To bring less could cause insult. Insult could mean war. I don't know whether or not Mehana was telling it true and whether trading had ever been discussed, or if he was simply telling people what he knew could make this man an acceptable match for Pirinoa, an acceptable tribal man.

At that time, hapu desired Pakeha traders to become a part of them in order to give them easier access to goods that they prized. But even if trade had been mentioned merely to impress, those listening would have understood the possibilities. There was no doubt Billy was a seaman. They all knew he'd worked the trading routes. It was true also that Tangaroa had handed him on to their shore, when on a stormy night a vessel had broken up on rocks around the coast from there. While others had drowned struggling against the currents, Billy had let himself be taken out to sea to be brought back further down to where people had gathered as he walked out of the receding morning tide. The people had given him food, he'd slept for a morning on the sand, then he'd gone, making his way round the shore. Why would Tangaroa have delivered him if this match wasn't meant to be?

Mehana continued to speak about this business of trading. He spoke of intended trading routes, intended goods and where main supplies would come from. When he'd done as good a job as he could he sat down.

Talk went from one to the other for the rest of the day until the feelings and thoughts of the people were plain, and in favour of Billy Silk. The fact was that the people had failed to find a match for Pirinoa and the situation could be saved in this way without embarrassment, because it was Pirinoa's wish.

Billy was asked through Mehana: 'Do you have a wife in this country, or any other country?'

'There's no wife in any country,' Mehana replied.

'Do you have children in this country or any other country?' they asked.

'There are no children,' Mehana said.

'We will marry you to Pirinoa,' they said. 'You'll be part of this hapu. You'll live as we live.'

Now it wasn't until this moment that Billy Silk, through Mehana, knew what this whole day was about. How do we know today what his response was? How do we know that the response was not straight from the lips of Mehana.

'He agrees to it,' Mehana said.

'When you marry her,' Billy was told, 'you'll have land to live on and timber for a house and a trading vessel. Your children will be our own children and will inherit rights in the same way as their mother has inherited. They'll be brought up in our way and our custom. If we find that you have a wife or children elsewhere, we'll kill you. If you deal in land, or sign any paper to do with land, we'll kill you. If you ever leave her, we'll kill you. If you don't treat her as we've treated her, we'll kill you.'

'He agrees to it,' Mehana said.

Not long after that, Pirinoa and Billy Silk were married. People of the many hapu came bringing their gifts. Celebrations and speech-making continued all day and through most of the night, then Pirinoa and Billy Silk were taken to a sleeping house to sleep together.

The story that Pirinoa had to tell the grandmothers the next day would have been the story that was proper to tell. It would have been borne out by what the grandmothers had been able to hear and maybe see – a story of voices, laughter and lovemaking. It was all true, but I believe Pirinoa never told the full story until years later.

Perhaps the events of the day and the night had been too much for Billy Silk, perhaps he was a shy man. Most likely he was drunk. Later events showed that it was not lack of interest that caused him to lie down and go into a sound sleep as soon as he and Pirinoa were left alone.

What a dilemma for her! This was the night of her marriage and yet her marriage had not been made. How would she, in the light of day, be able to face the grandmothers who would know at a glance that the marriage had not been made. Billy Silk, by insulting them all in this way, could be killed, but that would not reduce her shame. There he was, lying like a fallen tree. There was their marriage house as quiet as the time of Te Kore.

There was nothing to encourage the grandmothers sitting about outside the house listening, and if one of them parted the reeds to look in through the wall to see what all the silence was about, even by the glimmer of new moonlight, and no matter how close she put herself up against Billy Silk, they would know. So she lay herself on top of Billy Silk to give a better shape to what might be seen through the walls. Billy lay under her, gently snoring.

But it was there, while she lay over him, with his warmth beneath her and his breath on her shoulder, that her anxiety began to leave her. Soon she was throbbing and swollen as though she had just come up from the deep of an icy river – but still he was asleep, any eye would see it. So she put her hands down between their two bodies and began to squeeze. Billy woke with a yell, his raho began to spring in her hands and he came into her, both of them surprised and quick. And married.

They lay back with their hearts beating. 'It's all right this,' he said, which were the first words spoken between them. 'It's all right this, so make me an oar again.' If she didn't know those words it didn't matter. He took her hands down, laughing. She laughed too, and handled him. Then they whispered and laughed and rolled under and over each other with enough noise, enough times, to divert the marriage-makers until daylight.

12

TE PAANIA

'You're going to Wellington,' my mother said after I was tipped out of
school. 'Got money for your fare, and for you to board for three months
with Dad's cousin. There's a two-week course you can go on. After that
you got two and a half months to get you a job.'

'What course is it?' I asked.

'You got to stay there, got to get a job. If you don't get a job yourself
you got to make someone help you get one.'

'What course is it?'

'Don't know, you just got to behave yourself and do it.' She was
sweating and ugly and pretending to lack understanding.

'We got other mouths to feed,' my father said for the second time.

I thought it might be a typing course that I was being sent to do, but
instead it was a deruralisation course, an attempt at making a country
frog into a city frog, an attempt at making a native frog exotic. That's
what I understand now.

We learned how to catch buses, buy tickets, fill out forms and
applications, use the telephone. Learned about walking smartly and
sitting with our knees together, about how to enter a room and how to
behave at interviews.

Learned that our clothes were all wrong.

My two new dresses, sewn for me by our neighbour, were much too full, too long in the skirt, too high at the neck. They had too much material in the sleeves. On catching sight of myself in a mirror in a furniture shop during one of our orientation walks I thought I looked upholstered. I was one of those La-Z-Boy chairs.

Mrs Gerrard, who was the woman helping us look for work, didn't like my chances of finding a job because I was only fifteen and had no formal qualifications. 'And you could be twelve, looking at you, Te Paania,' she said. I liked her. I liked the way she called me Te Paania the way that no teacher ever had.

'I have to get a job,' I said. 'Have to find one myself or get someone to help me. My parents have other mouths to feed.' I was my mother, sweating and ugly and beginning to have understanding.

'If we don't find something by the time the course is finished,' Mrs Gerrard said, 'you can come and see me each morning and we'll both keep looking.'

Two weeks before my three months was up Mrs Gerrard said she was sending me to an office downtown for work experience. The office assistant was in hospital and someone was needed for two weeks, just to help out. 'You never know what might happen,' she said.

My job was to collect tapes from the bosses and put them into the central dictaphone for the typing pool of twenty-six typists. I had to log the tapes in, log them out again and deliver copy back to the bosses. Easy. I did it fast and easy.

The other assistant never returned to work. After two weeks the job was mine.

So there I was with a job that wasn't in the freezing works. There I was out of the house, out of the town, feeding my own mouth but remembering to keep it shut in other ways, running from here to there and back again.

And when I ran myself out of work on some afternoons, the typists, who were all very old, would send me on messages, since I was the one who wouldn't be missed by any boss that happened to walk through. I kept my mouth shut and went out to buy lollies and cigarettes for them, and to take husbands' suits to the drycleaners. I kept my mouth shut and organised sweepstakes, placed bets and collected divvies. Also I delivered love messages in an envelope to a man who waited under the station clock, who would give me an envelope to deliver on return. I kept my big mouth shut even though I always read the letters. Neither the man nor the woman ever challenged me, though they must have been able to tell that I'd opened their envelopes.

On some afternoons I was free to practise typing on an old typewriter there. Nobody took any notice of what I was doing except for a woman called Lorel who would chat to me now and again. She wore grey skirts, blouses with beaded collars, bunny wool cardigans, and had a pretty face packed with cream and powder that became slippery in the afternoons. One day she said, 'You should go to night school and learn properly.' I hadn't heard of night school but she talked to me about it and told me how to enrol.

That was how I came to attend night classes where I eventually passed my trade certificates, enabling me to become a part of the typing pool. Someone else was employed to run from here to there and back again, with tapes from the bosses and typing from the pool.

Tappity tap tap zing.

I'd been working as a typist for about three years, when one day a word processing machine appeared in the office, along with Jenny to operate it and to teach its operations to us.

Over the three years there had been some changes in equipment. Old typewriters had been replaced with new electronic ones, and there had been streamlining of filing. We had all adapted without difficulty to these changes, but this new machine, that it was said cost thousands of dollars, was not welcome at all (except that it excited *me,* but I kept my big mouth shut about that). This new machine, according to the women, could scramble everything you'd done or make hours of work disappear right in front of your eyes. None of the women wanted anything to do with the new equipment, and if the bosses were going to start bringing stuff like that into the office then they were going to resign, boots and all, find jobs elsewhere. Jenny wasn't welcome either.

So I opened my mouth just a little. 'Let me,' I said, but none of the bosses would answer me, hear me. I was too native, too froggy, too scary.

So I went back to night classes then opened my mouth a little more. 'I can do it,' I said.

'She can do it,' Jenny said. We kept on saying it until the bosses had to recognise me. 'All right, give her a go,' Anthony said.

After the typing pool was done away with, and after the office was refurbished with new carpets and drapes and work stations, I was upgraded into one of the new positions. And when Jenny left to have her baby I took over her position as training officer.

New suit and heels.

Howzat for a frog?

One day Shane walked in. He was a computer mechanic who had come to service the machines. 'Is there a caf?' he asked, whizzing his little screwdrivers and removing the covers.

'Tea and coffee only,' I said. 'Down a level and not till ten-thirty.' I thought he might hear my heart.

'No, I want food. A pie,' he said. 'I'm allowed fifteen minutes on my timesheet.' He was peering down onto a grid that looked something like a tiny city of streets and lights and buildings. He was the giant with the power in his hands.

'Down to the ground,' I said. 'Left through the plaza to the glass doors, two to the right – sandwiches, muffins, scones, rolls, pies, chips, that sort of stuff . . . Didn't you have breakfast?'

'Yes but . . .'

Giant and beautiful. Thin beauty. Small head with close-cropped black hair, smooth forehead, thin black eyebrows, round dark eyes, half-lidded as they slid back and forth across areas of the little city. Nose long and curved at the tip, skin a dark, even brown. Small shoulders, and from there the same width all the way down. Long arms and legs, long, bony fingers.

Unfrog.

Insect beauty.

He was wearing a long-sleeved white shirt, a pretty tie, dark trousers. His suit coat was draped over a chair. 'You've got some style,' I said. 'Is that a uniform?'

'Yes well . . . it's the dress code. Anything to do with computers is wanky.'

Man beauty.

'Are you all good-looking in your family?'

'Those of us still in one piece,' he said. 'Those with teeth,' lower lip pushing out, sullen. 'If I get this running and set up its tests, we could go down for coffee and a pie. Look at the printouts when we get back.'

'OK, I'll take an early break. Nothing I can do anyway.'

Boom boom.

'How long have you worked here?' he asked as we made our way to the lifts.

'Six years. Since I was fifteen.'

'Are you the boss yet?'

'*I* think so.'

He selected a pie and a bread roll and ordered coffee. I ordered hot chocolate because it was so impressive in its tall glass with its long spoon, its pink and white marshmallows, its sprinklings of cinnamon and chocolate and blobs of cream.

'Are you married or anything?' I asked.

'Nothing.'

About three months later Jenny called in with Shelley, who had been born prematurely and who was tiny and knowing. I walked round the office with her, unable to stop myself from smiling and patting, from lifting the scalloped edge of her knitted coat to examine what was underneath, from sniffing her head and her ears.

'So all systems on go,' Jenny said in a voice that made me feel she would have liked to have swapped places with me. 'I hope they upped you to trainer. That Anthony can be mean, you know.'

I walked to the lift sniffing and clucking, never thinking until later about what Jenny had said. I hadn't had a salary rise and needed to open my mouth about that.

The next morning I went to see Anthony, explaining that as I had taken over Jenny's job and had full responsibility for office staff training, I should be receiving a trainer's wage.

'I'll look into it,' Anthony said.

After a month, since I hadn't heard from him, I went to see Anthony again. 'You don't have School Certificate,' he said.

'But I have other certificates,' I reminded him. 'Certificates much more relevant to the job than School C. And there's more work now. I'm doing more work than when Jenny was here.'

Not bad for a frog.

'School Certificate's what you want for the next increment,' Anthony said, showing me the page in the pay manual.

'I know what's in the book,' I said. 'But I also know you're the boss. It's your decision and you can give me a raise if you decide to. If you want to pay me what I'm worth there's nothing stopping you.'

'But we don't have to, Paania.'

'Te Paania,' I said.

'We don't have to, Te Paania.'

In some ways it suited me to leave, which I managed to do without swearing. 'Stick your job, Anthony,' was all I said. 'See who else you can get at the price.'

I had not long moved out of my aunt's place and gone to live with Shane in an upstairs flat on the other side of town. I found a job nearby. It wasn't a permanent position and I was overqualified for it, but it was convenient for the time being.

And I was in love with this Shane, then pregnant, then married.

I kept the job right through to smash-up time.

13

KURA

It was with this birdnosed one, son of a high-born woman and a whaler, that goodness began. Grandfather Tumanako didn't know that goodness was a thief.

This goodness was passed on to my mother, who passed it on to me. Some of us have kept it, kept our faces shut away ever since then. Others couldn't. Others have inherited wilful wildness from outstepping Pirinoa and adventuring Billy Silk.

Yet the wilfulness was not entirely lost in me. Somewhere in me was the spirit of Pirinoa and Billy, only it was hidden away. I had practised and practised goodness until I believed my camouflage was me – but somewhere down inside was the spirit, or a little core of it, bandaged round and round.

Shane? He could never shut an eye or keep his mouth silent, even though he never knew quite what to see or say. He was misfitted and wild, but also didn't know what to do about this goodness that kept hounding him. In the end he had to smash it at my feet in order to make my eyes spring open; in order to prise my lips apart; in order that I could be cured of my thieving ways and this goodness; in order that I could begin to unravel the sticky, twining cloths that kept wildness, like hidden treasure, trapped within.

For seventy-three years I've been looking into the squint-eyed portrait of this beaked grandfather, and used to think that one eye was opened wide and startled because of his birth and the circumstances that he found himself in, while the other was screwed half down by suspicion as he wondered what to make of the world.

But it was as I was growing up that I came to understand the real meaning of the half-shut eye. Yes, he was warning us that following generations would have to keep one eye unseeing, keep lips sealed in order to survive. That was his message, which I know came from goodness, love for us – but also from uncertainty because the world had changed forever. I believed the message once, but only because hard goodness had set itself within me too. Grandfather didn't know that goodness could rob the children's children.

This birdnosed boy, who was given the name of Tumanako, was Pirinoa's and Billy Silk's only living child, several children preceding him having died at birth because of the cursing of Pirinoa by a jealous enemy.

It was because of the strong incantations of a tohunga at his birth that Tumanako survived, and it was so that he could be kept safe from jealous harm that he was taken from the affected Pirinoa as soon as he was born, to be raised in the household of her mother's sister. A young woman with an infant of her own was brought into the household to be his nursing mother.

There were two grandmothers too, who were part of that family. They were the ones who had been Pirinoa's supporters when she had wanted to marry Billy Silk – and if it was true that there had been anyone listening through the raupo walls on the night Pirinoa and Billy were married, it would have been these two.

Both were women of high rank who had been matched from the time of birth to suitable male children, but there were too many wars, there was too much death. Their future husbands had gone to the ovens and stomachs of their enemies. Their sacred tattooed heads had been traded.

They were women for whom there were no men equal or suitable, and who had never married or had children. These two were left to pine for the children they'd never had, and to look after the children of others.

Once past child-bearing age themselves, they were able to protect younger women whose lineages could be affected by spite and revenge.

Yet these same grandmothers had not been able to keep Pirinoa from harm. This was talked about over and over when I was a child.

Our people, the old ones at the time of Pirinoa's parents and before, had enemies, enemies from far back, that they lived with in peace much of the time – when their lives were too full for war – but who they always knew were their enemies. This was something understood from season to season and generation to generation. If there had been a killing, if there had been insult or a broken agreement, there had to be repayment and more. Repayment could be made quickly, or the need to repay could bind the next generation or the next.

There was always something to avenge, and revenge was important in those times, part of a pattern laid down. It meant death, especially of chiefly people, victors giving insult to the living by cooking and eating the flesh of their chiefly dead. It meant the cutting off of heads to destroy tapu, the eating of the heart to demean, the swallowing of chiefly eyes – revenge turning on revenge.

Or revenge could be taken through potent ill-wishing and bad speaking – which could kill, make ill, or meddle in people's dreams.

When the Pakeha came in his pretty ships with their ugly cannons and guns, those old ones who were enemies to each other began to trade for muskets because vengeance was of such great importance to them. But it was only some people who had access to this trade. Others, unable to get muskets, were made vulnerable.

War became different after the coming of guns. Life became different. From that time on there was death like there never had been before. It was not death eyeball to eyeball now, or instant death – a heavy, sharp-edged club slicing through an enemy skull. It was not death here and there, this season or next, this generation or next, as it had been before. It was death from a distance, out of air, taking people from off clifftops, from out of water, from in amongst trees – and there were piles and piles of dead.

So many dead.

Too many dead for the death customs to be carried out in the way laid down, too many dead for the ovens and stomachs of the avengers. The all-important genealogies were being affected, whole families were disappearing, lands and food sources were being abandoned, negotiations were not able to take place, liaisons were not able to be made according to tradition. The world had changed forever.

After a time all became war weary. There had to be an end to war.

Pirinoa's parents were growing up when their mutual enemy acquired muskets. Her parents were of different hapu and had never met.

It was because of guns that Pirinoa's father's people, those remaining after battle, had to leave the land they'd been living on and move quickly south. Nearby, there were people with whom they had also had disagreements, and survival depended much on the goodwill of these neighbours. But these neighbours had also been devastated by the force of guns. They were Pirinoa's mother's people.

So the two peoples met to make peace and liaisons, and one of the first actions by Pirinoa's grandfather, father of her father, was to lay down on the meeting ground his most famous fighting weapon. This was his taiaha named Tu-te-wehi, which had killed many chiefs and which was known throughout the territories.

Gifts were exchanged and treaties were made in the way that was customary, and as a final seal, so that these negotiations would be binding forever, the two peoples married their genealogies and their lands together through the union of the highest-born daughter of one family, with the highest-born son of the other.

Pirinoa was the eldest child of this union, holding the senior lines of the two peoples. There was no one equal in genealogy to Pirinoa in our line, and never has been again. She was alone in her chiefly descendancy, and after the death of her parents was the one deferred to in matters of land and all other issues of importance. Genealogy was everything to them. It was because of her high birth that Pirinoa was given authority over land from Awapango to Awakehua, and from the sea to the foothills and mountains. This is not to say that she owned the land in the way that is now meant, but it was she who defined the boundaries and who discussed exchanges of rights at different seasons, who allowed neighbouring peoples to live on land or fish certain reaches of the rivers, set up their eel weirs, hunt or garden in particular places. She knew the sites and the happenings of the many events of her time and before. It's not that other people didn't know these things, but only that her birthright gave her the authority.

Everything that was important, both to her mother's and father's people – land, birth, history – was held within her chiefliness. It made her a servant of the people.

They were hard times when she was born. The people had been humiliated by this enemy with guns. Their chiefs and their children had been stacked into the ovens and loaded into the stomachs of their enemies, or their dead had had to be left rotting on cliff faces, across water, in amongst trees. The death ceremonies could not be carried out according to the ways laid down.

Also, ancestral land had been left without its cooking fires, and although Pirinoa's father's people's wish was to return there one day, it was not possible for the moment. Cementing their alliance was important then. Survival was everything.

The only Pakeha seen in those times were those who called in to do trade. They were made welcome for the goods they brought and Pirinoa's people began trading in flax fibre.

It was a poor existence. They left the sunny slopes where they had been living and built their houses near the low, damp swamplands where the flax grew. Because much time and energy was used in cutting, carting and scraping flax, there was not proper time for hunting and fishing. There was little time to tend gardens. All of the fibre was being used for trade and there was none left for the making of clothes and matting, no time to do things in the old way. The exchange and the contact brought them mainly clothing, blankets, tobacco and rum. But it brought illnesses too, sicknesses that they'd never had before. They became weak, they were much poorer than they had ever been, and although they did everything they could to remain at peace by allowing safe passage through their lands, there was always the possibility of attack.

This is in the time when Pirinoa was a child. Her parents had other children but none of them survived those difficult days. Life was a little better when the trade in flax lessened and there was a demand for pigs and kumara.

Later, in the time when Tumanako was a boy and the land and climate were found to be suitable, the people began to grow maize, barley and rye. They built a large mill and began to prosper. In fact theirs was rich and desirable land in Pakeha eyes and there were many attempts at purchase. 'Will our grandchildren live in the wind?' was what Pirinoa's grandfather said to those who came with guns, pots, pipes, blankets and beads to exchange for a name or a mark on a sale deed. These words of his were repeated often when I was young, but were whispered in a secret kind of way, not spoken out proudly in the way I believe Pirinoa's grandfather would have spoken them. Goodness had set itself in amongst the people.

Nevertheless Pakeha had settled on some of the land because it suited Pirinoa's people to have them living nearby. A store and a post office were built, and the people also allowed a road to be made and helped build that road. However, they kept the authority of the land and wouldn't sell it. They didn't want to steal from their grandchildren's children. Closer to where they lived, other land was set aside for a church and a school. The church was quickly built. Some years later came the school. It was what the people wanted. The old ones didn't know then that a school could kill their children, that a church could shrink people's souls into tiny knotted balls which would become wrapped and hidden in layer upon layer of windings inside them.

Throughout the country Pakeha were increasing in numbers. Guns, alcohol and blankets had done all right for some of them, who had exchanged these for land, and who believed a man could own land in the same way as he owned his coat. He believed that he, one person, could possess land and everything on that land by taking a signature from someone who didn't own land in that way. Or he believed he could take land by drawing lines on paper. For him it was a way laid down. There was fighting and trouble between Maori and Pakeha over this.

But eventually there was a treaty made between the Maori people and the Queen of England so that all this stealing and fighting would stop. All those old deals and lines on paper that the Pakeha had made were now null and void, or supposed to be. The Pakeha couldn't go and get land off the Maori any more. All stolen land had to be returned to the Maori people and all land was now under the Crown's protection, or supposed to be. Only the Crown could buy land; that is, only if Maori wanted to sell it.

Also, because of this treaty there would be a government. There would be laws. Maori would stop their warring and their grievances against each other. Pakeha would stop stealing land. Maori and Pakeha would not fight each other any more. All the trouble would end and there would be peace forever.

It was not only Pirinoa's people who had begun trading. By this time many hapu had begun to prosper. They had bought ploughs and carts and other farm equipment. They owned horses, cattle and pigs, and grew grain and vegetables. Some had bought ships and went round the coastlines trading, or went to and from Sydney, there being a gold rush in Australia and a demand for produce.

Tumanako was growing up in those days of prosperity.

However, after the treaty was signed there *was* more stealing of land, much worse than before. Pakeha were now arriving in shiploads from across the sea and they had been promised land by the settler government. And although some Maori had sold land, or given land to Pakeha, it was not enough for them. They wanted more land, they wanted the best land, they wanted all the land.

So now this new government became the biggest stealer of land, making more and more laws to steal by. Once they had the land they sold it to the new settlers and made themselves wealthy.

There could be no peace then. The treaty was broken. There was terrible fighting as Maori tried to stay on land that was all of life to them, and which was a way laid down. They couldn't live in the wind. They couldn't give away their grandchildren's lives. They couldn't give away their own authority, because what would be the point in peace and prosperity? What would be the point in life?

The Imperial Army, with its muskets and cannons and horses, came in behind the new laws to flatten the Maori people, to imprison them, then to take further lands to punish them for fighting for their lives.

War was different again, not only because of the muskets and cannons, the horses, the piles and piles of dead, but also because this was fighting without season. Soldiers of the Imperial Army did not have to plant or harvest, or to leave battles because the birds were fat and the eels and mullet were running. But the Maori people could starve in a war without seasons, people could starve without land, people could starve living in the wind.

Tumanako had grown up by then. He didn't go to war as some of his relatives did. When he learned that his great-grandfather had put his taiaha down on the ground, he understood this to be a sign that they should give up war forever. He believed it. It was his goodness. There was the half-shut eye.

With these new laws, first it was the area that Pirinoa's father's people had run from – land which held the bones of their ancestors – that was taken. This first was a law that the settler government had made to steal unoccupied areas which they described as wastelands.

Later, their mill and their houses were burnt down, canoes became targets for soldiers and their cannons, and more of the land was taken. The people were being punished because some of Tumanako's uncles and cousins, along with Billy Silk, all with their two eyes wide and anger as a treasure in their hearts, went to assist relatives in war against the soldiers. Although the great-grandfather's taiaha had been laid down, not all felt bound by this action in the way that Tumanako did.

The people rebuilt their houses on coastal land, all around where my house is now, and lived mainly from the sea. It wasn't good land for grain but they grew vegetables and raised pigs there. It was a poor existence. They were thin, they were few, they were dying. They kept themselves good there with alcohol and the church.

For over seventy years I have looked into the squint-eyed portrait of Grandfather Tumanako and have been able to see down through his eyes and into his boy's heart.

What I saw, what I grew to see as I grew, was a boy, only child of a whaler and a chiefly woman of many jurisdictions, always surrounded by adults, with older boy cousins as companions, who took part in the adult life around him. Although he was dressed in the English gentleman fashion that people had adopted by then he was brought up in the ways of his mother's people. In good times and bad, in changing times, he was his mother's son, a son of her people, and because of his chiefly lineage was expected to know the genealogies and the songs and recitations that went with them. He had to know the territories and the histories and was expected to be present at the long meetings where matters of importance were discussed, where talk went on for a night and a day, a night and a day, a night and a day, until all talk had unwound itself.

He had to grow up in the laws and the lores, to know the sites and the signs. He had to understand the changing times and to know what advantages could be taken of the changing world.

But he couldn't stop Pakeha laws being made. The people had no say in that. He couldn't stop the tides of new people arriving.

It was after the death of Pirinoa that a new law was brought in to make Maori people own land in the coat-owning way. Tumanako had grown up and had children of his own.

The government didn't like land to be in the hands of whole groups of people. They didn't like it to be in the hands of grandchildren's children – children who hadn't yet been born. It was difficult for them to steal from so many owners. So they set up a Land Court to make it easier for themselves. This court drew up titles to pieces of land, making three or four men the new owners. This is how Tumanako and two of his relatives became owners, in the coat-owning way, of land they really knew was for everyone – land from river to river, from the coast to the hills and beyond. If they hadn't accepted these titles the land would have been taken away.

But Tumanako had been brought up as his mother's son, goodness wasn't too hard in him then, so he took little notice of the paper to do with this land. People built their houses on the land and worked the gardens there as they were used to doing. They kept their knowledge of the boundaries, kept the stories of what had happened. They survived.

*

It was after Tumanako's death that goodness and obedience turned us against ourselves. Individuals began to apply to the courts for land to be broken up into further separate titles because that's how it was done in the new law. But in order to do this people had to spend weeks away from home to be at court sittings in order to secure titles, and this was unaffordable. There were survey expenses to be paid too. Huge debts built up, which people could only pay off in land. Some people, just as Tumanako had done before his death, tried to retrieve stolen lands in the courts but the laws were too strong. There were more and more laws being brought in and people were humiliated by them. Some ignored the laws and went to live on land that they thought they should have a right to live on. When they wouldn't move they were imprisoned. Others, living in the wind, built up debts with storekeepers and innkeepers which could only be paid off in land. But if the wind-livers had no titles, it was often paid off, in land, by relatives who did.

In among families there was a circle of bitterness which turned, from season to season and generation to generation, into bitterness against each other, people laying blame on one another for what had been lost to them. Some of them kept their titles, while some of them sold land or gave it away, wanting nothing more to do with it because it was the cause of too much trouble.

They lived in poverty and sickness and peace. Goodness and silence had set itself in amongst the people, and even though the stories were still told they were told in whispers, kept as secrets amongst themselves, to become stories of shame. People became more and more silent, because if they spoke they would harm their children. They had stolen their grandchildren's lives.

The land on the coast, where our few houses are, where the church is and where the school used to be, is what remains of land that once stretched beyond the township, beyond the sheep and dairy farmlands, to the parklands and reserves and the mountains. A few of us have stayed in our little houses on the ragtails of that land. Others – many, many others – like the singing grandfather of Te Paania, had to go, live in the wind. Some come home to be buried, some do not.

And for all those years I forgot there was another self handed down to me from Pirinoa and Billy. The wild. We have to find it in ourselves in order to move beyond survival.

But who had struck out at Pirinoa? It was her womb that was affected, jealous spite attempting to cut off her chiefly line. If she had never had a child, that would have been the end. House empty. House lost. Those who had ill-wished her would have had their way.

How had it happened? It's true that her people had enemies. It's true that because of wars, disagreements and reprisals, her people moved about from place to place, which could have left them open to bad-eye and speaking. It's true that they were visited by, and gave hospitality to, neighbouring peoples who had not always been allies. But Pirinoa was a protected one. There were always women, past child-bearing age, who surrounded her when there were strangers present. She was never taken anywhere without the rituals performed that would keep her safe. Also, amongst her own people there were experts who knew how to return potency and ill-will to its senders. She was protected in every way.

On the other hand Pirinoa was wilful. She was the one who kept the wildness, cherished it, for us. That's what I see when I look back to her through the grandfather's eyes. The world around her was changing and she liked to step out into it. There was no one who could command her because she was alone in her genealogy – not free but fearless, perhaps giving herself too much freedom in those very different times, leaving herself open to spite and potent ill-wishing.

Or had she transgressed? This is something never spoken about in regard to Pirinoa. No, never. Had she brought ill upon herself? What did the old mothers know? Why were they so in favour of her marriage to Billy Silk? Was it because he was a man without family and that there could be no reprisal if it was found that this special high-born daughter had already been with a man? What did they already know when they took Pirinoa aside to prepare her for her wedding night? We cannot know that now, there was no whisper of it. I speak like this only because my lips have been parted.

But there was nothing more important to the old mothers, and to the people, than that Pirinoa should have children. Without children her chiefly descendancy would have ended. If Pirinoa was to have only one child, this child must, in a time when there was so much death and so much change, safely grow to be a man. If there was something to know about Pirinoa the knowledge stayed with the grandmothers who knew what it was like to pine for their children.

And oh, I know how the people would have cared for her while this baby grew inside her. They would have travelled far inland to find the most delicious forest foods for her, they would've gone to the furthest fishing grounds and the special river places for her. She would've had the grandmothers to massage her and tend to her from the time she conceived until her baby was born, and from that time on.

At first I didn't remember, but now I do, that when I was a young woman having a child my aunt came to live with us so that she could attend to me. I remember that relatives visited, bringing special dishes. Then in my own way I came to tend to Te Paania when she was expecting her second child, bringing food from the sea, a tree, the massage oil.

14

MAHAKI

He'd just got in the door when he heard the gate swing, the footsteps on the path, a jangle, as though someone had sent the bin lid flying. Then he recognised the voice, the laugh. Dave was two steps ahead of him going out and gathering in Te Paania, who they'd hardly heard from since she moved from the house of sharpened pencils to the house of rooms and gardens, with a lover that she liked.

They'd received the first letter not long after she'd left hospital, telling of the visit with Kura and the family, what had taken place there and what was happening now: '. . . I feel her against me as I lie awake in the dark,' she'd said at the end of the letter, 'every breath, every shudder, every movement. Then when I finally sleep, I wake, again and again, to her crying. Am I nuts? When I hold her she snuggles into me, sniffles and snuffles. Up against my shoulder she squeaks and squirms with wind – burps and sleeps. I feel her right through me, smell her baby smell. Or sometimes it's her baby mess and baby pee, or her milky sick-up that I smell. I'm crazy.

'But I'm not unhappy as I get myself moving about and feel myself getting stronger. My life's good but I do need her, just as I need others – Grandfather, Mum, Dad, the kids, little Brooke. I need their daily lives.

'Also I believe she needs me. I'll never get over what was *done*. What was done is worse than anything, far worse than pain, much deeper than loss. I need to make it up to her. She's *owed*?'

He and Dave had read the letter over and over, happy because it showed her trust in them and helped them with their own grief – because for him and Dave too a baby had died, though they'd had no claim except in their hearts. When they'd gone to visit Te Paania in hospital they hadn't been able to talk about what had happened. It was as though the ache and the loneliness that they felt, and the anger at what had taken place, were feelings they'd had no right to. Then the letter had come, confiding in them, trusting them. It helped. It was a relief.

'Why has Baby been mutilated? I want to know, I have to know,' he'd said that day, striding down the corridor after the doctor.

'You need to keep your voice down. You need to watch your language,' the doctor had said – as though what was being asked was less important than how.

'I don't care for your language either,' he'd said, 'but that's not the point . . .'

'What is the point?'

'My clients have a right to know. We could be taking this matter to court.'

'You wouldn't have a leg to stand on,' the doctor had said and Mahaki knew it was true.

After some further discussion that hadn't got him anywhere he'd gone to find Kura, who hadn't wanted an inquiry, wouldn't lay a complaint, only wanted to get away, take Baby home. He'd felt helpless, useless, angry. The next day Dave had driven up to get him, and a day later they'd attended the funeral of the baby and Shane – where he and Dave had been outside the inner grieving of the family. They'd been treated like special visitors, but how would anyone know about their involvement with Te Paania and Baby? How could they know about Dave's excitement and their plans?

Letters had come once a week from Te Paania, telling them of her progress as she managed to walk a little further each day. Eventually she'd been able to get along without crutches and to take a daily walk into town where she'd meet people she knew – aunties, uncles, cousins, friends: '. . . people I grew up with, went to school with. It's good for me, they're all good for me. You know – distracting.'

They were cheerful letters, giving funny accounts of her father's illegal business, or descriptions of when the God Squad came to town. They were about Brooke, about what she could say and do, and about a baby girl who could kick, then roll, then sit, then crawl; who smiled, gurgled, laughed, grew teeth, pulled herself up to stand.

After they'd come back from the funeral he'd taken the carton of notes into the bedroom, along with the file boxes, and put them out of sight in the wardrobe. Hadn't been able to face the stuff – body parts, genes, buying and selling and theft. He'd felt as though he was looking at two containers full of pages on which the story of their own disfigured baby was being told. Meanwhile, at the office, more material was piling up. He hadn't been able to bring himself to read it.

Also there was the upstairs flat, the bedroom where they'd begun stripping down walls. Hadn't been able to face that either. Dave had put the cans of paint, colour charts, sandpaper, brushes and rollers away in the cupboard under the stairs. Then there were Te Paania and Shane's belongings, as well as a drawer full of baby clothes. They'd left it all as it was. Locked the door.

Something else that had been on his mind was that the old man had been ringing, wondering when he was coming up to continue with the taping. The trouble was that he hadn't been able to keep up work on the tapes he'd already done. Hadn't got far with that Council either. He'd have to get up there soon, take Dave with him.

Good, get away for a weekend.

In the letter they'd received before Te Paania had left her parents' house she'd announced that she was better: 'Pins have been removed and I'm getting along fine. The plate in my arm doesn't come out for another six months but it's no bother. Good use of the arm and able to do my bit round here.

'How do I really know I'm better? Because I'm bored. Really. Bored, bored, bored. Awful huh? I feel ashamed about that. It was a good town while I needed it, all the familiarity here for me to sink into, all the attention of family and friends etc. But now I'm so-o, so-o, bored. I'd be OK if there was work here, any sort of work, but there's nix.

'Still crazy. There's been an outbreak of meningitis here. You would've heard about it on the news when two pre-schoolers died. Scary . . . Do you realise it's been two years?'

What haunted him now wasn't someone's carelessness with a baby who had died. It wasn't that the baby's eyes had been removed for whatever reason, or that language had been used in an offending way. Nor was it because of the use of the supermarket bag. In his time, and in his work, he'd come across all sorts of carelessness, mistakes, inadequacies that had caused people to be at loggerheads with each other. There'd been many times when misjudgments and misunderstandings had led to drama and trauma. He'd made his own booboos too.

In his type of work there was always a cross-cultural mismatch – people not comprehending what other people were saying or thinking because they each came from a different experience and understanding.

So what got to him now was not so much what had been done on that day, but simply that no one at that hospital had cared enough. It was as if he, Kura, Niecy and Darcy were a bunch of oddities, waiting for a thing to take home and bury, for no good reason. It was as though they were not quite people, and therefore their lives didn't matter, as if they were not capable of suffering, had no right to suffer, no cause to feel distressed.

There was human error that was part of being human, but there were attitudes that he could only think of as being less than human.

And there you were – each group of people seeing the other as having something missing from being human. The trouble was that it was the little people who bore the brunt of that. To come from a background of being white, Christian and so-called 'civilised', was to be right; was to have the power of law and state and wealth, a certain way of thinking and feeling on your side.

They'd written to Te Paania after receiving the 'bored' letter, telling her to come home: 'Everything's still here. We've kept the flat free. But if you don't like the idea of being on your own come and stay downstairs with us.' She'd replied saying she'd come. 'All I need is a job,' she'd said.

It was after that that he and Dave had opened up the upstairs flat again and spent a few weekends painting and papering. Ready if she wanted it. Ready to be let to someone else if she chose to live downstairs with them.

But she hadn't come.

By the time she rang she'd left her parents' place and found a job she liked, found a tower to live in. 'Decided I should try living on my own, with my own ghosts,' she'd said. 'I've never lived alone. It might be good for me, might be something I need to do . . .'

'. . . a big mistake,' she'd written three months later, 'One (unghost) person in one whole house is ridiculous – just not meant to be. No, no, no, not how human beings are meant to live as far as I can see. Can't put up with this concrete prison much longer, but I like the job and want to see my contract out.

'After that? I'll make a move, look for another place, see if Mae and Brooke will come and live with me – though it sounds as though Mae's found herself a fella. Should I do the same? Or . . .?'

15

TE PAANIA

During the first weeks at home I spent much of my time in the living room – during the day resting, or talking to Mae or Grandfather. At night I would lie awake, staring into the room's corners or watching moonlight come in, lopsided, through rifts in the curtains. All the time I would be listening, and when I went to sleep at last, would fall into dreams on the unfinished edges of wooden bridges which half spanned the yellow river, where people with injuries floated by on doors of many descriptions. Doors of cupboards, houses, refrigerators and cars. Doors made of wood and metal and glass.

These dream people felt no pain and were hopeful of reaching the other side. Some had rigged sack or shirt sails, while others poled along, using the handles of shovels and brooms. Above them, above where I stood, the sky was filled with children who used their arms as wings, and who spoke in bird voices as they sped by.

On the other side of the river was a large house which I thought could be reached by crossing the bridges. My footsteps staggered and echoed on the boards, but in the end I found every bridge to be incomplete. I stood at the edges of them in the hot wind stirred by the vibrating arm-wings. I called, without voice, to the people sailing and poling by.

In the mornings I would sit against pillows in an armchair while the family saw themselves out the door.

I was grateful for the noise of them hurrying from room to room while they kept up their arguments and conversations, and while the sound of the washing machine thumped through the house. On the way out, each one would look in and speak to me.

Mae would come in with Brooke whose bib and face would be crusty with rusks and Weetbix. She'd put her on the floor while she went to run the bath and get the towels and clothes ready. I'd get myself up to go and watch this bathing, which took place amid plastic containers and fish and boats and frogs.

Soapy baby.

And my eight-year-old sister leaning in, knowing all the sounds to make, the words to say, the baby places to wash.

I thought of her getting ready for school, lunch and book in a bag, crying over a broken pencil, eyes squeezed shut and mouth open, new teeth sawing their way through gums.

Eighteen.

Sleeves rolled to the shoulders.

Baby arms.

My own baby was too small for a bath like that. There was a rug on the floor in the living room where I could spread a towel. Beside the towel I could put the baby bath. I would undress my baby, wrap her, lay her along my arm with her head resting on my palm. I'd hold her over the water, washing her face, working my fingers in the facecloth to clean the fatty creases and the curls of her ears. I'd squeeze water from the cloth to wet her head, then soap my hand to rub through her hair.

I'd rinse off the soap, unwrap her and let her down into the water. Her neck and head would rest on my wrist while I gripped her round her shoulder and armpit with my thumb and two fingers. She could be a thin, dark insect perhaps, or a fat, spotty frog pleased with water. I'd move her legs, jiggle her hands, while she made her gurgling noises, then turn her to wash the back of her neck, her back, her blue patch, her buttocks and legs. I'd turn her again, swim her. We'd talk and play.

Then I'd take her out and dry every bit of her, every place, dressing her in clean clothes. She'd turn her head and move her mouth into me.

On the settee Brooke would grin at me with four teeth and bumpy gums, one cheek red and flaky. She'd take her bottle in long, dozy swallows and soon fall asleep.

On fine afternoons I'd walk to the end of the street with Mae and Brooke, who would then continue on to the shops. Later I was able to accompany them all the way into this town that my mother's scrubbing and cleaning had bought me out of. I'd look for signs of my baby in the faces of relatives. I'd compare her with babies of the same age and think about what she needed, what I'd buy for her, what I could do for her, how I'd protect her from fevers, from the epidemic, from being hurled through windscreens of cars. I'd think about what she would look like at four months, or five, though I could never understand this clearly.

I had often seen parents who didn't look at all like each other, but who had a child so completely like both of them that it was uncanny – a child with a face that was as triangular as his mother's and as round as his father's, whose skin was both dark and pale, whose eyes were grey or brown depending on which of the parents you saw looking at you from in them. Another child could have a mouth that was both small and large, lips that pulled themselves into a little socket but which opened to something of a letterbox slot whenever she laughed or smiled. It was the father's mouth metamorphosing into the mother's – not a mixture of one and the other, but completely both at once.

When I pondered on this I would wonder if my child could be at once Shane and me – a handsome frog, dappled, yet smooth and dark brown; a thin apple with eyes that were at once hooded and protruding, at once black and amber; hair that could be both wavy and straight.

At other times I made her into a little Shane, thin and dark, with a small chiselled face which had shadow and light passing constantly over and through it, as though always seen by the light of burning. Here was this Shane-child growing, gurgling, bubbling, talking to me; rolling and sitting; crawling and wearing holes in the knees of her stretch-'n'-grows; pulling herself up to stand. Once a week I would write to Mahaki and Dave and tell them all these things.

During this time I was happy to be home. The young loungers

outside the takeaway shops, kept good by Cokes and pies, were all part of me. Old school friends, who had become fat or thin, kept good by bad teeth, dope, beatings, welfare and pregnancy were part of me too. These were the people who could mend me, give me rest from crying, change the nature of my dreams.

I was happy at first to sit listening to the street preachers who called me sister, and to the band of singers with their fine harmonies – kept good by hymns, repentance, the coming of the Lord. At first I thought that I could belong there again.

But once the pain was gone, once the scars had faded and I could move about easily, I realised I could never buy back into the ghost of a town with my own ghosts in it, where I walked each day with my ghost of a baby.

Who was I now?

Mother, sister, daughter?

Frog, ghost, friend?

I needed work. There was none in the town, so I decided to ring the firm I'd worked for to see if there were any vacancies.

'You disappeared,' said Glen, 'We knew you were in hospital, knew you'd gone home from there but didn't know where.'

'I got the flowers.'

'No, no jobs here. We've had the consultants in and we're doing a hatchet job. Downsizing – which means throwing out the old ones and getting in new ones for half the money.'

'Have *you* been hatcheted?'

'Moved. North, head office. And . . . there's something there, suitable, if you want to apply, if you want to move that way.' He read out the job advertisement and said he'd get me a reference from Maggie. 'We missed you,' he said, 'coming in with your hair wet, smiling.'

Three weeks later I went to a job interview. Three days after that I learned that my application had been successful. I moved to Auckland.

'It's an utter shambles,' Glen said. 'There's this whole place to sort out. By next week I'm supposed to be on the road. Bloody hell, don't know what they've been up to, it's upside down. Just as well you're here. You're the only one I'd trust to get this place up to scratch. Holy shit, no wonder the branches are all out on a limb.'

Glen had a wide, pale forehead and a sheet of corrugated black hair. From his forehead his eyelids drooped, his face thinned. His cheeks folded and bunched round the sides of his mouth, making him look sorrowful. 'I don't suppose I'll be here much at all,' he said. 'Big boss wants me out on the road. But I'm trying to persuade him there won't be so much need for travel if we update our systems. Got to get me a life.' He went drooping away.

Office manager?

It was work that I enjoyed and I intended making it a big part of my life. It would keep the ghosts out, keep the loneliness at bay. I'd never lived alone before – though in another way I was never alone now.

I found a flat close enough for me to be able to walk to work. It was situated in an apartment block that looked like a contemporary castle, rising out of the ground in coloured flutes and cones – or like a bunch of sharpened pencils in a desk holder.

It was a skimpy, expensive place of moulded concrete and stucco, with a small kitchen and living area downstairs. There was a narrow metal staircase spiralling up to a thin bedroom. Next to the bedroom was an all-in-one washhouse and bathroom. It was fully furnished for one.

Entrance was through a paved yard, via a heavy door. There was a back door of wired glass that opened on to an enclosed, card-sized garden. It was comfortable enough for me I thought, but not a suitable place for children.

Ghost mother?

I moved in, knowing as soon as I closed the door that this was not for me.

'Home to my shoe box,' I said to Glen one night when we'd both been working late completing folders for his conference in Sydney.

'Is it so small?' he asked. 'Those places look quite big from the outside.'

'They're all walls. Thick walls. All right for me I suppose . . . No good for kids.'

'Which kids?'

'Any kids. If my sister came to stay Brooke would hate it there. There'd be no space for her. There's no light. The walls are all dark and spotlighty. Shelf lamps and all that sort of drama.'

'But handy to work.'

'Especially when there are extra hours. Don't mind extra hours, something to do.'

'It's nights,' he said. 'You bust a gut all day, or you're on the road for a week. You get home and wonder what it's all about. Don't want to bother thinking about food – buying it, cooking it . . .'

'Having stuff in the fridge . . .'

'I go out usually. Asian – Indian, Thai, Vietnamese.'

'I usually get something from the deli. Heat and eat.'

'And I eat too fast when I'm on my own.'

'Me too.'

'Don't want to eat so fast, just want to blob out, have a slow eat, take my time, enjoy . . .'

'I hog in like it's the last day of food.'

'Should've got a smaller place too, like you. Don't know why I got a whole house and a damn garden, I'm never there to do anything. Couldn't garden to save myself.'

'You thought there'd be someone to come and live with you.'

'Fat chance. Anyway I don't blame her, she's better off out of it. No good at relationships. I always complain about being on the road but I suppose that's my real life after all. As soon as I get stuck in a house with someone, anyone, I want out. Jesus.'

Then I wondered what it would be like to live with him, be in a house with him, have a garden together, be in bed with him. The idea made me laugh.

'What's funny?'

'It'd be better than nothing,' I said.

'What would?'

'Anyway, Mae and Brooke might come and stay for a while if they can stand it. I should look for something more suitable, cheaper.'

'We should swap, shouldn't we?'

'I was thinking about what you said.' He was standing inside my triple-locking door on the night he returned from Sydney. He looked so downcast and funny standing there that I put my arms up round his neck, pulled his head down and kissed him. He smelled like Air New Zealand lollies and looked completely surprised. 'I thought you might like to go out. Turkish,' he said. 'There's a place I go . . .'

'What do you think about us staying here, stuffing up a couple of pita breads, warming them, eating them. At the same time, or after that, we could throw a couple of brandies into ourselves.'

'That'll do fine,' he said, with a face that had turned itself completely upside down. 'I'll shift the car. Out there on the footpath over a yellow line. I'll get wine.'

'Go to the chemist,' I yelled up the footpath to the back of him, and saw the back of him break up laughing.

'Yes it's small,' he said, leaning back from under the dining light, nursing his brandy and letting his eyes move round before they came back to me.

'It is,' I said. 'But anything's possible.'

'Do you think so?'

'I'll show you round,' I said, starting up the tinny, curly stairs. 'Or do you think the staircase . . . ?' He started laughing behind me.

It was such a relief to make someone laugh, and then to make love.

Lover?

'Maybe it could work out,' he said after we'd been together for a few days. 'Maybe I could . . .'

'Don't worry about it,' I said. 'I'm not in it for the duration.' He thought about that for a while.

'Are we talking about finito, now?' he asked. 'Or are we talking days, weeks?'

'Let's try weeks, perhaps months, but not years,' I said. 'Let's not talk about love.'

'I'm away a lot of the time . . .'

'It's OK . . .'

'And it's going to get worse – Hong Kong, Thailand . . .'

'It suits me . . .'

'Better than nothing?'

'By far.'

I moved to his place, which was in a garden part of the city, in a house surrounded by lawns and trees and flowers. It was one of the older, smaller houses in the street, a property that you could imagine would soon go up for sale. The new owners, keen on the suburb but not on the house, would have something built that was more in line with other homes of the area.

It was the largest space I'd ever lived in, and as I soon found out, the emptiest and quietest, especially when Glen was away. I thought of Mae and Brooke coming to stay. I thought of my baby and Brooke playing in the rooms and in the trees. Better than nothing, but Glen wasn't one with whom I could share these thoughts.

One day I said to my child, 'Maybe it would be easier if there were two of you,' and decided that before Glen and I parted, I'd have another baby. I decided to make this my own business and didn't discuss the matter with Glen. He didn't notice me growing, didn't know I was pregnant until I told him. It made him thoughtful.

'I suppose I could . . .'

'Weeks and months but not years,' I reminded him.

'Yes . . .'

'I need this, you don't.' I thought he seemed relieved.

'Talk about it when I get back,' he said. He was preparing to go to Asia and was to be away for six weeks.

I knew that I shouldn't wait until he returned. If I did I knew we'd find enough liking for each other, and enough reason, to make us decide to stay together – which would be a decision not right for either of us.

A week after he left I gave notice. Three weeks later I left the job. I wrote two letters and packed my clothes.

The next morning I put on a loose, jingly dress, which was the only one that would fit me comfortably by then. I locked the house and went out on to Rathbone Drive, in frog weather, with a pack on my back, holding a ghosty daughter by the hand.

Dawn rolled out ahead of us on the long road. Dark tree shapes and black houses spun by. Four dog feet and a pair of Adidas came our way, splatting out drops.

Lappity lap lap zing.

Frog in black and white movie.

In wet dawn, starring.

Fade.

Up to cinecolour on Highborn Crescent. The rain stopped and there was pinkish light. There were fruit and flowers dropping on wet lawns all the way to Jellicoe Park. We stood in the middle of it.

Escapees.

Stars.

Boom boom.

People were on their way to work, to town, to another place. But they were only extras, ha, not part of the real story.

Down.

Down we went. On a roll. Getting faster until this daughter pulled me by the arm. Rolling, until my big belly crimped and cramped. I was being kicked to hell by this sprog.

OK.

I slowed down. I was not, after all, a lone star. I promised that we would soon be in a gentle bus, being borne sweetly along in it.

At the end of the bus journey we stepped out on to a railway platform, the three of us, hungry, but too early. So I bought a big, hot munch and lovely grimy coffee. We sat and waited.

When the time was right I found a taxi. We were taken along familiar streets in it, stepped out of it, clicked the gate and walked the path.

Frog star days.

16

TAWERA

She complains that I forget her, that I won't move over in the bed or make room on my chair for her. She doesn't like me to play with other kids, or talk to others. She gets me into trouble.

'You're twelve,' I said one morning during maths time. 'You're not supposed to be here. You're supposed to be in Room Ten with older children.' She gave me a real hard shove with her elbow. 'You're supposed to be doing Book Five mathematics and to read chapter books by now,' I said. 'You're supposed to smoke on the way to school hiding the cigarette backwards in your hand. After school you should have a paper round so that you can have pocket-money. You could be in love.'

'Quieten down in Group Two please,' the teacher said.

'How can I be in another class if no one knows me there?' my sister said. 'Who is there in another class to be my eyes? How can I smoke, have a paper round or be in love when I know nothing about all that?'

Our group was meant to be the quiet group that day. We were working in our books, practising accuracy, speed and neatness. I wanted to get three stars, but she was getting in my ears, interrupting all the time.

'How do you expect me to learn mathematics if you won't speak to me? How can I have my life and my education if you won't help?'

'You should listen to the teacher in the first place,' I said. It wasn't a good thing to say.

'I do listen. I do have ears in case you hadn't noticed,' my sister said, her voice becoming squeaky. 'I *can* hear you know. But how do I know what you're doing if you don't tell me?'

'How can we get three stars if you keep shoving and interrupting?'

'And how do I know you're getting our answers right if you won't say?'

So I began explaining each step of the calculations, knowing we'd miss out on getting a star for speed and that the talking was going to get me into trouble. To make matters worse she wasn't at all satisfied with my explanations. She was giving me bummage. 'Can I see? Can I see? You don't want me to have my learning. What sort of a brother are you? What sort of eyes are you? You go off thinking, all by yourself.'

'They'll hear us,' I whispered.

'So I embarrass you now that you're eight years old, now that you're so clever?' she said in an awful voice, 'You want to be the only educated one in the family. I'm rubbish am I? Wastecare, am I? Little jerk.' I felt bad.

'You're my sister, I'm your brother, I'm your eyes,' I said.

'Are you sure?'

'Yes.'

'Sure?'

'Yesss.'

'Group Two's supposed to be the quiet group today,' the teacher said.

I took my sister's hand and began tracing numbers, explaining every little thing. I tried speaking inside my mouth, leaving a little gap for the words to come out, but although I didn't move my lips at all the teacher still heard. I was relieved when the bell rang.

At morning break my sister and I went to play in a tree, away from all the children who were playing soccer and other games. I thought it was best that way.

'It's a tree like a lot of the other trees that I've described to you,' I said. 'It's not a very tall tree – about the height of our bedroom wall. If you feel along here, that's what the bark feels like. Put your hands round here, that's how round the biggest branches are. But the littlest branches are small enough to circle your finger and thumb round. If you touch here you can feel the size of the leaves and how smooth they are. The bark is grey like elephant skin. The leaves are green like January's eyes.'

'Grey, green, the colour of elephants, the colour of January's eyes? What's that supposed to mean?' my sister asked, but she wasn't angry. We were having fun up in the tree. 'Why is it you never tell me properly about the colours?'

'I don't know how to tell you about colours,' I said.

'Think of something then, you can do it.'

So I pegged myself onto a nice comfortable branch and thought about how it was all up to me to think of words and sentences for colours. It was a good feeling to know that these words and sentences could be any that I wanted them to be. Here I was, in charge of all the colours of the world. 'Grey,' I said, 'is like putting your tongue out and licking a window, starting from the bottom and going right up to the top.'

'That's good,' she said. 'What about green?'

'Green is like sticking a pin in your arm.'

'I know about licking windows,' she said, 'but I don't know what sticking a pin in is like.' So I undid my Ronald McDonald badge and gave her a jab by her elbow.

'I don't like green,' she said. 'I don't like the eyes of January, though I do like elephants and licking windows. I think grey is a good colour ... Let's play elephants?'

'Elephants can't climb trees,' I said, hoping she would want to get down so that we could play soccer.

'These ones can,' she said. So we played tree-climbing elephants until the bell went. We put our clothes back on, jumped down from the tree and ran back to our classroom.

'Tawera was up in a tree with no clothes on,' Florrie said to the teacher when we went inside. But Florrie is always so bad – putting buttons up her nose and paper in her ears, nosing into everyone's business, pinching sandwiches and telling lies – that the teacher took no notice of her. 'Pick your jersey up Florrie dear,' she said, 'and go and sit down please.'

135

'You didn't tell me the name of the tree,' my sister said as we went to unpeg our My Family posters from the string. She said it in an uncomplaining way.

'I don't know the name of it,' I said. 'But after school we'll get some leaves to take home and show to Mum. We'll look for it in Mahaki and Dave's books, read all about it.' Delia was putting out crayons and paints.

'All right tell me all about this now,' my sister said as we began work on our posters. 'Yesterday you didn't explain properly, just mumbled all the time.'

'Right at the front,' I said, 'are the two biggest and oldest ones. One's that great-great-great-great-grandmother. She's wearing a long dress, a feather cloak and a greenstone. She has two feathers in her hair. The other one is the great-great-great-great-grandfather with big abs and pecs who rode on a whale.'

'Squeezed his balls at their wedding.'

'Behind them is the grandfather with a funny eye and the nose of a bird. Alongside him there's the grandmother. Lots more up, up, up the paper.'

'You're mumbling.'

'Gran Kura, Mum . . .'

'Shane?'

'Glen . . .'

'He's a dork.'

'January . . .'

'I knew you'd say her, always flinging herself upside down.'

While we were working on our poster I found that the teacher had believed Florrie after all. She pulled a chair up beside us and sat down. 'If it's true that you took off all your clothes,' she said, 'I'd better explain that it's something you can't do at school without there being trouble.'

'It's how we play elephants,' I said.

'I see, but still you can't play that game at school. People – children, parents, teachers – will complain about anyone who's without their clothes.'

'I understand,' I said.

'And you need to work more quietly. Who do you talk to, Tawera?'

But I couldn't answer that. 'Anyway,' she said, smiling at me, 'you have a wonderful family. You're such a wonderful artist.'

'Yes, who do you talk to Tawera?' the kids said when the teacher had gone. I didn't answer. I'd decided to draw January upside down, doing one of her handstands – her face the wrong way up, eyes blinking backwards, hair floating up, nose holes showing. But the kids kept staring. 'Tell us who.'

'Nobody,' I said. I shouldn't have said that, what a dig I received.

'I didn't mean it,' I said.

And the kids said 'Errrrr?' in a funny way, their voices starting low down, rising until they were sitting on the tips of pins. They looked out of the sides of their eyes at each other. I felt so disappointed with this that I refused to give any more descriptions, no matter how much pinching and poking went on.

Mariana came to collect our posters and we tidied away the crayons and paint.

While we were waiting for the bell to ring I began to think about my problems. There were things I needed to sort out.

Think, think, think, and then I got it.

What I realised was that when you're no longer four years old, or five, or six or seven, you can learn to read with your eyes. I mean, when you get to be eight you don't need to point to each word and say it out loud. You can read in your mind, like Mum does, staring at her papers or her screen.

'I'll talk to you in my mind,' I said to my sister without opening my lips, without using any voice.

'What do you mean?' she said.

Wow.

'Like what I just did. Spoke words into your mind without opening my mouth.' I was excited.

'Please yourself. Makes no difference to me.'

After that I thought about the problem of friends and games. 'We'll have friends together,' I said with my mind, 'and when we play soccer, you can think what to do and I'll do the actions. You can be the brains.' She liked that. It was very important.

'No leaving me out,' she said. 'No leaving me on the sideline with all those dogs.'

Mum stopped what she was doing and removed the headphones. She looked at the leaves we'd brought home. I was amazed by what she told me. 'They're from a karaka tree,' she said. 'We used to make bubble pipes with the green berries. Cut them in half, scoop out the kernel and it's like a little cup. Make a hole in the side of it with an old nail, then look about in the dry grass for a good piece of straw to fit in the hole. We'd shake up a piece of soap in a tin of warm water and blow all these bubbles. Bubbles all over the show . . . When the berries were ripe we'd eat the orange skin.'

'Orange? Orange is pulling every finger and making every knuckle go crack . . . Where's Gran?' I asked.

'Down cooking with Dave.'

'We're going down to get a book.'

'Have a shower. Wash your legs . . .'

'No, I have to read the book straight away.' I went out the door and downstairs before Mum could say anything else.

Gran hugged me with her little arms, pressing her wrists against my wings so as not to touch me with floury hands. She was getting smaller because of all the stories that had leaked out of her. On the bench in front of her were squares of dough ready for frying.

Dave was making stroganoff, whipping noisy strips of meat round in a pan. There were chopped onions and sliced mushrooms on a board. His face was steamed. 'Late home,' he said. 'Playing soccer, muddy knees.'

I showed him the leaves. 'Karaka tree,' I said, proud of my knowledge. 'I need a book.'

'We made porridge when the berries were ripe,' Gran Kura said. 'We put them in sugarbags and left them in running water for days before cooking them in kerosene tins. Hours and hours, so we wouldn't get sick from the poison.'

I went to get the book, but was distracted from that by Dave's window that was spread out on his work table. When it was finished it would be put in my room, where light would break through it in all different colours. Dave had cut all the pieces and laid them all out to show the pattern. 'Now that I've learned to explain colours properly,' I said to my sister, 'I'll be able to give you a better description.

'If you stretch your arms out and touch this corner and this corner, you can tell the height of the window. If you touch here and here, you'll know how wide it is.

'Diagonally, here to here, there's a wavy yellow strip, like a flowing river. Yellow is touching a number two hair shave with the palm of your hand. On the top side of the yellow river, filling that whole triangle, are diamonds in a dark blue sky — like the everlasting stars. Dark blue is when you pull down your bottom eyelids and let hard, cold wind blow on your soft eye meat.'

'What colour are the diamonds?'

'No-colour, see-through . . . It's a hand on any cat's purr.'

'Go on then.'

'On the bottom side of the river you can touch the outlines of trees of different sizes. Pin green they are. Amongst the trees are red and orange flames, as though there are people walking about with lanterns. Red is someone blowing a long sound on a conch before the dancing begins. Orange . . .'

'Is pulling every finger and making every knuckle go crack.'

'That's right, that's good,' I said. I think she was pleased with this praise. I think she was happy with my descriptions.

We went to the shelves where Mahaki and Dave keep their tapes and CDs. There's a space at the bottom for books that are too big to go on the narrower shelves. In *Native Trees of New Zealand* we found a picture showing a tree just like the one at school. There were close-ups of the leaves as well as of the green and orange berries. Plenty of information too.

'It's right Mum,' I said, when she came in. 'It's a karaka tree with broad green leaves, and green berries which ripen to a bright orange in late summer. It doesn't say anything about eating orange berries or making bubble pipes from the green ones.'

'The people who wrote the book don't know about those things,' she said.

'You're clever, Mum. You're clever too, Gran Kura. "Kernel deadly poison," it says here.'

'If anyone ate the porridge before it was cooked properly,' Gran said, 'they'd drop to the ground and their eyes would roll back and look inside their heads. Foam would come bubbling out of their mouths because they were beginning to turn inside out.'

'Like the aliens on *Skeptiks Three*, who grew from the trunks of pyro plants, pouring sticky green stuff from their mouths to trap Lixia?'

'Yes. If anyone got sick you had to take them down to the beach and bury them up to their necks in sand, packing the sand down hard so they'd stop shaking and jerking. You had to stop them from bending themselves backwards, trying to place their foreheads onto the soles of their feet in imitation of the moon.'

Mahaki came in and I held the book up to him.

'Bring it here. Show me,' he said as he sat down.

'I'm sitting by Mahaki,' my sister said.

'You sit one side and I'll sit the other,' I said. However when we sat she squeezed herself between Mahaki and me. I wasn't too pleased. Anyway, we had a good discussion while Dave, Gran and Mum put food on the table. 'Come on kids,' Dave said.

When we'd finished eating I suddenly felt niggly and tired. What I wanted to do was curl up on the settee and go to sleep in my tiger blanket, as I often did in weekends when Mahaki and Dave didn't need to get up early for work. But it wasn't a weekend. In fact it was only Monday.

'We'd better get you into the shower,' Mum said, which made me feel really upset and sorry for myself.

All those stairs, all that washing.

All those complaints and accusations about not being a proper brother. All that being up a tree instead of playing soccer, being told on by that cute Florrie, being told off by the teacher.

All that sideways looking. All that thinking and planning and having to remember to talk in my head. All that being pinched and poked and shoved and squeezed. It wasn't fair at all. I had to blame someone. 'What do you care Mum,' I said. 'You didn't even have a very good reason for making me. It was only so I could babysit my big sister, keep *her* off your back, out of your hair, out of your eyes, your head, your ears.'

'There you go,' my sister said. 'Talking like I'm not here, thinking I can't hear because my eyes are in my stomach.'

'Shut up Big Ears.' I'd had enough of her.

'Wanting all the attention for yourself.'

'I needed you,' Mum said. She looked shocked.

'You're everything to us,' said Dave.

This was pretty good stuff. I wanted to make the most of it. 'And there wasn't any good reason for leaving my father now that I know the story. He might've liked me, bought me a Sega or a horse or a dog, taken me to Thailand.'

'We didn't know you wanted a Sega,' Mahaki said.

'And a horse and a dog,' I said.

'Come on sweetheart,' Dave said, 'I'll backy you up.'

All right. I ignored the pinching and poking and climbed up on Dave's back, locking my arms round his neck, curling my legs round his waist, laying my face against him. Up the stairs we went.

Dave turned the shower on, helped me undress, and I stepped in. He reached in to soap me. The wet hair on his arms flattened and glinted, making his arms look like the backs of two stroked cats. He rubbed me with a big towel and helped me on with my pyjamas.

By the time I got into bed I felt good and sleepy. I didn't mind making plenty of room in the bed for my sister, didn't mind sharing the blankets and pillows with her.

Later in the week Mum had something to say to me that had been on her mind since the night of my grumpy mood. 'About your father,' she said, 'and what you said about me not having a good reason for leaving. He and I both knew we weren't in it for the long haul. I knew it was the right time to go. You and I would've been alone now if I'd stayed. If we'd gone to Thailand we'd have been alone in Thailand by now. I wanted us to have a family, one that was right for you. I wanted your father and I to remain good friends.'

'I know, I know.'

'About your sister . . . It's true . . .'

'Mum, Mum, you don't have to explain. But geez, Mum, "Better than nothing?" How do you think that makes me feel?'

'Well . . .'

'And are you sure you didn't sex me on the stairs?'

'That was just a joke. No, I've never been interested in anything uncomfortable . . . And I hadn't even thought of you then.' She laughed and opened her arms to me. 'Come on Bubs . . .'

Well OK.

I climbed on to Mum's knee, leaned against her and put my face in her neck. I spread myself on her lap, deliberately taking up all the room. After all, my sister was the one who was always telling me I had a dorky father, as if Shane was so hot.

Then I sat up. 'Mum, you're right up with the telling of it now,' I said. 'You've caught up to me – that boulevard, bumping along, those aliens, those reversible dancers. I know the rest. But tell us about this work you do with earphones clapped over your ears, eyes bugging out behind your glasses making you look like a creature – not a mother, not even a frog. Like something that's more than frog, beyond frog. What sends you in the middle of the night down the stairs, knocking on Dave and Mahaki's door?'

17

TE PAANIA

Beyond frog?

It's wildness that makes my eyes bug out. It's my bugging-out eyes that enable me to see wildly, according to Gran Kura. This same wild-seeing caused the leapings from my throat when I was at school, and later launched me into the arms of Shane. 'You recognised him as someone who would rescue you from too much goodness,' Gran said.

And it's the same wild knowing, according to her, that made me refuse to sit in an alien garden suburb. It brought me instead to where there was a family, a school safe for my children that wouldn't kill them or teach them to die.

But how could I – who had been saved from the meatworks by my mother's labour and my father's words, who'd had hick town extracted at fifteen and who'd nightclassed herself through to office management – believe that all Gran said was so? I'd been made, hadn't I? I only see what I see, which is ordinary enough, plain enough to me.

'No one saved you, or made you, except yourself and what's in you,' Gran said. 'There's been nothing extracted, not at fifteen, not anytime. You were born with your kind of knowing, otherwise how would you have understood, at school, that there were lies being told, when there were others like me who were too good to understand it? How did you understand that you were too smart for those examination papers? How did you know what to say to Annabelle? Like with Pirinoa, no one can order you.'

'We've come to ask what your school has to offer our child,' I said to Annabelle in her office where extra chairs had been brought in. Mahaki and Dave had taken an afternoon off work so that they could come with Gran and me to find the answer to this and other questions.

I'd never before met anyone called Annabelle, who was small behind her large, orderly desk. Her hair was short and reddish-grey, kept back from her face with a brown band. Her makeup was orange-toned, sparse, hasty, token. She wore an olive green trouser suit over an orange blouse. Round her neck were several strings of beads that would please and interest children.

Behind her on the wall were masks coloured with paint and crayon, and decorated with bottle tops, curled paper, twigs and leaves. The mask-makers were Awhina, Jaylene, Morehu, Sasha, Saana, Mahu, Jonus.

Holes for eyes.

Annabelle's eyes were something. They narrowed and flickered when I asked the question. Her face lit, uncreasing itself. 'Oh no,' she said. 'Not mine.' She stood with a handful of papers. 'I'll get these sent, get Jacqui to take the calls. 'Scuse a minute.'

It wasn't the first school we'd visited, though it was the one just down the road from where we lived. We'd gone first to a school on the other side of the hill near to a Kohanga Reo.

Because of the existence of the Kohanga Reo we'd expected to find what we were looking for there. *My* school this, *my* school that, the principal had kept saying. *My* school has a job to do. *My* school and *my* teachers treat everyone the same. I knew immediately that this was no place for our children, but the visit helped me to know the first question I wanted to ask Annabelle.

'What I mean is,' said Annabelle as she came back in, 'the school belongs to kids and the community, doesn't it? Was that a trick question? Our job is to deliver curricula based on the needs of our kids. Well that's the theory. Here ...' She stood and took a ring-binder from a shelf, undid the catch and removed wads of paper from it. 'Get you a copy so you can read, see what we're on about ...' She left the room again.

'All easier said than done,' she announced when she returned. 'But we can only try, ask for help when we need it. Ask what your child needs and what you expect from the school, for your kid. Then we can just do our darnedest ... So what? Come on, tell me.'

'Want him to be ... OK ...'

'Taken into account ...'

'Not hurt ...'

'Happy ...'

'Come on, more, more, that's only square one. It's not enough,' she said, rolling her hands in front of her as if she were hyping up an audience. They were little hands, pale and freckled, with big blue veins worming under the skin.

'The world,' Dave said.

'His learning.'

'And everything else besides.'

'There's more than just surviving.'

'That's better,' she said, rewarding us with smiles.

'Tawera speaks two languages. Riripeti's death was quick and mine was slow,' Gran Kura said.

The first sentence of what Gran said was translated for Annabelle by Mahaki, who went on to describe Gran as a Maori language activist who had made a decision never to speak in English.

'Ha,' said Annabelle bumping up in her seat. 'I love days like this.' Her hands, with outspread fingers, came up in front of her face then trickled downwards to her lap. 'I can see it all falling into place.'

She brought her hands back to the desk, threaded her fingers together and screwed her eyes into us. 'Well now, listen to this. I've been having meetings with the Kohanga Reo parents on the other side of the tunnel. There hasn't been a Kohanga set up on this side yet. Don't know why. I think we deserve one. Anyway, the parents have approached me because they've had no joy from their own primary school over there –

which means that when their Kohanga kids turn five they leave their Maori language behind. They go into a school that's resisting the setting up of an immersion class, or bilingual – or whatever it would be called. They've had a few fights with Lesley over there, and a few fights with the board.

'Now they've come to us. It fits, you see. We have a twenty per cent Maori roll here. We've tried to put programmes in place, kapa haka, etcetera, but it's not enough. No *depth*. We're keen to have a whanau class, whether it be total immersion or bilingual. With the children coming from Kohanga we'll have numbers, enough kids for an extra teacher.

'So what are we doing about all this?' Annabelle thumbed through a pile of folders on her desk, pulled one out and spread a hand across the cover of it. 'We've advertised for a teacher for next year, that's what. I thought that would be the difficult bit, you know, getting someone who's a trained teacher who's also fluent in Maori. It's a problem apparently. But . . .' Annabelle opened the folder, flicked pages, flicked her eyes. 'Here we have two applicants. One's a young man graduating from T'Coll at the end of the year – fluent speaker, according to the application. The other's a woman I met when she was an ITM. She's marvellous and wonderful.

'Well, at the time of all the big education cost-cutting exercises she became chained to a desk – as a lot of people did. No longer allowed to get out in the field. She hates it. Rather be back in a classroom working twice as hard, getting less money. I know we'd be lucky if we could get her.'

She shut the folder. Her eyes went to the clock on the wall. 'God I've done it again, done all the talking. We teachers are all hyper . . . Can't help it, talk to me . . . Ask me . . .'

There was little chance to do that. Annabelle lifted the phone and called through to someone saying that she was going to be late, then stood and went out, returning with the pile of information that had been copied for us.

Many of our questions had been pre-empted. Some of our fears had been allayed. Now we would read. We would discuss with each other, find more questions and attend board meetings.

Whether we decided to send Tawera to school or not, it seemed there was something new for Gran to do.

'Mrs Haunui,' Annabelle said to her, 'when we interview our applicants would you be interested in being on our interview panel as someone to judge language competency? Mrs Haunui, when we get this all under way at the beginning of next year we know that resources are going to be scarce. We envisage employing someone on a part-time basis to help the teacher, three to five hours a week, someone skilled in the language. Would you consider putting in an application?'

'Ah I love days like this,' she said again just as we were leaving. 'When things turn on their heads and you have a look at all the treasure that falls.'

Perhaps in my heart I didn't want to find the school to our liking. From time to time, as Tawera was growing, we'd talked about keeping him home. I would've liked being his teacher – something for me to do that I could feel right about doing. Because it wasn't just that I had come to see schools as unsafe places, I was apprehensive in other ways too, wondering what I would do with my days. I didn't want to return to work, which I thought of now as part of a past, something I'd moved away from in order to make life different.

'Dressing for the office in high collars, shoulder pads, skinny skirts and the right shoes isn't me any more,' I said to Gran Kura. 'Going out to work for bosses just isn't me.'

'You're you, no matter where,' she said. 'No matter what the clothes.'

She was talking about froggy camouflage – which is a ripple on water, stalks of criss-crossed grass, patterns on wood and stone, raindrops on mud, imprints of old leaves and flowers on the ground, eyes sitting, as floating bubbles, on the pond's surface. It was something keeping its true self underneath, yet the 'not hidden' is true also.

'Not like us,' Gran said. 'Trying and trying not to be who we were. When we put makeup on our faces it was to cover the colour, to cover the ugly, cover the bad. We really meant it. We didn't want to be these bad, ugly people, speaking this heathen language. We wanted instead to be these good people, wanted our children not to be who they were. No, no, not to be their ancestors. We did what we were told. When we were told to sing, we sang. When we were told to kneel, we knelt. When we were told to move our houses we moved them.

'We didn't know our children would refuse to be who we were trying to make them be. We didn't know they would demand their names, or that they would tear the place apart searching for what we had hidden from them. We didn't know they would blame us. You're lucky to be so evil.'

'You think I'm under-using it? This evil?' I asked, not really clear about what I was asking.

'Everything we do, everything that happens, is a preparation for something,' she said. 'Look at me now. It's only now I know what I should do because Riripeti died, or because of Shane and Baby. It's only now I can rid myself of this sickness, so that in the end I can have a healthy death. It'll come to you, you'll see.'

It did come. I didn't have to be concerned about what I would do with my days. My life became busier than it had ever been. Work came to me. It absorbed me, made my eyes bug out.

'Up to my ears,' Mahaki said one night. 'We're overloaded at the office. Just can't find enough time for the real stuff.'

Three or four times a year Mahaki had been going to visit his grandfather to make tape recordings of the old man's stories. This was the 'real stuff'. It was because of what he had learned during these recording sessions that Mahaki decided something needed to be done about an area of land in his home territory, known as Anapuke.

'Gone on long enough,' he said, pacing as he does, frowning as he does, curls falling round his big face. He was rolling his hands like Annabelle. 'Old man's agitated, got it on his mind. And what's the use of me being a bloody lawyer if I can't do something, waste of bloody time . . . Anyway, tapes.' He stopped pacing and sat down opposite me. 'They need transcribing, big backlog, wanted to do it myself . . .'

'Give them to me . . .'

'Max had a go but it needs someone with a knowledge of the

language, someone used to the old people's voices and the way they speak – in whichever language.'

'I'll have a go . . .'

'The old man switches from one to the other.'

'Bring me one of your machines, and a transcriber with a foot control.'

'I'm pushing for a meeting with the Town Council, well, pushing for the Council chiefs to come and meet with the people.' He was up pacing again. 'But they're just being bloody-minded, insisting that we send a delegation down to their offices instead. The people are fed up with that, going there with delegations. It's time that lot had a bomb up them . . . Mightn't need to do all the tapes, just certain ones, or certain parts . . .'

'I'll do them all. Otherwise what's the use of me being a bloody office girl if I can't do something, waste of bloody time.'

He stopped pacing and his grooved forehead smoothed itself. He laughed. 'I'll bring the tapes tomorrow, and the equipment. Outdated, not what you're used to . . .'

'Or as Gran Kura would say, why was I pushed out of house and home, why did I see a notice on the board of a supermarket, why did I walk out in the rain, etcetera, etcetera?'

'I get it.' Then he said, 'It's all becoming one.'

The tapes took my breath away. Bugged me. Led me to realise I should be taping and transcribing Gran Kura's stories too, which is what we began to do.

It was three years before the meeting between the Town Council and Mahaki's people took place, and it was when I began transcribing the tapes from that meeting that I began to understand what Mahaki meant when he said it was all becoming one – the old stories, the new stories, Anapuke and the eyes.

18

MAHAKI

Once most of the people were in, Mahaki set up the tape recorder and went to sit down. Through the window there was a good view of Anapuke. He let his eyes move up its sloping edge, along the scooped ridge and down the steep face, settling his thoughts. Beside him, his cousin Maraea was talking, arm in a sling, hair in sprigs. He couldn't make the effort to keep up with what she was saying.

The men from the Council had already been formally welcomed and given morning tea. Now they were being escorted in like royalty. Chairs and a long table had been brought in for them. The heaters were going. The old man followed them in and sat in an armchair that had been placed by the door.

There was a buzz, but Mahaki couldn't share in the excitement. It worried him – everyone on a high because they trusted what was going to happen, really believed that Anapuke was going to be handed back, right then, just like that, after forty years of asking and being ignored. Well, he was suspicious about the message he'd received that the Council wanted to come and negotiate the return of Anapuke. Knew there'd be a catch somewhere. And it made him feel sick watching his smiling elders organising chairs, tables and gas heaters for the two men, after stuffing them with food.

'Piss me off,' Maraea said.

Elders? Councillors? But maybe he shouldn't be such a cynic. It was a start, wasn't it? It was an achievement getting the Council men there, even if it was only to begin negotiations.

'Well, wait and see I suppose. See if it's going to be better than a slap over the ear with a wet fish,' Maraea said. Kani, sitting on the mattress opposite, was eyeing round to see if everyone was ready. He rolled his big weight on to his knees, stood and began a karakia. The prayers wheezed out of him. 'He looks like an avocado,' Maraea said.

Kani went on to introduce the men from the Council, who were Bob and Colin. Then the old man stood to speak, frail, his voice just audible. Mahaki went over and shifted the recorder closer towards him. Bob and Colin leaned forward to listen.

'I was a boy then, twelve years, too young for war. Older brothers, cousins, all that, gone. That's me, a boy of twelve standing. Next day a twelve-year man. Ploughing, planting, sledging water, dragging down wood, but never mind.'

He could see the old man was going to tell it all, could see the Council blokes resigning themselves. He wished the old man wouldn't bother. Bob and Colin wouldn't know what he was going on about and wouldn't care either. Away from the old man for a few years you could forget too – how to listen, how to hear, especially when the old man was speaking in English as he was having to do now. You had to open your skull, peel off and peel off, listen. He'd heard it all before, though there was always something new to listen for.

'There was this old man Hori who talk to me about Anapuke. Well that hill, that Anapuke, you don't hardly talk about. It's from the far, old times, when there's only the Maori.

'Us kids all know you don't go there. No. You go there it's trouble. But how can we go there anyway? No pathway and big swampland all around, and it's far. Far to us childrens.

'And you don't look there. If our eyes go that way we don't leave them that way. No. We look another way. You don't look at Anapuke or a ghost will come. You don't talk about Anapuke or a ghost will come.

'But now here's this Hori talking to me, a boy, about Anapuke. He's a man to give you a fright. Only small, same size as me a twelve-year boy, bandy leg, ragged and grey, his head on sideways, put like that by a ghost when he's a baby, looking at me one red eye up and one down. One ear listen to the ground and the other listen to the sky. What for? I don't know what for he's talking to me, a boy, about this Anapuke. But then I think it's because this boy's a man now. All this boy's brothers and cousins gone across the world and don't come back. "All round is caves," this Hori say to me. "In all of them, bones. Hill of the dead."'

Maybe it was a good thing after all that the old man was on his feet, but not for the sake of the councillors. Mahaki could see that most of the people had never heard any of this, not the younger ones anyway. They'd moved forward so they could take in every word, their faces held up like chalices as the old man told of the caves and recited the names of the ancestors who sat looking at the sun.

'Well I live my life a bit more and here's another big war. Old enough to be a soldier. Old man Hori ninety-eight. He cries, begs me. I know it's wrong to go and leave him, know I won't see him again. No. I think I'm this brave man going to war, paying back for the brothers and cousins. Stupid. Off I go.'

He could see the councillors wilting, the heat making their eyes droop. They'd probably like the heaters turned off or shifted, but think it mightn't be right to get up or ask anyone, while the old man was talking. They perked up a little when he began speaking about the act that eventually saw Anapuke become Council property. He described to them the many meetings that the people had held in their attempts to have Anapuke returned.

Hated it when he was a kid – all those meetings. Instead of going off to play with other children he'd been made to attend. The old man had made him sit, held him by the ear, every now and again giving it a wiggle. Hours and hours. Boring stuff to a kid. Tape running out. He went to turn it over.

'We come here today because Anapuke got to return to the people, got to, because now there's a new business.'

What new business? What was itching the old man now?

*

'I won't go into history,' Bob said. 'That has been done eloquently already and it's something you all know about better than we do. As you know, Council employees come and go, but you people have been here a long time. Will be here a long time yet, no doubt. You've had a long-time desire to see Block 165G10 returned to you. Council holds records showing how and when this property was purchased. Council holds certificate of title. Although we have found no record of payment being made, we can assure you that it was policy at the time for people to be paid for their land, either through transaction or through compensation being awarded.

'Now we're not here to debate the pros and cons of the Maori Affairs Act that at the time made it compulsory for land not in use to be sold to the Crown. We're not here to discuss the Public Works Act that made land available to the Crown for railways or roads or defence or community good. Past injustices, or otherwise, are not our concern at the present time. What we are concerned with now is what is the best solution for all of us, for now and for the future, as regards 165G10. As has been said there has never been a use for the land, and we, frankly, have no use for it now. It would be far too expensive for us to develop it ourselves, and though we believe we could sell to developers for a good price we think that this may not be a good solution under the circumstances.'

Jesus, they were going to offer it to them for sale. Sell it back to them. That'd wipe the smiles off the aunties. That'd make the cream cakes redundant.

'We need to take all of our best interests into account and see what can be done to realise your hopes and to satisfy the needs of our Council. We believe we have a solution . . .' Bob paused, turned to say something to Colin, opened the folder on the table in front of him. 'We've come here today to offer you, the people here, first option on the land. We'd be happy to let 165G10 go at government valuation price if you wish to purchase – government valuation price of course being a fraction of what could be obtained for this block of land on the open market.'

Silence.

'That's our proposal, ladies and gentlemen. You may have questions to ask, or matters you wish to bring up for discussion.'

Silence.

People waited, faces moved back into the shadows. Keep calm, Mahaki. He traced down the steep face of Anapuke. Halfway down and far to the left was the first cave. Nose of the dog. Ancestors sat, looked at the sun. Along the face of the dog, on the tip of its ears, was the second.

Enough silence to make the two men fidget their papers and shift on their chairs. He watched as they leaned together. Their mouths moved. One head nodded once, the other twice. Colin stood.

'Of course we're not looking for an immediate response. We'd be pleased to answer any questions. Government valuation on 163G10 would be as of December last year. It may be negotiable. Terms could be looked at.'

Silence.

Colin sat, then stood again. 'As Bob has said there may be matters you wish to discuss. There may be questions.'

Down the long neck to a point two-thirds along the ledge that formed the back of the dog was the third spot. Around and under the dog's no-tailed backside, on the tuft, there was the fourth.

Kani was on his feet, eyeing round, waiting.

Silence.

Along, up the underside of the long neck, tucked under there was the fifth cave – and back to the nose. Kani cleared his throat.

'We've heard the gentlemen. They've put an option before us to do with this land of our ancestors. Have we any questions? Do we want to discuss any matters concerning this option? The meeting is open to all our thoughts and expressions.'

All joined up. Follow the dots and you'll find who's hidden in the hillside. Legless dog. He was still a student when the old man had begun naming the places, showing him the legless dog. He'd been told the names of all the ancestors too, but he'd been unable to remember them – there'd never been enough time and his brain was too used to book learning. Not a move from the old man.

What new business?

Not a movement anywhere. It looked as if they'd have to try and

154

take the matter to court, but what would the courts make of the old man's evidence? Who would there be to understand it, or believe him?

Now Maraea, beside him, was standing, flapping her sling.

'OK. Who are these rip-offs? Why are we letting them come here asking us if we want to buy our own land – land that was stolen in the first place? Why did we stuff them with cream cakes and press our ihu to their ihu just to have them insult us? Kick them out. Go on. Award them the order of the boot.'

They call the wind Maraea.

People came out of their silence and began talking. Bob and Colin were fixated in half-smiles, unable to move their eyes.

'I agree with my cousin,' Abe from the shadowed corner opposite was saying. 'We didn't come here to hear this, we come here to have that land handed back. No buying, selling, nothing like that.'

'It's not the usual thing, is it,' Ani said, 'for stolen goods to be sold back to the owners?'

People up on their feet, angry, challenging.

Court? It was a worry. If they built a case on Anapuke being a sacred site the courts would want their own kind of proof. There's no way the old man would want anyone nosing round on Anapuke disturbing the dead. He could imagine the old man being asked in court how he knew about the burial caves and him saying Hori told him. All the eyeballs would fix themselves then, boring holes in the walls in an effort not to roll heavenwards.

And he could imagine the old man on his feet telling them, 'I am the proof. In here,' pointing to his head, perhaps reciting the names, believing that would make them understand. But even the use of that word 'sacred' was off-putting. It was a word people pretended about when they were trying to be sensitive and knowledgeable.

Now the old man was up again. Mahaki went forward to change the tape and reset the recorder. He wished the old man had stayed seated. Bob and Colin were sitting back in their chairs looking patient, keeping their eyes still as if refraining from looking at their watches.

'You get out with your helicopters now. Right now, so we know our ancestors' patterns will not be separated from their bone and their blood.

'Separated? What for? So you can have new words to put in a book, so you can tell yourselves what place a Maori was born from, what journey we take to here, who give us our tongue . . .'

The new business, what the researchers and scientists were up to – patenting, genetic bits and pieces. Didn't know how the old man got on to that.

'. . . I come from the ground I tell you. No need to disturb the ancestors to tell you that. I come from the ground and the heavens. I come from the ground and the heavens in the most most faraway place. I come from the ground and the heavens in the longest longest time ago. I come from the ground and the heavens from the place deep deep felt in my heart, and my tongue come with me. Don't you kill our ancestors. Don't kill our childrens . . .'

Grandfather giving it his best shot, what he believed to be his utmost contribution to their understanding – but the Council men didn't have a clue what he was going on about, sitting there like wood.

Now the old man had forgotten to keep speaking in English. He'd switched languages. Colin and Bob looked affronted. They could afford the odd flicker of impatience now because the old bloke was definitely gaga, they thought. They leaned on their elbows, leaned back, leaned forward, together, as though they'd been synchronised. But what do they hear anyway, those who haven't learned to turn what is said in order to examine the underside?

Back to English again, or a mixture, voice fading.

Mahaki tried to put his mind to what would happen if they took the matter to court. He thought that rather than go for the sacred site option, it might be better to build a case on the people's insistence that the land had never been sold in the first place, that there'd never been payment, either because of purchase or through compensation. But it was a shaky business going to court, and expensive. Too expensive. They'd have to try and prove fraud. That would be just about impossible.

'We hear what you're saying,' Bob said as the old man sat down.

'Patronising bullshit,' Maraea, beside him, said.

Silence.

Kani was sliding his eyes round the room to see how many chins were up, how many eyebrows flicking.

Plenty.

All.

'Thank you, gentlemen,' he said. 'It's time we let you go back to your desks. Our father here has definite thoughts and we haven't sensed any disagreement with those thoughts from among us. However, we need our own time to consider the option you've put before us, and also to consider what other options there might be.'

Order of the boot.

'Cool, huh?' Maraea said as Kani showed the two men out.

'Pretty good for an avocado.'

Bob and Colin were smiling their way out, trying not to quicken their steps, bending their heads towards each other as though in serious conversation.

19

KURA

There was Rebecca who gave birth to my brother and me. We loved her. She had a husband who we also loved. These two were deep in our hearts but we didn't know the full reason why this was so until the death ceremonies took place, which is when the stories were fully told.

Rebecca, who gave birth to us, gave birth to six children altogether. Four were from her own husband.

Our own mother, who was Rebecca's sister, never did give birth.

Our own father was our own father.

Grandfather Tumanako was the only one of his line, being saved from death by strong incantations. Without him our direct line to our great ancestor would have ended. This mattered deeply to the people. It was everything to them.

From the time he was born, Grandfather's future was thought about and discussed, and when he was a small boy there was a marriage arrangement made with a daughter from a related hapu. The daughter was called Maharahara. It was she who carried me back from death when I was a child. It was she who, from our verandah, sent Jack on his way with his axe. It was she who abandoned me.

Grandfather Tumanako and Grandmother Maharahara had nine

living children, the precious offspring, holding the life force. They were the way forward, the hope, the continuation, the way of survival.

But although Grandfather and Grandmother had nine children, their grandchildren were few. Of the nine children, four died before they had children of their own. One had three children but all died – two of measles and one of fear. Our mother and our mother's sister, and her two remaining brothers, had ten living children among them.

When our mother grew up, the old custom was followed and a marriage was arranged. She was to be married to someone she had never met, being told of his existence only when it was time for wedding preparations to begin. It was a proper arrangement for someone like her.

Preparations for the wedding began in all the hapu to which she had connections. Crops were set aside, animals were fattened, the church was painted, the sleeping house was made ready to accommodate all the visitors who would be coming. Arrangements were made for the setting up of a large marquee which would be used for the wedding feast. Our mother was taken to a dressmaker who made a wedding dress of white satin. The dressmaker also made gowns for eight bridesmaids, because no part of the family could be left out as far as bridesmaids and groomsmen were concerned. Frocks and outfits were made for my mother and brought to her from relatives everywhere, everyone wanting to give their utmost for this wedding.

Hers was the first wedding amongst Grandfather's and Grand-mother's children. Her two older brothers had drowned two years before, now this wedding was bringing new life and new hope to everyone. It was a joy to the people.

Also, as it happened, it was a joy to our mother and father because they fell in love and were happy together.

Our father's people arrived with him the day before the wedding. There was a day and night of speech-making and singing, and giving of money and gifts. Also visitors had brought cartloads of supplies – bags of potatoes and kumara, boxes of canned meat and fruit, drums of smoked mullet and eel and all sorts of baking and preserves – to add to what was already there. Our mother was kept at home that day. She met our father for the first time when she was taken to the church the next morning. It was right for someone like her.

After the wedding and the big marriage feast, plans were made for the couple to take a journey to our father's home-place to visit all the old people, the sick people and those who had been unable to attend the wedding. These ones wanted to welcome the newly married couple and to have an opportunity also to give their gifts. This marriage gave hope to people. It was precious in their hearts.

Our father's family was also a family that had been affected by sickness and death. Children were of great importance to them too. Everywhere the young couple went people would say to our mother, 'You're taking Joshua away from here. That's all right but let us have one of your children.' Or they'd say, 'Remember us first when you name your children.'

When all the visiting was over, our parents returned to live with Grandfather and Grandmother.

Marriage had also been discussed for my mother's brothers, and also for her sister, who was the youngest in the family. And it was when it came to sister Rebecca, who was eventually to become our birth mother, that arrangements did not go as people had planned.

Rebecca fell in love with a man of no reputation who did not meet with family approval. She was told to forget him, told not to waste her lineage on a man whose hands hung empty at his sides. Rebecca said nothing and stayed quietly at home for some weeks. One morning the family woke to find her gone.

The brothers were sent out to look for her and they found her at last, with the man, living at the home of one of his relatives. The relatives said to the brothers, 'Ask your family to accept this marriage because it's already done. Tell them their grandchild is already made.' So our grandparents had to give their approval, but after the child was born they made Rebecca come home and have a wedding in the church. The church was of great importance to them. Marriage in the eyes of the Lord was important.

After the wedding Rebecca returned to her husband's relatives to live. They built their own little ponga house by the river.

This all happened five years after our own parents' marriage. Some of the brothers had had children by then. Soon this younger sister's first child was born, but our own parents were still without children.

They remained childless for fifteen years. Our mother became listless and ill because of it. She lived in sorrow, is what we were told. People wondered what she had done to attract the lingering of what had affected her grandmother, Pirinoa.

There was even some talk of Mother and Father parting, whispers that our father's people wanted him to have another wife. But he didn't want another wife, and there were many who wouldn't have agreed with this anyway, knowing it would have been Christian sin. People prayed for them.

Then one day Mother and Father prepared for a journey. They loaded a wagon with clothes, supplies and blankets, and told people they were going to stay with sister Rebecca for a while. People believed our mother was going to her sister's to choose one of the children to bring home and raise as her own.

It was a day's journey to the river crossing. They drove the horses and wagon through the river shallows to the other side where they were met by Tiaki, Rebecca's husband, who had seen them from the hill slopes. He helped them unhitch the wagon and load their belongings on to the horses. They walked the horses along the river tracks to the house. It was dark by then. Rebecca and Tiaki knew that Mother and Father had come there for a special reason. There was a right time for speaking.

During the first days after our parents arrived there were visits to be made and foodstuffs to distribute. There were conversations that had to take place, time that had to be spent.

Then one afternoon when they had all come into the cooking shelter, when the fire had been stirred up and the children were watching the rain, there was enough silence to know that it was the right time. Our mother said to her sister, 'I've come to bring you my husband so that you can bear our child.'

'You've come to ask for one of our children to take home and bring up as your own,' Rebecca said.

'I've come to bring you my husband so that you can bear our child,' our mother said again.

'You've come to ask us to have a child for you,' Rebecca said.

'I've come to bring my husband to you so that he can have a child that is his,' she said. 'And so that this child will have the same ancestry that our own child would have.'

Rebecca and Tiaki, sitting side by side, didn't move, didn't look up, didn't say anything. Our mother and father, seated opposite them, watched, listened to the rain, listened to the fire spitting, the kettle boiling, the water hissing on the stones. They let their tears run down and they waited, not moving even when the fire died and the baby cried. They waited until Rebecca said, 'I can't refuse you, you're my older sister. I can't refuse you, you'll die without your children.' They waited. Nobody spoke. Tiaki went out to walk in the rain.

After he'd gone the fire was stoked and the children were given bread, but no one discussed what had been said.

Later, when the children were asleep, the three sat by the fire waiting for Tiaki. When he returned he stood in the doorway and said, 'I love my wife, therefore I have to agree. I've taken her away from her people, therefore I have to agree. I'm a man without lands, therefore I have to agree. My name doesn't come from the heavens, therefore I have to agree.' There was rain on his face.

This wasn't something new our parents were doing. It was one of the old ways – a sister bearing a child to her childless sister's husband, so that both their own and the husband's genealogies were kept in that child. It was important to them. What the ancestors gave deep in themselves, the spirit of them, the life of them handed down, was important to them. It was what life was all about. It was survival. Everything that was done was done because of the ancestors and because of the children's children. Just as it was in the time of Pirinoa.

But also in the time of Pirinoa and even later, it had been the aim of enemies to spoil all that, to demean ancestry by the eating of a heart or the swallowing of chiefly eyes, to destroy tapu by the cutting off of sacred heads, to desecrate by making people into food.

Now times had changed, which is why our parents went about this matter somewhat secretly, not family to family in the old way. They were aware of Christian sin.

The next day Tiaki told them he was going away to live in the bush for a while. Our father and mother stayed with Rebecca until she became pregnant. Tiaki returned and they went home. When it was time for me to be born they went back to Rebecca and Tiaki's, staying there until I was weaned.

A year later our mother took our father to her sister again and my brother was conceived and born. 'We'll always remember you,' our mother said to Tiaki. 'Your first children are older brothers and sisters to our own. We'll always remember that. You and my sister are in our hearts.'

So we grew up with a special love for Rebecca and Tiaki, always knowing we should honour their children above ourselves. We always knew that Rebecca was a mother in our deepest affection and that Tiaki was a father who we greatly honoured. But we didn't know the full reason, because although we called them 'whaea' and 'matua', this was nothing unusual. All of our mother's and father's sisters and female cousins were mothers to us. We called them all whaea. All of our mother's and father's brothers and male cousins were fathers to us. We called them all matua.

None of what had taken place was talked about as we were growing up, or not in our hearing. I don't know if it was because we were so completely our parents' children that it was not necessary to speak of it, or whether it was hidden from us because of Christian sin.

But at the deaths of our own parents and the deaths of our birth mother and her husband, the stories were told. Because how could the most important honouring be properly done if they hadn't been told? Our own parents died some years before Rebecca and Tiaki, then Tiaki died; a year later, Rebecca.

When Rebecca died my brother and I had a strong desire to bring her home to bury her beside our mother in her ancestral place, so we went to ask for her. A large group of us went. All our people of status, all of our good speakers with all of their strong arguments came with us, saying that we wanted to take Ripeka back to her home, back to her family, her land, her standing place, the place where her placenta was buried. We knew we had a right.

But Tiaki's family was strong too. They told us that Rebecca had been cast aside by us in the early days, that we had looked down on her husband. They said they wanted to bury her by her husband who had always loved her, and that in this they had the support of her first children. The talk went back and forth, back and forth all morning, until we were finally told, 'It will need many more of you to pick her up and take her.' We stopped then. We had no intention of pushing the family aside and attempting to snatch the dead Rebecca away, even though we had a right. Everything had been said. We knew we'd done the best we could. We would've been ashamed if we'd felt we'd let her go easily. After that my brother and I were given places of honour beside her until the day of her burial.

20

MAHAKI

A few hours' drive ahead of him on a wet road. Take it slow and hope he wouldn't be picked up for the state of his tyres. It wasn't quite the scenario he'd imagined for himself when he'd decided to become a lawyer, envisaging himself sparking and dramatic in polished wood rooms on behalf of wronged clientele, money dropping into his pockets.

Enough for a nice house for Mum, himself and Sis. All the bills paid. Nice things – though he'd never been quite sure what 'nice things' meant. Vaguely – dinner sets, glass ornaments and bundles of towels, a good car. He'd pull into one of the roadside stands and get apples to take home.

So a couple of years into his law degree, when Mum had gone to live with Harry and Sis had started going out with Tui, he'd felt abandoned. So much so that he'd dropped out of university and gone back to live with the old man for a year and a half, wondering what life was all about.

Well courtroom dramas weren't a patch on what they'd just been through in the wharenui, especially after the exit of Bob and Colin. The anger had all spilled out. 'Don't you let them,' the old man had said. 'You all don't let them if I'm not here. They eat you if you let them.'

It was mostly the older ones who'd wanted to take the case to court, though he could sense their doubts about that even while the talk was going on. Whether the land had been paid for or not wouldn't be a big issue in court, wouldn't be able to be proved one way or the other.

The cousins wanted to go to Anapuke, right now, and camp. Occupy the land. Plenty of discussion on how that could be done. He could see it was likely to come to occupation if they couldn't persuade the Bobs and the Colins into a different understanding. Big difficulties with occupation though, that no one else had thought of. He hadn't had a chance to speak about these – or hadn't dared.

When he'd had his own opportunity to speak he'd explained the new market-driven environment that government departments and agencies were now in, the big budget cuts and all the rationalisation that was going on. While he was talking he'd been able to hear himself, how he sounded, and he'd tried to change gear. 'Departments now have to be cost-effective, got to find money. So one of the things they're doing is looking round to see what they can sell off. That's what Bob and Colin were doing here today. The only reason they came to us, instead of having us come to them, was because they need a sale. What they said about getting a higher price on the open market is mainly bullshit I think, because there wouldn't be any likely buyers. But they know *we* want the land. So now that it suits their interests they're trying to get what money they can from us.'

He'd recommended that a letter be written to Council outlining reasons why the land should be returned without cost, a letter in which they should point out that the land had never been sold in the first place and that no records of payment had been produced. 'We could also point out that we've never received any rent for the land over the years,' he'd said, 'while at the same time being deprived of use. We could ask questions as to how these matters would be regarded in court and how they would be presented in the media.' He'd suggested that the letter could be followed, after a few days, by a delegation, in the hope that Council could be persuaded. Council had, after all, admitted they had no use for the land.

It was at that point that Abe had stood up and said, 'You sound just like a bloody lawyer. Talk, talk, talk. All talk. Giving us shit. Send another letter, send another delegation? No. If we want to set up camp we'll set up camp. If I have to go on my own I go on my own. Stop bullshitting. Who's side are you on, anyway?'

Boot on the other foot. He, who was regarded as a stirrer round the courts, a pain in the backside among law authorities because of the work he did amongst his own people, and because he was constantly holding the Treaty of Waitangi under establishment noses, was now getting rubbished by his own relations. Plenty of support for Abe too, from Maraea and others. 'No more letters, there's been enough of those.'

'No more delegations, there's been enough, unless we want to get the knee-capper delegation in.'

'Just say the word.'

'And since when have the media done us any favours?'

They'd given him a real hard time. He'd had to sit down and keep his mouth shut while the debate went on. Court or direct action? It had gone on for hours, round the house, then round again, flaring in disagreement every now and again.

It was well into the night by the time Kani stood. 'We're interested in all the possibilities being discussed here,' he'd said. 'We'll keep talking if that's what we need to do. But since Anapuke won't go walkabout, and since we've been on his case nearly fifty years, perhaps we can be patient a little longer. Perhaps we can take up all the actions that have been mentioned. I'd like further comment from our nephew here.'

So he'd found himself on his feet again. 'Occupation,' he'd said, 'would need to occur as soon as possible as a deterrent to prospective buyers. No one'll want to buy if they think there's controversy. But I see some problems to do with occupation . . .'

'Never mind the problems . . .'

'All right, court?'

Big problems there too, the biggest one being that they were unlikely to win, but he hadn't wanted to say that or they'd have thought he was on the wrong side for sure. There'd have been another eruption. 'A last resort,' he'd said. 'It takes time, takes money . . . But let's get back to what some of the aunties and uncles have been saying . . .'

Because it seemed the older people weren't against occupation of the land, neither were they all for going to court. What they were emphatic about was that they wanted the world to know the truth. They didn't like it when they were called bludgers and landgrabbers, didn't want anyone to think they were being greedy and unreasonable. They wanted it to be seen that their claims were fair and thought that this was more likely to be shown through the courts. At the same time they knew there was no money for court, could see that the younger people were not going to allow the time it took to get the matter before the courts.

'There could be other ways of getting the message across — pamphlets, the media,' he'd said. All of this had been discussed quite eagerly.

Then he'd got back to the matter of the letter and the delegation. Dangerous ground. There'd been a murmur. 'Just so that when the time comes to occupy the land or talk to the media we can say that all proper channels have been tried,' he'd said. 'And so that Council won't be able to say they weren't warned.'

In the end they'd all agreed — with a but and a but and a but. He'd felt bruised by the time he got back home with the old man long after midnight.

But it was good to be home again. Of all the places he'd lived when he was a boy this was the place he thought of as home. Maori Affairs house, little box. Two concrete steps up to a tiny porch, where there'd been two hooks low down where he and Sis could hang their bomber jackets. There was board to stand their gumboots on.

The porch led into a narrow wash-house where there'd been a wringer mounted between the two concrete tubs, beside them a copper on a concrete slab. Tubs were still there but the copper had been taken out to make room for a washing machine. The bathroom at the end of the wash-house, which earlier had been just big enough for a bath and basin, had been extended to include an inside lavatory.

The door from the wash-house opened into a square kitchen where the wood range was usually going. Floor covered in blue linoleum with the pattern worn away. There'd been a big cupboard, with vents covered in wire scrim, that let air flow through from outside. In it, bluish mutton sat on a big oval dish with skin on it hardening. There was always milk clotting in the milk billy, butter on the turn, tins of rendered fat. A smell to it, like muddy banks. The cupboard had been taken out to make room for a fridge, and though the old wood range was still there an electric stove had been put in. Same wood table with the wooden form against the wall, but there were a couple of new chairs as well. When they'd needed more seating in the old days the old man had sent him out to bring in beer crates from the wood shed.

Behind the kitchen was a small living room, though he remembered that in the past most of the 'living' was done in the kitchen where, if they weren't eating or working, they'd be sitting round the table talking or playing cards. The kitchen was where the parties went on too. The living room was where people slept when there was a crowd. A bare room in the old days, an old sofa and two chairs being the only furniture. On the mantelpiece, along with photographs, there'd been an inscribed red vase that someone had brought home from the Centennial Exhibition. Now there was a whole collection of furniture. Photographs everywhere.

Off the kitchen and living rooms were the three little bedrooms.

He could hardly remember his grandmother, who'd died when he was little. It was after that, and after their father had left them, that their mother had taken them back to live with the old man and Aunty Maata. They'd stayed there for five years. Mum and Sis shared one of the bedrooms but his bed had always been in the old man's room, where it was even now.

After they'd gone to bed the old man had talked for most of the rest of the night, telling him the dog, telling him the ancestors, a dust is all, I won't be here and you got to do this, do that. He'd tried to keep himself awake, could almost feel his ear being held.

But he'd had the last word with the old man in the end and it had made them both feel better. 'Father, if we're going to occupy Anapuke you better bloody stay alive because you're coming too,' he'd said. The old man had laughed, brightened, and they'd both gone to sleep.

So what was agreed to was that a letter would be sent to Council, then a delegation, both within a timeframe. If there was no joy with that they'd take up occupation. 'If that doesn't turn things round we just stay on until we get arrested,' he'd said. 'Then they'll have to take *us* to court.

But mightn't want the embarrassment. Might be able to persuade them to just do the paperwork and save their faces.'

But, but, but.

'But we got to see that letter, or any letter, before you send it.'

'But we want some of us younger ones in that delegation so we can have our say.'

'But you got to tell us everything.'

'Two weeks. Two weeks max, then . . .'

Then worse excitement ahead, sitting out on a rock.

Not what he'd imagined for himself in the early days. He'd seen himself in partnership by now, in a subdued office with polished wood furniture, toned walls and furnishings, their own library, everything on line – bringing home more than apples.

The thought of all that made him smile now. Those sorts of places didn't interest him – all furniture and air-conditioning. In fact going into them often made him feel like laughing, as though he'd entered into some kind of parody, a send-up of himself. The community office with posters covering the cracks in the walls, that survived on grants and donations, suited him. Wall-to-wall stress, but at least he was doing work that he wanted to do. For people that needed him. Always needing to be needed. Huh.

One thing he hadn't known in those younger days, something which had seemed out of reach even of his imagination after Mum and Sis had gone their own ways, was where he would find love. He'd always expected to look after his mother and his sister, had thought the three of them would always be together. Not that Mum and Sis had really deserted him, even though that's how he'd felt at the time.

Years coming to terms. Years discovering himself, discovering the world. But it was really when he'd started living with Dave that he'd begun to understand real rejection – by friends and family, including Mum and Sis at first. Huh, you could spend your life feeling rejected.

They'd met at an after-game function at a rugby club during his own rugby-playing days, his days of denial, when he'd been disguised by brawn and uniform. Dave, too elegant not to be a target, was looking for a way out, soon realising there wasn't one – until Mahaki had rescued him. He'd seen what was happening and pretended Dave was his cousin even though they'd never met. 'Come on cuz, we gotta go,' he'd said in the middle of an announcement of winners of a hamper raffle. They'd escaped. Both drunk, but club colours and clothing had got them through the streets safely.

Another hour should see him home.

And this 'Action Anapuke' was now going to take all of his time. He'd have to give up the claims research that he was doing, which was about the only paid work that he had. Then there was the 'new business' that he'd been working away at over the years – conference papers he was supposed to be preparing. He'd been asked to be one of the NGO reps in Geneva too. He'd have to flag it.

New old business. A few things the old man had said had given him new perspectives – but now there wouldn't be time.

But, but, but.

'But no holding back.'

'But you better be there, beginning to end.'

'But you better be there when the arrests happen.'

A lot on him, heavy on him, but they were going to win somehow. Had to. Otherwise there'd be such a sense of failure among the people that they'd never recover from it. One more failure to add.

Yet it took so little to give people hope that it seemed hope itself was almost dangerous, as when Bob and Colin had come. It had been something great to some of the older ones, almost as if they'd needed patronage, needed someone else's authentication. Then the big let-down. There was a two-headed, or many-headed monster existing in the people, something sitting down, submissive, dependent and dull. Standing with that was something else – alive, pained, raw, showing its teeth.

But.

This was his own 'but', a 'but' that he hadn't dared bring into the discussion at midnight. Anapuke was such an inaccessible place, so out of the way, that who was there to care whether Anapuke was occupied or not? Council could choose to ignore them and who else would notice? He could see themselves camped out for months. No one even asking why. 'No holding back,' his cousins had said, but if he'd brought this concern out late at night he'd have been accused of trying to talk them out of their decisions. They'd all have been divided again. Probably there would've been a group heading for Anapuke right now – not well prepared, not well informed, probably not even knowing how to get there.

Lights coming up. Light rain still falling.

It was survival at stake. Always had been, and in this case not just survival of his particular whanau.

However if they could pull it off, get Anapuke returned, it would be a great thing for people throughout the country – give everyone a boost. A lot on him, heavy on him, but they were going to do it one way or another, otherwise he might as well have been a bank teller.

Wet road up hill. Dark windscreen. Creaking wipers making twin fans.

21

TE PAANIA

'Don't worry about transcribing them,' Mahaki said to me as he came in on the morning after his return. He had the two tapes and a piece of paper in one hand, a bag of apples swinging in the other.

'I will, I'll do them,' I said.

'Only if you want to, otherwise if you just label and log . . .'

'I'll do them. Itching for the next episode.'

He put the apples on the bench and the tapes on the desk.

'And there's a letter that's got to be faxed to Maraea at the Health Centre.' He waved the notes, put them down beside the tapes then began walking back and forth with his hands cupped in front of him as though he could be judging the weight of two of the Braeburns. 'She's going to get four or five others to read it before they give us the go-ahead. Phone us tonight and she'll get it posted tomorrow if everything's OK . . . We'll need a file for Anapuke. Going to be a heap of stuff . . . if that's all right.'

'No problem,' I said. I poured coffee.

'I could be out sitting on a rock by the end of the month.' I could see he hadn't slept.

'Coffee?' I asked, but he didn't answer. He kept on pacing, telling what had happened between the people and the Council at the meeting. Gran came in from the bedroom and sat back in the cushions on the settee to listen. I passed the coffee to her. Her eyes followed him.

'It's just that I can't see Council, you know, bothering,' he said, frowning down on these virtual apples. 'They'll go off and try to find their money some other way. Leave us sitting there . . .'

'Turning into stones.'

'Well, such an out-of-the-way place no one'd notice, no one'd bother.'

'If you got the media along . . .?'

'We could try and rark them up but don't think they'll be interested either.'

'Why not somewhere else then . . .?'

'And spooky . . . you know. The way we've been brought up you don't go anywhere near Anapuke . . . It's a nightmare.'

'Like arms falling off,' said Tawera coming in from the bathroom with his hair jelled and combed but his face unwashed. 'And a head rolling along the road while people stand on the footpaths and watch with enormous red mouths, laughing, yah huh huh, yah huh huh, yah huh huh, yah huh huh.'

Mahaki stopped weighing fruit. The frown ran itself back into his head. He opened his arms and Tawera stepped in with his sleepy face. They hugged walking, Tawera's feet on top of Mahaki's, sharing legs. Yah huh huh. Then Tawera leaned back making space for the sister – legs seen and unseen, walking.

'Why not somewhere else?' I said again.

'Ha that's her,' Gran said.

'Not your rock,' I said. 'Somewhere . . .'

'Meaning?' Mahaki said over the heads, still walking. 'You're saying . . . what?'

'One of their sacred sites.'

'Evil, see that?' Gran said.

Mahaki stopped walking. 'Like what, like where?'

'I don't know, tell me.'

'Like the cathedral?' Mahaki said. 'That's if there was a cathedral . . . or Council Chambers, mayoral lawns . . .'

Tawera stepped down, went to the bench and began shaking cornies into a bowl. I noticed that his clothes were too small for him. He'd pulled the bottoms of his track pants down to his shins, which was as far as they would go. The waistband of his track top had drawn up, pulling the bottom of his T-shirt with it so that two inches of his bony back was showing. He sat down and began crunching while I poured fresh coffee for Mahaki.

'Te Ra Park,' Mahaki said. He sat, took a mouthful of coffee. 'You mean go there, get in their faces . . .'

'Something like that.' I popped bread down in the toaster, pointed at it, raised my eyebrows at him.

'Yes please,' he said. 'Haven't eaten . . . So? Te Paania we could . . . I reckon it's brilliant.'

Not bad for a frog.

On the wall beside my desk were rows of shelves that Dave had put up for me. Over the time since I'd begun the work that Mahaki had been bringing home, these shelves were filling with boxes of transcriptions. Much of this was from his grandfather. Each time Mahaki went to visit him I would look forward to the new tapes that I'd have to work on. It was work that I found challenging, deeply interesting, almost addictive. Sometimes Gran and I would work on them together. She'd help with the translation of passages that I found difficult, or we'd discuss ideas that were new to me, or elusive.

But also growing in numbers on the shelves were the boxes of transcribed stories and information from Gran Kura herself. I was behind with this work but I'd labelled and itemised the tapes and made copies for other members of the family.

When Gran Kura had first left the home where she'd lived all her life, it was because her life had changed. It was because she'd seen, or now understood, that there was something more she needed to do. Although our mid-city house was now her base, she had gone, from time to time, to spend time with other members of the family too. Also, once a year she'd gone to stay with her daughter Vera, who had never understood her decision to leave home in the first place.

As she grew older this travelling became difficult, especially once she began her part-time work with the school. So the tapes had become more and more important. Once copies were ready she'd take them to the Post Shop and send them away in bubble bags. The tapes had stirred people. Gran had stirred them, as she had stirred us. Darcy had begun finding out about land titles. He and others had begun language classes. There'd been meetings where a claim to the Tribunal had been discussed. Now research had begun.

In the meantime, here I was at the centre of all this activity. It was like sitting on a stone in the middle of a pond with all the different aspects of my life moving out in ever-widening circles about me. I was engaged, eyes out, surrounded by voices – actual, or on tape or on paper. Even with Tawera and his sister away at school, Mahaki and Dave at work and Gran sometimes out working or walking, the house was never empty.

That morning I typed up the fax message to Mr Geddes and Mr Lawrence of the Council. My old office equipment didn't include a fax machine, and since there was a strong wind and heavy rain that morning I decided to wait until the weather cleared before going out to send it.

I began work on the tapes and the morning went by.

When I left my desk in the early afternoon the weather still hadn't improved, so I put the fax message into a large envelope, tucked it down inside my jacket and went out into the storm.

My feet, familiar with the ruts and patchwork of the cracking footpath, odd-stepped on the high parts so that my old shoes wouldn't take in water. The southerly at my back was dealing up rain. Fences went by me, blue bags ready for pick-up, debris, a flummoxed sparrow. The gutters ran, powerlines pitched about in the clapping wind. There was a whiff of freesias.

Under the dairy verandah was a dry patch where I paused for a moment. 'Mother's Dirty Lover' the *Truth* board said, while out on the footpath stand were oranges, bananas and apples in bins, and bunches of jonquils, single and double, up to their necks in dark blue buckets. Wet cars surged uphill as I made my way down.

'What do you think of it?' the chemist asked.

'Wild.'

The machine ticked the pages through to Maraea at the Health Centre. I paid and went out, headlong into the teeth.

It wasn't until everyone was in bed that night that I returned to my transcribing. I wasn't far into the work when I shut the word processor down so that I could just listen, seated in desk light, head in the dark.

What I heard gogged my eyes out well beyond frog – new business, old business.

It was my business.

22

KURA

There was a man who was a ghost. He was an uncle to my father and lived in the place where my father was born.

Also, he was great-grandfather to the niece, who brought on to my verandah the suitcase that opened itself in the night, giving me to understand that I was going on a journey and that my life had changed. This ghost was an old man when I was a child.

As well as being great-grandfather to the niece, this man-who-was-a-ghost was the niece's great-great-granduncle as well. I didn't know his name. No one called him Grandfather.

He was seldom seen, but occasionally at one of the gatherings we would notice him pulling wood from the manuka stands, sawing the wood into lengths and piling it on to the stacks.

We'd see him rubbing fat over the big pots, and once they were filled, setting them here and there on the stones of the fireplaces, shifting them from time to time. He'd feed the wood in, turning the embers, moving in and out of smoke, keeping the water hot and the pots simmering. We never heard his voice.

He had a wide face, and a forehead that was deeply marked with a scar that resembled the bone inside a herring. His short white beard had been trimmed across flat so that his face looked square. There was no life in his face, no light in his eyes because he was a ghost.

When he walked he pulled one leg along, and when he sat this leg stuck out stiff in front of him. He wore soldier boots, and soldier pants tied at the bottoms with rope, though he was too old to have been a soldier. He wore shirts without collars, done up tight against his throat, and a ragged panama pulled down over his forehead. Sweat poured down. He was smoked and wet and smelled of pork fat. He melted by the fires.

When in the meeting house he sat or moved about in the shadows. I never once heard him greeted in there.

From where we lived it was a day's walk to get to the home place of my father, though a runner going by the hill tracks to take a message could leave home at half water and be there by the time the tide was full.

Or our father – at times when he'd had a dream of a grandfather, mother, sister or brother – setting out at daybreak to find out why he was being called, could be there before the dew had left the river banks.

There was flu when I was six – bad, bad flu – and my father had a dream. The dream was of his mother standing on a strange hillside, calling to him. In the morning he set out to see her. There was streaky colour coming above the hills as we watched him leave, believing we would not see him now for two or three days, perhaps two or three weeks. We were surprised, on our way to school that morning, when we saw our father returning, crying.

He had reached the top of the rise on the way to his mother's house when a cousin called to him to go back home because people there were sick with influenza. At first father couldn't hear the message that was being called to him and continued on his way down. When he finally heard what was being called he wanted to rush down to see what was happening to his mother and the people, but his cousin kept calling to him, 'Go home, go home, your mother doesn't want to see you.'

Our father didn't want to return home. He didn't yet know the seriousness of the terrible sickness that had come to the people. He called to the cousin that he was coming. That was when his cousin picked up a gun that he had left lying in the grass and held it under his own chin. 'If I can't do the job I was sent to do,' he said, 'I might as well be dead.'

Our father turned back up the hill and came home.

Despite this, the flu eventually came to our settlement too. It was a bad time. My brother and I stayed at our grandmother's house while our mother went out to help nurse the sick and look after the babies of sick families. Our father went out to bury the dead. We were lucky to remain alive.

After the flu was over there were children left without parents. It was then that our mother brought home two baby girls, Hinemoana and Matewai, who became our adopted sisters.

Apart from the times when we stayed home because of sickness or tragedy, there were journeys that we made each summer to visit our father's relatives and to exchange foodstuffs with them.

In preparation for this journey we would spend evenings fishing for conger eel, which we would smoke and pack into a drum. At every low tide we'd gather paua to be preserved in tins of pork fat, and loads of sea lettuce which we'd spread to dry in the sun. The day before leaving we'd collect bags of pipi and pupu, which we'd keep in seawater until it was time to go.

On the day we were to leave, all the goods would be loaded on to two sledges for the horses to pull. Some of the lighter goods were loaded into a dinghy to be taken by water.

It was always a day of early high tide that was chosen for the journey. We'd set out when the tide was up, sledges sliding over the slippery tussock at the top of the beach. We'd have a pet pig trotting along with us, sometimes two.

By the time we reached the next bay the tide would be on its way out. The sun would be getting itself right up. There was a stream there. We'd drink from it then continue on, all of us with something to carry – little kids on shoulders, babies on the backs of their aunties – until we came to the next bay where we'd stop and rest. We'd swim, and eat bread and plums. The dinghy would be there already, the rowers resting in the shade.

When the tide was right down low we'd go and get crayfish from the holes in the rocks, put them into bags and into the dinghy. We'd pick up our loads and off we'd go again, salty, getting tired, with the most difficult part of the journey in front of us.

The sun would be hard on us all the way from then on, and from there on the tracks were rough – deeply furrowed in some places, soft and boggy in places where water seeped from the banks. Children would be sent ahead to collect armfuls of rushes to lay over the tracks to make them smooth for the sledges.

At the last bay some of our relatives would be waiting. We'd unhitch the sledges at the last creek and follow the horses into a clearing of long grass and shade. The horses would be left there until we made our return journey.

From there the drums and bags had to be carried up the narrow tracks of a rocky face, and down through manuka scrub to a dirt track where someone would be waiting with fresh horses. We'd follow the river through bush tracks, coming eventually to the clearing where the houses were, where the rest of the people waited.

We'd stay there for a week or more and when it was time to go home we'd load up with freshwater eels, pigeon, wild pork, mutton, corn and all the things that had been prepared for us.

In the summer that I was twelve, the man-who-was-a-ghost died.

The morning after our arrival, in the year that I was twelve, we children and some of the mothers dressed to go to church then set out for Grandmother Rina's place where church was held. Grandmother Rina was a sister to the man-who-was-a-ghost though I didn't know that then. He didn't live at her house but stayed alone in a house made of nikau, close to the river's edge. No one went near.

There had been drinking and celebrating all night, but now the cooking fires were dead. There were flies collecting on leavings, and dogs and pigs were nosing and snouting into bones. There were cows with full udders waiting by the verandahs to be milked. Bodies were strewn like the dead under trees. Only the birds to make a noise.

By the time we returned from church the fires had been tidied and lit, there was a beer barrel sitting in the low branches of a tree and the celebrations were continuing. The drinkers were calling us to come and save them, and our mothers pulled faces at them as we went to change our clothes. The dress that I wore to church was one that had been made for me from offcuts of bridesmaids' gowns, by the woman who made dresses.

That afternoon, as we were making our way along the riverbank to the waterfall, we saw the-man-who-was-a-ghost on the other side of the river with cooking tins beside him. He was swirling stones in a tin to clean it. At the waterfall we washed and swam and played in the pools until the sun started to go down. As we were returning, we saw the man-who-was-a-ghost lying among the tins with his feet in the water. We hurried past. We told no one about the man because no one ever spoke of him.

The next morning one of the uncles went from house to house saying, 'Kua mate a Rorikohatu.' That was the first time I'd heard the name of the man. He was dead.

So the ghost had died, yet no one came out of their houses. There was no commotion.

Not long afterwards we saw four men with shovels climbing the hill to the burial place. And in the afternoon, although we were not allowed to watch, my cousins and I, from where we were hiding behind the cooking shelter, saw the dead ghost being carried up the hill in a blanket. There was no commotion. The men carrying him were making it uphill as fast as their legs would go.

From then until it was time to go home I stayed near the adults to hear what would be said about this strange thing that had happened, but although the man-already-a-ghost had died and been buried, no one spoke of it. On the long walk home a week later I kept close to my parents so that I could listen to their whisperings. Nothing was said about what had taken place.

When we arrived home in the red sky, our grandmother, and others who had not come with us, were waiting by the red water. We were busy until dark sharing out the goods we'd brought back, and instead of going home to our own house we went to stay with Grandmother who had beds ready for us.

It was that night, when I was pretending to be asleep at

Grandmother's place, that I heard my mother say to my father, 'No one cried.'

'No,' my father said, as though in his sleep.

'For the man,' my mother said.

'No.'

'Buried without a minister,' she said.

'Because he was father of his niece's baby,' our father said, waking and sitting himself up. 'And because nobody killed him.'

My father was one of the men who had gone to look for the niece, who was then fourteen years old. This was some years before my father and mother were married. The niece had gone into the bush to hide, no one knew why.

When they found her and brought her home everyone could see that her stomach was big, and out.

'Who gave you that?' her grandmother wanted to know.

'Rorikohatu,' the niece said, naming her mother's brother, naming the grandmother's son.

Some of the men went looking for Rorikohatu to kill him. They found him, they didn't quite kill him, but he was always a dead man after that.

The girl, Roena, had already been promised in marriage to someone, but now that couldn't be. She stayed with her parents and the baby was brought up as a brother within the family.

It wasn't until ten years later that I saw where the man-who-was-a-ghost had been buried. There was a road by then, and a new railway station only a short horse-ride away. We could board the train, and after two stops, be at the home-place of my father. It was a different life.

It wasn't a better life. No. There was no work for people. There was no market for the drystock that we ran. So we made big gardens and it was work, work, work, for mothers and fathers, old people, children, from early to late. We sent our vegetables to market and they rotted there. We took our vegetables round by horse and wagon but no one had money to pay. So we gave the vegetables away, sometimes being given something in return.

But our cupboard was the sea. Our cupboard was the land too, even though more and more of the land had gone. It was possible to be ragged and to live in a dilapidated house. It was possible to be hungry, but not quite to starve. It wasn't until the war came that there was work for people.

I was up at the graveside at the burial of our father's brother when I first saw the dead ghost's grave. It was down the steep side of the hill, outside the graveyard fence in unconsecrated ground. It had no cross. It had no stone.

23

TE PAANIA

I'd never asked why.

Others had asked. Mahaki had demanded down corridors. Cousins had talked among themselves. At the graveside the cousins had given me their answers – answers I'd scarcely listened to then. I hadn't looked for truth in them, hadn't turned them to look at the underside.

What had become of wild?

I took the earphones off, turning the tape back to listen to this new, old business that was my business.

It was past midnight, and while I was listening Gran Kura came in from the bedroom. She had a night-life of her own on talkback radio with Nga Ruru. She'd come out to use the phone. I switched the recorder off.

'What was it?' she asked when she'd finished, 'about helicopters and bones?'

'What the scientists and researchers are up to, I suppose,' I said. I pulled a chair across for her, shifted the light, switched the recorder on again.

'... so the bones of our ancestors will not be thieved for medicines, so we know our ancestors will not be used for experimentations, so we know our ancestors' patterns will not be separated from their bones for the Pakeha to go and make money or to make things for them to use, or to make things better for them, or so that they can be known for putting a Maori in a sheep or rising a Maori up from a dust . . .

'. . . take spirit from blood, cut our dust, murder our dust because a wheua, a toto, a hupe, a makawe is all . . .'

'It's right,' Gran said. 'One bit and you got the whole thing.' It seemed an ordinary enough thought to her. I wanted her to stay and talk because there was so much going on in my head, but her mind was with Nga Ruru. She was looking forward to responses to her call. She returned to her bedroom as the tape neared its end.

'You meddle with our bones, try to make us buy our bones from you, might as well shoot us all.' The voice was tired, fading.

'. . .give our land back now or shoot us like you do before, or like we do to each other before . . .'

The last few sentences were faint, squeezed into the end of the tape. I wound back, putting the headphones on to hear them more easily.

'Burn our house. Take our food. Break our canoe. Like before. An eye is all . . .'

Is all?

I put the headphones down, feeling as though my head was coming out through my eyes. I took the tape from the player, made my way downstairs in the dark and knocked on Dave and Mahaki's door.

A cantle of light from beneath the door became a lit room as the door opened. Dave was there with Mahaki behind him.

'Look at you . . .'

'What is it?'

'Is Boy all right?'

'The new business,' I said.

Dave brought me in and seated me, put a cushion at my back, took strands of my hair and threaded them back behind my ears. 'All that awful stuff,' he said.

'Murdering our dust . . .'

'Don't know what got him on to that,' Mahaki said, pulling the heater round and flicking the switches. 'Saw a helicopter hanging round Anapuke most likely. Got worried and started nutting

186

things out for himself. Been on his mind ever since . . .'

'A few bits of bone . . .'

'And you've got the whole blueprint.'

'That's what Gran Kura said.'

'Don't know why you had to give our mate all that gory stuff,' Dave said to Mahaki.

'Well I haven't . . . not yet,' said Mahaki.

'It puts him in a temper,' Dave said to me as he went to the kitchen. 'Now it'll put you in a temper.'

'They're finding new bits and pieces in isolated communities,' Mahaki said. 'Something different out there in the way of gene lines – and that's what us watchdogs are jumping up and down about.'

My head was still full of the words of the tape. I was finding it difficult to keep up with what he was saying.

'There's already been mapping of tribal people – those who're dying out, in different parts of the world,' he said. 'Their genetic bits are about to become some scientist's big discovery. They're after endangered species . . . Up for grabs, up for patenting, up for sale, but no proper processes . . .'

'Drops of blood.'

'Scary stuff – research going on in military labs, or your bits being taken and altered or reproduced, transferred into plants or animals, kept in labs long after you're gone, things like that.'

'Dead and alive, both at once,' Dave said. 'Puts him in a temper.' He handed me a cup of coffee. 'Calm you down or spin you right out, one or the other.'

'Anyway this is where the old man's hit the nail on the head,' Mahaki said. 'Something I never thought of until he said . . . I mean, we're not on the map of targeted people – too impure. But after listening to him I'm thinking that if researchers could get their hands on tissue from our old tupapaku from the caves they could have a ball analysing us. Like they're doing with stuff taken from museums – remains of ancient peoples . . .'

'Hair, all that.'

'Looking for the big answers, or the cure-all for God knows what.'

'An eye is all?'

'I know . . . It's what got me started on all this. No one would answer me.'

'And I never . . .'

'Well not then . . .'

Mahaki went to the bedroom and returned with a stack of boxes. 'The blood, sweat and tears stuff. I was going to ask you. Years ago actually, but I let it go for a while. Anyway, supposed to be writing up papers and now there won't be time. If you go through these you'll understand what he's on about.' He went to the shelves and returned with a videotape. 'Have a look at this and you'll get an idea of what the bio-prospectors are up to, the Gene Kings . . .'

'All those things people said,' I said, thinking again of the morning at the graveside. 'Medicines, research, experiments, markets . . .'

'What other answers are there?' he said. 'I mean you can understand what some of these guys are on about, benefits to mankind and so on. But at one conference I was at they were talking about people's genes being a free resource like air and water, that is until they get pounced on and patented. It's rough business.'

'My business.'

'It's about people having a say in their own lives, about sovereignty.'

'So it's time . . .'

'My time to get back to my village. Your time to look for eyes, find out what's happening out there in the world of invention and gene lines. New business, old business, but it's all the same business . . .'

'Whether it's land or fish . . .'

'Or loot from graves . . .'

'Or eyes . . .'

'That little hospital was small fry really, but the attitudes were the same. They were allowed to because they were allowed to. Law allowed them. Power allowed them. We had no right to say no, or yes, because we weren't people. Baby wasn't a baby, wasn't the family's baby. Baby was a body, and legally belonged to the medical superintendent.'

24

TAWERA

'You're such a smartarse,' she said, banging me so hard that I stumbled, let go of the feathers and fell on the footpath. 'Gab, gab, gab to all those stupid kids, concert, concert, concert.'

'What're you on about?'

'How do I know what's going on? How do I know what it looks like?'

'What what looks like?' I asked, standing and brushing myself down.

'The stupid Tawhaki outfit.'

'You only have to ask.'

'You only have to ask, you only have to ask,' she said in a horrible singsong voice.

When I opened the door, Mum, who had been watching from the window, was coming down the stairs. 'What happened?' she asked. At the bottom of the stairs were boxes and blankets ready for our trip to Te Ra Park later in the week, so I tried to distract her by talking about that as I took off my shoes and went with her up the stairs. And when I escaped to the bathroom to put Savlon on my knees and patch up my elbows, I could hear her and Gran talking about me. They became silent when I came back out, staring at me in a worried kind of way. I hurried through afternoon tea and went off to my bedroom to practise.

But before I started the songs and the lines, this is how I described to my sister the costume I would wear in the concert. 'There's a rapaki which ties round my waist, made of strong cloth from a piece of brown curtain. It's fringed at the bottom and covers the whole of the elephant face nearly to the knees.' I placed my hands here and there on her as I described the rapaki. 'It's decorated with foil coils and sparkling strips of material with sequins sewn to them. Blue, green, red and silver. Blue is ...'

'I know, I know. I know blue, green and red. Just tell me silver.'

'Silver's a squeaky fart.' I thought she would enjoy that. I thought she would like squeaky fart silver, thought I was explaining everything very well, but I noticed that her lips were pushed out so hard that her chin had dents in it, and that she kept turning her head away from me.

'From the top of my left shoulder,' I said, 'across my heart and down to the edge of my ribs on the right-hand side, there will be a flash of squeaky fart lightning. There'll be flashes on the upper parts of my arms, as well as from armpits to waist. My hair will be done in a topknot. In the topknot will be three white feathers. I'll have a moko drawn on my face – which was done in the olden days with bone chisels, cutting patterns into the skin in a painful way before the dark green dye was rubbed in.' I thought she might like that piece of information.

With my finger I traced the spirals of how I thought my moko would be – on her cheeks, the sides of her nose and on her forehead. I patterned her top lip and chin in a way I have seen in paintings and drawings of splendid chiefs. Was she happy with this? She gave me such an unexpected push that I bumped my head on the drawer and banged my elbow on the bed.

'What's up?' our mother called.

'Nothing,' I called back. Then I said to my sister, 'What was that for?'

'How can you be Tawhaki?' she said.

'I was chosen, wasn't I, by the teachers and the kids. The teachers and kids think I'm the right one to play the part of Tawhaki. They think my voice is good.'

'I was chosen, wasn't I,' she said in a squeaky, horrible voice, her mouth in a wide slit, her head rocking from side to side. 'The teachers and the kids think I'm the right one to play the part of Tawhaki. They think my voice is good.'

Then with her mouth back in its usual shape, in her usual edgy voice she said, 'I heard the story. I heard the teacher tell about Tawhaki. That's why I asked. Tawhaki was the most beautiful man ever seen. He had a face chiselled from dark sea rock, hair as long and as black as a deep, shadowed river alive with eels. His body was as if it had been shaped from the ochre hillside. Lightning flashed from his armpits, and with each step he took thunder rolled across the land.'

'So?'

'So how can you be Tawhaki?'

I didn't answer her. I began practising my songs because I didn't want to listen to her any more.

'Dreamer,' she said, giving me another push. This time I stumbled and sat down hard on the floor.

'What's going on?' said our mother from the doorway.

'I fell,' I said.

'You don't just fall.' She was frowning as she reached out a hand to help me up, trying to think of something more to say. But all she said was, 'Dave's home.'

'Mahaki's ringing tonight,' I said, following her out.

'You're spotted and not very brown at all,' my sister said on our way downstairs. 'You've got pingpong eyes, warts on your knees and legs like the handles of axes. You told me all that yourself, showed me, made me touch your warty knees. Can you make lightning flash from your armpits? Can you walk like thunder?'

'Acting. You know acting? It's when . . .'

'I know all that. I know about acting.' She grabbed me by the arms and dug her fingers in. 'I'm the one who should be Tawhaki – brown as rocks and dark as rivers, singing and dancing, going on journeys, flashing and booming.' She let go of me, pulled her hands back to her shoulders then thrust her arms forward, flicking all her fingers out stiffly. 'Zap, zap,' she went, but above my head, because she didn't know how small I had made myself as I sat down on a stair, clutching my arms across myself.

'Angel, what's wrong?' said Dave from the bottom of the stairs.

'I slipped,' I said.

He stood me up and looked into my face. 'Where's it sore?' he asked.

'Nowhere.'

'So who can I be?' she said later when we were in bed. 'Who can I be in the concert?' I didn't know how to answer her.

She couldn't be one of the pukeko, who, even though they had beautiful feathers, lived in swamps, had stick legs, big feet and fire prints on their heads. She would never agree to that. She couldn't be one of the Ponaturi who were far too ugly, or Tawhaki's sister, or Shore Daughter, or Woman-With-Crooked-Fingernails. She couldn't be Eel or Man-Who-Showed-The-Way or Woman-Who-Sat-By-The-Door. Of course not. Those parts were all being played by other children.

'Come on,' she said. 'Tell me.'

'Why don't you stop hassling me. Use your own brain for a change.'

She pulled my hair so hard that it made tears pop into my eyes. I stuck my thumb knuckle into my mouth, biting into it so that I wouldn't make a noise. After a while she let go and didn't say anything more for a long time. Didn't move. I thought she was asleep. 'You think just because I don't have eyes that I don't cry,' she said.

And even though I realised what she was doing, even though I knew that she was trying to hurt me, that she was bullying and blackmailing me, my heart was squeezed.

'No,' I said.

'Yesss.'

'All right . . .'

'All right what?'

'All right I'll think of something.'

'Nothing dumb,' she said and in a moment was asleep.

But I was awake with this squeezed heart bumping inside me. I was looking into the night, which was like a high, dark wall.

Awake, awake, awake.

Then after a long time I did think of something and was able to go to sleep.

'Tell me,' she said in the morning.

'What's the matter, Hunbun?' my mother said to me. 'Are you sick, are you tired or something?'

'Tell me,' my sister said.

'Was there a dream that came hurting you?' Gran Kura asked.

'I'm getting ready for school,' I said to them and shut the bedroom door. 'Tawhaki Unseen,' I said to my sister.

'How come?'

'There are two Tawhakis.'

'That's not what I heard.'

'Two. Seen and Unseen. They have incantations to make themselves invisible and back again to visible. You know the part where they go to the house of the Ponaturi and ...'

'OK, OK, I remember. What will I wear?'

'Same as me.'

'Hair?'

'Topknot and feathers.'

'And what will I do? How will I act in the play?'

'We'll be together,' I said. 'Journeying together, singing together, dancing together, saying the words together. But when it's time for Tawhaki to be unseen, then Tawhaki Visible disappears and the people see Tawhaki Invisible instead.'

She thought about it for a long time, 'That's all right then,' she said. Whew.

'How did you get those?' my mother asked when she was helping us to get ready to be Tawhaki. They were little green and yellow bruises she was talking about, in rows on my arms, which I'd been hiding with long sleeves. 'I fell in the bedroom,' I said. 'I stumbled on the stairs.'

'But how could you fall and stumble? You don't just fall and stumble. They look like finger marks. And that on your hand is like a bite, as though someone's dug their teeth in.'

'From school,' I said. 'Playing hard games.' I could see she didn't believe me. I could see she was mystified. 'It's all right Mum,' I said, 'they'll be covered with lightning flashes. Put our lightning on.'

Mum did outlines of lightning on our body and arms, then filled these in with silver. She did a neat job of it, though the underarm ones became a little smudged because of my wriggling and giggling. It made Mum laugh too. We had such a good time getting us ready to be Tawhaki, so I hoped she'd forgotten about the bruises.

When we were ready Dave took us to school in the van. Mahaki wasn't with us because he was away at an occupation of Te Ra Park. We'd seen him talking into a cellphone on the television news.

In the hall, chairs had been put out for the parents and a floor space had been left at the front of the room for our performance. The backdrop was a big black curtain which was like night, or space, decorated with moon and stars, Mars, Saturn, comets and lightning.

To one side was our teacher sitting on a baby chair. On a coffee table beside her were the overhead projector, an old flax basket and all her pieces of coloured cellophane. Opposite her was Kawea's father with a tape deck, purerehua, drum, cymbals, and dried peas in an ice-cream container.

Everything was ready.

It was dark at first. There was mysterious music from a tape, and stormy rain sounds that Kawea's dad was making by swirling the peas in the container. Our teacher put orange cellophane under the loose weaving of the basket and moved it round and round on the projector. Orange light began flickering across the moons, comets and stars.

Now it was time for the waking of the pukeko, who were Deanie and Kara and other little children, in black tights and tops, bright blue feathers attached to their arms. People clapped for them as they danced with their big feet, flapping their wings, wiggling their tails and angling their red heads in all kinds of ways. 'Ke, ke, ke,' they said.

They formed a circle with their wings outspread. When they broke from the circle and danced away, there we were, Tawhaki Seen and Tawhaki Unseen, in yellow cellophane light, the purerehua making a tornado sound as we began our song:

194

On the hill that trembles
In the splintered valley
Tawhaki walks
And this is his song

People clapped and cheered for us as the singers formed in behind us to help us with our story:

From those armpits flashing
From those footsteps striking
While the moon is breaking
He lights the darkened sea.

We were going on a journey to find our mother and to avenge the death of our father.

The first part of our journey was to take us across the sea. There was sea music and green and blue cellophane light. The waves, made by Juney and Awa with a long piece of silky painted cloth, were growing larger and more dangerous, but the singers sang the song of our sister, Pupumainono, *'On the wave tops stepping, not in the hungry hollows,'* taking us safely across to the other side.

Over there we fell in love with Hinetuatai. We did our falling-in-love dance and sang our love songs amid the dancing lights, but we didn't forget our journey.

We left Hinetuatai on the shore, travelling for many days until we met a woman sitting by a pool tying her hair in knots. Her fingernails were so crooked that when she pointed the way to us, we went in the wrong direction. The singers had to sing us back on to the right pathway, *'This way is that way, that way is this way,'* were the words of the crooked fingernail song.

Once we'd got on to the road again we met Tuna Roa, who, although he gave us no directions, sang us songs of great encouragement and gave us good advice. He gave us incantations to make Tawhaki invisible, then visible again.

Eventually we met a man who showed us the night-time house of the Ponaturi. These Ponaturi, who couldn't live in light, were from another country which was at the dark bottom of the ocean. At night time the Ponaturi would leave their country and come ashore to their sleeping house, but they would have to go from there before the first light of dawn to run back into the darkness of the sea. It was the Ponaturi who had stolen our mother and killed our father, putting his bones in a basket to hang in the rafters of this night-time house of theirs.

There we went creeping, creeping, in the full daylight made by our teacher. There were our little tiptoe sounds made by Kawea's father with his drumsticks, and there were the singers whispering our creeping song.

But what did we hear as we approached the house? We heard tap and tap. Rattle, rattle. Rattle, rattle, tap and tap. It was our father's bones talking to us from the rafters of the house. They had recognised us and were welcoming us.

And who was this approaching on the pathway? It was our mother whose name was no longer Urutonga, but who was known instead as Te Tatau, The Door. She was a slave of the Ponaturi now and her job was to sit all night by the door to watch for daylight. 'Don't stay here,' she said after she'd greeted us. 'Go, before the Ponaturi return at nightfall or you'll be killed for sure. These Ponaturi are ferocious.'

We told her that we had strong incantations by which to become invisible, and that we had been given some good advice. So she said, 'All right then, stay. I'll help you to cover all the cracks and chinks in the walls of the house so that no light will get in. The Ponaturi will be tricked into sleeping late.' So we began our gathering dance, picking our bundles of dry rushes and reeds, sealing every chink in the house so that no light could enter. When that was done the singers began our incantation of invisibility.

There was the drum roll.

There was the light, sweeping and swirling.

There was the dark flash and the cymbal crash that vanished me behind the curtain.

And there, for everyone to see, was Tawhaki Invisible. The people clapped and cheered for her as she danced and danced in the sweeping, swirling light until the sun went down.

But now, here were the Ponaturi, running up from the shore in the dark, wearing their fluorescent outfits, their fluorescent ugly masks, their fluorescent wild hair, pushing their way into the sleeping house and lying down to sleep in piles, not knowing that Tawhaki Unseen was among them.

All night long they groaned and moaned and snored. Before dawn one of them called, 'Te Tatau, Te Tatau, is it about to be morning?'

'No, no, it's nowhere near morning yet. Sleep well,' our mother called. A while later, when it was already cellophane dawn and the singers were singing the sun-rising song, another of them called, 'Why is this night so long? Te Tatau, I'm sure I can hear the birds singing. Should we be going now?'

'Not yet,' she called. 'The night is still deep. I'll call you when it's time.'

The red sun rose and the light turned first to orange and yellow, then to full, clear day. The little drum roll started up. There came the black flash, the cymbal crash, the white light. And there was Tawhaki Visible. The people clapped and cheered for us.

'You can get up now,' called Te Tatau to the Ponaturi as she helped Tawhaki Seen and Tawhaki Unseen to pull the rushes and reeds from the cracks and openings.

The Ponaturi ran from the house, trapped by light, falling and dying of light. That was the end of them, except for one who was good at leaping.

We took the basket containing our father's bones and journeyed with our mother – in streaks of lightning, in Tawhaki music, in storms and drumming thunder – back to our own country. The people whistled and clapped and cheered. Everyone was happy with that.

The next day when I was doing my picture of Tawhaki Seen and Unseen, I painted him as brown as rocks, as dark as rivers, with hair of eels that swam down from his topknot, right out to the edges of the paper. I swirled his face with moko, gave him wide shoulders, a big chest and the strongest arms and legs that I could do. Then I decided to dress him in Superman clothes, with lightning cracking down from his armpits and flashing out from under his Superman boots. He looked good, I think. As I worked I described everything. We were both happy with that.

25

MAHAKI

They arrived while it was still dark and assembled at one of the walk-in entrances to Te Ra Park. Not enough light yet to see the flowerbeds and pathways, or to make out the Arts Centre Buildings, the Fitness Centre, the adjacent shops and warehouses. Behind them were the dark shapes of the Council Chambers and the commerce buildings.

He felt relieved now that the day had come – at the same time nervous. But at least he knew they were well prepared, that they'd taken enough time to talk and plan and organise.

After the visit to the Council Offices by the delegation, and because there'd been no profitable discussion, there'd been a group wanting to go immediately to Anapuke. The Staunch Brigade – hard-nosed and uncompromising. It was tender.

He'd tried to choose words carefully when he'd first put forward the idea of an occupation on a site more visible than that of Anapuke, hoping people wouldn't think he was trying to cause delay or to undermine the operation – hoping they all understood by then whose side he was on. The idea had met with silence at first. He'd thought everything was about to blow.

However, the silence ran out. People began talking and planning, having seen the sense of the idea. And after the old man had had his say they all knew that Te Ra Park was the right place.

'It's sloping land before the road come,' the old man had said. 'From the main road down. Now flat and filled, flower and grass. One of those land put aside that time when government put aside no-good land for us and take the rest for them.' It was the tenths he was talking about, one of the portions of land that was meant to stay with the people when the rest was taken. It seemed it had been made into a city park instead.

The old man had gone on to talk about the rest of the land too, on and on until there was an eruption from the younger people. The hard core began talking about laying claim to all Council property, so called, as they watched the old man's cupped hand pointing in every direction. 'This family there to there. This family there to there. Crops there to there. Homes there to there. Bones moved there to there . . .'

But at last they'd come back to arrangements for occupying the park in order to make known their demand for the return of Anapuke. 'Anapuke first,' they'd said. 'Then once we're set up on the park we want the grandmothers and grandfathers to tell us the rest.' It was talk they wanted, information. Other action could wait until later.

OK. Te Ra Park was the right place, but an occupation in the middle of town was a far different matter from an occupation on a remote hillside. It scared some of them, himself included.

'Don't want trouble in our town,' some had said.

'Don't want our kids, anyone, hurt.'

'Don't want to hurt anyone.'

'We work in the checkout, the bank, the shop, the garage, the school.'

'We got to tell people why.'

'Don't want to feel shamed.'

And there'd been arguing. 'Haven't got time to waste educating others,' the younger people had said. 'A job to do and now's the time, no messing around.'

'Anyway why should we be shamed? What've we done?'

Almost a walk-out, a split, some wanting to act immediately, others willing to wait. But Mahaki had discovered that the impatience was not so much because of a desire to get on to the land in a hurry, but because of fear that interest would dissipate if they didn't act quickly – or that there would be a loss of nerve, a loss of momentum.

In the end there'd been an acceptance, a slowing down, as the young people had seen how much crucial support could be lost if they didn't spend the time needed to get everything together properly. There'd be the public to deal with, the city fathers, the media, the police, visitors.

Also there were issues of security, discipline and emergency that had to be talked through. There had to be standards.

'No booze, no drugs.'

'No one getting stroppy.'

'Got to be all right for the kids.'

'Safe.'

'Has to be a pamphlet to give out to the people of the town, explaining.'

'OK, so we better not go off half-arsed. But . . .'

'But you all better be there, early morning, afternoon, after work, night. Whenever. And . . .'

'And why don't we all have a good time while we're about it? Because it's a great thing, isn't it?'

The mood had changed. There'd been excitement as they'd discussed bringing singers in, people to speak to them, the kapa haka groups. For a while it seemed almost as if the original reason for the occupation had been forgotten.

At one meeting Kui Maata had stood and begun what seemed like a ramble about their old meeting house, telling some of its stories, telling how their old house used to care for them.

A silence had followed, people wondering whether she was for or against. Was she saying they should be staying home and being happy with what they had. He'd had to listen, flap his ears, turn what was being said, look at the underside.

'Well it's true. I think it's quite right,' Maraea had said. 'I mean there's old people. There's kids. It's good to have a house – if it's possible.'

Before this they'd been talking of pitching tents, bringing in caravans. Good ears, Maraea. 'Tents could blow away,' she'd said, 'There we are waking up in our beds and all the joggers spotting us without our lipstick on. Or the rain comes down and there's Mayor Perkins gawking out his window at all this half-drowned whanau.'

More excitement. The skilled ones among them had begun telling what was needed to construct a house and described how it could be pre-built and trucked in.

'Put up on site in a few hours if we got enough builders.'

'Demo timber and disassembled car cases.'

'Pallets. We know where we can get a few loads of those.'

Now here they all were in the dark, ready to walk in and take over, trucks and vehicles and trailers parked up ready to be driven on for work to begin. Abe had adzed a figure out of a railway sleeper. It was to be their pou, the first thing in the ground.

Abe and his helpers were ready with it now, near the front of the assembled group, and light, picked up from street lighting, was reflecting from the shell eyes of it.

Kui Maata and Kui Horiana, leading them, were on the move now, clearing the way with their voices. Eerie, even to him. Past and present all in a moment, is what it felt like. Yet it wasn't the past or the present but the future that was pulling them as they began to move forward.

There were cars lighting the roads now as they walked the park's circumference, past the gardens, the stands of pohutukawa, the ti kouka, the toilets, the kids' playground and back to where they'd started. The shovels went in, and in a moment the pou was standing there. It had taken them six weeks. Now here they were, their pou with his feet in the place that they would dig their own feet into for the next weeks, months, however long it took. No going back.

He went with the others to begin unloading the trucks. First there were the four centre posts. There was enough light now to see the spray spots that Abe and the others had marked out the day before. The spades went into the ground, the dirt piled up and the posts went in.

The unloading continued as the frame of the house went up and the tents were erected. He found himself with a hammer in his hand being shown where to knock the nails in. Later, when the walls were up, he'd get the window from the boot of his car. 'Put it in the house,' Dave said. 'Give our window a bit of history. We'll get it back later.'

There were a few joggers out. They looked across but didn't stop. Lights on in some of the buildings, cars pulling in over at the gym.

'Going to be a show, is there?' two backpackers on their way to the main road wanted to know. He gave them a pamphlet. They left, trying to read it in the half light.

A police car pulled in, the car door shut and an officer walked in between the beds of flowers, waiting as a truck with a load of pallets backed past. Mahaki put the hammer down, dodged in under a tent flap to pick up pamphlets, then made his way across.

'You're all up early,' the officer said.

'Hi Clive,' said Abe going past.

'Hi Abe . . . What's going on?'

'We're occupying our land here in order to draw Council's attention to particular injustices to do with sacred sites at Anapuke,' Mahaki said. 'Information in here,' he handed a leaflet to the officer.

'Got a permit?'

'We've granted ourselves one.' The officer headed back to the car with the leaflet.

People were beginning to arrive at work now. Some stopped, accepted or refused a pamphlet, and continued on. The walls of the house were up and the roof was going on, one of the generators had come to life and there was water on a gas ring being brought to the boil in the kai tent.

At nine o'clock the leaflets were distributed round the shops and offices of the town. By nine-thirty the first of the reporters had arrived, wanting to know what actions had been planned.

'Those actions that will keep ourselves well and comfortable, informed and entertained while we await a Council decision,' Mahaki said.

'What if Council goes against you?'

'We'll await a new decision.'

'And if they dig their toes in, what then? What further actions have been planned?'

'We'll extend our buildings and make them fit for colder weather.'

'If police are sent in will that justify tougher action on your part?'

'We don't believe it's a police matter. We don't believe we should be arrested for setting up house on our own land.'

'The matter of ownership will be seen differently by the authorities, don't you reckon?'

'We'll not voluntarily leave here until we know Anapuke is safe.'

'Not voluntarily. So you think ...?'

He hadn't realised how much into negatives the reporters were. They didn't want the kind of information the pamphlets gave – not so far, anyway. Sounded as though they wanted a riot. He'd offered to do an article for the press but they'd turned him down. He wondered how he was going to steer attention towards the real issues.

There were photographers around by the time the first interview was finished, and the television news crew came along in time to set up for the arrival of a truckload of mattresses.

How far will you go?

Do you intend to solicit the help of local gangs?

Solicit?

What defence measures do you have in place? Who's in control? Have barricades been discussed at all?

They were dissatisfied with his responses and after they'd finished talking to him they went scouting for others to interview. But these others were too busy with their own tasks and kept referring them back.

He could see now that the media tent they'd set up was going to be too small. He'd have to do something about additional space. They needed to be keeping their own records too, needed walkie-talkies and a cellphone.

'Gives you the guts-ache, doesn't it?' said Verna, coming up beside him, 'Faces at windows and now, lunchtime, they're all out having a gawk. Went to school with half of them.'

'Mm, full frontal here all right.'

'Anyway ... Come and have a bite.'

All set up and operating. Gas cookers, fridge rattling away, trestle tables, wash-up area. Good. Stew and bread. Te Rina looked in. 'Message from the mayor. He's on his way back from Queenstown,' she said. 'Wants to meet with us after four.'

'Good, send him an invite. Do you think five?'

'OK.'

'Tea at six-thirty,' Maude said.

After tea he'd take the old man home, have a shower and come back. They'd decided there was no need for them all to stay every night, though there were some who wanted to do that. They'd rostered themselves, hoping there'd be visiting supporters needing the beds once everything was under way, especially in the weekends. Dave and the family. He ladled food on to his plate. Wished he could've been home for the school production.

'Now there's all these denim jacket guys out here with their pencils ready,' Te Rina said.

'They can wait, Mahaki. Have your kai.'

'And some John Lennon caps and specs setting up cameras.'

'Eat, Mahaki.'

'So. I'm very sorry ladies and gentlemen,' the mayor said, 'but we can't have this, can we? We cannot have unauthorised constructions on Council property and tents all over the place, blocking the passage of citizens on their way to work or play. I do understand your concern about your land but this is absolutely the wrong way of going about the matter, absolutely.

'As you know, I met with a delegation of your elders in January. There were some young people among them too. I explained the position to your elders and they assured me they understood what I was saying. I know they were in agreement. I believe that they understood that we are trying to do what is fair for everybody. I'm sure they'll be disappointed when they find out about all this . . .'

'The elders are here . . .'

'Also, I've had the pleasure of visiting you on your own marae on several auspicious occasions. I've followed the protocols and respected your traditions. I want you to all now respect the Council marae and the traditions of this town. I want you to respect the wishes of your own elders too, many of whom have a high standing in this town, and who I believe may be embarrassed once they find out what's happening . . .'

'They're here too . . .'

'I don't think I need to say more. I expect and trust that all of you will have removed yourselves, your buildings and your bits and pieces by tomorrow morning. After that has happened I want you to come and see me. We can talk these things through. We can always talk. As I've said, as I explained to the delegation, my door is always open.'

Like speaking out a stereotype of himself. But it was good. It was gold. It was funny. It helped them over their jitters, dug their feet in. After he'd gone, people who may have felt on edge before, now relaxed. 'How come he didn't see you e Koro, e Kui?'

'He saw, it's just we look young.'

'Absolutely.'

The guitars came out, the singing and dancing began.

> *My eyes are dim, I cannot see,*
> *I have not brought my specs with me,*
> *Ringa ringa pakia, waewae takahia,*
> *Ringa ringa e torona, kei waho,*
> *Hoki mai.*

Acting out stereotypes of themselves.

26

TE PAANIA

Curry and salt thrown in, but still you know it's fish.

Or frog.

But there's hibernation and a time beyond hibernation. There's a time beyond survival, a time beyond the taking of the eyes.

Sometimes it is your own being, who you are, that causes your life to change – when suddenly, but not from choice, you must breathe in air instead of water. Sometimes your life becomes different through fate or accident – through your being left or right of the extended arm, or by you being in a car, on a road, with a certain person at a certain time. Sometimes there's something deliberate that you've done to cause change – deliberate and planned – like deciding to have a child, or like putting your belongings on your back and walking out into a froggy morning.

But sometimes change comes to you. Although you haven't sought it, it is as though you have waited for it, expected it without knowing what it will be. It was as Gran Kura said when she spoke of what has happened already, what has been done already, being a preparation for something else. You find that you're on the same journey, even though this new path is as yet unfamiliar and unexplored.

I worked through the files, sorting, logging, reading and making notes. During the day I worked until I heard the bell ring for the end of school, and later continued until well into the night, going to bed feeling rinsed and somehow elongated – staring into the dark with my bones lengthening inside me. I'd fall into dreams of the forest man.

In the dream the man was staked out in a dry bush clearing, in a country strange to me, where the trees around were black as though painted. These trees were hung with pulsating fruits in the shapes of hearts, diamonds, clubs and spades, which eventually burst. From them emerged flocks of glassy mosquitos which left the trees and descended to drink the blood of the man. When they'd gone, flying to somewhere beyond the forest, the man would stand as flat as paper and walk a robot walk. He wore the clothes of Tawhaki. It was as though I could take him in my arms.

I knew I had to work myself beyond these dreams and this terror. How? There comes a time. What did I know in the mind of my heart? What did I see with my own stomach eyes? What would help me to move beyond the knocking in my bones?

Frog in horror movie.

What would I do?

All I could do was croak.

Not croak as in die, but croak as in croak – open mouth, make sound. Froggy to the rescue, didah didah didah. Well, hardly that, but I would be part of it, part of the voice. I'd have my croak to add.

When the bell rang for the end of school I would leave my desk and go to the window to watch for Tawera. Gran Kura, who by now had had to give up her work at the school, would join me at the window, waiting for me to tell her what I could see.

'Tell me,' she said, on the day before the school production, 'has he got his jacket and shoes? Does he walk with friends? Is he bringing feathers?'

On the arm of the settee was the rapaki which she'd been making. She'd been waiting for Tawera to bring home feathers which she wanted to tie in a bundle to hang from the waistband, then it would be complete.

'The shoes are on his feet,' I said. 'His jacket's tied round his waist by the sleeves. He's with other kids and he's walking backwards and talking. Everyone's talking, no one's listening . . . Feathers? Yes, there's something in his hand.'

At the crossing they waited, bunched together behind the school patrol barrier. The white arm with its red disc extended. They crossed and divided, going their different ways. The orange bag began its way uphill, along with purple bag and blue bag.

'With Kawea and Donise,' I said.

'Yes, I see them now.'

He stood by the gate at Kawea and Donise's place until his two friends had walked and talked themselves to their door. Then he came hurrying up the hill and was nearly home when we saw him trip sideways and fall.

'It goes too far,' Gran Kura said.

I watched him pick himself up, brush himself and gather up the feathers. I left the window to go down and meet him.

At the bottom of the stairs there was the box we'd packed with canned foods, packets of cereal, pasta and noodles. There were clothes, towels, sleeping bags and the tiger blanket, all ready.

'Like a holiday, Mum,' he said as he came in the door, dropping his bag, removing his shoes by toeing off the heels.

'What happened?' I asked.

'I fell,' he said.

Have I given you misery, I wanted to ask.

'There's a playground there,' was what I said. 'On Saturday there'll be bands playing.' I put my arm round him, which seemed to be all I could do. Even so, as we walked upstairs with our arms about each other he edged away to make room for his sister.

'Feathers,' he said, holding them out to Gran Kura when he went in. She put her arm out for him to sit beside her, rocked him against her. 'It goes too far,' she said. He stood and went to the bathroom, not allowing her to go on.

'I know what he has to do. I know what I have to say to him,' said Gran Kura when he'd gone. I put bread in the toaster, put out milk, butter, Marmite, peanut butter and the box of Milo, made a pot of tea.

'It goes too far. I can't leave it unsaid for too much longer.' She was a bird, feathered, bright-eyed, anxious.

'He'd never agree,' I said.

When he came back in he had creamy knees and plaster on both elbows.

'I know what you have to do,' Gran Kura said.

'Silver,' he said, cutting off words and taking a package from his bag, 'to lightning me. A pen for my face.' He put milk into a cup, spooned Milo into it, whipped it round, gulped it and came up with a milky-brown moustache. Then he buttered a piece of toast, spread it with Marmite and began taking large bites, swallowing crusts hardly bitten into, thrusting his head forward, eyes popping out.

Subject closed.

So Gran held up the rapaki. 'It's nearly done,' she said. 'Lightning Man.'

'Tomorrow,' he said, happy with the costume. He finished the Milo and went off to his bedroom to practise.

I returned to my desk trying to hold to the edge of what I was writing, pulling myself towards it, but there was too much cutting across my mind, a discussion going on, bumping and banging in the bedroom.

'What's up?' I called.

'Nothing.'

So I listened for a while, then when I heard him singing, edged my way back to the work because there was an idea I wanted to follow through before I put it away . . . *permitted through their own decree* . . . Door downstairs, Dave returning . . . *manipulation of law and power* . . . *desire made law* . . . High, good voice . . . *splintered valley* . . . *while the moon* . . . A scuffle and a bang.

Have I done this to you? Have I given you misery?

I left what I was doing and went to the bedroom where I found him sitting on the floor. 'What's going on?'

'I fell.'

But how could he just fall? I helped him up not knowing what I should do or say. 'Dave's home,' I said.

It was the next evening when he was dressing for the concert that I saw how hurt he was, but he wouldn't let me ask. He was too happy and excited to talk about all that, so I put it all aside. We sat on the floor in the kitchen and laughed and laughed while I lightninged him before we went downstairs to Dave. It was a night and a half.

27

MAHAKI

Mahaki picked up the towel with his gear rolled in it and made his way out between the rows of mattresses. Most still occupied, but cooks up and gone. Abe and others out already.

As he started off across the park he could see them ahead of him in the half light – Abe, the Reverend, Jossy, the two Anis, Makere, and Jill the journalist who was seeking the inside story.

He sprinted to catch up and they ran the three blocks together, arriving just as the lights were coming on. Ashley, at the counter, waved at their season passes as they clicked, one by one, through the gate.

'All fine this morning?'

'Fine, yep.'

Up-your-nose chlorine. He put the bundle on a chair, took off his shoes and shirt and bellyflopped in, others smacking the surface, cracking it open in the lanes along from him.

He began kicking forward, face down, elbow back. Straightened his arm and pulled down. Bubbles filled the spaces between his fingers. A fan of white formed as his arm pushed against the water and pulled back. Right left, right left, head to the side, mouthful of air. Used to be good at it. Not now. Lost his speed, but he was finding the rhythm OK.

Their days had fallen into a rhythm too, now that they'd got over one or two hitches and learned to listen.

'What's this word "occupation"?' Kui Maata had asked at their talk session on their second night. And she'd spoken again about a house, about the people who had lived there making their gardens, about an old man who grew gourds. One by one the older ones had stood to support her, telling their own stories. They all knew that 'occupation' was a fancy word that showed lack of understanding.

From then on they'd dropped the word 'occupation' from their minds and their vocabulary. They weren't occupying land, they were resident on their tribal property – living there. He'd had to rewrite his leaflets. Even the word 'peaceful' that he'd used so deliberately in front of 'occupation' now seemed redundant, something that should be assumed along with ownership and with living in a place. They'd had to untwine their brains.

The other problem was one of management. On the first two days they'd had the whole world coming at them from all sides – some to support, some to condemn, some out of curiosity – but too many, too many to handle. They'd soon realised that setting up so they could do things in their own way, under their own terms, was important in getting their days at Te Ra running smoothly. The next morning they'd put up an open gateway so that visitors would know where they would be met and brought in, or where they should gather to be called in the usual way. After that they'd felt at home. Easy.

And people were happy, enjoyed being together. Talk was what they wanted, which he noticed always came down to two things – whakapapa and whenua. Who, related to whom, from where. This, in turn, became, who am I and where do I fit in. After that it was, I'm X from Y, Hori from Rori. Someone. It made the faces different. After the faces changed there'd come a more real politicisation.

And fun.

Celebration. New songs and new stuff – rap, tai chi and line dancing. Kids doing it, oldies having a go. People enjoying themselves. Talk, information, those evening sessions.

Plenty of other positives too. Anything they needed they'd been able to get, including cots and highchairs, tape recorders and video cameras.

Plenty of messages and moral support, which didn't mean there was nothing to worry about. There was always anger sitting in themselves somewhere. It could always fly, go wrong.

Out there their actions had brought out anger, some of the hatred that usually just chewed itself along under the skin. There'd been threats from locals, retaliation around town, name-calling, kids getting into fights at school. Also there was the twangy talkback radio stuff that they'd all decided not to listen to any more. There were letters to editors that they didn't have to read, or which they could read and just allow to swim over the top of them.

It wasn't all hatred. Sometimes hurt, bewilderment, people taking their action as a personal affront. Hadn't they grown up together? Hadn't they been in the same rugby team? Hadn't they always been good friends? As though this made them enemies now, opponents.

They'd tried to get it across that it was laws, not people, that were the enemy, that it was justice at stake; or that it was fear inside people that was the enemy, not the people themselves. Getting land entitlement to unwanted land was all they were asking for, and that couldn't hurt anyone.

There'd been an angry outburst over those three bits of wood though, the gateway.

'That crowd down there telling us where we go, where we stand, what we do on our own park.'

'Stamping all over us with their big black boots.'

'Jumping to their tune now.'

'We got rights too, us honkies.' There'd been more calls for the police to come and kick them all out – '. . .all those dole bludgers, thieves, radicals and stirrers with their criminal supporters.'

In spite of all that, visitors had been compliant about the gateway.

The police bosses had been OK too – patient, professional, making their carefully worded announcements over television every two or three days. It was the young cops who were jumpy and dangerous, likely to lose their heads while waiting for a law and an order to act under. Council hadn't delivered either so far – he didn't know why. Probably delving through their files looking for ways to deal with the situation without embarrassing themselves. Mayor Perkins had already tried to get them to remove themselves by promising 'top level' discussions about the land, but they couldn't agree to that or they'd be back to square one – delegations, discussions, procrastination, stalemate.

Big crowd expected today so they couldn't spend too long, a couple more lengths should do. Ani and Ani were already out, heading for the showers. After breakfast the next relay would be down for their swims and showers. Later, parents and kids, some of the cooks, others, stretching the town facility. Not too welcome at times, since some were using the showers but not the pools. Attendants were getting sour.

Well there was nothing wrong with it, they paid the same as everyone else.

Or perhaps not quite the same. Season passes had been swapping hands, passes for passing. Still, the centre would be doing better than usual. Businesses round town, especially supermarkets, would be making extra bucks too. In the lane next to him Abe emerged from under his ropes of hair, pulling himself up the ladder. Time to go.

Mahaki lathered his face and balanced his mirror against the soap in the soap-holder. He bent his knees to see into it and began edging his razor over his chin a little at a time. Abe, next to him, was shunting the last dollops of shampoo out of the plastic bottle. He pushed the button to start the water going.

Morning karakia was just finishing when they arrived back at the house, which might mean that as latecomers they'd been only partially blessed. No matter, the day had been set right. He put his toilet gear into his bag, rolled his sleeping bag, stacked his mattress and went to hang out his towel and shorts before going over to breakfast.

'How goes it with the press gang?' Rev asked as they went to the end of the table and sat down.

'Hoping they'd give it a break for the weekend, especially the local guys,' Mahaki said.

'Giving you a hard time?'

'Well, wasting my time. We're wasting each other's time. I'm sick of the same old irrelevant questions and they're sick of getting what they think of as non-responses. I got on better with the overseas people, the

Japanese, Germans, the BBC – more interested in reasons and history than in sniffing out a blood bath or bringing up questions of separatism, apartheid, special privilege – all that old stuff that seems to sit like spiders in people's minds.'

'Too close to home for some.'

'There was the koori woman, Maureen, and Dwayne and Drew from Canada. Clicked straight away. Plenty in common, plenty to talk about. Easy. But the home crowd? I just can't put the answers in a way that they can understand or take seriously. They think I'm having them on. Seems there's nothing within their own experience to match, give them a clue as to what I'm talking about. All they really want to know is where we keep the weapons and who's the ringleader.'

'They're wet behind the ears. Should send a few old hacks.'

'No meeting place, not even a collision spot. As though the questions are out of whack with any answers I can give and vice versa. They seem to me to be not listening. On the other hand I must seem to them to be evading, or lying through my teeth. They're sick of it, I'm sick of it. Spend my time better helping the cooks.'

'Or talking to Jill here,' Rev said as Jill and Makere came to join them. 'Someone with more of a commitment.'

'Well it wasn't weapons I was interested in,' Jill said. 'I can believe there's no stash of weapons. And as for *ring*leaders, I wouldn't put it that way. But *leaders*? Yes, I wanted to find out who was masterminding or mistressminding all of this. Couldn't see how all this could happen without at least an organising committee.'

'Have you found out who the big boss is?'

'There isn't one. People are just used to the group dynamic, used to having crowds around. Slot themselves into the things that they're good at. Anyone can turn a hand.'

'If not they go on a fast learning track, or they pack up and go home.'

'As for the old people . . . well, they're an enigma.'

'It's grass-roots knowledge that has to be valued – otherwise we're gone. But I know what you mean . . . you can dislocate your neck trying to listen to the elders sometimes.'

'It's worth the effort, I've decided.'

216

'So you'll be doing a story on how we get it all together – pics of people carrying cabbages, hacking up meat, eating and sleeping?'

'No. My curiosity's satisfied about all that. I want to have a decent go at backgrounding the issues, getting viewpoints if I can.'

He stood, gathered dishes and took them out to the tubs. 'Move over.'

'Thought I was never gonna hear the words,' Toi, up to his elbows in dishes, said, 'Come on scrubber . . . food . . . eat. The new shift's come in.'

'Left us the worst ones, huh? Pots, plastics and bloody ladles.'

'Chuck'm at the wall.'

'No wall.'

They were washing down benches and scouring the wash bowls when Te Rina came across to tell them that the visitors were being called in at ten. 'Big crowd waiting already. *Star* and *News* tried to jump the gun but I told them there was no one available to talk to them. Told them they could go back out and come in with the visitors at ten.'

'Maybe they'll go home, go to the beach instead.'

He could see Kura up front with the other grandmothers leading the visitors on – wispy. But just seeing her was good, seeing the confidence of those who'd lived beyond fear, beyond ego, who couldn't be reduced by criticism, threat, or anything at all. The grandfathers too, further back, in their best clothes, warm shirts, natty shoes.

Far back he could see Dave's head, above all the other heads – as though floating. Deep forehead and hanging face – Jesus-looking, though brown and unbearded. Long neck that swapped light and shadow amongst its tubes and flutes and grooves, not that he could see all that from this distance. Green jacket with the collar turned up brought up the colour of his baggy, dog-eared eyes. He watched Dave turn every so often to speak to Tawera who was still out of sight, though every now and again there was a glimpse of the orange backpack. He looked for Te Paania, saw her amongst the younger women not far ahead of Tawera and Dave.

And who else was making their way forward? He tuned his ears to the callers to see if he could pick up on who all the visitors were. Some

217

were known, some had identified themselves in the countercall – people of this place, people of that place, then the call to the four winds. He recognised some of them.

Star and *News*.

Local gang 'boys' – some his own age or older – booted, jacketed, patched, rolling their shoulders as they walked. One of them was his cousin Tam, and there was the big one, Judy, from school days – though he wouldn't have known him if Abe, beside him, hadn't said who it was.

Judy had been small in those days, asthmatic. Spent his in-school hours drawing snakes in blue and red biro up his arm. Head of the snake on the back of his hand – red mouth, red dripping fangs, then the long snake body coiling up his skinny arm to his shoulder. Chains all over himself too, crossing his chest, round his neck, wrists and ankles. Always in trouble for nicking pens. Bush of black hair, which was something he and Judy had had in common.

He looked for the old Judy inside this new body, which was wide at the shoulders, meaty in front. More neck than he needed for the size of his head. Walked-on face. No bush of hair now – no hair at all. And now that the group had come closer he could see the gang insignia tattooed on Judy's forehead, the tattooed chain round his big neck. The real thing.

The people dispersed to sit down while the speeches took place, some going to the seating that had been arranged, others going to sit on the groundsheets that had been spread here and there on the grass. He could see Tawera now, big eyes, big teeth, bright face, going with Dave and Te Paania to sit under one of the trees, shifting himself to make room for naughty big sister.

Mahaki put on overalls and boots, left Dave and Te Paania to fetch their belongings and went to where the hangi had been put down. There were more tents popping up everywhere, people all over the place having a good time. Tawera was away with the young ones watching the bands being set up.

He took a shovel and joined the men round the mound as they began shovelling the soil away from the hangi, releasing steam. As they neared the top layer of covers they began to work more carefully, shaving the dirt down and away.

'Garage down Bessie Street,' said Judy beside him. 'Crowd down there knocking up signs.'

Mahaki stepped in, peeled back one of the covers, stepped back, turning his face away from the heat and carrying the bag to the water drum. Didn't know what Judy was getting at.

'Never seen them myself,' said Judy backing off with another of the bags, passing it behind him. 'It was the boys, been jacking round, seen them.'

They stepped in and back, continuing to remove the bags, then rested while others scraped aside the stones that were anchoring the main cover. Steam.

Top layer of pumpkin and spuds under a wrapping of singed cabbage leaves. Always a relief to find that it had all happened in there, that the hot rocks had done the job.

' "Boot out bludgers", "Hauhau thugs" and shit like that,' Judy said.

Some of the men who had gloves on stepped in in twos to pick up the baskets. Mahaki followed Judy to the water drum where they folded wet bags to make pads for their hands. They lifted a basket between them and began a fast walk together to where the benches had been set up. People with big knives began slicing the mutton, pork and chicken, heaping it into oven dishes which were set down by the vegetable baskets for serving.

Placards were what Judy was talking about. There was going to be a march or a picket.

'Army style,' Mattie was announcing. 'Get your plates here, file past here and here, and we load, aim, fire. Got it?' Voice over the speaker was blessing food as he stepped out of the boots and overalls thinking about the picketers, hoping they would keep to the periphery, or maybe just march through the town. Well, little chance of that but at least now they'd had warning. He'd better see Kani, get everyone together and discuss how best to ignore whatever might happen, just get on with their day.

'You staying?' he asked Judy.

'Nah. Come for a jack, come for a feed, then that's us.'

28

TAWERA

Jewels, falling in slow motion. Slomo slomo slomo. That was before the crack on the head. And after that? Well . . . Well . . .

After that there were heads way above looking down. My mother, Gran, my sister, other people, me.

Me, looking down? Looking down at someone.

At me.

'I'm there, with you,' I said to my sister.

'No you're not,' she said.

'I'm you. We're joined. We're one.'

'No, Stupid.'

'Yes. I'm you, you're me. We're one – Visible and Invisible. I'm there with you.'

'Don't be nuts. I'm me, you're you, and you're nowhere near here – nothing like it. You're still who you are, still where you were.'

'That's not true. I can see. I can tell . . .'

'It was only a crack on the head you know.'

'I saw the colours sailing – pin, conch, hair shave, cat's purr, wind on the eye meat, knuckle cracking . . .'

'Why don't you just say the colour names now that I know all that . . .'

'It's more fun.'

'Anyway, it was only a bottle through a window. It wasn't as if it was a smash-up with a truck – steel folding, tyres bursting, bones snapping and heads cracking. It wasn't thump, thump, thump, pumping out blood spurting into the dark red sky. Conch, conch. Screaming, moaning . . .'

'There you go, conch, conch . . . Anyway, how would you know?'

'. . .One cockeyed headlight giving us a sideways glimpse of CARY CARRIER CO . . .'

'How would you know . . .?'

'I still had eyes then, remember . . . Petrol dripping. Dee doo, dee doo, dee doo, cop car, cop car, cop car. Ambulances. Fire engines, flashing lights, fire. Dee doo, dee doo, dee doo . . .'

'Anyway, getting back to my situation here. Listen to me. I was hit, I fell, I died.'

'Died? Bullshit. I mean . . . have a look. What do you see?'

'Kura, Mum, you, me, others.'

'See, the same as always.'

'But you're me. I'm you. I died.'

'You nowhere near died.'

'Well I must be nearly dead because I can't hear their voices. I'm getting there, getting close to being dead. All I can see are mouths opening and shutting. I can't hear a thing.'

'Your ears haven't caught up yet.'

'And who's this touching me?'

'Bridget.'

'She keeps disappearing. Bridget Seen and Unseen. I must be nearly . . .'

'You're not. There's a road. If you were nearly dead you'd see it. You're not even at the beginning of it.'

'You haven't told me about that before.'

'You never asked.'

'You might be bullshitting me.'

'No, no. It's true. You'd be walking along the roadway and you'd see all the different people gathered at their houses, all the different houses – people gossiping, laughing, playing games, laying out cards, decorating themselves while they waited. You'd hear singing and see dancing.

There'd be people having turns up in the lookouts where they keep watch night and day – except that there's no night and day, there's perfumed light and weightless air. Do you smell it, feel it? Do you see all that? Do you hear the people calling?'

'No.'

'So there, dummy, you're nowhere near dead.'

'Well I don't believe you. How would you know?'

'Of course I know, I do, I do, I know all about it. I went there, remember, walked the road, heard them calling me, found the right place, went through the welcome ceremonies. I was there . . .'

'So how come . . .?'

'There was someone there at the ceremonies who felt sorry for our mother. She told the people to send me back, so they did. It was only supposed to be for a little while. They're keeping my place for me.'

'I think you must be telling lies.'

'Why would I . . .?'

'Let's go there then. Take me there. Prove it.'

'Don't be an egg. I mean what about Mum and Gran, Dave, Mahaki, your father, our cousins, the teachers, the kids, all these people here? How do you think they'd feel if I took you there? They'd never forgive me.'

'You don't usually care about how they feel. How come you're caring about that now?'

'I have got a heart you know, no one cut that out of me. Otherwise I would've been gone long ago, wouldn't I? I mean . . . the way I get treated sometimes . . .'

'The way *you* get treated? That's a good one . . .'

'I can go back any time I want. You say it and I'm off. You tell me to piss off, I'm gone, ouda hia . . . Anyway, as I said, you're nowhere near. You've got minor injuries . . .'

'All right, you could just show me, take me there. I could just go there, watch the people somersaulting and cartwheeling along the road that has been spread with flowers and strung with coloured lights and banners. Or I could see them just plainly walking, or resting with their dreams visible above their heads . . .'

'I never said that . . . Geez, you make things up. And anyway I can't, couldn't even if I wanted to, you're facing the wrong way.'

'I could turn.'

'You can't turn. A few glass splinters and a bump on the head is not enough to turn you. Can you feel the bump? Is it sore?'

'Yes.'

'Feel those glass bits sticking into you?'

'Yes.'

'Well if you were facing *that* way you wouldn't be sore at all, see. You'd be walking soft air and perfumed light, you'd hear the conches bugling from the hilltops and hear the people singing.'

'I don't think it's fair . . .'

'Son?'

'Anyway can you hear Mum now, talking to you?'

'Yes.'

'Answer her.'

'Son.'

'What, Mum?'

'Talk to Bridget.'

'Are you sore, Tawera?'

'A bit.'

'Where?'

'My head.'

'Here, where I'm touching?'

'Yes.'

'Anywhere else on your head?'

'No.'

'Anywhere else on your body.'

'I think so.'

'What does it feel like?'

'Green, like little pins.'

'Anything else?'

'I don't think so.'

'OK.'

'Son we're taking you to the hospital. Dave and Maraea have

gone to bring the van round, they won't be long.'

'All right Mum.'

'And we're just going to shift you on to the stretcher, carry you like that, OK?'

'OK, Bridget.'

'Keep yourself as straight as you can and we'll slide you.'

'See, I told you I must be nearly dead, they're carrying me like a killed pig.'

'Stupid. They've put you on the stretcher because of the glass. They don't want to touch you because of the glass. The back of you is all right, but the front of you has got bits of glass sticking in it, holes all over, punctured – pin, conch, hair shave, cat's purr, knuckle crack, eye meat . . .'

'Shut up.'

'Dave's window is sticking in you. Little bits all the way down. The rest is scattered all over the place and some of it's in Mahaki's face . . .'

'Shut up.'

'He's out in the dark looking.'

'And why is Maraea driving? Why isn't Dave driving?'

'Dave's too upset.'

'Yes, well it was a beautiful, pretty window. It took him years.'

'Geez you're a stupid, dumb idiot.'

29

TE PAANIA

'*B*lack inside,' sang Tocker cracking down on her guitar, knocking out of it, upending it, beating it down, beating up, clattering and squeaking it, '*but I'm a rainbow when you look at me, Black inside but I'm a rainbow . . .*'

Tawera jumped up from the blanket we'd spread on the ground and ran towards the area in front of the stage, dodging in and out between the seats and ground covers as though he'd been called. He joined the people who were dancing, his arms like whips, his tender knees knocking, spreading, crossing, and his boy hips winding and unwinding. His big eyes, his big smile and his happy, brown, peppered face made me feel stabbed.

Tick-tock Tocker held her guitar to one side to give herself space at the microphone, dangled the instrument by its neck hitting across its strings, '*I have no labels*'. Her face floated out from her body, her calling mouth floated out from her face. Her voice came hitting, '*There are no excuses . . .*'

I could have followed Tawera and danced, or could've joined in conversations. Instead I lay down on the blanket and closed my eyes. People, voices, old friendly blanket, '*no explanashuns . . .*'

Stabbed, but in no ugly way, this heart, this red ace, this target –

225

though joy and sadness are sometimes too close, too much at one to be opposites. They're mirror twins, so alike that you have to know in which direction you're looking to be able to tell the difference. *'Stepping out, here we are . . .'* The big eye-in-the-sky winked its warmth down.

> *Not going to wait forever . . .*
> *Here we are . . .*
> *Mary Marilyn and me . . .*
> *As soon as I*
> *Find my dancing shoes . . .*

By the time I sat up again Tawera had found playmates and was going with them towards the swings, giving me a wave. Over by the fence Abe was walking up and down speaking into his walkie-talkie. Small, neat package, bunch of dreadlocks tied back, faded and gingerish, sparse black beard. The next band was setting up and Dave was coming towards me. He'd been doing a little espionage down Bessie Street, a little drive-by snoop.

'Do you think I should be in love?' I asked Dave.

'Yep,' he said.

'With who?'

'Whoever you like . . . but let's look him over first.'

'It was just a mood.'

Applause greeted the start up of the reggae beat. Dreadbreed — shades, caps and colours — beginning with their *Get up, get up, get up, get on up* theme song. Dave pulled me to my feet and we went to join the dancers — *Shout out, shout out, shout out, shout out loud.*

'Four people and a van-load of painted up signs is all I saw,' Dave said, 'but I suppose they'll meet up with others along the way . . .'

'Keep our fingers crossed.' *Shout out, shout out, shout out, shout out proud. Pee-ee-pul, Pee-ee-pul, Pee-ee-pul . . .* The vocalists stepped in to the mikes in turn, stepped back, stepped in together. The crowd joined in, *Pee ee pul, Pee ee pul, Pee ee pul, Get up, get up, get up, get on up, Shout out, shout out, shout out, shout out proud . . .*

'It's them, Mum,' Tawera said, coming back from the play area just

226

as Dave and I were about to sit down. 'What we were told.' He was tilting his head towards the road, obediently not looking.

Out on the road, in the direction of the play area, we could see the tips of the placards. We watched as the group made its way along to gather outside the fence with their banners and signs. Dave and I needed to be obedient too, so we turned our backs and kept on dancing as the chanting began – *Out out out, Out out out*.

But the picketers had chosen a bad day and a bad time. There were too many of us for them to want to come any closer. Too many *Pee-ee-pul, Pee-ee-pul*. The band, that had been about to finish, decided to stay. We danced, with the sounds building, until the *Out out out, Out out out* shout of the picketers seemed to fall into the rhythm of the music and be part of it.

Later, the protesters walked in file round the circumference of the park before leaving. The band packed its gear away and we all went across for the evening meal and prayers.

There are some moments that, when you look back on them, appear in memory as stills – framed montages – each frame in sequence slotting into position for your viewing, even though you are, yourself, part of the view within that frame.

It was dark by the time we'd finished eating, and after helping with the clearing up we went across to the sleeping house where Mahaki showed us the mattresses where we were to sleep. 'Under Dave's window,' he said.

There was talking and movement in the house, people were going in and out, or settling on to the mattresses, parents were getting children ready for bed and there were some children asleep already. Someone was strumming a guitar. There was a group of people singing.

In the first of these framed montages, Mahaki and Tawera were standing side by side, but a little apart from each other, at the foot of the mattress. They were looking up at Dave's window which had light shining through it from somewhere outside. I too was looking up at the window, but had come in after the others and was standing back from Mahaki and Tawera. We were seeing the window upright and lit, in a way that we hadn't seen it while it had been lying on a table over the years. Gran Kura, who had come in with me, had stepped to one side to speak to someone she knew. Dave was sitting back on his mattress with his bag, holding the tag of the zip between his finger and thumb.

In the next frame Tawera and Mahaki had moved closer together. Mahaki's arm was round Tawera's shoulder. They were still looking up at the window. Dave had turned his head to one side to speak to someone and had a towel in his hand. Gran Kura was sitting on the end of the mattress of the woman she knew. I had taken a step forward, still looking up.

The window was exploding.

The third frame in memory is of Tawera on the floor, Dave and I kneeling beside him, Gran looking across, Mahaki half turned towards the door.

After that there was movement, shouting, running, children awake and crying, a voice calling for Bridget.

The next day the Sunday paper gave front-page coverage to Saturday's events. There was a close-up photograph of one of the Dreadbreed vocalists at the mike, and a wide shot of the crowd. There was a close-up of an open-mouthed picketer and a back view of Judy.

There was a shot of Abe under police escort, and beside it a close-up of a man's bleeding face. There was a half-page report under the headline *Band Plays On as Te Ra Turns Bloody*.

30

MAHAKI

He gripped Tawera's shoulders, turning him, while at the same time bringing him to the floor – but not quickly enough. He could hear people running, Abe's voice calling, and once outside he could see Abe and four or five others sprinting across the park. He went after them.

Ahead of Abe and the others, two men scrambled over the fence, disappearing in darkness for a moment before coming into sight again as they ran across the road. They were lost to view once more as they slid down the grassed bank, which Mahaki knew led to the Fitness Centre carpark. For a moment he saw Abe silhouetted at the top of the bank. A second later he saw him flying.

By the time he reached the carpark Abe was on top of the man he'd tackled. He had him pinned, had a knee in his back and was pumping his face up and down on the paving. Mahaki went to help Jase and Hani as they took hold of Abe by the arms and dragged him to his feet. There were people converging, a camera flashing, a police car pulling in. The other runner had returned and was turning the broken-faced man over.

Down at the police station Mahaki presented himself as Abe's lawyer.

'You need a doctor,' the duty officer said.

'I want to see my client.'

'All cut up, bro,' Jase and Hani said. 'Get back and clean up.'

'Abe . . .'

'We'll look after Abe. Ring someone, come and get you.'

But he didn't want to ring anyone. He went out and began running through town towards the civic centre, hoping he wouldn't meet anyone, hoping Tawera was all right.

The glass had been cleared and the window boarded up by the time he arrived. The old man was up waiting with Kani, Ani, Maraea, Jill and a few others.

'Bridget rang back from A and E,' Ani said. 'Tawera's all right. Cuts are superficial and they've been treated. They're keeping him in for observation because of the knock on the head.'

'I'll go over and have a look.'

'Let's have a photo before you clean up,' Jill said. 'You might want it for something.'

'I'll drive you,' Ani said.

'Well, there are things,' he said to Jill. 'Media's going to have a ball . . .'

But it was another two weeks before he had time to speak to Jill. There'd been an escalation of feeling among people in the town and he'd been out doing his best to help scale it down. He'd tried to talk to the picketers, who, though they didn't return to the park, were now keeping up a constant presence at the Council Chambers demanding an eviction. He'd done his best with the media, but realised there was more and more pressure on police to clear the park, as well as on politicians to intervene.

Police were jumpy, and since neither the Council nor the politicians had given any orders, they'd decided to make their presence felt by issuing a search warrant, saying that known criminals had been spotted amongst the occupiers. They'd come in early one morning and taken away a cricket bat, a crowbar, an axe and two skinning knives. Cannabis had been found in a van that had broken down on site, and Mardy was arrested for obstruction when she sat on her belongings in an effort to stop police going through them.

'It's getting near the time,' he said to Jill. 'Cops, Council and public are so jittery there'll be an eviction order soon. We'll have to decide whether to stay and be arrested, or whether to change tack. Anyway, we're having a talk about it this afternoon.'

'How do you think you'd go in court?'

'If we get arrested and go to court we'll only be defending trespass, obstruction, things like that. If we try to take our own case . . .'

'You think you'll lose?'

'If we go to court we'll have to show there's been fraud – you know, prove the Council got certificate of title through skulduggery or theft.'

'Well it sounds as though there *was* fraud. No deed of sale, no payment . . .'

'But no evidence that there wasn't payment either – and no one's likely to take Grandfather's word. He says there was money offered but people wouldn't take it. It'd be like selling their ancestors. We believe him, others won't. Anyway I don't think the law actually required payment. It was either you sell us your land or we take it.'

'So certificate of title is the trump card, even though the law it was obtained under is now generally accepted as being unfair?'

'Yes. But I don't know about "generally accepted". Hardly anyone's aware of the law and what it did to people.'

'You think I might be able to help?'

'If we could turn public opinion it might help, if we could highlight unfairness . . .'

'In this red-necked district?'

'Mm. Well, if we could get the Council even more on the back foot it would be an advantage. I mean the only reason there's been no eviction so far is that the Council doesn't want court action. They don't want all their bungling to come out in court. They've tried everything. Bribery – you leave Te Ra Park peacefully and then we'll talk about Anapuke. When that didn't work they sent a smiling delegation, supported by their chosen kaumatua, who came down to try and big chief us. That was followed by a succession of Maori bureaucrats sent down to negotiate – without being given anything to negotiate with, I might add. They seemed to think the importance of their positions would impress us somehow.'

'And all this time Council's had the best press.'

'Yes, but I reckon there's a percentage of support out there. I reckon that support could increase if we could get our views highlighted and discussed. We need further impact on Council, more pressure on them. They're already shaky.

'If everyone could understand that land was taken under an unfair law, that there's no record of payment and that people refused payment, it could make a big difference I think. On top of that they could be told that Council doesn't want the land anyway, only wants to sell it to top up their coffers. There's a chance it could lead to an out-of-court settlement, that Council could just decide to return Anapuke to save itself embarrassment.'

'What I'm working on is an article for *UTMOST*,' Jill said, 'where I hope to examine all sides of all the issues. It's not what you need – small circulation and probably won't even come out till the spring issue. You need something immediate, something everyone'll read. Dailies don't use freelancers like me. I could probably get something into the Sunday paper, or work on one of my mates to do it . . . but it wouldn't be able to be too one-sided, you understand.'

'No. Just to get our points across, no matter how you want to balance it with other material. The "sacred site" aspect has never been seriously put forward either. We haven't emphasised that because the old man doesn't want attention drawn to it. I don't blame him. We're going to be talking about it at our meeting later – whether or not we should add all that into the equation.'

A heated meeting. Obvious from the beginning that walking off when the eviction notice came wasn't an option.

'We want everyone here when the time comes, in the house.'

'Not budging.'

'They'll have to drag us out.'

He'd pointed out that the problem of having everyone arrested was that the courts wouldn't want to deal with so many people. Trespass and obstruction were minor charges which the courts might decide to dismiss.

'Getting taken to court was your idea,' he was reminded, and he'd had to put his view carefully to people, to explain what could happen and how difficult it would be to prove fraud. 'I'm saying it might be better to either shame the Council into giving Anapuke back, in an out-of-court agreement, through the threat of court, or to embarrass them through the courts, hoping that the court'll see our side of it.'

'Well, we're not moving from here.' That was the main theme from young and old.

In the end it was agreed that selected people would remain to obstruct the dismantling of the house. After being arrested and charged they'd build their defence on the argument that as far as they were concerned, they were on their own inherited land, not breaking any law. They'd say they'd taken up residence to draw attention to their need to have Anapuke returned to them, pointing out that they had over many years and in many ways tried 'proper channels' in order to get the land back. Now there was no other course open to them. They would stress that the matter was urgent at this particular time, since the Council had recently offered the land for sale.

As a strategy they decided they'd call on large numbers of witnesses, hoping that during the course of drawn-out proceedings, the fairness of what they were asking would be shown. Once the order to vacate was given, all but the few remaining in the house would watch proceedings from outside the fence. Rev would drum up a few witnesses from his congregation as well.

After the eviction was over they'd set up new occupations outside the courtrooms, as well as in and around the Council offices. Maraea's flat would be used as a base for issuing information and statements, and people from out of town would be accommodated in the homes of locals.

'I know the way there,' the old man had said at the meeting. A big step for him. 'We can prove. We can take a person there.'

31

KURA

There was a woman who was good at making dresses. She had an old husband, one daughter and three sons.

This maker of dresses only needed to see a picture of a dress, or see someone wearing a dress, and she could make one the same. Any kind of dress that anyone wanted she was able to make. The dresses would always be made to fit perfectly. Whatever material was brought to her – lawn, cotton, linen, satin, taffeta, velvet, organdie – she could make something beautiful with it. There was nothing in the way of making dresses that the woman could not do.

She and her husband had pigs and sheep on their farm, and a large garden where they grew potatoes, squash and cabbages. The woman didn't work on the land but spent her days making clothes for people. She was always the one to be asked to make the bridal gowns and bridesmaids' dresses when there was a wedding. She made confirmation frocks, presentation gowns and outfits for special occasions.

Out of the left-over pieces of material that people brought to her she made patchwork dresses for little girls, decorating them with tucks and ricrac and ruffles and binding. These became our best dresses. We had a home dress which was any size and any shape, and old. We had a school dress, handed down, big and long, with hems that could be let down or taken up, to last for several years. And then we had our best dress, made for us by this maker of dresses, but which we hardly ever wore.

From the time she was a little girl the woman's daughter took an interest in this making of dresses too, and by the age of twelve was almost as good a seamstress as her mother.

The dress for my confirmation, that the woman made for me when I was fifteen, was of white organdie with a lawn underdress. It had a ruffled collar and long, full sleeves, gathered and buttoned at the wrists. It had a satin waist sash which the woman made from pieces left over from a wedding frock. When we arrived with the material the woman and her daughter were flying their needles round the hems of bridesmaid dresses made of pink taffeta.

The daughter, who was called Millie, was four years older than me, and it was about a year after my confirmation that Millie was married. The old father had died and two of the brothers had married and moved away to other districts.

The third brother had married also, but had built his own house nearby and had opened up adjoining land. He and his wife, with some help from Millie and her mother, were now struggling to keep the double property in order. Monday, who Millie was to marry, had the reputation of being a hard-working man. He was to be a welcome addition to the family.

Millie was of medium height and wide build. She had a big lovely face and a slow, serious manner that made her seem ill-tempered. Her husband was half a head shorter than she was, also wide in build, also serious in his manner – though no one would have put his quiet ways down to ill-temper. He was older than Millie by ten years.

When the engagement was announced, remembering the work that Millie and her mother had done for them over the years, people vied with each other to be allowed to provide materials for the wedding dresses and outfits. Pennies were collected among families. In fact everything that was needed for the wedding was provided by the different ones. It was Millie's family's turn to be on the receiving end.

Millie's wedding dress was the most beautiful we'd seen. It was of white satin with a high neckline and stand-up collar. It had long, fitted sleeves and a fitted bodice which was shirred at the shoulders. There were fine pintucks inserted with lace from shoulders to waist. The skirt was shaped over the waistline, gradually widening to the hem. She had a full-length net veil.

There were eight bridesmaids in blue satin dresses of a similar style, but with lace-trimmed puff sleeves and flared full-length skirts. The wedding day was a day when everyone, including these two serious people, was full of smiles.

Their eldest child was eleven when Millie first met Harvey. Harvey was a young soldier who had come from training camp to spend his leave at the home of one of Millie's cousins. We all attended the social evenings that were put on for the soldiers, and if Harvey did dance more with Millie than with the rest of us, no one noticed. If these two did talk secretly at that time, no one knew.

But Millie and Harvey wrote to each other from that time on, which is something no one realised until later. And when Harvey went on final leave before being posted overseas, Millie went to join him, leaving her three children with her mother and husband. No one knew where she was.

After the soldiers had gone she didn't wish to return to her husband, her mother, her children and the making of dresses. She found work in a factory, making soldier uniforms, and took a room in a boarding house where she intended waiting for the end of the war and Harvey. But when it became obvious that Millie was pregnant the owner of the boarding house put her belongings out on the landing and let her room to someone else. In a similar manner she was put out of her job, and though she tried for other lodgings and other work, there was no one who would accommodate or employ her. There wasn't any alternative but to go home. She didn't know what would happen to her.

Once Monday's family found out that she was home they made preparations to come and take what was theirs and what was owed to them.

A week after her return we saw Monday's people coming, at first nothing but a shimmer at the furthest visible point along the beach.

It was a hot day. The trees were out in crimson flower. The

birds were ringing and gonging in them like bells.

As they came nearer we saw that there were about a hundred people, most walking, some on horseback. They'd brought a horse and dray. They had their dogs with them.

When they arrived near to where the houses began, they left the shore and began making their way across the paddocks, calling and stamping and shouting, to the house where Millie sat in the middle of the verandah in a very fine dress that did not hide her pregnancy. The birds went silent in the trees.

To either side of her, but standing apart where they could be clearly seen, were her mother and her brother. Her husband stood away to the side of the house with his dog beside him.

'We've come to take you home,' Monday's family said to him. 'We've come for you and your children, and to claim what you, and we, are owed.'

Some went to round up the sheep and collect the pigs, chickens, horses and the two milking cows. Others gathered together the shovels, spades, axes and farm implements and stacked them on the dray, while others went into the house collecting furniture, linen, blankets, curtains, crockery, pots and kettles, baskets, jewellery, food, preserves and clothes. Everything that was in the house was taken, except for photographs.

Then the people left with the man and his children, the animals and the drayload of goods.

All this time Millie and her mother and brother had waited without moving or speaking. All this time we had watched from the fences, knowing we couldn't interfere.

From then, Millie, her mother and her brother had to start their lives again, which they were able to do now without blame. Later Millie's children were able to visit her, but they never lived with her again.

Harvey never returned from the war.

32

TE PAANIA

'Shall I take you to a doctor?' I asked Gran Kura, whose eyes burned. In some lights it seemed as though her bones had come to the outside, webbing and overlaying her skin.

'Of course not,' she said. 'What good would that do?'

It was on my tongue to ask, 'Shall we take you home?' but I didn't ask it.

'Anyway,' she said, 'what's the trouble? Isn't my tongue still clacking in my head?'

So Tawera and I went to town and bought a new coloured jacket for her that could be folded small, put in a bag and pulled out still looking smart. It cheered us up and she was pleased with it. We went to the markets to look for food that she would enjoy, but she would only have a few mouthfuls of fish, a bite or two of buttered bread and her cups of milky tea.

Every night Mahaki rang to keep us up to date with what was going on at the park. On television we'd seen the hand of a policeman on Mardy's head bobbing her into the police car, followed by a sweeping shot of the Council men and their tame chiefs talking to Kui Horiana and Kani. There'd been plenty of footage covering the activities of the picketers at the Council buildings, while headlines in the newspapers began more and more to highlight Council reluctance and police inactivity. Getting hot, according to Mahaki.

It was three months after they'd taken possession of Te Ra that news came that the 'occupiers' had been served an eviction notice. They'd been given ten days to clear the park.

'I won't be thrown in jail after all,' Mahaki said over the phone. 'They want me to stay out of it so I can prepare the defence for court. Got to do some delving into files, see what I can find.'

'We'll bring the van up and help move the gear,' I said, at the same time wondering whether Gran Kura would be able to make the journey.

'Maraea wants you to come and help set up an office at her place,' he said. 'And give a hand with some new leaflets for the campaign.'

'I know what you have to do,' Gran Kura said to Tawera, 'because it goes on too long and it goes too far.' I stopped what I was doing to listen. Tawera was felt-penning a large picture of Michael Jordan, Bulls 45, doing a lay-up. Michael, in his red outfit, was airborne on blue and yellow squiggles and arrows, his head thrust back, eyeing the ring. His large hand, on the end of a muscled, out-thrust arm, palmed a ball that trailed black and orange flame.

I thought Tawera might try to change the subject, as he usually did when Gran wanted to talk about what we'd seen happening, or thought he might make up some excuse to leave what he was doing and go outside.

'But Gran, it isn't what you think,' he said. He stopped fire-colouring long enough to look at her.

'You can't be soft about it,' she said. 'Because it's your life and your self.'

'It isn't what you think,' he said again.

'You have to open your mouth and swear,' she said, 'your worst. Tell it to get out, tell it off properly, that's what you do.'

'Give it heaps?'

'As loud and as bad as you can.'

'Like piss off. Like pokokohua, taurekareka, arsehole pig?'

'Yes. Although I'm sorry about pig,' she said. 'Pigs were our pets, our babies. We carried the little ones, cuddled them. They followed us. We took them swimming. It was our job to feed them and keep them away from the gardens. We always cried when the fires were lit and we heard our pets squealing. We cried and cried when that knife went in, the blood poured into a bucket and there was no more noise. Pigs were the very special gift you could give when someone died, or when there was a marriage or a christening. I feel sorry about pig because animals are much older than we are.'

'I'd forgotten about that,' he said. 'I'd have to leave off pig.'

'Anyway, all the rest of it, as hard as you can,' she said. 'Loud and hard, but the biggest thing is that you have to mean it. You have to mean what you say. You have to chase it with your words. Gone.'

'Not "it", "her",' he said.

'Well I don't want to pick on anyone in particular,' Gran said. 'I don't want to offend anyone. Just want to say it's the way you do it. It's what you have to do when you need to. I can't go ahead and die without telling you. I know it could mean your life.'

'I understand,' he said, rattling through the felt pens, testing, discarding, selecting, 'I do understand. But how could I? Gran, how could I? And even if I did, how could I mean it?'

Gran had nothing to say to that, but she watched as in the sky of the stadium Tawera began to outline in large block letters Michael Jordan's name.

'I've found out,' he said as he began colouring in the words, 'that there are lots of brothers and sisters who argue and fight. They watch each other to see who has more milk in a cup, and one of them says, "She's got more than me," or "He's got more than me." And the mother says, "No, they're both the same." But the kids argue and get mad and don't even want the milk any more. They won't drink it.

'Or if there's a blue cup and a red cup they both want the red one. They try to pull the red cup off each other and the milk gets spilled, then the mother or father won't let them have any milk at all. Sometimes one of them is glad when the parent won't let either of them have any milk because that one didn't really want milk in the first place.'

The lettering was breaking into stars and each letter had a yellow tail, like a comet. He began working these bright tails out to the edges of the paper.

'It seems to be true what you're saying,' Gran said.

'Sometimes when the sister and her brother are playing board games or card games, the one that's losing the game gets upset because she keeps getting swallowed by a coloured snake, or isn't quick enough to shout SNAP. So she tips the board, or scatters the cards, or won't give the dice for the brother to have a turn.

'When Kawea and Donise's mum was taking them in the car to the airport to pick up their dad, Kawea said, "I'm sitting in front," but Donise ran and got into the front seat first. He pushed in beside her and she tried to shove him out. "You can't both be in front," their mum said. She told Kawea to get in the back and said he could be in the front on the way home. He said no, because dad would be in the front on the way home. So his mum said, "Well you can be in the front next time we go somewhere," and he said, "I don't want to be in the front next time we go somewhere, I want to be in the back." Then his mum got mad and made him get in the back. Made him. She pointed her finger at him, pointed to the back seat and he couldn't ignore her. He was crying in the back seat of the car. Only Donise smiled and waved to me as they drove away.'

'I'll have to think about all this you're telling me,' Gran said, leaning back into the cushions of the settee with lids, transparent, down over her eyes, 'Go on,' she said.

'Sometimes Mahara used to get whingy and aggro because Mahi would wake up in the night and get into Niecy's bed. She'd wake up and find herself alone in their bedroom and get upset.

'Other times it's different. Sometimes brothers and sisters just share the Lego, or play elephants, or save something for each other when they have a treat. Or they agree who can be Michael Jordan or Scottie Pippen and talk agreeably about who they like on TV.'

He stopped talking as he concentrated on finishing the picture, looking it over to make sure there was no white paper showing through.

'Gran, this poster is for you,' he said when he'd finished. 'Michael is six foot six inches tall and was born on February the seventeenth, 1963.'

'Now that I've thought about it,' she said, 'I suppose it means you have a true sister. I suppose it means she has a true brother.'

'He went to High School in Wilmington, North Carolina, and to College at the University of NC. He's the best basketball player in the universe. His old number was 23 and his comeback number is 45.'

'You and your sister do all the things that brothers and sisters are allowed to do these days, so I suppose what you're saying is right.'

'There's nothing to worry about with me,' he said, signing his name in an especially dashing way at the bottom of the picture. 'My family is a good family. I have a happy childhood.'

Mahaki rang asking us not to come until the eviction was over.

'You think it'll be rough?' I asked.

'Shouldn't be,' he said. 'We've told the police we won't make trouble, which doesn't mean they believe us, I suppose . . . But there'll be detours, cordons, car searches, reinforcements . . .'

'Overkill.'

'Riot squad . . .'

'We'll keep out of it then,' I said. 'Anyway I don't know if Gran can travel. We might have to stay . . . Maybe just Dave.'

'Fading,' Mahaki said.

'We'll see . . .'

'If she wants to come there's plenty of room at Maraea's.'

Television coverage on eviction day was peripheral. All roads to the park had been cordoned off, shops and offices had remained closed, the streets had been cleared, reporters and camera crews hadn't been allowed near. There were a few longshots of police being bussed into the area, and of the riot squad on standby.

'We could stay home,' I said to Gran. 'Dave'll take the van . . .'

'But why else would I have new clothes?' she said.

At Maraea's house we watched home video of the Commissioner of Police giving orders over a loudhailer to what looked like a large crowd of people in front of the house.

'About a hundred and fifty of us,' Maraea said. 'We'd been squeezed together all night, sharing mattresses. Didn't get much sleep, but knew if any of us went home to sleep we wouldn't be allowed back.'

Following the order there was an exodus that the camera tried to show. Feet and backs of people leaving, making their way through police lines singing. 'Bawling too,' Maraea said. 'None of us wanted to go. It was hard, especially leaving those old people.'

When the camera returned it showed the twenty people who had remained, among them the three elders including Mahaki's grandfather. These were the twenty finally arrested, the camera wobbling each one away into a police van, returning to pick up the next. The old people made their way quietly to the vans under escort, while the younger ones had to be handcuffed, dragged and carried. The last to be taken were Mardy, who had climbed up onto the roof, and Abe, who had chained himself to the pou.

We installed a computer and printer in Maraea's front room and moved her shell collection from the mantelpiece so that we could arrange files there. Ani P and I went through and sorted the boxes of papers and newspaper cuttings that had accumulated. We gave them to Gran and Tawera to put into clearfiles. I was surprised, at one stage of that first afternoon, to see Gran eating banana cake.

The next day we designed a pamphlet for the new campaign while Maraea made phone calls, arranging meetings of all those who were to be involved. By the time we left for home on the third day, Maraea's house was receiving coverage as being the new headquarters of land grievance activity.

The journey had done Gran Kura no harm. 'Count me in,' she said one afternoon while we waited for the news to come on.

'Here it is,' Tawera said, zapping the volume up on Channel One.

'The next stage,' Maraea, with her bundle of leaflets, was saying, 'is to make people aware of the reasons we're asking that Block 165G10 be returned to its rightful owners.'

'The rightful owners being?'

'Ourselves, descendants of our common ancestor. Genealogy

shown on the back of this . . .'

'And on what grounds?'

'Bullet points here: Land not sold in the first place. Special spiritual significance . . .' There was a cut to footage showing responses to the pamphlet from people round town.

'It's a load of rubbish.'

'I reckon they've got a point.'

'Don't know what they're on about, we're all New Zealanders, aren't we?'

'They should all go out and get haircuts and get jobs.'

'The Council should give it back. Yes, definitely.'

'Council has declined to comment,' said the interviewer, 'but will issue a statement at a later date.' There was a final shot of the picket taking place outside the Council offices.

By the next week the picket line had grown, 'Getting too big,' Mahaki told us when he rang. 'Got a few stroppy ones joining in, got to keep the lid on.' They were wanting to keep the pressure on Council, but not so much that Council couldn't back down. 'Court in a month's time. Watch for Jill's article on Sunday,' he said.

33

TAWERA

I expected arseholes.

Following the discussion that I'd had with Gran, I thought my sister's mouth would make itself square and her voice would come out of it ugly. 'Talking about me as if I wasn't there,' I thought she would say in an awful singsong way. 'Saying "her" as though I can't be hurt, as though I can't hear.' On and on, 'I have got feelings, have got ears you know.' All that.

I thought I'd be covered in pinches.

She didn't say anything about the conversation for days and days, and when she did it wasn't arseholes, nowhere near.

We were walking down the rickety hill, the lumpy footpaths, too steep and cracked to skate down. I had our tied-together rollerblades round my neck. It was a snappy, cold day, walking barefoot.

'What happens next?' she asked.

'Next, what after?'

'When kids get older and help themselves to milk from the fridge without having to ask. Or when they have friends their own age to play games with. What about when they don't want to get into their parents' bed any more and aren't bothered about the front seats of cars?'

I sat on the lip of the drive that led into the school grounds, pulled on blue socks, put my feet into the boots and began lacing them. 'I don't think I know about all that,' I said.

'Well, let's talk about it.'

'OK.'

'I think when kids get older they have milk when they want it,' she said. 'Not because the other one's having some.'

'I agree with that,' I said. 'And if they *are* both having milk, they don't bother looking to see how much the other one's got. They're too busy thinking about their hair, or some problem.'

I pushed off along the drive and on to the asphalted play area, building up speed.

Round the play area we went, across the carpark, along the paths and round the buildings. 'When they have friends their own age to play card games with,' I said, 'even if they lose, they just say, "Get you next time," or something like that.'

'And I don't think the older ones want to get into their parents' beds, or in the front seats of cars any more,' she said. 'Because parents can see their thoughts . . . Our last year,' she said as we stopped to look in through our classroom window.

The chairs were up on the desks, there was new work up on the board, and there was a coating of white dust over everything. A black-and-yellow wasp crawled over a chalky apple. I told her all of this. 'Our last year,' she said again.

'They're looking for a college for us to go to,' I said.

'You'll be all right,' she said, but I didn't know why she said it.

We rolled back down the drive and out on to the footpath, weaving in and out between the Saturday shoppers, to the crossing. We clumped across to the strip of garden area between the two one-way roads and began to roll again – past flax bushes rattling their tongues, opened out roses, shrubs that had gone spiky and brown. I described all this to her even though she didn't seem to be listening.

'The kids with their own thoughts,' she said, 'sometimes still play Lego, but it's mostly only when they want to show a little cousin what to do.'

'They don't play elephants any more.'

246

'But they still say who they like on television, think about who they want to be.'

'They watch the basketball games and save up for the caps and singlets, which the mother says are a rip-off.'

'They still have their cards and albums even though they don't look at them any more.'

Round Queen Victoria we went, past the war memorial, while cars and Cityline buses went by. We rested for a while, getting breath, keeping steady by holding the branch of a tree. Patchy lawn, and on the bare places, skinny sparrows on twig legs, jumping.

Across the roads on either side were the car sales with flags, signs, bargains. Picture theatre, Liquorland, undertakers, KFC. People in jackets, cold and hunting. She knew all this.

'Do they like each other?' she asked.

'Who?'

'The brother and sister who are older now?'

'I think so.'

We were on our way again, clumping back over the crossing, stopping to look in the window of the tricky picture shop where there were magic-eye pictures and holograms on display.

A new hologram showed a silver eagle with wings reflecting pink, purple, green and yellow as it moved in flight. Another showed a hunter carrying a gun, a pair of rabbits hanging round his neck like rollerblades. When he moved he became his own skeleton. 'Hologran,' I said, which amused us as we moved on again, 'Hollow Gran.'

Off we went, zigging, zagging, then clunking up the road to the tunnel. 'And I think they go and live somewhere else,' she said. 'Sometimes nearby, sometimes far away from each other ... But what happens if they go and live somewhere so far away that they know they'll never see each other again?'

'I think they'll miss each other.'

'But they'll still know. They'll still remember ... We're not supposed to come this far,' she said as we entered the tunnel with lights like oranges. She'd never worried about that before. We rolled along the footpath, high on the tunnel wall, while below us the cars boomed.

Out the other side we flew down a sharp slope, braking near the bottom, grabbing hold of a black-and-white pole. I told her about the pole, describing it as we turned on to the long undulating street of liquorice allsorts houses. 'He still knows he's got a sister,' she said. 'She still knows she's got a brother. They'll be all right.'

I was tired of all this talk of brothers and sisters, and when I'd finished describing all the lolly houses I asked, 'Why aren't you giving me arseholes from that time Gran and I talked about you?'

'When I was twelve,' she said, 'you reckoned I should be in love, have a paper round, smoke on the way home from school.'

'But that was years ago. Why be mad about that now? It was only because I was annoyed and couldn't get on with the maths exercises. Anyway, that was before I discovered that we could talk into each other's minds. Anyway . . .'

'You don't have to be defensive. All I was going to say is, you're twelve, nearly a man now. You could be in love, have a job, all that . . . But what I really want to tell you is, you won't have to swear . . . use those words.'

'I won't. I wasn't going to. How could I? Didn't you hear me? You don't have to be mad about that.'

'Who said I was mad?'

'You keep changing the subject.'

'No I don't. All those brothers and sisters . . .'

'I don't want to talk about that any more.'

'They grow up and go and live in other houses . . .'

'We already said that.'

'They have other friends, and partners. They go out with friends. They fall in love. They're still a family and always remember each other, but they don't want to be lovers.'

'How do you know that?'

'I've thought about it.'

'So what?'

'So, you'll be in love, with someone like January . . .'

'I was a kid then.'

'Someone *like*, I said. Not January, someone *like*.'

Past the houses were the pine plantation, the rugby park and the community hall. We flew by them down the long sloping road. 'They don't want someone getting in between,' she said.

'Who don't?'

'The lovers. They don't want someone listening to them saying, "You're the most beautiful man in the world and I love you."'

'Yuk.'

'They won't want anyone there when they kiss.'

'What're you going on about?'

'They don't want the brother or sister there while they take each other's clothes off, drop them on the floor and kiss each other naked and falling.'

'You didn't see that.'

'You described it to me. Then he puts it in . . .'

'They don't show that part.'

'But everyone knows . . . And they ride and dive around, sweating and blowing and grunting, like tennis players or wood choppers . . . Where are we now?'

'Going past the college, nearly at the bottom of the hill.'

'We're not allowed this far.'

'You've never worried about that before.'

At the end of the long slope I sat, removed the rollerblades, tying the laces and hanging them round my neck like rabbits. We waited for a break in the traffic and crossed the road where we took a little track through manuka and kakaho, until we came to a place where a creek ran down. We played there for a while. I described everything to her.

'I think it's time we went home,' she said. She'd never ever said anything like that.

'All right,' I said.

Just as we were leaving I saw a stick that I liked. It was knobbly and interesting, and although it was wet and muddy I decided to take it home.

We started barefoot up the slope towards the tunnel. As we walked I told her what I might do with the stick. 'I'm sixteen,' she said, as though she hadn't heard anything I'd told her. 'I want to talk about what we were discussing when you were full of glass, about where you thought you were going . . . about the road . . .'

'So, I made a mistake . . .'

'It was a long road, like this one that you described to me, but without the traffic and lights and wires, without poles and pipes and all that asphalt. There were people walking and dancing and singing along it, looking to this side and that, listening for their names. It was a yellow road, its surface worn smooth by all the travellers . . .'

'Did someone describe it to you?'

'I had eyes for most of the journey, but eyes weren't needed there anyway. And I understood colours even though I couldn't name them.

'There were trees either side of the road. They were nothing like the trees you've described to me. They were flat on both sides, moving backwards and forwards, and from side to side, like seaweed. Their roots were like hands, clinging to stones. You didn't *have* to walk or dance along. Instead you could swim or surf or skate or blade, without needing boards or wheels. You could swim or fly.'

'Thin gravity,' I said.

'Not all were moving. Some, at the beginning of the road hadn't made up their minds. They were looking back, hesitating, sitting there thinking about it.

'There were some standing in groups chatting, laughing, tossing for it. Their heads fell back as the coins went spinning up, their eyes looking high to where the sun might be. But there was no sun, even though there was light. The coins were the sun, catching a glimmer, then dropping. The heads bowed. Eyes looked down to see who had been chosen. "You. You. You're the one." They'd laugh and point at one of them. "No, no. Come on, two out of three." "No, you. You're the one. Goodbye." They'd laugh, waving that one up the road. That one would start off slowly then begin to run, finding it easy after all.

'At the top of the long slope there was a place to climb down – if you wanted to climb down. Otherwise you could fall, or jump, or dive, or fly. Easy. Then you just kept on going.'

'If we could do that now we'd soon be home,' I said. 'Uphill and down we'd go, up and down, whizzing along not touching the ground, with propellers on our heels and elbows.'

'I never said that . . . But on and on. Walking, running, greeting someone, feeling someone's elbow bump you as they hurried past, looking this way, that way, waving to the ones up in the lookouts, listening for your name.

'Then hearing it – Baby No-eyes.

'I waited by the gateway to be called to my welcome ceremony.'

We ran, shouting through the tunnel of oranges to make our voices echo. The cars and vans below started up question and answer with their horns. These sounds deformed inside the curve of the tunnel, nearly breaking our ears.

'I was on loan,' she said. 'Although our mother didn't miss me at first, she later heard words that changed that. After my welcome ceremony, the woman who felt sorry for our mother sent me back. I was only on loan because Mum needed me, but it was meant to be just for a few years. Then you came.'

' "I see her," I said, when Mum and I became undolled. "I see her with two holes in her head." ' I was happy to be discussing this.

She said, 'We had to be a family because it was what our mother wanted. There had to be a family and a childhood.'

We climbed the school wall to make a short cut through. 'Our last year,' she said.

'I already know that. They're looking for a college for us to attend. You keep changing the subject.'

'Not that. Not school,' she said.

'What are you talking about then?'

'You're nearly a man,' she said, and although I niggled and nagged at her she wouldn't say any more.

So I thought and thought about all she'd said, all we'd talked about. I thought about my family and my childhood and about being a man.

It was turning out to be far worse than arseholes.

34

KURA

There was a teapot with a dent by its nose. The knob of its lid had cracked and broken off from too much use, but a new wobbly knob had been made from the cut-down cork of a port bottle. There was a piece of wire to keep this new knob in place. We took the teapot with us when we went from house to house because we wanted a new roof for the church.

Here we were with not many people at all. They were dead, or had gone away to find work. I too was old enough to go and find work, but was the one allowed to stay and look after grandmother and the church. I was old enough to be married by then.

Grandmother, although her body and arms were strong for someone so very old, was unable to carry anything heavier than a dish in her hands. I cleaned floors for her, collected the wood, milked her cow and carried dishwater and washing water out to her gardens. I brought water for the copper, rubbed the clothes and put them through the mangle on wash days. I sandsoaped the boards of the lavatory and washed them down. Well, her hands were like bunches of flax pods which, after the summer is over, have twisted and burst themselves out in all directions.

I didn't look after the church on my own, of course not. Every third Saturday of the month – that was the day before our Sunday service –

we'd go along and sweep out the sand and rub the floor round the altar and under the pews with polishing cloths. Then we'd pull little children up and down the aisle on bags to bring up the shine. We'd dust the pews, the font, the ledges, and give the pulpit a good rub. We did it for God.

My cousin Tilly and I were the ones who cleaned the plaque and the altar brass. There were little spots and dribbles of wax that we had to pick from the candlesticks before we dabbed and rubbed the Brasso on them. We liked the thick, black smudges on our cleaning rags that gave off the smell of God. We liked the way our fingers went cold.

We'd leave the streaky candlesticks while we cleaned the plaque of dedication, and the two vases that had been made from fired-off bombs, then with soft, clean cloths we'd begin the polishing. This was God's work truly.

The last task inside the church was done by our mother. She would spread the starched cloth over the altar and set on it the shining candlesticks and the bomb-case vases in which she had arranged flowers and foliage. She did this work as though it was a reward for herself.

Outside there were the grounds to tidy, a gate to mend, cobwebs to brush away, another nail needed in the roof. There we were every month, all over our church, inside and out, getting everything ready for God.

But the house of God was leaking. With every rain there were puddles to wipe up, new places where we had to put tins to catch drips, new damp patches on the walls. No matter how many nails were hammered in to keep the roof iron down, and no matter how much patching was done, still the rain came in.

Even though our own houses leaked, were broken and patched and needed paint, we knew this was not good enough for a God who saw everything. How could we beg his forgiveness? How could we sing the praises of the Lord if we let the rain come into his house. We had to get funds for a roof, so we raised money from card games going from house to house. We wanted a porch too, to stop water blowing in under the door. A porch would be a place where brides could step into, a place where wet coats could hang to dry, a place where a stranger could be welcomed.

What did the church look like then? It was a box with a sharp tin roof. It was without a porch and was painted white like it is now. It had a red roof, a red door, a red steeple with a bell in it. The steeple was a small wooden stand with its own sharp tin roof. One night the steeple blew down in a storm and that was when we replaced it with the wooden cross.

The bell was put away for many years, then was put up again under the eaves when the new porch was added in time for a christening of children. Its voice was different now because of a crack on its head caused when it had fallen at the time of the storm. Later when the porch was renovated the bell was taken over to the meeting house and hung at the end of the bargeboard where it is now.

It was the older people who played cards, sometimes in the houses or on the verandahs, or out under the trees. It was their enjoyment, their noise, their talk and arguments. They played any day or night, or at any waiting time, unable to think of it as sin.

So each week for the roof, poker games would be arranged at one of our houses. People would arrive on a Saturday afternoon bringing the teapot with them. The games would begin, going on all afternoon and through the night. There'd be a few hours' sleep and they'd begin again.

While my cousins and I kept the fires going, brewed tea, cooked beggars-that-float and made sandwiches, the games went on. The players yelled and laughed. Pennies and silvers jumped and jingled as people banged down their pairs and flushes, their full hands, their bluffs, their straights and ace-highs. Sixpence out of every half crown of winnings went into kitty, or threepence out of every half at the big tables. 'This for the winner, this for the roof, Kitty's away.' That's how our roof piled up.

At night we lit the lamps and candles and the games went on. Into the teapot we put three hands of tea, then filled it with boiling water from the tin on the fire, adding milk from the billy and big spoonfuls of sugar. We did this many times a day. Also we rolled cigarettes, emptied the ash tins and kept the fireplace clean. While we did these tasks we had our own gossiping, teasing fun.

I was too young to be interested in playing cards but I was too old not to be married.

There'd been no arrangement made for me because in those days we wanted to follow our hearts. Also our parents wanted us to marry Pakeha, so that we would be rich and get on in the world, and so that we would not be so dark and ugly. They wanted our children to be fair.

There was someone who I thought I might marry, and who people expected I might marry. His name was Maiki Johnson, but he married Beryl Patterson, the storekeeper's daughter. No Maori wife for him.

Who else was there? There was Jack Hepetema who did fencing for Pakeha farmers and who sent messages to me. I didn't like the messages, didn't like his loud mouth or the way he stared. I didn't like Jack Hepetema.

So why did I marry him?

I married him out of my own goodness, because my family thought I should marry. He was from a known family and good-looking enough, they said. As well as that he was able to support me and I wouldn't have to leave home. I would still be the one allowed to look after my grandmother.

But not long after I was married, my grandmother did something that it took me a long time to understand. 'The house is yours now,' she said one day. 'I'm going to live with your mother, who, now that you're married, has been asking for me. I go with nothing, leaving everything here with you because of the way your grandfather was buried.'

How ashamed I was that I hadn't looked after my grandmother properly. It was my job and now she was leaving me. I couldn't think what I'd done wrong, and when I asked her, all she said was, 'Why would I leave it all with you if I thought you'd done wrong?'

When the Birdnosed One died, all that had been gifted to him was buried with him. There were the feather and dog-hair cloaks, greenstone and whalebone patu, earrings and neck ornaments. There was the sacred taiaha called Tu-te-wehi that had been laid down in the time of Pirinoa. These were all the things that had been given when he was born and during the time when he was growing. The circumstances of his birth and life were too unordinary for those gifts to be separated from him now. He was too unordinary, born of someone too unordinary, and there was no one else unordinary enough to touch those unordinary gifts.

There were letters and writings and books that were buried, along with his pipes, his bedding and clothing, and his mandolin. After he was buried men stayed by his graveside with guns to guard his burial place.

So what was left in the house after the death of our grandfather, apart from household things, was what my grandmother had brought with her into marriage. Her kiwi-feather cloaks, her head feathers and hair combs, her taaniko bags and sashes, her carved box of jewellery. Then there was the hei pounamu that grandfather had put round her neck before he died, which was a gift from Pirinoa to the children's children. She had given all of these treasures into my care now so that they wouldn't be put with her when she died. She said to me before she left the house, 'Don't worry, I won't come back looking for anything after I'm dead, and no one will blame you for what I've done.'

Our grandmother was changing the custom by allowing her unordinary self to be buried with nothing. She did it because there was so little left for the children's children.

When she died there were heirlooms to go on her casket, there were portraits and photographs to surround her, but these were not her personal items. They were the usual treasures, kept by the family for those occasions, and put away again afterwards. They were the same ones we put with Shane and Baby, the same that will be brought out when my time comes. Only her clothes and bedding went with her.

But Grandmother lived another six years after she left me to my husband and her house. Jack and I had five children. One day, when Peter, the eldest, was five, I went to my mother's place and said to my grandmother, 'I don't like my husband. He gets drunk, gets on other women and comes home putting his fists into me in places where bruises don't show.'

'We shouldn't have allowed it,' Grandmother said, 'We shouldn't have let you have a husband like that. We shouldn't have let your children have a father like that.'

She came back to the house with me and we waited. We waited three days before Jack came home, and when we heard his boots on the shingle she went out to the verandah to wait for him, telling me to remain inside. 'Get anything that's yours,' she said to him. 'Then go.

Don't come back.' He said nothing. He took his axe and left.

Three weeks later I gave birth to Francis. I had Cousin Tilly come to live with me. The new roof had been on the church three years, the roof of cards, and that year, the year of Francis's christening, was the year the porch was built, with a bell under its eaves singing a croaky song. Grandmother died at the end of that year. We think she was a hundred and four years old. Another year later I heard of the death of Jack Hepetema.

People were now talking about a carpet for the aisle so that grandparents and babies would be warm, so a bride would not slip, so her gown would not trail on the boards. But there were fewer and fewer pennies, fewer and fewer people. They'd died or were gone, their houses were empty and falling, the church had a roof and a porch but not a congregation, and the minister visited only twice a year.

Six years later I fished a new husband out of the water.

Unless the weather was bad we spent part of every day getting food from the sea. It was how we lived.

On the day I fished my husband we'd all been down at low tide getting pipi. It wasn't a good enough day to go out in a dinghy to fish, but as the tide came in people began to throw their lines out from the beach. My cousin and I decided to take some of the older children round to the next bay to collect firewood.

The next bay is sheltered by high cliffs, and the sea there was calmer than the bay we'd left. So we weren't surprised to see a little dinghy far out at one of the fishing spots, but only wondered where the fisherman had come from, knowing he hadn't come from our way.

We filled all the bags with smaller pieces of wood, then began dragging logs and bigger branches to pile next to the tracks. There was a style to this piling, starting from a square of the largest pieces laid out on the ground. The next layer was of a square of shorter pieces, each layer becoming smaller and smaller, with the smallest layer on top. It was a mountain. The mountains were left like that waiting until we brought a horse and sledge to pull the wood home.

It was while we were building our mountains that I noticed the little boat coming slowly, crookedly, towards shore. I couldn't make out this strange movement of the boat until I went down to watch and saw that the rower had only one oar. He would stand in the boat and use the one oar like a paddle – one side then the other – to get on course. Then he'd put the blade of the oar in at the back of the boat, jigging it from side to side to push the boat forward. But progress was slow. The paddler was fighting the drift of the tide. He'd put the anchor down every so often to give himself a rest, then he'd try again, paddling paddling, shunting shunting, but the water wasn't letting him come towards the beach, which was the only good landing place.

He had to give up that idea and allow the water to take him towards the rocks where he would try to find a way in.

There he was using his wits, being pulled towards this rock, that rock, pushing off from this rock, that rock, with his one oar, making his way along. I knew he was looking for the zigzag channel that would let his boat in without breaking it. I knew also that the channel wasn't visible from where he was, and that he could easily pass it by. But from the beach the channel was easy for me to see.

I hurried out over the rocks and stood by the channel entrance. Soon he saw me and understood why I was waving to him. There he came, towards me using his wits, out and forward, out and forward, a little at a time.

When he was close enough he let the boat drift out. He turned towards where I was, stood and planted his feet, and as a wave rose, gave one big pull to nose his boat into this gap that he could now see. Yelling, laughing and using his wits, he pushed off this side and that side, to get himself into the neck of the channel, swooping and weaving through it.

Right then, right there, I was in love with this small man with skin like wet rocks, feet planted, shouting and using his wits, shooting through the channel. He was wearing army pants and a football jersey. He was wet and laughing.

Who was he? He was my father's orphan.

'Thought my boat was gone,' he called as he jumped out and we

258

began running the boat ashore. 'Thought my fish were gone.' In the bottom of the boat was a load of snapper and the broken oar.

When we were children I'd known him. When he was eight his parents, grandparents and brothers and sisters had all died in the flu epidemic and he'd been brought to my father's people by a man married to my father's cousin. His name was Mahi Haunui but we called him Marty Hau. When Marty was about twelve my father's cousin-in-law died and it was difficult for our aunty, his wife, to look after their large family. My father asked if he could have Marty, but instead the cousin-in-law's family came back to claim him.

I didn't see him again until I fished him.

We carried the boat up to high ground, the children helped us to thread all the fish on to strips of flax, and we set out on the tracks, leaving our mountains, pulling our sacks of kindling.

The family was pleased with us with our necklets of fish because the fish hadn't been biting in our bay that day. My father cried over Marty and took him home, saying that it was his turn to have his cousin's foster child now, even if this child was now a man. Marty had been to war and back again. He'd lived here, there and everywhere since then.

Marty became our main fisherman from that time. Robert was eleven, Ellen was ten, Margaret was eight, Matthew was six and Francis was five.

'I've got nothing,' Marty said to me one day, 'but I want to get married. I want you and I to get married. If we married and moved to town I might find work.'

But I couldn't move to town. I had a house to look after and had charge of my grandmother's things. 'All right, I'll get work in the brickworks,' he said.

We married and he worked in the brickworks for five years, waking at four in the morning to be in time for the early train to get him to work. He would arrive home in the dark, covered in red dust from the works and soot from the train. After five years I wanted him to stop. It was no good. His chest was too bad. We had Vera who was a year old.

But it was all right. Times were better. After Marty stopped working in the brickworks he was able to become a fisherman again. The children and I were his helpers. We had a little van and Marty took our fish to town. That's when he became known as Marty Fish. We built up our gardens and that's how we lived. He was the love of my life.

Twenty years after I fished him he died out on the verandah trying to get breath. The verandah post was where he leaned, the ledge was what he held on to, the wall was there to support us while we lifted him under the arms.

He was gone. My love, my orphan, my fish.

It seemed not long after that the children had gone too. All the people had gone, most of the houses had gone. There I was, just me, my grandmother's house, the treasures, my family looking down at me from the walls, an empty church, my quiet tongue.

But I wasn't forgotten. No. People came to talk, children and grandchildren came to stay, my brother's sons came to mend my house – to give it new windows and make a beautiful kitchen for me. Eventually my daughter, Vera, returned to live in my childhood place.

One day Shane came stepping.

I know how the teapot got a dent by its nose. It happened when a ghost was watching Tilly and me from by the willow tree when we were on our way back to Grandmother's house in the dark. We'd gone to get the teapot because a card game had started up. Tilly threw the teapot at the ghost but it hit only the tree. When we told this serious story to the card-playing parents and grandparents, they said, 'Her again,' and laughed, and kept on playing.

I suppose it's time for me to go home now.

35

TE PAANIA

'Do you mean now, this week?' I asked. 'Or in a month or two? Sometime in the new year?'

'As soon as you're ready,' she said. 'I don't want to leave it too late to walk into my house on my own two feet, otherwise how will *they* feel?'

The days were warming up. The weatherbeaten cabbage tree with its flogged leaves was showing signs of a straggly early flowering. We'd pulled creepers away from it and removed stones from round its feet, hoping that would help it grow more healthily. It made no difference, still it straggled. The pohutukawa by the back door was thirteen years old. It had new lime-coloured leaves and milky buds, and in a crack in our rickety path a seedling had taken root. 'Look at you coming up through concrete, what do you care?' Gran said to it. By the steps the flax bush was shooting a green wavy stalk from its centre.

We had clipped the taupata hedge to let more warmth into this puny yard of ours. The winter had been stormy and cold. Gran hadn't been out since our trip to Te Ra Park, but I would take a break from my work and go and sit with her in the yard on a fine afternoon, waiting for Tawera to come home from school. Gran seemed to enjoy these times in the crowded yard as much as I did, talking to Tawera and to the trees.

*

'Or on my own three feet,' she said.

Tawera had brought home a muddy stick from somewhere. He'd scrubbed and scraped it, to find that underneath the dirt was a good piece of manuka. He tidied the splayed end of it with a knife and one Saturday morning went shopping for new pens. When he came home he began drawing figures on the stick. He worked on one end of it all afternoon, then leaned it against the door frame to dry.

The stick remained there all winter. Sometimes Tawera would leave it for a week or more, but would always come back to it, taking it up to begin drawing again. I couldn't help noticing how quiet he'd been since our return from the park. There were quiet conversations but no more quarrels.

The cuts on his face and arms, which had taken a week to heal, had left no scars. The lump on his head had gone down after a few days, and though he was left with bruising, this quickly faded.

'Are you all right,' I kept asking, and I'd try to talk to him about that night, worried about how it had affected him.

'I'm all right,' he'd say. 'Only sorry about the window.'

By the end of winter, there we all were up and down the stick, the ghosts and the unghosts – Dave the angel, Mahaki the swimmer, Tawera and Gran the singers and dancers. And there I was, springing from the knees with my elbows hooked up in the air as if playing a saxophone.

'This family can all help me to walk,' Gran Kura said to Tawera after he'd polished the stick and given it to her, and that's what she used to help her walk from that time on. She helped herself up and down stairs with it, helped herself in and out of bed with it, and used it when she was showering and dressing.

'It's not that I can't have your help,' she said, in case she was offending us by being so independent. 'But I do like my stick. It's like having a new bone to hold me up.' Sometimes she called the stick her big family, or her other leg.

'As soon as you're ready,' she said again. 'Because if I let myself die here, Pita and Bon will think they haven't done well. They'll think they haven't looked after the house or the garden properly, or that I'm accusing them of not caring for grandmother's things. They'll think they haven't done the job they've been given if I don't go home in time. What would they think if I never came back to the room they've always kept ready for me. What would they think if I never came home to my verandah?'

'Whatever you want Gran,' I said. It was as though she thought we'd have to be persuaded.

'And how would Vera feel, my daughter, who never wanted me to come away in the first place, who has never understood why I left my home and who, ever since then, has begged me to return? Think how hurt she and her family would be if I let myself die here. They'd blame you, thinking you'd prevented me from returning.'

'I'll ring Dave,' I said, 'and we'll write a message to Mahaki.'

'The trouble it would be,' she said, 'taking me all that way dead. You wouldn't be able to take me past this marae and that marae without calling in. You'd all be worn out before the burial. All that expense too . . .'

'Do you want to ring Vera, tell them we're coming?'

'Otherwise the verandah might as well have been made into a patio.'

All through the winter we'd been having daily contact with Mahaki through e-mail, keeping up to date with all that had happened since the eviction.

On the day of the arrests, the elders and those who had only trespass charges against them had been released on police bail. By morning the charges against them had been dropped. Abe, Mardy, Hani, Ani J and Makere had been charged with trespass, resisting arrest and obstruction, and had remained in custody until their court appearance the next morning when they pleaded not guilty.

Over the weeks that followed Mahaki built up the defence in preparation for the case. 'People are hyped up and hopeful,' he said, 'but I think we need to do something different if we're to get anywhere. Need a new approach. I keep hearing the older people saying how they want everyone to know, want the courts and the whole world to hear their story. It makes me wonder if they really *believe* that we can get this land back. Or did they give up this idea long ago? Are they just humouring us now, thinking that they'll never get Anapuke back but at least there's a chance to let everyone know the story. Like having the story told is better than nothing. There's one part of me that puts all that "tell the world" stuff aside not as important, soft option, cop-out. There's another part of me warning myself that I should take heed, keep my ears out and flapping, have faith and go for it.'

We looked forward each evening, after Dave came home, to opening up our mail, reading the day's notes from Mahaki, then writing our replies. These early letters from Mahaki were uneasy. He was undecided. Then as the first day of court came near there was a change of plan. 'We've decided to let Abe and Co defend themselves,' Mahaki wrote, 'and I'll be their coach on the sideline. We'll take a gamble on getting the stories told and getting the old people in the witness box, which should get plenty of media coverage. We'll have to see what happens after that. If I keep out of it there'll be more tolerance by the judge (I hope), of evidence being allowed that's only minimally related to the charge of trespass – more opportunity for it to all come out.'

'But how can it?' I wrote. 'How can a defence of trespass etc lead to a return of land?'

Before I could receive a reply to that question there was another change of plan.

'We're going for broke,' Mahaki wrote. 'We're changing the pleas to guilty and taking the opportunity to make a plea in mitigation, using "cultural considerations". I believe now that getting the stories told *is* the way to go . . .'

'But how can a mitigation plea . . .?'

'It's not that telling our story – in defence of trespass, resisting arrest, obstruction, or in a plea for mitigation – in itself will get land back through the courts. It's going to be what goes on outside and around the court that matters. As well as getting the stories told in court, and in that way looking to gain court sympathy, we'll be giving out information with the hope of gaining a measure of public support. We want to embarrass Council into returning the land, which we can show they really don't want, and which no one else will touch now anyway, given the controversy and likelihood of further trouble.

'Actually by the time we've finished I believe the Council will want rid of Anapuke and will feel they've got off lightly if they can do that with as little fuss as possible. Information coming out now is showing how remiss their office has been in their documentation over the years. Another reason they'll feel they've got off lightly is because the reserves put aside for our people, that is, the "tenths", have been eroded, absorbed, sold or leased for peppercorn rents. We've got good evidence. Also the timing is right in regard to the question of rents, as there's already a national focus on this in other places. Government has recently admitted there's been injustice and what they've described as "less than honest dealings" which have led to disinheritance. The courts have ordered that something be done about it. Yes, Council, after we make them aware that we are on to all this, might be relieved and grateful that we are focusing only on the return of Anapuke (for now, ha ha).

'We want our court presentations and evidence to lead to positive discussions with Council, backed up by hints that we may take the matter to court, to the Race Relations Tribunal, the World Court, or whatever else we can think of to hang over them. Also they know that there's always the possibility that we'll re-occupy Te Ra, or possibly organise another picket, or a sit-in of Council chambers.

'There are some positives regarding public interest and interview opportunities. Maraea's doing a great job. Jill's article has really helped. Also we've had an offer from an anthropologist who is an authority on sacred sites. She can research an area through history, culture, habitation etc, and through comparison and deduction (and I don't know what else); can make a report showing the strong likelihood, or otherwise, of a specific piece of land being a place of burial. This is without actually going on to the site – but we could take her there if we have to. Anyway she's working on it now, out of her own interest, and maybe her report will be useful in the long run.'

After the court case had started we received messages from Mahaki in which he described elders speaking about what Anapuke meant to the people, and about the efforts that had been made, over the years, to have this piece of land returned to them. He thought that the court and the judge tolerated the evidence well. It was a big surprise though, after the judge asked if any of the letters were to be made available, when the old lady Horiana said she had them at home.

'Well, they weren't the exact letters, or exact copies,' Mahaki wrote. 'They were practice letters that Horiana, with the help of others, had written before sending the final drafts: "We the people of . . . ask you the people of the Council to return our sacred land. This land has not been sold to you and the people have received no payment. The people do not want payment. No. The people want the land returned . . ."

' "We have not received any reply to your letter . . ."

' "We invite you to come . . ."

' "We wish to come and meet with you . . ." They were impressive in their own way. The old faces, old voices, were even more impressive.'

From the time of Horiana's letters, media attention picked up and we looked forward to the TV news hour, the reports from court and the TV and radio interviews that took place daily.

'. . .Judge Setson seems to have a genuine interest in the circumstances,' Mahaki wrote. 'He's been questioning witnesses and seeking information on "cultural considerations". He's been precise over the details of the argument that there's been a breach of Treaty principles. Looking forward, with great hope, to his summary and findings on Monday.'

It was on the evening that we received this letter from Mahaki that we mailed back telling him that we were preparing to take Kura home.

There's a time when you must leave water to breathe air. There's accident and action that make life different from what it was before, and there's always a waiting and a preparation for what might be expected, though unknown.

Also there's change that comes not through accident or action. It's expected but not waited for, though from time to time you see it limping and struggling towards you. There's no reversal. In the end you accept what's coming and you look full into its face.

'I should rescue you from there,' Gran Kura said to the seedling in the crack of the path as we made our way to where Tawera and Dave had the van packed and waiting, 'But it's the wrong time of year. When there's more water in the ground someone will get you and bring you to me.' It was a fine bright day, though the rays from the sun that was pulling itself up above the hills had not yet reached the yard.

'My sister's going too,' Tawera said to Gran as we helped her into the front seat. Her hands were black, her feet were cold, her bones had become hollow.

It wasn't the first time Tawera had said this, 'My sister's going too.' There was something different about the way he was using words. 'You'll be all right,' Gran Kura said.

Or perhaps I hadn't understood what he was saying. There was something different in his face.

'She always comes,' I said. 'Where we go, she comes.'

'Going,' he said, 'not coming. Coming with us. Then with Gran Kura, going.'

'Going?'

'There, where all the people go, where she was before, swimming along the roads, flying off clifftops, across oceans, getting there.'

We were driving through one set of green lights then another, slowly in the morning traffic, keeping in the left lane with the sun slipping between buildings, glossing up city gardens – reflecting from windows, signs and facades. People were stepping it out on footpaths and overhead ramps, going to work, pleased with sunshine. It was as though it was an ordinary day.

As we drove in, Aunt Vera and Bon came down off the verandah followed by Niecy with Mahara and Mahi and others who lived in the nearby town. Word had got round. Uncle Joe, Pita and Gordon were crossing the paddock with January and some of the other children.

So it was a warm homecoming with the sun standing straight – a flipped coin – the flowers lifting up, the trees catching light in bundles. There were people crying, fetching bags, wanting to walk her, lift her, do something about this ghost of a returning person. But up she went onto her verandah with her stick, taking her time, her tongue clicking and clacking against the bones in her head.

'The two of them,' said Tawera from his unbearable face. 'The two of them together, going.'

'What can I do?' I asked.

'Nothing.'

We cleared the living room and put mattresses down so that we could all be in the house and take turns sitting with Gran Kura during the night. 'Don't wait by me,' she said that night, 'Go to sleep. I'm not going anywhere yet.'

'How do we know?' Joe asked. 'You might sneak off while we're not looking.'

'How would we feel if we let you go like that?' Bon asked.

'All right,' she said, and went into a heavy sleep, hardly stirring until next morning when she woke and said, 'Don't take me to the church, the church of cards.'

She closed her eyes as though asleep again, but in a little while helped herself up, took her own time to wash and dress, and came into the kitchen where we were preparing food for the day. She was able to take two bites from a piece of Louise cake and drink a cup of tea, then she jabbed her stick at the floor and, hand over hand, climbed it until there she was standing like a bent pin.

'You make us sick doing that,' her daughter Vera said. 'Coming home and expecting to do everything for yourself.' Kura said nothing. She made her way down the passage under the eye of the winking grandfather, and out on to the verandah.

We put her chair in the shade of the clematis which was a mat of dark foliage with flowers out on it, full and starry like a drop of night sky behind her. It covered one end of the verandah, twining itself up the downpipe and threatening to bring the spouting down. Although it was a warm day she needed a blanket round her.

In the afternoon she went down into the garden, which was buttery with sun, where she looked into the faces of flowers and muttered in and out amongst the trees. Visitors came and went, or came and stayed, all bringing food. They filled the house and verandah and walked about in the garden. It was becoming difficult to find enough refrigerator or shelf space for food.

Tawera had gone down to the beach to swim with January and the other children. They stayed away for most of the day and when they came back I was pleased to see how he'd brightened. I hadn't seen him playing and talking like this for a long time. It was a noisy, happy day.

Later, when we put out the bowls of meat, puha and potatoes, the pies and pizzas, the fish and salads, bread and cakes, he said out of his bright face, 'It's like a lovely party, Mum,' then, with a mouthful said, 'They're at the beginning, the two of them, but they haven't turned round. They don't want to. Gran's waiting for something and my sister's waiting for her. Or maybe she's scared, or maybe sorry for us. She talks in riddles. There are others, further on, tossing dollars to find out "yes" or "no". They're being given the shove and don't care, not scared of anything.'

'Not of anything?'

'No.'

'That's all right then, isn't it?'

He was looking at me as though waiting for me to say more. I was trying hard to think of the right thing. Gran had already gone inside allowing Vera to help her get ready for bed and brush her hair with a baby brush.

In the living room the mattresses were being pulled out from against the wall. Little kids were being put down on them. Tawera and I were carrying dishes and scraping plates ready for washing. 'You've been good eyes all your life,' I said. 'There's been a family and a childhood.'

Frog eyes.

Large brown freckles on a thin brown face. Wide frog mouth with something of a smile. He was happy enough with what I said. Later I heard him laughing while he was talking to Mahaki on the phone.

'Crossing our fingers,' Mahaki said when I took the phone. 'Hoping Setson will give us a good go tomorrow.'

That night Kura woke several times. She sat propped up on pillows and wanted the light on. She moved her eyes about without speaking. Her tongue was silent in her head, making me wonder if we would hear from her again.

The window was open to the warm night air and moths came in flickering dizzily round the light. Beyond the window, beyond the verandah, the insects twittered, while further out, the sea bunkered up the sand. We could see a slice of it catching an edge of light from a last bit of moon.

We did hear from her again. The next morning she woke, and though she didn't get out of bed, she was bright and talkative for a while, almost as though she felt she should entertain us.

In the afternoon I went to get the paper, and by the time I arrived home Kura was lying back with her eyes closed. 'They've been discharged without conviction,' I said. She opened her eyes and closed them again, seeming neither asleep nor awake as I read the column out to her.

Judge Setson had been 'able to understand, and have some sympathy for the position that a group of usually law-abiding citizens had come to, because of historical events . . .' Those before him had 'brought forward witnesses who had given credible spoken and documentary evidence regarding efforts over the years to regain and retain land of important cultural significance to themselves and the hapu of which they were part.' Witnesses had spoken about 'general disinheritance, caused particularly by the Public Works Act of 1928 and the Maori Affairs Act of 1953, and the ensuing deprivation to three generations of people.'

They had argued that 'land taken for purposes for which it was never used, breached the principles of the Treaty of Waitangi.' They had explained that 'no claim for the land in question could be made to the Waitangi Tribunal as it was not Crown land,' and went on to say that 'after giving the matter much consideration, and after consultation with elders, they had been unable to think of any other way to draw attention to what they considered an injustice, than to take the action that they consequently took . . .' There was a photograph of the five leaving the courtroom under the heading 'Discharged Without Conviction.'

Kura opened her eyes when I finished reading, though said nothing. But that night when Mahaki arrived, pleased with the events of the morning, she said, 'I listened to the story.'

The next morning she said, as though there'd been no days in between since the first morning, 'No not the church of cards. The marae is far enough, just take me there.'

These weren't her last words. Her last words were whispered – mumbling, complaining, urgent, and what sounded like swearing – into Tawera's rocking ear.

36

TAWERA

Last words?

Last words.

It's been three years and I haven't told anyone about those last words. Mum, Nan Vera, Koro Joe – all of them are still waiting I think. Or maybe they've forgotten about it by now.

I haven't forgotten. It was awful. I was put into this no-win situation and it wasn't fair. Gran in one ear, my sister in the other, my head nearly falling off swinging between them. They made me say it, made my head nod, forced that word out of me – 'Ye . . . Yesss.' Geez it was horrible.

I'll tell all about it later.

Maybe.

All right, I will, but later.

Because there *are* other last words you know, even though they may not be so final. There's catching up to be done. You can't just leave everything dangling, and Mum's not much help lately.

Let's see.

Mahaki and Anapuke and all that? Well it was like a great big party after our friends were discharged. I don't mean a party with food, music, dressing up, wine and beer, flowers and presents and all that. No, but there was just something happy going on all the time. We had all these visitors, new friends – Abe, Maraea, the Anis, Sue, Rev, old people, young people, kids, Janet – calling in to see us, especially Abe. He and Mum have got a thing going, part-time lovers. Mahaki was home a lot of the time too. That was good.

Actually there *were* presents, wine, music and flowers etc, but spread over days and weeks, not all in one big party lot.

Also these friends, and Mahaki, were popping up on television all the time, or popping out of the newspapers telling their stories. We kept seeing them everywhere, hearing about them, reading about them. Everyone was talking about them. The old grandmothers and grandfathers were there too, on TV, in the newspapers etc. Mahaki said they'd been kidding the councillors along, saying back to them some of the things they'd said earlier: 'Come on, Malcolm and John, our families have always been friends.'

'My kids were at school with Hazel and Bernard.'

'I was a five-eighths for Central when you were out on the wing.'

Then, kindly, they would say, 'We don't want to take you to court, to the Race Relations Tribunal, the World Court, ha ha. We don't want to occupy our land again, we want to stay home and look after our electric blankets. Come on it's up to you, we all want to vote for you in the next election.' All that.

Kindly?

Well, yes. Let's say kindly.

But of course no one could ignore the big men round town either, or the little and big voices round the country. We couldn't ignore their faces or their words. 'It'll be the thin edge of the wedge,' they were saying.

'If you give in to these lawbreakers, these terrorists, let them hold you to ransom the floodgates will open.'

'We'll all be shoved off our land . . .'

'And all you Council blokes'll get the shove come next election.'

Council was meat. There they were dangling, but what they feared most was another occupation that would undoubtedly coincide with by-elections.

So, in the end they did it, came across and decided to return

Anapuke, using Janet Hewson's report to help them. 'We have no choice,' they said, 'now that Anapuke has been shown to be, in all likelihood, a sacred site, and in light of recent understandings and recent judge's comments, which of course we take seriously, we believe it is timely that this block of land should be returned.' The land was to be made a Maori Reservation for burial ground purposes, and for the cultural and historical interest of its original owners and their descendants.

Of course there was a big blow-up from the 'floodgate' and 'thin-end-of-the-wedge' people, Council members getting flak, being threatened, one resigning, one getting the shove at the election. Flak, threats, hate mail to Mahaki and others too, but Mahaki didn't worry, he'd had it all before. The trouble was it kept him away from home. He stayed away from us for two months longer than he would have, because he didn't want anyone to know about his family. Families get threatened sometimes, he reckons. Anyway, it was some months before the paperwork was done and finally put through the Land Court, but this was it, this was it. It was like a big party.

By the time it all went through, Mahaki's old grandfather had died, but never mind Mahaki said, because the old man lived long enough to know it was all going to happen. He was happy. It was all right.

So there were these good, busy times, party times, that happened in blocks and chunks, where there was noise and hurry and all the rooms were filled. That was good.

In between these blocks and chunks, there were times, with Gran Kura and my sister gone off together to live in another place and another house, that there were great mountains of quiet, great mountains of time, great mountains of space to deal with. It was awful.

Where was noise? Gran's voice, all her stories, were now silent, and the stick that I made for her, though it would sometimes wriggle and now and again tap itself against the wall, was mainly standing quiet by the door. There were no more conversations with my sister, no more quarrels, no more instructions and directions into each other's minds. And what about the squeaks and squeals and singsong voices, the slips

274

and trips, the bumping on the stairs? None of that now. All gone.

What about time? There it was – limping along, limping along. There were huge globs of it left over. I'd get up, put on the grey and red uniform ready to go to this new school. I'd have breakfast, slowly, but the same breakfast as always. I'd pack my lunch, check everything, and then I'd wait. I'd wait, wait, wait, for it to be time to go. All this time – squares of it, balls of it, lumps of it – sitting all about me, on top of me, while I waited until it was all right to leave. I'd dawdle, dawdle, dawdle until I arrived at Kawea and Donise's house. They'd come out of their door, out of the gate, hurrying, still doing up their bags, unable to find enough of time. And there I was, waiting.

Time would speed itself up once we started walking, but only a little. There was no double-talking to do, though Kawea and Donise and I did have important matters to discuss because the three of us intended starting up a band.

At school I would sit through long periods of time with all the work done – no one to explain it all to. Done. Finito. Finis. I'd wait, wait, wait – wanting time to ping itself across this big, wide river of itself to overtake me, or take over me, or take me over. Or even slap me down, as when someone ahead of you in the trees forgets to hold the bunches of foliage aside and lets them fly back, hitting and stinging you. It can happen with a swinging door if you don't watch out. There I would sit, sit, sit, hoping that time would take me by surprise.

And what about space?

Spaze.

In between the comings and goings of family and friends, the rooms would grow. There were too many of these rooms. They were too large. There were empty chairs, an empty bed, and me with one bed all to myself. It was strange.

Mum and I changed the furniture round in an effort to get our small space back. We took Gran's bed into the living room and made a seat of it, then shifted the office machines and furniture into Gran's old room. It seemed better for a while, until Mahaki and Dave came up to see what we'd done. They said, 'No, it's no good rattling around up here. Why have two kitchens, two washing machines, two half-filled fridges, two vacuum cleaners, one office up here and another downtown. We'll sell some of this stuff, then we'll clean out the study and the spare room downstairs. This up here can be offices and studios.' Mum and I agreed with that. It was better.

But there's more to discuss about spaze.

I found it difficult to remember to sleep in the middle of the bed. It was a lonely place there in the middle. Also it was difficult at school to sit properly on a chair and to remember that there was a whole desktop to spread my books and pens across. When playing soccer, there were all these little gaps that I could fit myself through, because there was only me. I didn't have to move back when hugging, or sit with a gap between Mum and me, Dave or Mahaki and me, on the settee. I could keep a book close to my face and read it to myself. I could examine a bus ticket or a fly. It was terrible.

I could go out and play Space Invaders, which I had previously given up doing because of complaints about me not moving over, keeping the games all to myself, not explaining properly, not being a proper brother. I'd given up a lot of things, come to think of it.

Spaze Invaderz, Time Invaderz, Invaderz of Silentz.

Which reminds me about my Horror Face. Faze.

Later.

What about Mum? Besides being a part-time lover, she's also a speaker and a traveller. She's getting up noses and under skins, stepping out. I went with her to her first convention, which took place downtown on the first Friday of the first school holidays after I started my new school. 'I'll come with you Mum,' I said, not wanting to be left alone with all those time, space and silence mountains.

Off we went on this eerie day that was moving but not breathing. I mean, there were people about the streets; shopkeepers were in amongst their racks and behind their counters; offices, factories and warehouses were open and vehicles were going up and down the roads. But there was no breath. Coloured flags, strung up around the saleyards, hung still. Trees were without a movement of even one leaf, the tongues of flax didn't speak or whisper, flowers were without expression. There were no birds hopping, or flying, or twittering, or tweaking at bits. Gone. No birds.

Up above, the sky was like a flat, grey lid the colour of cement, and completely unmoving. It could crack. It could open. Something could come ouda there, beam us up, my mother and me. We could be invaded, then returned with all memory erased, to take over the world.

Just kidding.

We turned a corner, making our cold way past warm cooking smells of Bar and Grille, Bar and Espresso, Oriental City and Missy's Patisserie. We were heating up. The picture theatre went by, Family Fun Arcade, Auction Rooms, Lucky Corner and the TAB. 'I don't know about this,' Mum said. 'I'm OK at setting up systems, showing people what to do. I'm OK talking about all that.'

'You'll be all right, Mum,' I said.

She'd bought a new waistcoat from the Op Shop – deep blue, patterned with red and black whirls. She'd washed and ironed a blouse she liked from her working days, which was of white chenille with full sleeves, buttoning at the wrists with flat pearly buttons. Same buttons down the front – one snipped from the bottom tuck-in part of the blouse to replace one missing at the collar. Her black trou were from working days too – waist tucks and wide legs – brushed and pressed, waist button shifted to give more room. Her old boots had been brushed up and had new laces. She'd dabbed on a few dobs of makeup. Not enough to hide herself, no, just the right amount to make her laugh, blink at herself in the mirror, wink at me behind her big glasses. I was in love with her.

We waited at the crossing by the brick toilets, next to a spiral of dog doo and a pole covered in show advertisements. I clung up the pole until the buzzer went and the striding green man came up on the lights. We crossed, passing by the Arabian Oasis with its hatch down, painted all over in palm trees and temples. La Casa Pasta, Mexican Party, The Fat Lady's Arms.

Getting hotter, we turned into the street that I like where there are buildings with their insides being taken out in all sorts of different ways. In among these are a mixture of new and old places. There are the fruit and vegetable shops with bins stacked high with perfect oranges and apples and seasonal fruits; tables of cut and uncut watermelon, rock and pie melon; bundles of silverbeet, spinach, spring onions and parsley; boxes of onions, carrots, potatoes; stands of cabbages and lettuces with their wet green hearts on display. There are new and second-hand book and music shops, Krafty Korner where I buy my paints and pens. There are galleries – down in concrete basements or up the wooden stairs. There's Pierced and Tattooed, the Bucket Waterfall, Xtacy Gear.

There's the busker with his guitar and amps and speakers. I put him in one of my paintings – the way he stood, the way he angled his guitar, the way his head dropped back, his tossing hair, his tight black clothes. Behind him is the butcher's window with its trays of steaks, roasts, chops, schnitzel and cutlets, strings of sausages and salami. But there's one of those eggs beside him in the painting that I did . . . it's a problem.

Later about these eggs.

Nearly there.

Hot.

'We shouldn't have walked, I'll have sweaty underarms and a melted face,' Mum said in front of tall glass doors that slid themselves open to let us into a grand foyer of palms and pink carpet and marble reception counters.

Great globes of light fixtures hung from the ceiling on gold stems at all different levels, like a sculpture. There was water sliding down a rock formation into a ming blue pond. 'It makes me want to pee,' Mum said, 'and also I want to look at my face. I want to fan under my arms.'

We found the toilets where she went her way and I went mine. When she came out she'd straightened her clothes and damped her hair. She was smiling and fabulous. 'Don't know if I can handle all this,' she said, but she looked as though she could.

'*On the hill that trembles, In the splintered valley . . .*' I sang as we mounted the majestic stair. 'Ha ha ha,' she went.

Mounted?

Majestic?

Well, these stairs were sweeping, and wide. They curved to heaven. Eight abreast could've gone up those stairs. You could walk up them without hearing a footfall, and as you walked your feet were cushioned on them as if your feet were two things that were precious. There was a carved wooden banister, twenty centimetres through, supported by heavy posts that were topped by carved swirls – like soft-serve ice cream from Wendy's, or those whorls of dog doo that I mentioned.

At the top was another large foyer, and there, waiting, was a man with a hand out to shake Mum's and mine. 'The early session's running a little late,' he said. 'The speaker got a roasting but they're wrapping it up now. Fifteen-minute break and then you're on.' He was smiling kindly.

Kindly?

Yes, definitely. Kindly. 'I thought I heard singing,' he said with a shy, pleased face. There were others waiting in deep chairs and the man introduced us to them.

Along a far wall was a long table dressed in burgundy cloths with white cups laid out, urns with 'tea' and 'coffee' labels on them, white plates with biscuits on them – creme, chocolate chip, chocolate thins, iced wafers, shortbread, krispies and wheaten. There were white dishes of sugar with silver sugar tongs, white jugs, a white jar of spoons and white paper napkins. There were rows of glasses and tall jugs of water with mint and lemon floating. I'm so used to all this describing.

Soon all the people came whooshing out through the big wooden doors, talking fast and hard, some of them bolting, packet in hand, downstairs, outside, to smoke. The rest went fast forward to stand in line at the urns. They were people from all over the world. 'All over the world Mum,' I said, so impressed.

'This all gives me the shits,' she said.

'From those armpits flashing, From the footsteps striking, While the moon is breaking, He lights the darkened sea . . .'

'I was only Tawhaki's lightning painter remember.'

'Go for it, Mum.'

'I'm a frog,' she said, bending herself. 'Ha ha ha.'

There was the hall filling, and there was Mum going up on stage and getting a mike clipped on. There was a starving-looking man in a T-shirt doing something with cords and switches, after which there was careful light and a quietening down sound.

And there was Mum, centre stage, being introduced to us and stepping up to the lectern, placing her manila folder on it. She shuffled her notes, took a breath and began to read.

People round me began to creak their necks, straighten their legs out, bend them, straighten them again. It's no good, Mum. That's not it. Mum, Mum come on. Come on, Mum, what do you care?

Perhaps she heard me.

Perhaps I spoke into her mind.

Down she came from the lectern, leaving her papers behind, and there she was centre stage again. There she was wild, telling us about my sister. No more creaking and shuffling as she told about all that happened during that time while she was climbing back from the dead. After that she spoke about people's lives, and about different people having different knowledge of life, having different hearts and different understandings. She told it very well. 'This research interferes in a highly sacred domain of indigenous history, survival, and commitment to future generations,' she said. 'Genes are the ancestors within us.'

I thought she was clever, but some people became shuffly and impatient. They pressed their fingers underneath their chins and huffed down their noses. And it got worse, it got worse, because Mum started telling us off.

'Use your own people's genes,' she said. 'Or the genetic material of like-thinking and like-feeling people. Stop targeting remote communities just because their genes may have something different to offer. At least wait until there've been proper codes of ethical practices and legal confinements established, proper processes for consents to be obtained – processes acknowledging whole community and intergenerational ownership, processes free from extortion and pretext, processes that positively acknowledge the right to say no – of people who may be opposed to their genealogy being interfered with; who don't like the idea of their life patterns being taken and owned by someone else; who don't want the essence of themselves being altered or disposed of, or transferred into plants or animals or other humans. Stop pretending that indigenous people will benefit from this research.'

I thought she was great and there were people who clapped and cheered. There were others who were angry and got stuck into her, which I thought wasn't fair, though she handled it well, in my opinion.

'There'd be no progress at all,' someone said.

'Progress is people having clean water and enough food,' she replied. Good on you, Mum.

'There are answers out there in isolated communities.'

'The new frontier,' she said, and bent herself over laughing. 'And whose health problems are we talking about, answers for who? Ha ha ha.'

'Greater good, greater good,' red people were shouting.

'Which has little to do with numbers,' she said. 'It means the good of the rich, the good of wealthy nations, the good of scientists and researchers, the good of pharmaceutical companies, the good of those who have the might of states and the power of law to back them.' She was warmed up really – melting face and wet under the arms. 'None of it gives food or clean water to dying communities, saves their land and protects their resources, helps the Hagahai to survive.'

She was a wonderful star.

'That's my croak,' she said when she'd finished.

She came down from the stage in her new-laced, polished-up boots, and though some people didn't like her, others were in love with her, I could tell.

I was going to say 'not bad for a frog' but that's her line.

'Come on, Mum, you say it, come on it's your turn to tell.'

'No, keep it up son, you've got your eye on things. You're doing a great job. Also, you haven't finished. Remember what you said about later, later.'

Geez.

37

TAWERA

In love? Plenty of times. All the time. With cousins like January, with teachers, with friends who are girls, friends who are boys, always in love with someone.

Really in love? I don't think so. There are just these enormous feelings that make you feel nervous and sick, with either happiness or unhappiness, but you can't tell which. At those times it's as though happiness and unhappiness are one and the same, and as though satisfaction and dissatisfaction are the same too.

Weird. I don't want it, don't want the real thing, even though all my friends are falling head over heels, left right and centre.

Like Kawea. He spends hours on the phone talking to Monique. Sometimes Donise and I take off without him, rollerblading up through the tunnel, or down to the wharfs and round the bays. We meet up with other kids and terrorise the pavements.

You can get the same sort of feelings looking in mirrors dealing to zits.

Horror face. It's disgusting – a head, nose and chin full of pimples. Stand in front of the mirror, press your fingers down hard at either side of your forehead, squeeze towards the middle and all these bumps explode. It's frightful. There's this gory horror face looking out and you feel sick with happiness and unhappiness, satisfaction and dissatisfaction. Along with all that is a sense of both guilt and achievement that makes you want to laugh and cry.

Surfing's what I like. That's what I do when I go up to stay at Aunt Niecy's. Yes, coming in on waves, I suppose, is the best I've found so far if we're talking about enormous feelings – riding up there with your feet planted hard, working along, working along, keeping it all going till you get dumped. Out you go again to wait for the next big one, hii-aa. That's when you can understand that there probably is a difference between happiness and unhappiness, satisfaction and dissatisfaction. Hi-aa, hei-aa.

Painting and drawing? Well that always was and always will be.

Later, later.

Enough about me, I'm all right.

There hasn't been much about Dave.

Mahaki's often away, but I'm used to that. He and Maraea and Abe are working on getting reserve lands sorted out, finding out where they are, what rents are being paid. They're seeing what they can do about getting those rents increased now, instead of over the next forty-two years, which is the timing put on it by government. But also Mahaki's helping Niecy and Darcy, showing them how to do research for our people's land claims there. Gran's stories that Mum has recorded, are there to help them.

Mum's a traveller. I'm used to that. She'll be off to a conference in Fiji in three weeks' time. After that it's Geneva.

About Dave. Nothing's changed about Dave. I go down to his job every afternoon after school and help out, doing messages and putting things back in the right places on the shelves – rolls of wallpaper, sample books, kitchen and bathroom fittings, door and drawer handles, all that. Out the back there's the glass department, but I keep out of there. This is Jenkin Supplies where Dave's the manager.

From the shop I'm able to see Dave upstairs in his office on the half floor. It's a talking job that he has these days, and from what he tells me I think he misses the old days when he used to get round the city in his van, swinging round buildings, putting in windows.

We go home together, and whether Mum and Mahaki are there or not we have a good time. Nothing's changed about Dave. We put on our music, we talk about everything, we clean the van, go to the movies if we want to. There's time for all that. He warns me about life and looks after me.

I'm not saying I want to be looked after all the time, or that I want to listen all the time to warnings about life. But I know I'm fortunate to have something, someone, unchanged, even though I expect I myself will change. Something's rumbling in me. Don't know what I'll be like once I take in all of my tail.

All that's later.

Two winters ago, Dave and I bought a terracotta pot and filled it with potting mix. We lifted the seedling pohutukawa out of the crack in the path, settled it in the pot and looked after it. Later we all went – Mum, Mahaki, Dave and I – to the unveiling of headstones for Gran Kura, my sister and Shane. We took the tree there and planted it. It was good to be back home where everything's bubbling because of what they've been finding out about the land titles.

All right. Now to *those* two.

I still believe they could've talked to each other. There was only the depth of a shadow, like a breath, between them. At that time they were closer to each other than either of them were to me. They didn't need to involve me, or that's what I believed then. It was awful.

There we all were, having quite a good time really. There was Gran Kura, hanging on to life, hanging on, hanging on. Some said she was waiting for Mahaki to come, waiting to find out what happened in the courts. I thought that at first too, but no, that wasn't it.

Hanging on, hanging on, then I had to go and sit by her. It was me she wanted.

The lights were on all through the house, the doors and windows were open, there were people in every room and out on the verandah. There was a guitar plunking, a bit of singing every now and again, insects inside and out, the sound of the tide coming in. Jan and Mahi and I were thinking of sneaking off for a swim because it was so hot, but Gran Kura wanted me.

Me.

I had to sit by her. I had to bend my ear down low.

'She won't turn,' Gran Kura said into my ear. 'She won't budge. If we're to go together you'll have to send her.'

'It wasn't my idea,' I said.

'Go on, go on,' my sister said in my other ear. 'Send me.'

'It wasn't me who thought of it,' I said to her. 'It was nothing to do with me.'

'But you agreed.'

'No, I didn't agree at all.'

'About our different houses.'

'Brothers and sisters,' I said, 'And *their* different houses, not you and me in different houses.'

'You knew what I meant.'

'It doesn't mean I agreed.'

'You kind of agreed.'

'If I go alone I leave you with a handful,' Gran Kura said to me. 'It wouldn't be the right thing to do.'

'Talking about me as if I'm not here.'

'You'll have to send her.'

Gran didn't have much voice left, I had to put my ear right down. She didn't have much breath left, I could feel it like a moth on my skin.

'Never,' I said to Gran.

'You'll have to swear like she told you, use those words,' my sister said.

'Never.'

'You want me round your neck for the rest of your days? No time for friends, for schoolwork, for kissing and falling . . .'

'Shut up.'

'That won't do,' Gran Kura said. 'Harder, louder, much more than that.'

'No, never.'

'Pokokohua, taurekareka, as well as those English swearings,' she said. 'I won't say them, no, you won't catch me speaking English on my deathbed. Go on, shoo her off.'

'You heard, do as she says,' my sister said.

'Never.'

'Do it. You've got to get rid of me some time, you're thirteen . . .'

'What's that got to do with the price of fish?'

'Do you want me to stay, then?'

'Do you want to stay?'

'Do you want me to go?'

'Do you want to go?'

'I don't know.'

'What do you mean, you don't know? You always know what you want.'

'"Want" is different from "should",' she said.

'You've never worried about "should" before . . .'

'It's taken me a long time to find out about "should" . . .'

'I can't wait much longer,' Gran Kura said.

'So swear,' my sister said. 'Go on, your hardest. Tell me to piss off. Hard.'

'Never. So stop trying to make me make you. Stop trying to make me responsible . . .'

'All right, don't cry.'

'I wasn't.'

There was a long silence. Nothing, nothing, nothing. Then, 'All right,' my sister said. 'Don't swear if you don't want to . . . But I'll tell you what, just let me . . . Go on, let me, that'll be enough.'

'Let you?'

'Let me. Just say one word . . .'

'Looking the wrong way,' Gran Kura said.

'What word?'

'Say yes.'

'. . .won't turn, won't hold my hand . . .'

'Go on, go on . . .'

'Let you?'

'One word, go on . . .'

'All right, if you want me to.'

'Say it.'

'All right then.'

'Go on.'

'Mm.'

'That wasn't it.'

'Ymm . . .'

'That's not it.'

'Ye . . .'

'Getting there.'

'Yesss.'

It was awful. It wasn't fair. I was furious. I wouldn't, wouldn't cry.

Everyone else was bawling, wailing, praying, singing hymns, going in and out, ringing up, kissing Gran, talking to her, shutting her eyes, putting her teeth in, shutting her mouth, laying her down flat so she wouldn't be bent in her coffin. I was mad at all of them. The doctor came, the undertakers came, people came and went. I wouldn't talk to anyone. I went to sleep.

The next day we went down to the marae and waited for Koro Joe, Pita and Peter, along with this big crowd from here, there and everywhere, to bring Gran back from the undertakers. There was all the karanga ringing out, all the crying and wailing, the greenery waving. Not me.

They got her in, opened up the coffin, draped the cloaks, laid out all the greenstone and the whalebone – along with the grandmother's things – and put the photographs and portraits around: Birdnose and the grandmother, the two mothers and the father, Riripeti, Marty Fish, Shane, others. I didn't watch all this being done, but I had to see it eventually. I rolled myself in my old blanket on one of the mattresses, shut my eyes and wouldn't talk to anyone. I was a blanket with paper inside, or cobwebs, or seed pods, or grass stalks, or old leaves.

Nothing.

Well all this noise and activity stopped after a while and the speakers were getting to their feet having a crack at Gran Kura for going away and coming back on her last legs. They were getting it all going. When the call came from the kitchen for us all to go and eat, I pretended to be asleep. I stayed there while group after group of visitors came in and cried and wailed and talked and joked and sang and laughed, and I wouldn't stand in line for the hongi. Instead I stayed there rolled. They went out for cups of tea and cigarettes. I stayed there rolled.

And I thought of the two of them on the road. They could've been dancing, or flying, or rolling along on invisible wheels. Or the road itself could've been their conveyance, like an unending K Mart travelator, or a speeding beam.

But I don't think so. No. It was an ordinary country road of packed-down dirt – stony, dusty and potholed in some places, but washed away, covered in debris and fallen rock in others. It curved, it straightened, it undulated. There they were taking their own time in amongst the other travellers who were dancers, cartwheelers, riders, fliers – and motor-bikers without bikes, in sitting positions, as if on Harleys, taking the bends, whipping the straights, whooping up and down the undulations.

There they were, hooping along in the perfumed light and the weightless air.

Without me.

I was the one who'd been made to free them – of me of them, her of me of her. Geez.

All along that long road they went, until they came to the jumping-off place. There they went, holding hands, leaping, flying through the air together, then diving down, down, down, to become, from there on, swimmers or wave-steppers or little boats.

So what?

I was rolled there not being my usual self at all – not at all that staunch one, those good eyes, the one who always thought what to do.

Thirteen.

I was hungry too.

Just as I was thinking about this hunger and being staunch and being thirteen, January lay down by me and fixed her pin eyes on me. 'Come for a swim,' she said, so I unrolled myself and we sneaked out the side door while another lot of visitors was being called in.

We returned from the beach just as it was becoming dark. The visitors had already had their evening meal. The tables had been reset for us. There was a great smell of the puha and meat that was being brought to the tables in steaming bowls. I wanted to eat. I found I couldn't. I had a small piece of meat which seemed to stick halfway down. I couldn't get over how mad I was at being made to say a word. I went out to the wharenui and rolled myself again.

The next day I went out to the kitchen each time we were called for meals, but could eat only a little. That night I unrolled myself and sat up for the poroporoaki, listened to all the funny stories, tried to join in the singing, but I felt as though I still had that hunk of meat stuck somewhere down inside.

The following day at the burial I collapsed by the hole and had to be taken out of the urupa. Nan Vera had to leave her mother's graveside because she was the one who knew what to do with me. She put her mouth hard against my head and blew – front, back and sides, with her cheeks puffed out like balloons – not that I saw that or felt it. I was out to it, but I was told about it later. After that they gave me a good going over with water.

Nothing happened.

Shouted at me, 'Tawera, Tawera.' I heard the shouting, came to, and was given juice from a can of apricots to drink. After a while Nan Vera left me with Mum, Mahaki, Dave and some of the aunties, and went back to the burial to have a word with her mother. The dirt had all been shovelled in by the time she got back there.

I lay there feeling exhausted, thinking what was the use of being mad just because they, she, made me say a word. Yesss. Why should I be angry about that? After all I had to say it. I finally realised that. Of course I had to. It wouldn't have been fair to have let her go without me saying it, without me allowing her. If I'd let that happen I would've thought about it later and been sorry. It took me all those days to work that out, but that was it. I was all right.

Mostly.

We had a big dinner – meat and vegetables cooked in the hangi, dishes of seafood, bowls of salad, steam pudding with custard and cream, trifles, jellies, fruit. I had something of everything. The meat lump inside me had gone.

EPILOGUE

Last, last words.

This year I attend university where I study between the lines of history, seeking out its missing pages, believing this may be one of the journeys that will help me be an artist.

In the room upstairs that used to be my bedroom, there are pads, pens and paints, boxes of junk and piles of discarded paper from offices, while covering the walls are the drawings and paintings that have accumulated over my childhood years. I need these there looking at me, reminding me of what I could do. They are the works that I had the freedom to do when I was a boy, and which I know I'll be able to do again in a new and different way.

In those child times there were no spaces, nothing clean, no voids or chasms, no white paper remaining once I put down my brushes and pens. Every work was complete.

On the shelves, and in piles on the table where I work, are the scribbles and sketches and half-finished paintings that make up what I have done over the past few years – my attempt at capturing the bedraggled streets.

Of sun, dropping like bees between buildings to the buzzing footpaths and pavings where people walk in shorts and tees, or go about their deliveries or about their business. They are of singers and derelicts, of men and women with collars turned up, lugging vacuum cleaners up creaking, squeaking stairs. Of wind catching the people pulling their jackets about them as they step out from doorways with their baskets and briefcases and plastic bags. Of a boy and a girl weaving and wheeling among them.

They are of night light, and of rain falling on the night-lit city, fracturing colours into waterfalls of green, red and gold across the dark roads and pavements.

In one, a ship descends on the city from a broken sky.

But each of these sketches, drawings, paintings, holds a missing piece, a section of paper that is blank. Not one is complete. In each one, space pushes itself outward, and in doing so brings the eye towards it. Or on closed eyes it imprints on the retina, a patch that is dark and trembling, the size and shape of an egg.

Little egg.

Inner space. It aches inside me, and in the evenings when I go to my room intending to work, all I can do is stare at absence. I take up a pencil and put it down; take up a brush, lift a daub of paint on to the tip of it, and for long moments stand poised – like a dancer, perhaps a dart thrower, unable to invade, unable to bring my brush across those pure places. I don't know what to do.

So I put the pencil or the brush down and look all about the room for a sign to help me. I search first among the pictures and papers for a message, but don't find anything there. I swap this and that, move the table and the shelves, give a different angle to the lamp, talk in my mind, but none of this has any effect on little spazes. So I sit down to read for a while – the unsaid matters of history – but don't find what I'm looking for.

I turn to the window of plain glass, and from there look down on the ghosty yard seeing nothing new to speak to me. After a time I know that I must escape the quiet of the room.

I go out on to the streets to read the faces, the footprints, the walls and ways for just a word or two to come talking into me, just some sign, even if at first it may seem wayward, unrelated – curry or salt or agony thrown into the recipe, but still you know it's fish, or frog – to bring me back to me.

Searching for my own tag, own break out, own rulz.

One night I know I have found what I want, when down an alley between two concrete buildings, on a blue hatch door, I see two words written in red marker pen. I've not seen them there before.

Try Opposite.

The words are meant for me. Why would I have turned that way if they were not?

I make my way home, go upstairs and begin to work. But now, instead of trying to shrink the egg of space, I begin to enlarge it. Instead of ending with that little unbreachable gap I begin with it, embrace it, let it be there, make it be there, pushing my drawing further and further to the outskirts. I persist with this, night after night, until one night everything's gone, fallen from the edges of the paper.

Spaze.

Te Kore, the nothing.

My self sits inside me trembling as I prepare a new canvas, pin it to a board and let light fall on it. And so as not to be caught out by too much haste or too much sound, I move with great care and quietness as I place myself there in front of it – taking my breathing time.

Boom boom.

I squeeze fresh paint on to a saucer, lift a dob of it onto a fine brush and reach, breaching space with a drop of red.

Then I know.

Boom boom.

I begin to work the drop, pulling it down, adding colour, moulding it out at either side and stretching it outwards and upwards. There's a nose, curved at its tip, drawing outwards to thin darkened cheeks and down to a stretching jaw, a stretching open mouth, a widening, sinuous throat.

From there I go back to fill in the brow and to ease the black hair, strand by strand up into a high ponytail, working through to daylight. I can sleep then because I know I've been given my incantations – to make visible who was invisible.

Sister Seen.

In the scraped, clean place between her forehead and the high bones of her face I'll make the gashes, show the invasion. The wailing from her stretched mouth I'll paint in the form of the spirit figures – taniwha and marakihau – and her arms will reach out to something as untouchable as a receding dream.

And I'll become the invisible one, opposite, with a hand reaching forward. I'll be unseen – except that now and again I'll step in to meet her. We'll go rollerblading together in a place where she will be my eyes.

One day I'll bring back the edges of the city – the jugglers in coloured coats tossing limbs and hearts, the sniffers and paper sellers, the alleys, foyers, corridors, the pavements and the stairways, the ship falling from a concrete-coloured sky.

For now I'll work on this, my first incantation of visibility. It'll be inadequate because there's so much more for me to know, so many signs to follow, so many codes and omens to decipher, so much more absorbing of the tail, as I go, bumping along, or lap lapping, or karm karm or on a roll, hi-aa hei-aa.

Hi-aa hei-aa, plenty of that.

Feet at the beginning of a road.